ALSO BY JANELLE BROWN

All We Ever Wanted Was Everything

This Is Where We Live

This Is Where We Live

a novel

JANELLE BROWN

Spiegel & Grau

New York

2010

Published in the United States by Spiegel & Grau,
an imprint of The Random House Publishing Group,
a division of Random House, Inc., New York.

SPIEGEL & GRAU and Design is a registered trademark of Random House, Inc.

LIBRARY OF CONGRESS CATALOGING-IN-PUBLICATION DATA

Brown, Janelle.
This is where we live: a novel / Janelle Brown.
p. cm.
ISBN 978-0-385-52403-2
eBook ISBN 978-0-679-60384-9
1. Domestic fiction. I. Title.
PS3602.R698T47   2010   813'.6—dc22   2009048996

Printed in the United States of America on acid-free paper

www.spiegelandgrau.com

2 4 6 8 9 7 5 3 1

First Edition

Book design by Jo Anne Metsch

To Greg, now as then

This Is Where We Live

Claudia

SHE KNEW IT WAS COMING BEFORE SHE ACTUALLY FELT IT. SHE could sense it, this electric menace rumbling her way, the air suddenly heavy and full of static. Before she could even fix the word in her mind—*earthquake*—it had begun: a vibration that started in the soles of her feet, as if the linoleum tiles of the kitchen floor were quivering beneath her. Her world going suddenly liquid.

Claudia stood frozen at the sink, looking out the window at the sun, which remained inexplicably fixed in the sky just above the swaying eucalyptus trees. Her stomach leaped north—lodging somewhere in the general vicinity of her esophagus—as the mug on the counter began to shiver and then rattled its way toward the basin. The floor rippled before her. Outside, the ancient bougainvillea showered violet petals across the splintered deck.

"Earthquake!" she shouted, turning in toward the house.

It grew stronger. She could *hear* it—she'd never imagined that an earthquake would be this loud but it was, the earth creaking and grumbling, answered by the agitated chattering of their dishes and artwork and knickknacks. Below her, she felt their home wrenching against its foundation. Claudia couldn't recall whether she was supposed to run for the door or climb under a table or locate the triangle of life, whatever that was; anyway, these options all struck her as pathetically impotent responses to this monstrous twisting. Instead, she widened her stance and gripped the counter, reminded of a surfing lesson she'd taken a few years back. *It's just like a wave,* she thought. *You have to ride it out.*

Jeremy appeared in the dining room in his boxer shorts, holding a can of shaving cream. Half naked, the room breaking loose around him—pictures falling, chairs turning in nervous circles—he looked soft and thin and painfully vulnerable despite his height, but his voice, when he spoke, was firm. "Get in the doorway!"

She couldn't quite process his command, distracted by the exhilaration of this upside-down sensation, as if she'd climbed onto a roller-coaster ride without a safety belt. And then Jeremy was yanking her arm and drawing her into the doorway. He blocked her in with his body, pressing her up against the wooden frame. She felt his rapid heartbeat through the silk of her cocktail dress, the trembling house against her back. Together, they watched as their wineglasses marched, one by one, off a shelf to certain death on the floor.

The house jerked violently, making one last break for freedom. An enormous crash came from the living room and Claudia shrieked—less from fear than wonder and anticipation, a sense that in this next moment something might change forever. She visualized the concrete support beams that cantilevered their house over the canyon buckling and collapsing, leaving them buried under a pile of rubble. *We could die,* she understood, for the first time.

And then, just as suddenly, the earthquake was over, a dying echo as the ground once again grew solid beneath them.

Still, they stood there in the doorway for a long moment, suspended in time, wary. In the canyon, Claudia could hear dogs barking, the plaintive wail of a fire alarm, yet everything was strangely still, as if all of Los Angeles were holding its breath. For the first time she could remember, she felt connected to the entire invisible city, ten million people united in terror for fifteen glorious seconds. *I love it here,* she thought, absurdly.

Then the city exhaled, and the spell broke. A car drove by outside and a helicopter passed overhead and the squeals of children rose from the park at the bottom of the hill. Claudia looked up at Jeremy, feeling his pulse slowing against her chest. The panic had subsided, replaced by an effervescent sensation—perhaps the adrenaline of knowing that she'd just cheated death, perhaps just the return of the giddy mood that had buoyed her since she'd woken up that morning. A crystalline sort of joy washed over her, pure and blinding and sharp: for her husband, her home, her city, her life.

"Hi," she said to Jeremy's earlobe.

He shifted and gazed down at her, resting his forehead against hers. "You OK?" he asked, and ran his hands up and down her bare arms, checking for breaks or abrasions.

"I'm fine," she said. "In fact, I'm kind of turned on. Is that weird?"

Jeremy kissed her nose and then her upper lip and let his torso rest against hers. "Earthquakes are a known aphrodisiac," he said, his hand sliding toward the hem of her dress.

She kicked a piece of broken glass away with the toe of her sandal and tugged at the waistband of her husband's boxer shorts, fingering the damp skin trapped under the elastic. "Was that the biggest earthquake you've experienced?" she asked.

"Nineteen eighty-nine was far worse. This one was hardly a blip in comparison."

In the eight years that Claudia had lived in Los Angeles, she had been in a few earthquakes, but only little ones that vanished almost as soon as you noticed them. She would read the newspaper predictions— CALIFORNIA HAS MORE THAN 99% CHANCE OF A BIG EARTHQUAKE WITHIN 30 YEARS—with morbid anticipation. Back in Wisconsin, they'd had tornadoes and blizzards, but those marched in with trumpets blaring, giving you at least a few minutes to brace yourself and barricade the windows. A California earthquake had always seemed to her a more glamorous kind of natural disaster, an abrupt and thrilling narrative shift. She'd been waiting for this moment since she moved here for film school, and now that it had finally arrived and been deemed only adequate by the native, she was disappointed.

"Well, it felt big enough to me," she announced, as his fingers tugged at the skirt of her dress. She ran her hands up his bare back, riding the knobs of his spine. "For a moment there I thought the house might collapse and crush us both."

"Silly girl." His voice was low and phlegmy, his eyes winched shut. Water dripped on her face from his hair, still wet from his shower. "We weren't ever going to die."

"And if we had? Isn't this the moment when we're supposed to take stock and decide whether we'd be satisfied with our lives had we just met an untimely death?"

He wiggled a hand between her thighs. "Well, would you?"

She considered the question, distracted by his fingers. She let herself go limp and still Jeremy's body held her upright against the doorframe: She felt secure here, as if an anchor were tethering her, keeping her from drifting off into unsafe waters. "Yes," she said. "I'd be OK with dying today."

His hand stopped moving as he mulled this over. "That's morbid," he said. "But sure. I'll go with you, if we must."

The exchange hung there between them, lingering one tick of the clock too long.

"Though I'd rather put it off until after my movie premieres tonight, if you're trying to figure out the best time to do me in," Claudia finally added.

"Then I'll call off the hired assassins," he offered, deadpan, and she laughed, and the adrenaline took over again and they did it right there, amid the broken wineglasses and smudged linoleum, ignoring the ringing cellphones and the car alarms going off up the block; everything heightened by the sense of crisis averted, and the two of them together inviolable against even the motion of the earth.

After they finished, Jeremy disappeared into the living room as Claudia readjusted her dress and surveyed the damage in their kitchen: three wineglasses lost, a framed postcard on the floor, the handle broken off the mug in the sink. Above the stove, the botanical watercolors that they picked up at a flea market had tipped askew. In the plaster above the door, a fresh crack spidered across the wall. She reached up and put her finger in the raw gash, pried off a powdery chunk of plaster, and crumbled it in her hand. Patching the walls: another item she could add to that endless to-do list. The plaster walls were original to the house, which was built long before the days of Sheetrock; just as the plumbing that occasionally spat rust-colored water was original, along with the brick fireplace clogged with fifty years of soot, and the vintage O'Keefe & Merritt stove missing one of its orange Bakelite knobs, and the wood floors with gouges from the sofas of the previous owners, and the dubious gravity heater in the bedroom floor, which, with the turn of an ancient key, belched hot air from an open flame positioned precariously underneath the house. Their home was in a constant state of decay that they seemed incapable of arresting.

But Claudia adored this house with an irrational passion: Perhaps it wasn't the palatial Barbie Dream House she'd fantasized about when she was a little girl, but it was *hers,* an irrefutable sign pointing to her status in the world, a manifestation of the fact that she'd achieved something worth noting. They had seen at least twenty houses before they'd bought this one three years ago; each one more decrepit than the last, each more astonishing in the audacity of its listing price. Even for $600,000 their options had been severely limited—the first real estate agent they met had groaned when she heard their budget—and they were forced to creep farther and farther away from the center of Los Angeles to find anything within their price range. They'd looked here, in the isolated hills of Mount Washington, only reluctantly—Jeremy had worried that it was too far from a decent bar and restaurant, not even a grocery store within a ten-minute drive—but as soon as she walked inside, Claudia had known it would be their home. It was just like the ad had said:

> **Cozy two-bedroom bungalow nestled in a picturesque setting w/stunning canyon views. Warm wood floors, fireplace, big windows & a glass slider to breezy decks.**

So what if those two bedrooms were squeezed into twelve hundred square feet, and the glass slider was an addition from a dubious seventies remodel and didn't belong in a postwar cottage at all, and the exterior of the house had been painted a hideous shade of lavender? The house had claimed them as its own, seduced them so thoroughly with its *coved ceilings* and *sweeping vistas from the master bedroom* and *built-in bookshelves* that they hadn't even had to speak to each other at all, hadn't had to exchange any meaningful looks behind the real agent's back during the tour—they'd just known. This was the house from which they would be launching the rest of their lives: their artistic careers, their two-month-old marriage, their family. They'd put in a bid before the end of the day.

It was a marvel that they could afford the cottage at all: They'd had to go over their budget to outbid eleven other potential owners. But it was 2005, and mortgages were cheap and plentiful. Their broker didn't blink once when he looked at their income statements and saw a barely employed musician and an aspiring film director who had the ten percent necessary for a down payment only because of Jeremy's meager inheritance. Still, even with an ARM interest-only loan, they blew through Jeremy's inheritance within twenty months, began living on credit cards, and were saved just in time by a second financial windfall when Claudia sold her film at Sundance last January. That money was vanishing quickly, too. But soon the struggles would end altogether: Jeremy's new band's album was nearly done, and the payday that Claudia's agent had negotiated for her next film was so staggering—mid-six figures!—as to make their mortgage payments seem negligible.

Claudia swept the shards of glass up with a broom and carried the dustpan out the kitchen door to the garbage bins in the driveway. There she stood looking past the tangle of sage scrub and chaparral at the houses that cascaded down the mountain: a mix of ramshackle cottages with stained-glass baubles hanging in the windows that suggested Mount Washington's recent bohemian past and newly remodeled modernist behemoths that pointed to its more bourgeois future. Once, this neighborhood had been a stronghold of middle-class Mexican-American families, but the onslaught of gentrification was bringing a swift end to all that. These days, the token minorities tilted more toward Filipino and Korean; the primary evidence of the Spanish-speaking population that had gravitated toward the bottom of the hill was the *norteño* music that occasionally drifted up from the lowland parks. Even in the short time Jeremy and Claudia had lived in Mount Washington, the neighborhood had visibly changed. The ancient sculptor at the top of the street who fed the feral cats had died, and his peeling mid-century home had been reimagined by the new owner—a music producer who drove a BMW—as a three-story contemporary with water features. Next door to him, in a remodeled Craftsman that until recently had held a friendly Mexican family with six grown kids, lived a forty-ish couple who seemed to have two of everything: matching Priuses, matching twin babies, matching stainless commuter coffee mugs that they carried to their matching movie-industry jobs each day.

She turned around to see Dale, the gay violinist from two houses up, assessing the damage to his home. "You guys make it through OK?" she called up to him.

"Cracked foundation, I think. Looks like the house dropped an inch. Know a good contractor?" He looked past Claudia and then grimaced, disappearing back through a stand of sycamores. Claudia turned to see Dolores Hernandez, her neighbor from across the street, standing in the road and looking furious. A trash can had slid down the hill in the quake and capsized, toppling its contents on the path to her front door. Using a pink house slipper, Dolores palpated a Hefty bag that had ejected coffee grounds on her arid lawn.

"You see!" Dolores exclaimed, pointing a cigarette at a scattering of blackened banana peels and a decapitated American Girl doll. She looked up at Claudia and shook with indignation. "Your garbage, my house!"

Dolores had lived here forever, a stubborn holdout against the forces of change. Her house perched on the upward slope of the hill, a thickly stuccoed box whose strip of front yard had been paved with a forest of faded plastic pinwheels and toppled garden gnomes. Dolores did not strike Claudia as a garden gnome type, let alone a whimsical pinwheel sort of person. Tremendous in both age and girth, Dolores most closely resembled a landslide: wobbly jaw, pendulous breasts, a vast rear end pitted with fathomless craters, all that craggy flesh descending downward, downward, ultimately settling at the veined and purple ankles that Dolores squeezed into flesh-toned support hose.

"It's not our trash, Mrs. Hernandez," she said politely. She prodded at the doll with the toe of her sandal. "I think it might belong to the Olsons. We don't have kids, remember?"

This didn't satisfy Dolores. She put a hand on one mountainous hip and took a drag of her cigarette, her crevassed lips pursing tightly around the butt, her livery jaw ripping from the effort of inhaling. "You clean mess," she said. *"No es mi problemo. Estoy demasiado viejo."* Her eyes went hazy, and she blinked quickly, as if suppressing decades of pent-up emotion.

"I'm really very sorry," Claudia began, and then stopped, annoyed that she'd somehow been intimidated into an unwarranted apology. Claudia was always considerate of Dolores, even if she had to force herself. She made sure to wave at Dolores when she passed her in the street, she pushed holiday cards into her mail slot at Christmas, she even sometimes picked up the free *Mount Washington Monthly* from her driveway and delivered it right to her stoop so the old lady wouldn't have to walk too far. She and Jeremy never threw wild parties or had screaming fights. Maybe they did represent a change to the neighborhood that Dolores resented, but surely she could look beyond that and realize that they were really very *nice* people? What was it going to take to get a little civility from her? Did no one have manners anymore? That was one thing you could say about growing up in Mantanka, Wisconsin, in the heart of the genial Midwest, people were at least polite and responsive to friends and strangers alike, often to a fault, ready to cede their spot on the rescue boat in order to maintain overall peace on the *Titanic*. Here, in Los Angeles, each person was a war-ready fortress, cut off from the world by a moat of self-preservation. Even after almost a decade in this city, Claudia was still shocked sometimes when people blithely pushed in front of her in line at the movies, at their ability to pretend they hadn't just stepped on her toe in order to procure a better seat.

"I'll be happy to take care of it for you later," she said to Dolores. It seemed the kind of thing you should do for an elderly woman, even if you didn't particularly like her—just commonsense good manners. "But first I have to clean up my own house."

Dolores grunted and took another drag from her cigarette, tapping the ash on Claudia's shoe. Her wig slipped sideways on her head, revealing an inch of thinning scalp above her ear. Holding the cigarette between index and middle finger, she cocked her hand like a gun and pointed it at Claudia. "You!" she said, suddenly changing the subject. "*Husband* make noise! Terrible terrible music. Too loud I call police!"

"I'll tell him to play more quietly," said Claudia, backing away. Purple shadows were creeping up the canyon as the sun dipped behind the hills. It was growing late; they would need to leave soon if they were going to beat the traffic into town. "I'm very sorry, but I have to go now."

As she fled, Dolores traced her path with her cigarette. "*Espero que el terremoto les asuste a todos,*" Claudia heard her muttering, "*y que me dejen en paz.*"

Entering through the front door, Claudia heard Jeremy swearing under his breath. "I need help," he called, at the sound of her footsteps.

He was wrestling with his painting, which had jumped off the living room wall and lodged itself face down across the couch and coffee table. Of course. They had hung the artwork poorly. Claudia had known this even as they put it up three years earlier; perhaps it was antipathy for the unwieldy thing that had kept her mouth shut when Jeremy was fumbling with molly bolts. Claudia had always thought that the handyman gene was innate in men until she met her husband, in whose hands a hammer and nails were as useless as a mascara wand and eyelash curler. Her own skills were by no means expert—gleaned from afternoons working in her father's hardware stores, mostly—but somehow they'd struck an unspoken bargain that in this marriage she would be the fix-it girl while he took care of bills and cooking. Except for that painting. When it came to hanging that painting, she'd let him take the lead, and he'd botched it.

As she watched, Jeremy staggered backward under the weight of it and looked balefully at her. "Am I entertaining you?"

"Absolutely. Fantastic show. I give it two thumbs up." But she ran forward and grabbed the other edge, and together they righted the picture and lifted it back onto its nail. The enormous portrait—the only notable possession that Jeremy had brought to their marriage—was a violent field of greens, slashes of paint in hues of puce and fern and kelly, and in the very center a splintering male torso, naked and disembodied, rendered in pulsating shades of scarlet. The piece was entitled *Beautiful Boy,* and the naked *Boy* was Jeremy himself: Jeremy's exgirlfriend, Aoki, an artist of repute in New York, had painted it at the height of Jeremy's success as the lead singer for the (now-defunct) indie rock darlings This Invisible Spot. When she first met Jeremy, the fact that he had been a high-profile artist's favorite subject had given Claudia a kind of thrill—as if the glamour might rub off on her by sheer proximity—but her enthusiasm for the portrait quickly wore thin. She found herself comparing herself, unfavorably, to the notorious ex-girlfriend; she spent late nights Googling the names *Jeremy* and *Aoki* and agonizing over the fawning *Village Voice* profiles and eventually had to place herself on a permanent Aoki blackout, both for her own sanity and the good of their burgeoning relationship. Since their wedding, Aoki's name had rarely come up, and Claudia had managed, through impressive self-restraint, to immediately discard any magazine or newspaper that threatened to mention her, thereby erasing the woman's existence from her life entirely. Except for that painting. She remained plagued by its existence—not just its artistic merits (she'd never much liked abstract art) or that, at eight feet across and six feet high, it completely dominated their living room, but also, secretly, by the fact that it was physical proof of the elusive and possibly more exciting life that Jeremy had led before he met Claudia. Troubling evidence that he might, once, have been just as happy without her.

Even the adjacent wall of family photographs that they had selected and framed and hung as a kind of counterbalance to the presence of Aoki were completely dwarfed beside that painting. A fading snapshot of Claudia's parents back in Wisconsin, positioned in front of a smoking barbecue packed with grill-hatched wieners. A Sears studio portrait of her older sister's kids, unnaturally posed with teddy bears that did not belong to them. An otherworldly black-and-white photograph of Jeremy's mother, Jillian, her face stretched thin and luminescent over slashing cheekbones—the most haunting of a set of pictures that Jillian's photographer boyfriend had taken after her cancer diagnosis, a photo series Jillian had casually referred to as "the last sitting."

The biggest photograph, the one right in the middle, was their wedding portrait, the one with Claudia—her freckles masked by makeup and her brown curls for once tamed into something shiny and smooth (she had paid $200 for that privilege and never managed to replicate it)—giggling so hard she's slipping sideways in Jeremy's arms. In the photo, she looks like she's about to explode out of her white lace dress, her broad shoulders offended by the delicate fabric she has bound them in. Next to her, Jeremy has a sly, secretive grin, most likely due to having just poked Claudia in the side to make her laugh. He is wearing an eye-popping polka-dot bow tie and Converse with his tuxedo, a wardrobe choice that Claudia had willingly endorsed at the time but now somewhat regretted. During the frenzied months preceding the wedding, Jeremy had joked frequently about "buying their shares in the wedding industrial complex," and despite her agreement in principle—hadn't she suggested that they ask for donations to a breast cancer charity rather than crystal from Bloomingdale's? Hadn't she nixed the priest in favor of Jeremy's Universal Life Church–ordained godfather?—the closer they got to the ceremony the more she found that these jabs upset her, as if he wasn't taking any of this seriously. And so, at the altar, she had bitten her lip, waiting for the tradition-mocking surprise she was sure he had prepared for their vows. Instead, she had been shocked by how serious he had suddenly become, how achingly raw. "You took care of me when I needed it the most," he told her, his eyes wet, his throat closed with emotion. "I can think of nothing that will make me happier than to spend the rest of my life taking care of you too."

Now, as Jeremy fiddled with the painting, adjusting its tilt, Claudia flipped on the television. The newscasters on every station were speaking in stiff baritones to inflate the urgency of the anticlimactic news they were conveying. A biggish quake but not catastrophically big, 5.8 on the Richter scale, they said. No deaths reported, no injuries, not even a collapsed building. She scanned the channels, hunting for wreckage or panic in the streets, but the worst the news crews could locate was a wall of old bricks that had fallen off the side of an automotive dealership downtown. Pedestrians were walking around the pile in an orderly fashion, talking on cellphones. Sanity had reigned, despite the game doomsday face of the on-the-street reporter.

She picked up a copy of *Entertainment Weekly* that had slid off the coffee table to the floor. It was still folded open to the review of her film, and her eye immediately dropped to the summary paragraph, which she'd read so many times today that she nearly had it memorized:

Spare Parts' disaffected twenty-somethings tackle their relationship malaise with hilariously blunt banter and a few unexpected narrative turns, lifting this refreshing independent film clear of your standard romantic comedy clichés. Claudia Munger's witty prose and eye for the absurd hint at a gimlet-eyed auteur with a promising future.

Claudia glanced at the wall clock—it was past six. She jumped up. "We're going to be late to the premiere!"

Jeremy jerked back from the painting, which still listed to one side. "Already? Give me five minutes," he said, and then paused to examine her. "You're wearing the dress I gave you for Christmas."

She looked down at the cocktail dress, a draped purple silk with a daring neckline that had to be held in place with double-stick tape. "Is it overkill?"

"No. You look amazing. I'll wear my suit," he said, "so we can match."

But Claudia had already started to second-guess herself. "Maybe by dressing up too much, I'll jinx it," she said. "No one will show up, and then I'll look ridiculous standing around in a sexy cocktail dress in a movie theater all by myself."

Jeremy laughed. "Everyone shows up when there's free booze involved. Stop worrying. You're going to be huge."

Claudia ducked her head to hide her smile, letting her ego momentarily pave a thoroughfare over premiere-night jitters. Even at her most self-assured, she didn't like to speak her hopes out loud; the one, say, where her modest independent film became a blockbuster, leading the way to a bigger film, and then another, a whole career's worth, until eventually her name actually meant something to audiences and industry alike. Carter, her agent, seemed to think this was already a done deal, and signs so far had been positive—the effusive meetings with studio executives, the deal on the table for her next script, the glowing advance reviews for her film. Up ahead, just within reach, she could see the red carpet at Cannes, the appearance on *Charlie Rose,* the Oscar nominations, the million-dollar paydays, and the irrevocable personal validation that would come with that coveted gilded seal from Hollywood's elite. Maybe only a handful of directors could claim this kind of career, but on days like today, she believed she was capable of being one of them.

"There's a lot riding on this," she said. "Can you blame me for being jittery?"

"Well, I say it's your premiere. Wear whatever you want and don't worry about it."

He leaned in, and she felt his lips grazing her hair. "This is a big deal," she muttered into the warm flesh of his shoulder, still slightly tacky from their kitchen encounter.

"Of course it's a big deal," he said. "It's the beginning."

She squirmed away from him and examined herself in the mirror over the fireplace: Curls were already springing free from her hair clips and there was a smudge of dust across the front of her skirt. The girl in the mirror was all soft cheeks and wide doe eyes, the features of an overgrown baby, someone you might want to cuddle with but not someone you would take seriously as a *gimlet-eyed auteur*. She stared hard, trying to spy this woman. Instead, she saw a sporty, anxious elf.

"You look great," Jeremy said, behind her. "Don't-fuck-with-the-director great."

She turned back to Jeremy. "Wear the suit," she said. "And hurry."

They followed klieg lights across the city, their excitement growing as they drove toward the beams, only to discover, once they drew closer, that the lights were actually parked in front of a new sushi restaurant where a string of valets attended to a parade of luxury SUVs. Claudia's premiere, located at an aging movie theater a few blocks farther west, merited no light display, no tabloid television reporters, no screaming fans lined up for autographs, no limousines triple-parked in the street. Still, there was a red carpet flung across the sidewalk and a cluster of photographers standing by a logo wall; a table of pretty young publicists was handing out will-call tickets to a line of guests. Someone had arranged a brace of groomed shrubs at the foot of the carpet, and metal crowd-control barriers had been set up to keep out the desultory riffraff. A cluster of anonymous industry insider types, mostly in jeans or suits fresh from work, stood schmoozing outside the theater entrance. The atmosphere outside the theater crackled with anticipation and possibility, and the traffic on Wilshire Boulevard clotted as passing drivers slowed in the hopes of spotting Someone Significant.

Frankly, Claudia was grateful that there was a premiere at all. These days, with Hollywood still reverberating from last winter's strike, the lavish parties were limited strictly to tent-pole films with hundred-million-dollar marketing budgets. Claudia's was a low-budget movie with a small distributor—no Angelina or Jennifer or Will in a lead role, just an ensemble cast of semirecognizable indie-cinema stalwarts and television actresses. But her distributors, buoyed by advance reviews and a handful of Sundance awards and smelling the possibility of a breakout hit ("The next *Juno,*" Claudia had heard them say more than once, in recent weeks, occasionally swapping in *Lost in Translation* or *Garden State*), had ponied up the money for the free cocktails and the Mediterranean buffet and the rented carpet, so here she was, at her very own Hollywood premiere. Having attended so many of these events as a guest, where officious publicists typically funneled her straight past the red carpet toward the "nobody of importance" entrance, she found it hard to accept that this time the press line was waiting for *her.*

They parked a few blocks away and walked back toward the theater. Claudia's phone chimed persistently as congratulatory text messages and voice mails arrived from her parents and older sister back in Michigan, who had attended the Sundance festival in January but were forgoing the premiere. The evening air was soupy with late-July humidity; sweat dripped down the nape of her neck as they approached the red carpet. She reached out for Jeremy's hand, and Jeremy gripped hers back with a damp palm. By now, she could see her investors waving at her, the publicists smiling toothily in her direction. For a brief moment, as she stepped into the turning crowd, she remembered the sensation of walking down the aisle at her wedding, of a hundred eyes turned in her direction and the realization that this one day was inviolably *hers;* then she and Jeremy were swallowed up by the heat-seeking crowd, which had pinpointed Claudia as tonight's fuel source. There was her producer, grabbing her in a bear hug; and the stars of her film, doing interviews with a reporter from a film magazine; and a clutch of her friends, smiling from the sidelines as the flashes popped off around her.

The rest was a blur, just as her wedding had been three years earlier: a series of high-voltage encounters, each spinning off from the last, each one landing her at the next, as little by little she made her way across the red carpet and into the lobby and down the aisle of the theater; until finally she found herself sitting in a seat in the center of a crowded room as the lights went down and her own name floated up on the screen in four-foot-high letters: *Written and directed by Claudia Munger.*

The crowd applauded warmly; a few crew members whooped in the back of the room. As the opening sequences spun across the screen, Claudia found herself suppressing a hiccup of hysteria: It was all so bizarrely surreal. Really, if you'd told the other ninety-two members of Claudia's graduating class at Mantanka Senior High that their classmate would someday become a filmmaker who would attend her Holly-wood premiere accompanied by her famous-on-college-radio hus-band, they would have laughed in your face. Not just because people in Mantanka didn't tend to stray far from the confines of Kallington County, but because Claudia was not the likeliest candidate for even minor celebrity. Prematurely tall, slightly plump, and suffering from a vicious overbite (the result of a childhood car accident), adolescent Claudia had suffered as the target of the mean girls in her class, a gag-gle of acid-jeans-wearing, Whitesnake-listening, Sun-In-lightened featherbrains who used her as the butt of every joke. *Claude the Clod.* The torturous orthodontic headgear she wore throughout her junior and senior years—a byzantine contraption that encased her entire head in reflective steel—didn't help matters. Crippled by self-consciousness, Claudia spent the better part of high school locked in her bedroom, losing herself in classic movies that she watched on the VCR her par-ents had given her to compensate for their guilt about her dentistry.

But her orthodontist knew what he was doing. By the time she ar-rived at university, as far from Mantanka as she could imagine—which, at that point, was still only Madison—Claudia had lost the extra weight and the oral accessories and had, in their place, a perfect set of gleam-ing white teeth and a new understanding about the power of reinven-tion. She dyed her hair black, got a lizard tattoo on her ankle, and immersed herself in Alterna-Culture (Lite Version). What she wanted to be, she eventually decided, was a filmmaker. Not an actress—she didn't have that theatrical bent, and she would never be mistaken as the prettiest girl in the room—but the person behind the camera, the one who controlled what you saw on the screen. The visionary. To imagine an entire world and then just *will it* into being: That was power.

She'd thrown herself into college with the thrilled abandon of a prisoner released from long incarceration, joining every college film club she could imagine, becoming the president of the Cinema Society and the director of the university's StudentTV and finishing with a straight-A transcript that qualified her for the UCLA film program—even if it didn't get her the scholarship she needed to afford school. *That* she managed by living with her parents for two torturous years after college, working three jobs, and saving every cent until she could climb on a plane for Los Angeles with enough money in her pocket to pay for subsidized housing and a steady diet of burritos.

By any measure, her early years in Los Angeles were a success, a blur of well-received student films and house parties and love affairs with interesting if generally unavailable guys. But at the center of every accomplishment was always the fear that this Claudia, the attractive ambitious confident one, was somehow a fraud—that the real Claudia was the brace-wearing outcast hiding in her bedroom back in Mantanka. Hollywood was a town built on judgment—your body, your finances, your credentials, all were constantly on parade—and there were moments when she felt she couldn't bear the scrutiny: She was sure that if they really looked hard she would inevitably come up short. Even after she finished film school with a student Oscar for her experimental short and entered into a coveted (if humiliating) job as assistant to a narcissistic director of blockbuster supernatural thrillers, she felt she didn't quite belong here in the land of bluster and self-righteousness. Maybe she wasn't cut out for a life of perpetual anxiety.

Still, she churned out three earnest little scripts, passion projects that because of their so-very-edgy subject matter (prostitutes in North Dakota; suburban parents who murder their kids; a nonlinear drug addiction redemption story) were doomed never to be made. Her film-school friends told her she was crazy to be writing this sort of dark, arty fare. "Are you trying to defeat yourself? Do a broad comedy, get yourself established with the studios, and then go for the fringe indie stuff," her best friend, Esme, advised her. But she wanted to be successful *and* an artist; was that so unrealistic?

By the time her doctor diagnosed her with an ulcer, she had shown the drug-addiction script to a half-dozen film finance companies and received vaguely positive responses, a handful of rewrite suggestions, but no offers. *They are trying to kill me with encouragement,* she realized. Burned out, dead broke, and still single, she seriously began to consider packing it all in and going back to Wisconsin. Maybe the life that awaited her there—a conventional sort of job, marriage, kids, the whole middle-America Apple Pie package—wasn't so bad after all. At least she wouldn't be living a life of incessant rejection.

But then, just when she was beginning to tinker with the Wisconsin job listings on Craigslist, she showed up at a friend's barbecue at a run-down Craftsman in Venice. There, she found herself meeting the slightly sad eyes of the shaggy musician standing across the mud-stricken lawn and realized, to her surprise and great delight, that he was walking straight toward her.

The morning after their first date (a screening of *Bonnie & Clyde* in the Hollywood Forever Cemetery, talking until dawn on the roof of Jeremy's apartment building over a bottle of warming Chianti), she began writing a new script, this time starting from a place of inspired pragmatism. This one would be a comedy (*comedies sell*) with a boy-meets-girl story at its center (*everyone loves a love story*) and a cast in their twenties (*prime moviegoing demographic*). It would be more commercial but still sufficiently indie; and maybe it wasn't the original direction she'd intended to go with her career but it might actually get made. She would give it another try. More than anything, suddenly, she wanted to stay in LA.

Still, it took a year to cobble together the financing for the film, as she coaxed the money, one zero at a time, from friends and friends of friends and one miraculous Israeli hedge fund investor. Her budget was still so modest that she'd had to borrow her video camera from a friend; instead of a craft services table, her Aunt Betsy sent out home-baked cookies from Indiana; since Claudia couldn't afford stars, her lead ac-tress was a refugee from a television sitcom. Jeremy—by that point, her husband—served as production assistant, fetching her coffee and rubbing her feet when she got home from the set. They still went over budget, a shortfall she personally fronted on a series of credit cards. There were days when it felt like she'd just made an audacious losing bet.

But then *Spare Parts* was accepted into the Sundance Film Festival, and there her movie won a directing award and was nominated for two others, and finally she sold it to a respected film distributor for a sum that felt enormous to her (although, put into perspective, was probably the equivalent of one day's catering budget for the average Hollywood blockbuster). Sitting in her lawyer's hotel room overlooking the snowy Rockies on the day she signed the deal, she felt high—not just from the altitude up there in the mountains, but also from a certitude that she had never felt before. She had taken a gamble on her own future and drawn a winning hand despite the odds.

That was how she'd ultimately ended up here, in the packed lobby of this theater, surrounded by friends and film industry acquaintances and people who had worked on her movie and a vast number of complete strangers. The movie had finished screening; and even though there wasn't a standing ovation at the end, the audience cheered and sat through the entire credit sequence before making a beeline for the free bar. Now, the crowd drew together in small clusters, chatting and shaking hands and exchanging cards and then breaking apart to form new clusters, a hive of bees performing some kind of intricately orchestrated honey dance.

A group of grips loomed over the food tables, guzzling their sponsored-vodka cocktails as they double-dipped in the hummus. The suits stood in the corner, rapidly typing on their BlackBerries. Claudia's film-school peers, led by her friend Esme, stood in a protective semicircle around her, eyeing the strangers who approached. Jeremy was in position by the crudités with his friend and bandmate Daniel, who'd brought her a bouquet of yellow lilies. Even Jeremy's father, Max, had come out and shuffled around in his corduroys and flip-flops and untucked dress shirt, lingering lasciviously near a clutch of twentysomething actresses who played bit parts in the film.

Claudia stood in the center of it all, feeling vaguely like a stuffed pheasant in a display vitrine. It wasn't an unpleasant sensation. She was the axis around which the entire room seemed to turn. She arranged herself directly in front of her movie poster—SPARE PARTS in capital letters, the faces of her lead actors in profile against the Los Angeles skyline, the *Variety* quote ("Sharply funny. . . . Addictive!") just below—and dizzily accepted the congratulations, the pressed hands and overenthusiastic hugs. "Huge fan, huge fan," a total stranger whispered in her ear.

Standing at the center of all this adulation, it seemed perfectly reasonable to expect *Spare Parts* to be a hit. Didn't she have glowing reviews from *Variety* and *The Hollywood Reporter* and, now, *Entertainment Weekly*? Even the Academy Awards was dominated by plucky little independent films these days, especially upbeat ones like hers. Yes, *Spare Parts* was opening in only twenty-three theaters this weekend, but next weekend it was scheduled to open in two hundred more, and yet more after that. She was days away from signing a movie development deal with a major motion picture studio; her next film was going to be big budget, cast with stars, a serious endeavor about issues of real importance (human smuggling on the Mexican border!). Maybe she'd revive her drug addiction script next.

"Claudia, I'm so sorry I can't stay long, but the sitter's threatening to call the cops on the twins," she heard in her ear, and turned to see RC. RC's real name was Renata Calliope, but she'd been going by her initials for the last twenty-five years, ever since she arrived in Los Angeles as a fledgling screenwriter in her early twenties and realized that Hollywood didn't take women seriously. By now, RC's screenwriting credits—including a handful of award-winning films and a long-running television hospital drama—were high-profile enough that the androgynous moniker was no longer effective or necessary, but she often told Claudia about the delight she once took in showing up for a production meeting in a miniskirt and heels and seeing the profound confusion on the producer's faces when they realized they'd accidentally hired a chick to script-doctor their TV pilot.

These days, RC rarely wore heels. A mother of ten-year-old twin boys, she had traded in the stilettos for sneakers years earlier, and the skirts had been swapped out for a uniform of cargo pants with men's Hanes T-shirts. Compact, her graying hair cropped short, RC looked more like a teenage boy than a woman nearing fifty, but she spoke with the smoked rasp of a Depression-era film star. She was only fourteen years older than Claudia but seemed of a different era entirely, spawned by 1980s Hollywood, when women in the business had to grow a protective reptilian skin and carry their own set of steel balls in their purse to survive. Claudia had been seated next to RC at a Women in Film symposium at a student film festival years before; two hours and four glasses of wine later, RC had adopted Claudia as her occasional mentee and more frequent friend. When Claudia was struggling to get *Spare Parts* off the ground, it was RC who lent her an $8,000 HD DV camera, introduced her to the Israeli hedge fund manager who would eventually provide her financing, and talked her off more than one ledge.

Claudia hugged her, smelled Ivory soap and basil oil. "Jason isn't home with the kids?"

RC shook her head. "He's off shooting a reality show in Singapore. So, quickly, my thoughts about your film, before I have to run: The new ending you cut really worked; that was definitely the right decision. And I know you were worried about the second-act turn but I think—"

"*Claudia!*" Carter, Claudia's agent, slid up beside her and gripped her elbow with a moist palm, interrupting them. His pink tie was loosened and his balding pate gently reflected the overhead lights, and when he leaned in to Claudia the faint scent of cigarette smoke wafted from behind his cauliflowered ears. "There she is, the *auteur.* You saw that review, I assume?"

"Hi, Carter," RC said coolly.

"RC. Wouldn't be a premiere without you, now, would it." Carter bared thirty-two whitened teeth, skipping the requisite handshake.

Claudia cleared her throat. "Yes, the review. I saw it. A bit hyperbolic on their part," she said. "I'm hardly Truffaut."

"Well, as long as it sells tickets, right? Anyway, great notice. The people who matter will see it."

"I'll take that," she said. She hesitated, knowing she shouldn't be talking business at her own premiere, and then turned slightly away from RC to whisper in her agent's ear. "So, has Fox signed the final paperwork yet?"

He whispered back without lowering his voice at all, speaking for RC's benefit. "We have a sit-down with the lawyers lined up for Monday. But the way things are lining up for *Spare Parts,* I'm thinking we might even be able to drive the price up a bit. You haven't signed anything yet; so let's make them sweat, right? You're a hot property right now. I'll have you all set up by the end of the month. Trust me, OK?" He leaned away and smiled. "RC, shouldn't she trust me?"

"As far as she can throw you, absolutely," RC said. She shoved her hands in her pockets and rocked back and forth in her Keds.

"RC. Always such a card."

Jeremy and Esme had joined the circle now, carrying paper napkins filled with gooey baklava. They greeted RC, then turned in unison to offer Carter politely bland smiles, wary of the presence of the suit.

"Carter, this is my friend Esme, and I think you've already met my husband?"

Carter gripped Jeremy's shoulder instead of shaking the hand Jeremy had proffered. "Of course. Jeremy the rock star!"

"Ah, well, Carter," Jeremy said, one eyebrow raised. "I'm hardly a rock star. My band has to finish its album first." He loosened his tie reflexively, eyeing Carter's tailored suit. Dressed up like this, Jeremy appeared more defined, handsome in an unshowy, unkempt sort of way. Claudia often thought that he looked more like a second guitarist than the lead singer of a band—he didn't have the typical ostentatious sex appeal of the man with the microphone and generally hid behind overgrown hair and slouchy jeans. Still, he could wear a suit well when the occasion demanded it.

"But they're almost done, and the stuff they've done so far is fantastic," Claudia said. "Audiophone. They have a show at Spaceland next month—you should come. All of you."

RC laughed. "Only if you're planning to go on at seven. I don't make it past ten these days."

Carter reared backward as if Jeremy might somehow infect him. "I don't do music, sorry. But Jeremy, I can hook you up with the right people. Do you have a manager? We need to make sure you keep up with your wife, don't we?"

"That would be impossible," Jeremy demurred.

"He's already been more successful than I am," Claudia protested. "He used to be in This Invisible Spot—you've heard of them?" Beside her, she sensed Jeremy protesting against the attention.

"Oh, yes, of course," Carter said, unconvincingly. "I think my daughter has an album." He glanced at his wristwatch. "Speaking of, gotta run, but we'll confab on Monday, OK? Go celebrate; you deserve it. RC, lovely as always." He patted Claudia on the elbow, ignored Esme and Jeremy entirely, and made a beeline for the door, maneuvering around a table stacked with pyramids of brownies as he flipped the daisy wheel of his PDA.

" 'I don't do music,' " Jeremy repeated to himself, laughing. "Who doesn't *do* music?"

"I guess I should be thankful I didn't go into creative," Esme said, "if that's the kind of people you have to deal with every day." She nervously twisted her hair back into a ponytail, clipped it, and then released it. Esme had very expensive hair, thick and black and glossy, a high-maintenance curtain that only a marketing executive could afford. She was the only person in Claudia's class at UCLA film school who had come to her senses after graduation and taken a salaried job on the business side of moviemaking. These days, she worked eighty-hour weeks developing high-concept trailers for animated family films, which meant that Claudia rarely saw her except for the occasional Sunday morning coffee runs.

RC shook her head. "I really should find you a new agent. I remember when Carter was in the mailroom at William Morris; he was an insincere snake even back then. His type likes to devour nice girls like you as an *amuse-bouche* before the main course."

"As long as he gets the deals done, I'm not complaining," Claudia said. "I don't have any clout without him."

"You're selling yourself short," RC observed. Her cellphone began to bleat, and she sighed. "Crap. I've got to do some damage control, but call me tomorrow, OK? You two should come for dinner soon. As long as you don't mind takeout." She vanished toward the door.

Esme spun slowly, surveying the dwindling crowd, then turned back to Claudia. "Hey, film star, do you know anyone who might want to teach film appreciation to high school students?" she asked. "My mom just took a job as head of this private high school—Ennis Gates Academy, maybe you've heard of it, it's very artsy-fartsy—and she's looking for a teacher to replace one that just ran off with a student. Oops, right? She asked me for suggestions, but you're better connected to that world than I am, being that I'm just a corporate drudge these days."

Claudia didn't feel in the least bit connected to teaching, but she didn't want to tell Esme this. "They teach film appreciation to high school students?" she asked.

Esme wrinkled her nose. "It's LA. Of course they do. The school got some enormous endowment from a former student who made a bundle in real estate and started a film production company. Or was it investment banking? Can't remember. Anyway, they have a whole department, own their own film equipment, all that."

"Seriously? At my high school in Wisconsin they cut art classes because they didn't have enough money for the tempera paints."

Esme twisted her hair up into a ponytail again, holding it back with one hand. "Deprivation is a foreign concept to these kids. It's kind of sad—there's nothing to strive for, since they have access to everything already. Honestly, I shudder at the thought of my kids growing up in this town."

Claudia nodded. "Of course, you and Jeremy grew up here," she said.

"And look how I turned out," Esme observed.

"My mom let me battle it out in a public high school," Jeremy said. "But it's a lot worse now. I don't think we'll be able to do that with ours."

Claudia glanced at Jeremy, surprised that he had brought up the subject of children. The verdict early on had been "not until our careers take off and we're financially stable." Then again, they were almost there now, weren't they?

"Anyway, film teachers? Know one?"

Claudia reluctantly turned back to Esme. "What about Malcolm, the guy who won the Nichols award when we were in film school?"

Esme curled her lip. "Last time I heard, he was working at a coffee shop and applying to law school. He never even sold a script. . . . I'll figure it out. I just thought I should ask while I had you in front of me. Soon you won't even take my calls anymore. Your movie's going to be huge and I'll never see you again."

"You're the one working eighty-hour weeks," Claudia pointed out.

"This is true. I should quit."

The hummus plates were ravaged; the party was starting to thin out. Claudia squeezed Jeremy's arm and left her friends to get a last drink before the bar closed. She stood in line by herself, behind two middle-aged women in head-to-toe black carrying leather satchels laden with screenplays—development executives, in all likelihood. One had Chanel sunglasses perched on top of her head, so firmly anchored in her pageboy that they might have been surgically attached.

"Two million," Sunglasses was saying.

"No way," said the other. "It's going up against five other films this weekend, including *Batman*. It won't even break a half-mil. They should have released it in the spring when there's no other competition."

The bartender poured them matching glasses of white wine from a bottle of cheap chardonnay. "Female audiences will love it," Sunglasses continued.

"Women don't go to the movies anymore, remember? They don't *count*."

"That doesn't mean it's not a shame."

Claudia could feel her feet tremble in her stilettos; the room suddenly seemed to be slipping sideways. It was only when the two women froze in place, clutching their chardonnay with stiff fingers, and the bartender lurched forward to stabilize the vodka bottle display rattling on the bar, that Claudia realized that they were experiencing an aftershock. "Do you feel—" said Sunglasses, to no one in particular.

Claudia braced herself, expecting the worst—*you were silly to think you'd escape unscathed*—but the earthquake had already dribbled away, almost before it had even begun. The noise level in the room briefly dipped, before returning to an even louder volume: A minor after-shock, barely worth mentioning. The women smiled and turned away from the bar, noting Claudia's presence for the first time. Sunglasses stepped past, screwed her lips into a wretched smile, and moved quickly away. Her friend hesitated and then leaned in toward Claudia. "Loved the film," she said. "Best of luck." And then she fled, following her friend.

Claudia watched them disappear into the waning crowd. *Maybe they weren't talking about my movie,* she told herself. *Even if they were, Holly-wood is full of jaded cynics who are proved wrong every day.* Outside the theater's glass doors, a work crew was beginning to dismantle the crowd-control barriers. Busboys had cleared the trays of crudités away, leaving behind tablecloths stained with tzatziki drips and pita crumbs. Plastic cups littered every ledge, marked with lipstick and then aban-doned. Claudia moved back toward Esme and Jeremy, who had re-trieved their belongings and were waiting for her to say goodbye. She tried to smile back with the same tipsy contentment that she read on their faces, but it felt forced. The aftershock had left her decidedly shaken.

Carter's assistant had the annoying habit of turning every statement into a question. She also repeated Claudia's name compulsively, an an-noying tic that Claudia suspected was intentional, perhaps to make clients feel at ease. To Claudia's ear, it sounded patronizing. "Carter Curtis's office?" the assistant queried, her voice squeaky and distracted. "Oh, Claudia again? Claudia, I'm sorry, but he's in a meeting? I'll take a message?"

Claudia sat, breathing heavily into her end of the phone, trying to quell her anxiety. Carter's meeting was taking an inordinately long time—by her count, he had been in a meeting for fourteen days now, since she first called him on the Monday after her film premiere. It was apparently a meeting that lasted all day and all night, leaving him only enough time to fire off a three-word e-mail to her—"No news yet." That message had come a week ago, at two in the morning. She had heard nothing since.

"Just tell him I'm trying to get a status update on the Fox deal," she said.

Frantic typing on the other end. "The Fox deal? OK? Anything else, Claudia?"

"That's it," she said, and hung up.

She sat at her desk in their guest bedroom and looked out the window at the retaining wall, a ten-foot concrete edifice that kept the up-hill neighbor's yard from sliding down into theirs. If she craned her head, she could see the sky, painfully bright, with a brown scrim of haze collecting across the horizon. It was barely nine in the morning, but the early August heat had already settled on the house, baking into the walls and turning their home into an oven. Sweat trickled down Claudia's back, collecting in a puddle at the waistband of her pajamas. She leaned back in her chair and stared at the ceiling, fretting.

The audiences hadn't materialized. Maybe it was the earthquakes (unlikely) or maybe it *was* the fact that women didn't go to movies (possible) or maybe people just didn't like it (she hoped not), but re-gardless, the audiences never came out to see her film. Not the first night and not any other night. They had avoided it entirely, all opening weekend; had ignored the politely positive reviews in the Friday papers and Ebert's genial thumbs-up. Claudia had read the box office report that first post-premiere Monday (outside, an unusual summer storm, violent spatters of rain against the sliding glass door even though the temperature outside was still above ninety), letting her eyes scan farther down the list of films in release, and still farther, all the way to the very bottom of the page, where her film had lodged just above a documen-tary about freedom fighters in Gaza and just below a slapstick comedy about competitive air hockey starring Cheech Marin that had already been out for forty-two weeks. Total box office take: $39,000.

Reading the box office reports that morning, she felt something burrowing deep in her gut, a tiny worm of panic taking up residence. "But that's just one weekend. It's way too soon to know what your movie's going to do," Jeremy comforted her, and she reassured herself that he was right: There was plenty of time for word of mouth to gather and grow, and even if first-weekend grosses had been frankly dismal the film could still evolve into a bonafide sleeper hit over the course of the next months. The film hadn't even been released in most of America yet; it was in less than two dozen theaters! Once it was in wider release, once it received more press, it was possible that the rest of the country would finally catch on.

Except that the following weekend a half-dozen theaters bumped her film to make way for a Ben Stiller comedy. And then, this last weekend, instead of going wide as promised, her distributor yanked the film altogether, hoping to cut its losses. Just like that, less than three weeks after opening night, the film was gone. Almost as if it had never been made in the first place. Claudia wondered if she'd hallucinated the entire thing.

There would be other movies, she reminded herself. If all went as promised, she'd be directing a new one by the end of the year. Except that Carter wasn't returning her calls, which hardly seemed like a promising sign. She had never been an insomniac, but during the last two weeks, night after night, she had found herself awake at three in the morning. She would lie there in the dark, Jeremy placidly snoring beside her, and feel the increasingly familiar battle lines being drawn between body and mind: her thoughts setting off on a circuitous race course, denying her bleary body another night's sleep. Three o'clock in the morning had become her hour, the Hour of Claudia, Queen of Fret.

"Breakfast?" Claudia turned to see Jeremy in the doorway, with a plate of scrambled eggs in hand.

"Aren't you going to be late for work?" She reached out for the plate.

"Edgar's got meetings in New York this week, so I can go in at lunchtime and no one will notice. Honestly, I could skip work entirely and he wouldn't know the difference."

"Nice work ethic," she said. "Maybe you want to use this as an opportunity to patch the cracks from the earthquake?"

"That's your job." He flashed an apologetic grin. "I'm going to catch up on those bills. And I want to work on a new song."

"Oh? How close are you to finishing the album?" She immediately regretted the question. In the dozen times she had asked him this over the course of the last year, the answer had consistently been the same: "Soon." With each repetition the question sounded less like enthusiastic curiosity and more like wifely badgering. She didn't want to be that kind of wife—like her mom, always nagging her dad to mow the lawn or winterize the attic. Anyway, the album was dependent not just on Jeremy but on the other three members of his band. But with each passing month some of the air was let out of Claudia's excitement and she couldn't help but wonder why, exactly, the album was taking so damn long.

"We're close-ish," he said. He poked at an air bubble in the paint, a cheery cerulean color that she and Jeremy had applied themselves, somewhat sloppily.

At her elbow, the phone rang. She glanced at the caller ID: *Carter Curtis.* "Finally!" she muttered, grabbing for the phone.

"Tell him to get us that check soon." Jeremy tapped twice on the doorframe and then disappeared back into the living room.

Carter's voice on the other end was hollow and distant, as if he were speaking from one end of a tin can.

"Claudia? Carter."

"Please tell me you have the signed deal in front of you." She hunched over her desk, putting her nose close to a postcard that her parents had sent her from their recent RV trip to Mount Rushmore. George Washington stared back at her with stoic resignation.

Carter hesitated a half second too long, and in that moment Claudia knew. She lowered her forehead to the desk and braced herself.

"Unfortunately, no," he said. "Fox backed out."

Claudia could feel her breath fogging the surface of her desk. She squeezed her eyes closed, determined not to cry while on the phone with her agent.

"OK," she said. "Well, can we go back to Universal or Warner or any of the other studios who wanted to buy the script."

"That's what I've been doing all week. And they all passed."

"They suddenly don't like my script anymore? Didn't the executive at Warner call it 'Oscar bait' just last month?"

Carter sighed heavily. In the background, she could hear honking—he was in his car. "You know how it is in Hollywood, Claudia. They have no sense of perspective. They see a box office flop and run away in a panic."

She sat upright, wounded. "Flop?"

"Bad word choice, sorry." His words were muffled as he fumbled with his cellphone. "But look, Claudia, we both know *Spare Parts* didn't perform to expectations. I think it's a genius film, but honestly, the timing was off. Maybe it was just too *smart*. Audiences want popcorn fluff right now; they don't want to think. Maybe you should retool your new script as a comedy instead."

"But it's a drama about human smuggling in Mexico!"

"Then write something new." She could hear the impatience creeping into his voice. "It's murder out there. You've read the stories. There's no money anymore. The industry's in the tank. The studios are running scared from anything that looks like it might require audiences to use their brains."

"Pussies," she hissed, surprising herself.

"Yes. Pussies." There was a click on Carter's end of the line. "Hey, I have to take this call. But don't despair—get back to work writing. I'll be in touch, OK?"

The line went dead. She sat there, clutching the phone in her damp hand. From far away, she could hear the line beeping at her, and still she sat there, staring at a blank patch of wall across the room. She picked a pen off her desk and flung it. It left a black mark on the paint just above the light switch and then clattered uselessly to the floor.

"Jeremy?" She waited for Jeremy to appear in the doorway, but a minute passed with no sound of footsteps coming her way. She pushed herself out of her chair, letting her frustration run naturally downhill toward its only available outlet: her husband. Where was he when she needed him?

"Jeremy?" she called again, as she walked down the hall to the living room.

Jeremy was sitting at their scarred dining room table, surrounded by bills. He held a letter in his hand and didn't look up when she came in the room, not even when she crossed to stand directly before him. Vacillating between fury and misery, she felt the first tear escape from her right eye and dash down toward her nose.

"Well, that was—" she began, but then Jeremy looked up, and the rest of the tears dried up instantly. The last time she had seen him look this serious was when he told her his mother had less than a month to live: His face had the same flat quality, as if a horizontal line had been drawn across his features. He stared at her blankly.

"What is it?" she asked, wiping the solitary drop away.

"A notice of default," he said.

"Default on what?"

"Our house."

Somewhere in her chest, a trap door opened. "I don't understand."

Jeremy shook his head. "Well, the adjustable rate mortgage . . . it adjusted. Two months ago. Hard to believe we've already lived here three years. So we're a little behind." He shuffled the papers in his hand, stacking them neatly. "You know what? Don't worry about it."

"Wait—you haven't been paying the mortgage?" Claudia could hear her voice growing increasingly shrill.

Jeremy looked down at the letter on the top of the stack, as if it might tell him what to say. "Our payments more than doubled, to thirty-seven hundred a month. And our savings are gone, and my salary at BeTee wasn't covering expenses, and I figured the money from your deal was coming in soon so we could be a little late."

"Our mortgage doubled? And you didn't tell me? And you didn't pay it?" Repeating his words didn't imbue them with more logic.

"You were so stressed about your movie, I didn't want to worry you even more. Anyway, I didn't think it was a big deal to miss one or two payments. I used to do that all the time in my old place."

"Your old place was a *rental,* Jeremy. Your landlord was your *friend,*" she said. The meaning of the notice finally sank in: "Does this mean— the bank is foreclosing?"

Jeremy looked down at the letter in his hand. "I don't know. . . . There's all this junk mail that comes from the bank. . . ." His voice trailed off and he looked up at her, hopeful. "But we'll just pay it all off now. So. Did Carter have the deal signed? How soon are you getting paid?"

Claudia sat down heavily in a chair and stared up at the ceiling in supplication, noticing yet another new crack created there by the earthquake. The crack started at one corner, near the window, and darted diagonally across the room, ending just above the sliding glass door that led out to the deck. As Jeremy waited for an answer, Claudia lowered her gaze. She looked out the window past the tops of the eucalyptus trees. The wild grasses that grew up the hill across the way were the color of parchment paper, half dead from the sun, and the houses perched on the top of the hill looked like sentinels standing watch over a scorched earth. Farther out, the skyline of downtown shimmered in the summer heat. She stared long and hard at their view, as if waiting for the tectonic plates to shift once more, this time collapsing the world before her into rubble, once and for all.

Jeremy

THEIR LOAN CONSULTANT WAS UNFORTUNATELY HOT. TAMRA Goldsmith wore a tight black skirt, a filmy white blouse that suggested transparency without quite offering a glimpse of bra, and shiny black stiletto heels with red soles that flashed up at Jeremy like an extended tongue when she crossed her legs. Tamra was slender and poised and not that much older than they were, and when they sank down in the overstuffed chairs in front of her desk, Claudia seemed visibly to shrink before her. Jeremy pushed his own chair slightly back and away to telegraph to Claudia that the pretty banker was of no interest to him, even as he couldn't help noticing a hillock of tanned breast peeping from the top of Tamra's blouse. The mental exertions required by this—vague lust, connubial reassurance, discomfort at the need to be there in the first place—prevented Jeremy from really focusing on the first few minutes of their meeting.

Claudia sat next to him, a spiral notebook splayed open on her lap. Her pen hovered a scant millimeter over the paper, quivering with anticipation. She had dressed up for their meeting ("so she knows we're taking this seriously," she had said, a comment that Jeremy had found equal parts endearing and frightening) in a button-front blouse and a skirt of some sort of stretchy material that fit snugly across her thighs.

Tamra was typing on her computer and nibbling on her red-glossed lower lip. Behind her, he could see a security guard standing by the bank's double-doored vestibule, ushering customers in one by one. Red lights blinked on and off over the door, forbidding entry. A snaking line of customers stood waiting for their allotted time with a teller, sullenly facing forward, shifting as they read the news feed on the television monitor bolted to the wall. *Real estate prices down 18% in LA County. Gunman kills four in Monrovia. Police arrest teens for beating homeless woman. Jobless rate climbs to 5.7%.* Jeremy wondered if this was what it felt like to live in a maximum security prison.

Claudia finally broke the silence. "So we were thinking we would restructure our loan," she said, in what Jeremy recognized as her director's voice: friendly, firm, slightly bossy. "We were interested in finding out what options were available to us." To emphasize his wife's words, Jeremy offered Tamra an easygoing grin, the one that had always seemed to get him what he wanted in the past: one part dimple, one part self-effacing charm, one part happy-go-lucky reassurance. This smile had seduced jaded audiences in eleven countries, allowed him to live in friends' guest bedrooms for months at a time, earned him a free car upon arrival in Los Angeles; it even wooed his wife. Surely, it couldn't hurt to employ it now.

But Tamra sighed audibly. This was not a promising sound. "Interest-only adjustable-rate mortgages," she said. "The bane of my existence. I can't tell you how many people I've had in here in the last few months, panicking because their loans ballooned."

"But it's totally fixable," Jeremy offered, keeping his voice varnished with a shiny coat of optimism.

"Define fixable?"

Jeremy's smile tightened. "You tell me."

"Unfortunately, I don't have anything to tell you." Tamra offered a sympathetic smile, revealing red lipstick smudges across what were actually rather rabbity front teeth.

Claudia leaned in. "Wait. Are you saying we *can't* restructure our loan? Get an extension or a waiver or something?"

"If you like, you can fill out the paperwork for an extension request, and I'll submit it for processing. But I wouldn't count on it." Tamra sounded almost happy about this. Jeremy looked over at Claudia, marveling at this woman's flippancy. Was the banker *enjoying* this? It had to be a game; she was a sadist who was taking pleasure in torturing them—just a bit—before she took on the mantle of savior.

. Claudia fumbled with her notebook, flipping back and forth as she tried to read her own cramped notes. "OK," she said. The confidence in her voice was wavering; she sounded a touch querulous. "Well, what about refinancing? I read that mortgage rates are starting to drop. Maybe we could get a new loan with better terms?"

Tamra reached up to tuck a loose strand of brown hair behind her ear, nudging it back into her bun with a long glossy nail that had been tipped with a crescent of white. Fussy nails. Jeremy was finding her less attractive by the minute. He looked at his low-maintenance wife—all no-nonsense manicure and sexily disheveled curls and artfully invisible makeup—with a new appreciation. Jeremy wanted to get this over quickly so he could take her home and climb back into bed and spend the afternoon fucking and eating peppermint ice cream and watching old cartoons in the safety of their house.

"According to our records, we sent you a letter several months ago setting out your refinancing options. Any particular reason why you didn't take us up on our offer then? You're already two months behind on your payments."

Claudia looked at Jeremy. He felt himself shrinking under the women's shared gaze, as if by neglecting to read every single piece of mail the bank sent (and it sent so many! disclosure notices and monthly statements and privacy notifications and credit card solicitations!) he had caused this situation. Maybe he had. In fact, over the course of the last anxious week, he had been plagued by the unpleasant suspicion that this current mortgage mess was entirely his fault—he wasn't exactly a *provider*, and his approach to bill-paying was best described as a healthy serving of enthusiastic procrastination with a hasty chaser of last-minute panic. It was obvious now that he should have told Claudia when the mortgage ballooned, should have warned her they were missing payments, should never have listened to the gremlin in his head that told him if he ignored the situation it would somehow work itself out. Now, some internal husbandly impulse that he wasn't previously aware he possessed had kicked in; he felt the need to *fix things*. One way or another, he would extricate them from this mess.

"Yeah, there was a mix-up with the mail," he mumbled. "But we've only missed two mortgage payments! Refinancing is still an option, right?"

Tamra opened a binder and flipped through pages of cramped tables, cross-referencing what she saw there with the information on her computer screen. "No," she said. "Things are changing rather rapidly in the mortgage industry right now. So that's not a possibility anymore, at least not for a couple with your financial record. Your credit scores are low. I see you racked up a rather impressive credit card debt two years ago?"

"That was for my film," Claudia said. She leaned forward, gripping the polished edge of the desk. "We paid that off this spring, when I sold the movie."

"Well, all that matters is the score they give us, sorry."

"OK," Jeremy said, growing impatient. "Well, what about applying for a home equity loan, then."

Tamra laughed, a damp little snort of surprise. "Let me get this straight. You want me to lend you money to pay back the money we already lent you?" She shook her head. "Let's be realistic here. You have no savings of note, no investments that I am aware of, and no retirement accounts. You appear to be living month-to-month, yes?" She looked up and took their stoic silence as an affirmation. "Do you own anything of value other than the house?"

Claudia looked at Jeremy. "The painting, maybe. What do you think it's worth, twenty thousand?"

Jeremy shrank back in his seat, dodging her suggestion. "No way," he said, answering not Claudia's actual question but the implicit one she hadn't spoken out loud—*Would you be willing to sell it?*

"Well, that wouldn't help much anyway," said Tamra. "You need a long-term solution. I gather from the tax returns you have here that Jeremy is the only one of you with a salaried income. Jeremy, is this a career in which you can be expecting more financial upside in the short term?"

Jeremy felt his face redden, acutely aware that he didn't really have a proper career to be at the beginning of. It wasn't like there was a corporate ladder in T-shirt design that he was going to be climbing: There were only six employees at BeTee—the three Hondurans who did the screen printing and shipping, the woman who handled sales, him, and Edgar, and Edgar owned the place. In the last three years Jeremy had managed two raises, so that now he was making fifty-two thousand a year instead of forty, and his title had changed from Designer to Graphics Guru, but that was more of an in-joke between him and Edgar than a real promotion. As a day job it was bearable—and he certainly appreciated how easy it was—but it definitely was not something he considered a career. The *career* was his music, although the band was still stuck on song seven of their album, Daniel hadn't written new lyrics in a month, and Jeremy was starting to get concerned about the effect that their drummer's cocaine habit was having on their practice schedule.

"Not exactly, no," he said. He hated Tamra, his own age but somehow not his peer at all, with her expensive shoes and her computer spreadsheets and her long-term asset management plans. He hated that they had to sit here at all, at this woman's mercy. How had he ended up here?

Really, if you wanted to get nitpicky about it, the house had never been his idea in the first place. When Claudia first proposed the idea, a week after their wedding, he was horrified by the thought of mortgage payments and home repair and insurance. He had never really considered it—*real estate*—before; it had never seemed like something that fit his life. The places he'd lived when he was growing up had felt less like permanently fixed positions than temporary landing pads from which he and Jillian could launch a fresh assault on the world. There had been ashram stays in India and artists' retreats in San Miguel de Allende and New Age therapy conferences in Taos and a two-year stint in a student apartment in Davis while his mother finished her PhD in psychology, but there hadn't been anything resembling a long-term living situation until they settled into a rental bungalow in Venice during Jeremy's high school years (Jillian's only concession to "normalcy" for her son). And even that bungalow always felt uninhabited, with packing boxes that remained piled in the corners for years after they moved in. A house wasn't a value for Jillian; it was, simply, a necessity. Shelter, pure and simple.

Jeremy—a perpetual renter and couch surfer—had never bothered to take another view until Claudia changed his mind. Buying a house was a way for them to start a life that was about *them,* a newly married couple instead of two discrete individuals, she'd argued. An expression of their relationship, their aspirations, their vision of the world. It was what you were *supposed to do* at this point in your life. Anyway, mortgages were cheap. She'd run the numbers—if they got one of those interest-only adjustable rate loans everyone was offering, monthly payments would be negligible, even less than rent; with the real estate market going up 15 to 20 percent every year, they might even *make* money. Claudia had argued for it with a force of will that surprised him, and maybe because it was the first thing in their relationship that she had ever insisted upon, Jeremy didn't want to disappoint her. Frankly, it all sounded pretty good. Money for nothing. A house for free.

So he hadn't objected—not that first day, nor any other day during the two months it took them to locate the bungalow in Mount Washington. By that point, he'd become infected by her enthusiasm; he had the real estate bug bad. He found himself gushing about their new house's fantastic views, the quirky charm of its original details, the friendly neighborhood, the deer that occasionally ran down the street en route to the canyon. It could be their creative launching pad, they agreed; an artists' retreat like those little cabins in Laurel Canyon where Joni Mitchell and Frank Zappa lived and worked during the 1960s. He'd write his songs; she'd direct her movies; they'd have sunset parties on the deck and serve *mojitos* in jelly jars, culminating in impromptu late-night jam sessions. Paradise.

The fact that so many other people seemed to want the house—that they'd had to increase their offer twice, in order to outbid everyone else—simply cemented the fact that they'd done the smart thing. Claudia was right. The mortgage was manageable, the house value rocketed over the following years, and nothing had been sacrificed—not his ambitions, certainly not his lifestyle. It was a great house, even if it was a bit remote for his taste, and they'd fixed it up well. Really, he had kind of enjoyed the whole nesting thing: painting the walls periwinkle and lettuce, and going to the Rose Bowl flea market and IKEA to pick out furniture, and planting tomatoes in pots on the deck. They hosted several memorable summer barbecues. And if it all felt maybe a little *too* easy, he'd just chalked that up to his own ignorance about complicated financial matters.

Except that now it was clear that he should have listened to that initial warning bell. Because here they were, three years later, and it was clear they'd somehow tethered themselves to a boulder that was rolling downhill. He glanced down at Claudia's notepad. She'd written down: *Look into directing commercials. Roommate? Reduce monthly budget by 30%. Cancel dinner reservations Friday night. Lose: Cable, home phone line. Sell Jeremy's extra guitars? Yard sale.* The last item—*stable income!*—she'd underlined three times.

He turned his focus up toward his wife, who was now arguing with Tamra. She'd finally lost her temper, and the sound level of her voice was slowly rising, as if someone were stealthily turning up the dial on an amp. The people in line had turned to look at them, the most diverting entertainment in the bank. "So you're saying you can't do anything to help us?" Claudia said, with throaty indignance. "You're telling us we've wasted a half hour of our lives sitting here with you, while you gloated about our situation, and now you're unwilling to do anything?" Jeremy stared at his wife, surprised to see her lose her calm. This was new to him. He put his hand on Claudia's leg, both as a gesture of support and a plea for her to maybe tone it down a little bit. Getting confrontational wasn't going to help matters; he knew that much.

Tamra raised her hands and faced her palms to them, halting the torrent of abuse in its tracks. Her hands were soft and pink and plump. "I'm not gloating. I know you want to blame me, as the face of this institution, but it's nothing I can control. It's not that I'm unwilling—I would help if I could. But my hands are tied. I feed the numbers into the computer, and it tells me what I can and can't do." She looked tired, all of a sudden, and Jeremy could see ghostly traces of puffiness under her eyes, not quite masked by a layer of flesh-tone makeup. "It's just the reality of the mortgage industry right now. It's not like it used to be. Money is tight."

Claudia fell back in her seat, the anger dissipating as quickly as it came. She folded her arms tightly against her chest. "OK. Well, this is *our* reality," she said, in a voice of glum resignation. "We don't have enough cash on hand to cover the mortgage this month. Or next month. Not to mention the two back payments we already owe. So what happens next?"

"What happens next is foreclosure proceedings, Mrs. Munger." Tamra snapped her binder shut with a brisk finality. It was beginning to dawn on Jeremy that their situation was fairly simple after all: They needed more money, and they didn't have any. Unless Tamra miraculously decided to write them a personal check, he couldn't see how this meeting could ever have had have a positive outcome. They should never have come.

He gripped Claudia's knee harder, keeping her pressed against her seat. He could feel her straining under his hand with the impulse to flee this place as quickly as possible. But he wanted to give it one last shot, his best effort at being the family problem solver, the savior, the husband.

"Tamra," he began, putting every ounce of sincerity and solemnity he could muster into those two syllables. He fixed his eyes on the banker's with mute promise—of what, he wasn't sure. "Tamra, is there anything we can do in this situation? Anything at all?"

Tamra stood up, smoothing the black skirt down over her hips. She glanced at the bank's sign-in area, where a collection of sullen couples was seated on red vinyl divans, awaiting their turn with her. She proffered a stiff hand toward them, let it hang there in the air, unclaimed, as Jeremy and Claudia obediently rose from their seats. "My suggestion?" she said. "Get a better job."

They drove home in silence, Jeremy behind the wheel of the Jetta, Claudia sitting stiffly beside him, flipping back and forth through her notebook. She made little strangling noises under her breath, noises that Jeremy suspected were intended as an opening for him to ask what she was thinking. He glanced over to see her staring at her little apocalyptic jottings—*stable income!*—and flipped on the radio, as if this might somehow ward off the horror of those two words. The station was in the middle of a subscriber drive, and the DJs swapped banal platitudes about the joys of supporting public radio; but even this was preferable to the painful conversation that he feared would otherwise fill the void.

As they pulled onto the highway, he had the thought that sometimes struck him on occasions like this: *What Would Aoki Think?* Aoki, his own personal Jesus, an omniscient and certainly vengeful God, was always in the wings waiting to smite Jeremy with her unsolicited opinion. Even now, as he tried to dispel the memory of Tamra's lecture about the necessity of income management and a long-term savings plan, he could envision Aoki's disembodied moon face, her asymmetrical black bob whipping across her cheeks, getting stuck in her fuchsia lipstick, as she shook her head in dismay. *No no no no.* He hadn't actually seen Aoki in nearly four years, not since the day he went to retrieve his guitar from her studio and found she'd hacked it into twenty pieces, painted it Pepto-Bismol pink, and then reassembled it as an abstract sculpture entitled *Untitled 82: Fuck You Jeremy.* Still, Aoki was with him forever, judging him. And right now, he knew she would be laughing at him. He had committed the cardinal sin: He became boring.

Aoki was many things—slightly schizophrenic, maddeningly childish, disgustingly talented, and (above all) completely self-centered—but one thing that she was not, ever, was boring. The precious only child of Japanese immigrants who owned three sushi restaurants on Long Island, Aoki had been thrown out of four reform schools before her parents gave up and enrolled her in a New York art college at the age of seventeen. By the time Jeremy met her, twelve years later, she was mildly notorious within a certain downtown art set for her rococo paintings of classic cartoon characters in obscene sexual positions: Mickey Mouse sixty-nining Mary Worth. Dirty Sanchez Andy Capp.

Despite having attended the same New York arts college three years later, Jeremy had never heard of Aoki before the night she barged backstage after an early This Invisible Spot gig and presented herself to him. He was used to undeserved female attention—when you were the guitarist of an indie rock band, it came with the territory—but not like this. She wore a strapless white fake-fur dress of her own design, held together with strategic Velcro, which she ripped apart as he stood by the rancid cold-cut tray. The dress dropped to the floor, revealing slight breasts and a pair of faded Boba-Fett Underoos.

"So I've got this thing right now for transparent communication, OK?" she began, ignoring the flabbergasted groupies and his coughing bandmates, locking her dark eyes on Jeremy. "It's kind of a social experiment, but I saw you onstage and I thought, Hey, he's pretty cute and it would be fun to fuck him, so here I am. An offering. And this is what you get, nothing coy about it, so you can't complain I misled you later." The lewd content of her proposition contrasted with her high-pitched little-girl voice and the ridiculous underwear, rendering Jeremy speechless for the first time he could remember. No humorous observations, no self-effacing ripostes, no sly pop-culture references could stand up to the furious intensity of Aoki's will.

Jeremy thought she must be a little bit insane, but he admired the sheer ballsiness of the gesture, and he was stoned, so he took her up on her offer—not right then and there but about four hours later, after they'd shared two more joints and a pint of Wild Turkey and adjourned to her East Village flat. The force of Aoki's naked intention made him feel as if he'd looked in the mirror and discovered he was far more interesting than he had ever felt himself to be. He thought she'd somehow reinvented him, but he eventually realized, over the ensuing four years, that she'd devoured him instead, the way a scorpion eats its prey: paralyzing him and then swallowing him whole, beginning with his head.

He spent the first few years of the millennium blindly pursuing Aoki: through her two stints in rehab, three bouts of infidelity (two boys, one girl), and one attempted suicide. She was addicted to coke, and then heroin; probably sex too. And Jeremy was addicted to her, the way the space-time continuum seemed to flex and recoil when she stepped in a room. How else to explain why he benignly accepted her manic behavior, came to see it as perfectly normal? One day, he would come home and discover that she'd papered over their entire apartment (including windows, floor, and all major appliances) with smiley-face wallpaper that she'd found at a thrift store; the next he would find her naked on the fire escape, sobbing over the death of her parent's geriatric dachshund; the day after that, she would descend on the restaurant where he was waiting tables and talk him into quitting his job on the spot and flying to Berlin with her, where they slept in a squat with a group of Slovenian anarchists.

Aoki's life was a never-ending art project, lived as if an invisible audience were judging her work for originality and intensity of performance. Jeremy dutifully stepped into the role of muse and sidekick, a Zenlike counterweight for her unpredictable psychosis, the only person in Aoki's life who took her stunts in stride. She saw him, she said, as her savior, a role that both thrilled and exhausted him. After her second rehab stint, a brief period of freedom and sanity when Jeremy considered but ultimately rejected the thought of sneaking off to a foreign country before she returned, a freshly committed Aoki began a series of oil portraits, all of Jeremy—his hand, his torso, his neck, but never his entire face: intensely violent, quasi-spiritual, ten-foot tall paintings that finally launched her into critical art-world fame. There were shows in Tel Aviv and Rio. She cut her hair in a spiral around her head and took to wearing only clothes that were silver. Life with her was an amusement-park ride Jeremy couldn't seem to get off, even as the loop-de-loops nauseated him and the constant adrenaline threatened to give him a heart attack.

Besides, This Invisible Spot, too, was coming into its own. The band fired their atonal lead singer and promoted Jeremy from backup to lead; they hired an old friend of Aoki's, a manic Belgian named Anton, to write new material for them; they abandoned their melancholic slow-core sound, added a DJ, and began playing their songs at double speed. In 2003, they were signed to a prominent indie record label and released an album, *Feeling Fantastik*. It sold eighty thousand copies in the States, garnered raves from previously dismissive music critics, and briefly launched them to number two on the college charts. In America, they were respected; in Asia, they were huge. During that ill-fated February, the band toured in Singapore and Seoul and Tokyo, where they played to a crowd of ten thousand screaming *harajuko* girls and Aoki signed with a prestigious gallery. On a train to Kyoto, with his bandmates listening to their iPods in complicit silence and Aoki asleep with her head on his lap, Jeremy decided that he would propose to

Aoki at the Temple of the Golden Pavilion, just so that this hallucination—the frozen rice fields spinning past, the world unfurling before him—would never end. Except that when they got to Kyoto, Aoki disappeared for two days and returned so hung over that she spent the last leg of the trip vomiting blood in the bathroom. On the plane home, Aoki confessed that she'd been sleeping with Anton since Singapore. "He was seeking artistic inspiration, and I knew I could give it to him. It was really for the good of the whole band, including you," she explained to Jeremy, as if he would understand.

Considering his history, he might have given in to her twisted logic, if it hadn't been for the message on his answering machine when he finally arrived home, bleary and jet-lagged and shell-shocked. The message was from Jillian, his mother, informing him that she'd been diagnosed with stage-three breast cancer and her boyfriend had moved out because he couldn't handle the pressure of watching her die and would he mind coming out to Los Angeles to take care of her?

He moved a week later, quitting the band and breaking up with Aoki in an epic six-hour screaming match that ended with her threatening to jump off the Williamsburg Bridge if he got on the plane. He went anyway, and as he flew over the Great Plains toward the West Coast, looking down at the golden-brown fields that covered the country like a warm patchwork quilt, it was as if he'd expunged a poison from his bloodstream and was waking up, slowly, from a very long intoxication.

Things changed in LA, so rapidly that it felt like his years with Aoki in New York were a dream sequence from someone else's biopic. Reality was his sick mother, wasting away in her stuffy bungalow bedroom as she ejected an astonishing quantity of pus and blood and other vile secretions from her dying body. And there was a whole new social world for him to navigate, with long-neglected school friends like Daniel and Edgar. And then, only a few months after arriving home, there was Claudia. They'd met at the barbecue of a mutual friend, and he'd been struck by her immediately—not that she was the prettiest girl he'd met (though she was sexy in an endearing, guileless sort of way), but that she was so open, so free of artifice, in a way Aoki had never been. She didn't try to command attention but gathered it slowly to herself with easy humor and an earnestness that was foreign to him.

She was chronically insecure, there was no doubt about that. But underneath that nice-Midwestern-girl exterior was a stubborn streak and willful ambition. Bonus: she was creative, like Aoki, only *without* the exhausting chaos. Being with Claudia felt like being wrapped in a down duvet; it was comforting to be in a relationship of equals, one where he could sometimes—hell, *often*—even be at its center. During the endless months of Jillian's dying, he cried in Claudia's soft arms so many times that he eventually couldn't imagine ever living without them again.

He'd since lost touch with many of his friends from New York, including his bandmates, who had hired a new lead singer, renamed the band, released a second album that flopped, and finally disbanded when Anton died of a heroin overdose. Aoki's star had risen since their breakup; she was genuinely famous now, and he saw her name and face in hip lifestyle magazines every once in a while. He'd look at these photographs intently, trying to connect the woman in the pictures, blazing intention and icy confidence, with the screaming hysteric he'd left in a heap on her paint-splattered concrete floor. He threw these magazines away at work, so Claudia wouldn't run across them.

Otherwise, the only reminder he kept of their years together— besides the annoying voice that lingered in his head, judging him—was the painting hanging in the living room, an image of his own twisted torso reaching out for something just off-canvas. She'd given him the painting for his thirtieth birthday, right before they broke up. It was so monstrously monumental, so desperately needy, and so intensely personal that getting rid of it would be like throwing away a chunk of his own flesh. Even after everything had changed, he couldn't quite make that final break. So the painting hung there above the worn leather couch, a reminder of a Jeremy he no longer really recognized but sometimes missed, the way you get nostalgic for a long-lost college friend.

The last time he'd heard from Aoki was a letter she sent him when she found out about his wedding, three years ago. The message was scrawled in crayon, on the back of an old pen-and-ink sketch she'd made of him, sleeping.

jeremy she will never love you the way you need to be loved. you have bled my heart dry leaving me as empty as a ghost. i know i'm supposed to wish you all the happiness in the world but that would be a lie so i'm just going to say that someday you will remember that the only true love is devastation and you will realize that i will be with you forever.

She didn't sign it, an egotist to the end. He had almost shared the letter with Claudia, as a way of showing her how ridiculous the whole melodramatic episode with Aoki had really been, how over it all he really was, but then he thought better of it. He tucked the note in the back of a drawer and wiped it from his mind.

At least, that was the last time he'd heard from Aoki until two days ago, when he'd found an e-mail from her in his in-box. Just two sentences:

Coming to Los Angeles for a gallery retrospective this fall and would love to see you if for no other reason than to apologize in person. A lot has changed and I think I'm a much more pleasant person now, and at least 43% more sane.

He'd immediately closed the e-mail, shut down his computer, and walked away. But he hadn't deleted it, and he hadn't told Claudia about it, either.

Even now, as he swung up the hill toward their house, the car's wheels jolting across the potholes in the neglected asphalt and his wife silently fretting beside him, he could feel Aoki's e-mail tugging at him, demanding a response. Just thinking about it made his cranium throb, as if someone had wedged it in a vise and was slowly, meticulously, tightening the screws around his temples.

The world headquarters of BeTee sat above a discount copy shop in a rambling old Spanish building on an otherwise desolate strip of Hollywood Boulevard. BeTee had inherited this warren of rooms from a production company that went bankrupt producing straight-to-DVD fantasy films, and they had never bothered to remove the previous tenant's posters from the walls. In the foyer, DRAGON MAGICK greeted customers. Over Jeremy's desk loomed the sneering, black-vinyl-clad heroine of VIRAL VIXEN. Edgar, sitting directly behind Jeremy in their shared office, gazed at the surreal purple landscape of THE CRYSTAL

GATES. Under their chairs, the industrial carpet was marred with violent burn marks, suggesting that the previous occupants had not left happily, and the bathroom generally smelled like mold. But the view was unbroken all the way up to the HOLLYWOOD sign, and they'd dragged a clutch of folding chairs out onto the old iron fire escape, and sometimes he and Edgar would sit out there after work drinking canned Tecate and watching the sun set over the western hills.

It was the morning after the meeting with Tamra, and Jeremy couldn't draw. He sat hunched over his stylus for three hours, finally doodling a cartoon house with a happy stick-person family standing in the front yard. It was something a second-grader might render in finger paint: Mommy and Daddy and little androgynous stick child, all holding hands. Their smiling faces smirked back at him from his computer monitor: In stick-person land, houses were free and no one ever worried about money and everyone grinned even in their sleep.

The headline of the *Los Angeles Times* sitting on his desk read, FATHER KILLS FAMILY AND HIMSELF, DESPONDENT OVER FINANCIAL LOSSES. Jeremy dropped his stylus and scanned the first paragraph:

> The 45-year-old Agoura Hills financial manager who once made more than $1.2 million a year had lost his job. His luck playing the stock market ran out. His house was in foreclosure. On August 6, he purchased a gun. He wrote two suicide notes and a last will and testament. And then, sometime between Saturday night and Monday morning, he killed his wife, mother-in-law, and three sons, before turning the gun on himself.

Jeremy flipped the newspaper into the trash can. He spun around in his chair and addressed Edgar's back. "Any chance of another raise anytime soon?"

Edgar swiveled his own chair around to face him. Jeremy's friend was starting to go bald, and the tender areas of newly exposed skin at his hairline were pink with sunburn. The chambray button-down shirt that hung loose over his jeans didn't quite conceal a pale swell of gut that rose over his belt. Maybe it was the stress of running a company, but Edgar—a guy who, in college, had dyed his hair blue and pierced his ear with a safety pin—increasingly resembled a middle-aged man.

Edgar tapped a pencil against his nose and frowned. "I gave you a raise three months ago. A generous one, if I remember correctly?"

"You can afford another. The shirts are flying out the door. The company is hugely profitable."

"Yeah," said Edgar. "It's profitable because I'm a cheapskate."

"And because I'm a goddamn design *genius,* don't forget that," he reminded his friend. "Maybe I should find a job where my talents are actually appreciated." This was an empty threat, and Edgar knew it. All these years on, Jeremy still felt a debt of gratitude to his old college friend for so trustingly handing him a job for which he was probably completely unqualified despite two years of figurative drawing courses in college. Jeremy had arrived back in LA bruised and gun-shy from the demise of This Invisible Spot; it had taken nearly two years to finally gather the initiative to form a new band, and this job had been the patch that filled the hole where the music had been. These days, of course, it patched the hole where the money wasn't yet. Besides, who else but Edgar would put up with Jeremy's band practice schedules, his somewhat erratic work ethic, his habit of scribbling down music fragments when he should have been designing decals? Jeremy often felt guilty knowing that he would eventually reward his friend's loyalty by quitting this job when his band finally made it big. That didn't mean he wasn't going to take full advantage while he could.

Edgar rocked in his chair. "What if I took you out to lunch at Burrito King? Would that make you feel appreciated?"

"Can't," Jeremy said. "Having lunch with my dad."

"Fun times." Edgar lifted his legs and braced them against Jeremy's desk, rumpling a pile of sketches. "Hey, is everything OK? Any reason you're asking for another raise?"

Jeremy paused, resisting the temptation to fill Edgar in on the current crisis at home. Not today, he decided. He didn't want to be the honored guest at anybody else's pity party. "No," he said. "Nothing to get alarmed about."

"Whatever you say, my friend." Edgar dropped his legs and leaned in, peering over Jeremy's shoulder at the image on his computer monitor. "Hey, that's a bit rudimentary for a genius, don't you think? Stick people?"

"It's an ironic commentary on the American Dream."

"I thought we agreed the winter line was supposed to have an organic theme. Trees, birds, wildflowers, polar bears, that kind of stuff."

"Times are changing," Jeremy said. "No one gives a damn about polar bears anymore." But he hit the delete button, sending the stick family into trash-bin purgatory, before grabbing his wallet and heading out into the hot August noon to face his father.

Jeremy had never known his father to hold down an actual job; certainly, not one that required him to get up at a certain hour, put on a tie, or go to an office. "Instead of a vocation," Max Munger liked to say, "I prefer a vacation." Over the last forty years, Max had spent time as a screenwriter, a chef on the yacht of a Russian robber baron, an importer of Balinese furniture, a pot farmer, the kept husband of a Norwegian heiress, and a member of the Rolling Stones's entourage. He had never owned a home, although he had managed to father four children by three different wives in two different countries. At age sixty-one, he still wore the same military surplus army jacket that he had worn throughout the 1970s, now trendy with kids a third of his age, many of whom he still socialized with. His face was run across with crevasses, his watery blue eyes buried deep inside a canyon that had lodged itself between hairy eyebrows and bony cheeks. He peered out opaquely from there, and sometimes it was impossible to tell whether he was quietly judging the world around him or whether he was just so stoned he wasn't paying attention.

Max stuck out among the lunch crowd at this West Hollywood bistro, which primarily consisted of actresses sipping Arnold Palmers and frazzled production assistants wolfing down hamburgers between phone calls. The French Bistro was neither French nor a bistro, just a brunch joint with chopped salads and egg-white omelets. The aluminum tables on the covered patio were positioned exactly four feet away from a major east-west thoroughfare, a four-lane highway down which diesel buses and Navigators and Priuses hurtled at top speeds.

Anyone who dared to sit at these tables was not only consuming six liters of exhaust with their turkey burgers but would have to shout over the sounds of the traffic to be heard. And yet here Jeremy sat, having chosen this particular curbside table himself. The last few years back in Los Angeles had addled his brain; he had shed the New Yorker's cynical shell that he had once worked so hard to cultivate. He believed in out-door dining now. He believed in soy lattes. He wore shorts and flip-flops. He had even acquired a convertible, a dented European mid-century gas guzzler in sparkly green, and drove it with the top down even in the middle of winter. When his friends from New York came to visit, they made fun of him, said he'd gone soft and suburban, but in their stinging gibes he could detect a pang of envy, similar to the pang he sometimes felt when he listened to them talking about the benders they'd been on the week before, the random girls they'd hooked up with, the shows they'd been to at McCarren Pool.

"Marital troubles," Max offered, as an opening statement.

"Wait. You got married again?"

"No. You. You have marital troubles."

Jeremy looked down at his paper place mat, where the previous oc-cupant had doodled a purple daisy in stubby crayon. He aligned the paper with the edge of the table, seeking some kind of manageable order to counterbalance a conversation that had—as always with his father—immediately veered off course. "No! Things with Claudia are great. Why did you say that?"

"An invitation to lunch is an invitation to unload," Max said. He bared a wolfish smile for the waitress who was delivering their meals—flax-seed omelet and green tea for him, BLT and a boba tea for Jeremy. "Happy conversations happen over alcohol or sugar. Lunch is a virtu-ous sort of meal, problems that need to be witnessed in the stark light of day and all that."

Jeremy shifted uncomfortably in his chair, fumbling a piece of bacon out of the sandwich as a delay tactic. He hadn't wanted to go there yet. He wasn't sure he was even going to tell his father at all. He'd called

Max last night out of an impulsive, abstract desire for the presence of some sort of parental figure, and since Jillian wasn't around anymore Max would have to do. The minute he'd made the date, he'd regretted it. You didn't come to Max for solace of any sort—get-togethers with his father tended to be terse affairs, bracketed by Max's aimless self-satisfaction and Jeremy's uncharacteristic impatience—which was probably why Jeremy hadn't made real plans with his father in almost six months.

But looking at Max, now, he had a sudden epiphany. There was a ridiculously easy—if somewhat personally painful—solution to this problem, one Claudia hadn't even jotted down in her notebook. Why hadn't he thought of this sooner?

"I need to borrow some money," he blurted, "Claudia and I. Our mortgage went up and we need to find some more money fast or we'll lose the house."

Max threw his head back and released a wheezy whoop of glee, walloping the table with one fist for emphasis. "They got you on the house, did they? Why do you think I never bought one? Did I not teach you a thing?"

Jeremy didn't answer. He stared into the opaque depths of his boba tea, a drink he had chosen not because it tasted that good but because of its interactive appeal. It was not just a drink; it was a toy. He sucked hard, and a little nugget of tapioca shot up the straw to land on his tongue. It had the texture of dried glue, and he chewed on it vigorously, annoyed.

Max eyed him more soberly. "I taught you how to roll a joint. I remember that. You were fourteen and your mother nearly had a heart attack when you told her, you little snitch."

"And clearly that skill has been improving the quality of my life ever since," Jeremy said, failing to properly muster the appropriate sarcasm. It was true that his ability to roll perfect joints had served him well, once upon a time. The roller of joints was always at the center of things, the bestower of favors, all eyes eagerly focused on the paper in your hands, marveling at your ability to turn it tightly and swiftly into an aerodynamic tube. A well-rolled joint pleased your bandmates and helped you get girls. Not that this mattered much in his life these days.

"So how much do they have you for?" Max asked. He disassembled his flax-seed omelet, on the hunt for a solitary shiitake mushroom.

"We have to come up with an additional twenty-two hundred or so a month. I thought maybe we could borrow—six months' worth from you? About twelve or fifteen grand?" Fifteen grand didn't seem like an untenable number, but as he watched Max's eyes dart north with surprise, he began to wonder if maybe he'd underestimated how big the sum really was.

"And what happens after six months?"

"It gives us enough time to figure something else out," Jeremy said. "My band's almost done with our album, and once we get it finished we'll start making money. Or Claudia's next film could get off the ground first."

"Claudia is a sweet girl. Pretends to be an artist, but really she wants the same things her parents did: nice house, nice car, stable income, two-point-three children, vacations in Hawaii. Born and bred in conventionality and will never truly escape it. It's like a brand on her skin, S for square. Not her fault, probably." Max idly stirred the shredded omelet about on his plate.

"Stop it, Dad. That's not true." But he couldn't help thinking of Claudia's List of the Apocalypse—*stable income!*—with a twinge of terror.

"Is that what you want too?"

"I'm not asking for analysis of my marriage."

"No, you just want my money." Max winked and laughed hoarsely. He caravanned three lumps of sugar over to his green tea and thrashed the spoon about in the cup, making a racket.

Jeremy struggled to direct this discussion back on the rails. "Let's be serious here, OK? I know you have the money. Can you to loan it to us? We'll pay it back with interest."

Max sighed heavily. "Nothing would make me happier than having fifteen grand in my pocket to give you."

"Not give, loan," Jeremy interjected.

"Whatever, doesn't matter either way, I'm broke." He peered with dolorous eyes over the rim of his teacup, momentarily sincere. "Really, Jeremy, I'm sorry. I wish I could help."

Jeremy watched his brilliant proposal whisked suddenly away, like a newspaper caught in a strong wind. "You're broke? What happened to all that money you got in the divorce from Katya?"

"There wasn't as much as you'd think. She had good lawyers. And I made some bad investments. Tried my hand at day-trading. Not a wise idea, it turned out."

"I always figured you kept your money in a Swiss bank or tucked in a mattress."

Max grunted. "I sleep on a futon now." He sighed deeply, wiped the last curds of egg from his whiskers, and put the napkin on the table. "I'm going to have to find myself another rich wife one of these days."

"Now *that's* a healthy approach." Jeremy hunched over and shoveled the last crumbs of crust into his mouth, unwilling to meet his father's gaze. He felt petulant, against his own will and better judgment: He'd never asked much of his father, not when Max divorced Jillian and took off for that commune when Jeremy was only four; nor when Jillian died and Max could only make it back from Norway for two days for the funeral. Really, he'd been a goddamn saint, considering his father's neglect. And now he'd finally used his get-out-of-jail-free card, asked this one favor, and Max couldn't help him? Jeremy felt all those years of resentment flooding back—once again, he was the fourteen-year-old kid who had only distaste for the absentee dad who dropped in once every year or two with a backpack full of Free Mumia lapel pins or a custom-painted didgeridoo. Jeremy had thought he was over all that—that as an adult he'd finally gotten past the obvious Freudian abandonment hoo-ha and could actually admire his father's genial self-assurance and blunt honesty and generally haphazard approach to life. He sometimes even recognized how some of these traits had been passed through the chains of DNA into his own personality (and certainly this was a result of nature, not nurture, since his father had done almost no nurturing at all). Not now. Now he just wanted to slug him.

"Don't you judge me, kiddo. I'm the most content person you know. I'm doing just fine," Max said. "Your generation has such angst. We didn't worry about this kind of stuff. Mortgages! Retirement accounts! Therapy! Everyone in therapy. Talking talking talking and never doing.

How old are you—thirty-three now? Thirty-four? When I was your age, I was living with two women and a pet lion on a farm in upstate New York. I was blissfully happy."

"Yeah, I've heard about the lion before, Dad. It's a harder world these days. A lot more ways to fuck things up."

"Bullshit, Jeremy. Youth is timeless. You're only as old as you think you are, no matter what year it may be." Max stood, extricating a pouch of rolling tobacco from the thready back pocket of his corduroys. "Instead of running around trying to go even more deeply into debt than you already are, why don't you just lose the house?"

"Lose the house?" Jeremy imagined driving up to their front door only to find the house gone, vanished, aimlessly wandered off to a suburb in Arizona, with only the exposed cement foundation marking the fact that someone had once lived a life there.

"Sell it. Get rid of it, and then you and Claudia go jaunt around the world a bit, act like the kids you are. Live the moment."

Jeremy considered this in silence, stunned that he hadn't considered this obvious solution earlier. "Well, thanks for the fatherly wisdom," he finally muttered, but he was speaking to his father's back: Max was shuffling down the patio stairs and out into the sun. Jeremy watched as his father bent his craggy head over the cigarette in his hand and then exhaled a long, satisfied plume of smoke toward the bright midday sky. He found himself thinking, unexpectedly, how much Aoki would like his father. And also that, for once, his father had actually had a pretty good idea.

"*Sell* it?" Claudia stood in the living room with sandpaper in her hands from where she was attempting to patch the crack above the mantel. White plaster dust clung to her curls and settled in the hollows under her eyes, like the mask of a Kabuki performer. She'd covered the furniture in plastic sheeting, and the shrouded living room resembled a morgue, each amorphous lump a corpse waiting for identification. "Isn't that a bit extreme?"

Jeremy roamed about the room, ping-ponging from side to side, incapable of concealing his excitement. "This *is* pretty extreme, Claudia. We should get out now, before it's too late. Think of all the things we could do if we did!"

Claudia cupped the folded sandpaper in her palm. "Things like what?"

"We could travel around the world. Or move—say, to Barcelona! You'd love it there, all the great food and the music and the bars. And it's cheap! You'll write a new screenplay and I'll come up with a bunch of new songs to finish the album, and we'll bartend to pay the bills or something." This new plan that he'd hatched on the drive home sounded thrilling when spoken out loud. He imagined them unmooring themselves from this anchor of a house—this mistake they had clearly made—and drifting off to somewhere far less bounded by rules.

Claudia stared at him, perplexed. "You want to bartend? In Barcelona?"

"Doesn't it sound like more fun than being destitute here?"

She moved to the wall and slowly smoothed a hand across the spackle-filled fissure, checking the texture. "I don't know," she said, not looking at him. "It doesn't sound very realistic."

"OK. Fine." He couldn't prevent the peevishness that had crept into his voice. Didn't she realize that they were in danger of sinking with this house, becoming the buttoned-up people they'd always said they wouldn't be, just to save it? He summoned his backup reserve: "How about this: We sell the house and move into a cheaper rental."

Her voice was dry and hoarse. "I don't want to give up just like that. This is the moment when we're supposed to step up and fight. This is *our house* we're talking about."

"It's just a house."

"Let's discuss this rationally," Claudia began slowly, and he could tell by how carefully she articulated the words that she was trying to conceal her frustration, trying not to start a fight, trying in all likelihood not to annoy him more than she could tell he was already annoyed. Aoki used to scream at Jeremy for nothing at all—for buying the wrong ice cream flavor; for noticing a cute girl on the street—and their relationship had been defined by the totemic battles that were followed by explosive make-up sessions; in three years of marriage to Claudia, on the other hand, they had fought maybe a half-dozen times, always in a half-assed "I can understand where you're coming from *but*" kind of way. For a moment, he resented her for pandering to him like that, for being so *sympathetic* all the time. Sometimes Jeremy was acutely aware of how much Claudia adored him and how much he wished that she didn't: Not that he wanted her to stop loving him, just that it would be good for her to hate him a bit too. He didn't deserve unequivocal infatuation. Sometimes he just wanted her to scream at him, tell him what a shithead he was, but she never did.

"I *am* being rational. The bank plans to take it anyway, right? So where are we going to get the money to stop them, Claudia? Where? Because I don't think we can grow it in the vegetable garden." He stepped in closer. "I asked my father if we could borrow some money, you know."

"You did?" She peered into his face, trying to read what was written just under the surface. Up this close, he could smell wine on her breath. "Why didn't you tell me that's what you were going to do?"

He shrugged. "It didn't make any difference. He's broke."

Disappointment flickered across her face and vanished. "I guess I know where the *Let's move to Barcelona* idea came from, then. I can't say I really wanted to be in debt to your father anyway."

"Well, I thought it was a novel approach," he said. "It was certainly the path of least resistance. Maybe we could ask *your* parents?"

Claudia gave him a weary look. "My parents make a religion out of clipping coupons and hitting the free-sample tables at Costco, remember? They've been meticulously planning their retirement for years. I doubt they want to spend tens of thousands of dollars bailing out their irresponsible daughter."

"It was just an idea."

Claudia brushed hair out of her face with the back of her hand, releasing a shower of pixie dust to the floor, and then sat heavily on the couch. "We need to talk, Jeremy. I've been thinking a lot about what Tamra said. About being realistic about our financial situation. About starting to act like grown-ups."

Jeremy sat down on the edge of the armchair across from her, dreading where this was going. "Define grown-up?" He threw in a smile, hoping to lift the heaviness he felt descending on the room.

Claudia threw him a baleful look. "Look. We got ourselves into this mess because we acted like silly children, jumping in headfirst without a good backup plan. We've been waiting for our ship to come in for three years now, but you know what? I'm not sure it's coming anymore. We're stuck. Did you notice that the house down the street has been on the market for six months now? And it's *nicer* than ours. The real estate market is in free fall and we probably couldn't sell this place quickly if we tried, let alone get what we paid for it in the first place."

"So we declare bankruptcy. Or just walk away. Why not?"

"Because," she said, and he was alarmed to realize that her eyes were starting to pink over with tears, "I just can't *fail* like that. Think about it. I already lost my movie—and now the house, too? And what, we just tell our friends and our families that oops, we were stupid? We screwed up but hey, it's not our problem, we're just walking away? It's too *humiliating*." She rubbed at her watering eye with a dirty hand, succeeding only in transferring plaster dust to her cornea. Her left eye blinked convulsively with irritation. "Look, I'm just not ready to give up on our life. This"—and she gestured at the room around them—"we *made* this. Together. If we give it up now, what if we never have another chance again? *What if this is the apex of our lives and it's all downhill from here?*"

Jeremy couldn't stand to see her cry or, even less, to be the one making her cry. "OK, OK," he said, reaching out to squeeze her shoulder. "Don't cry. I was just trying to find the path of least resistance. Make it easier on us."

"There *is* no path of least resistance, Jeremy. Our best bet is to buckle down and dig ourselves out like responsible adults. And if that means making some sacrifices, so be it."

"So I guess this means you're not interested in a pet lion, then," Jeremy muttered, not liking this talk of sacrifices at all.

"A what?" Her voice was larded with impatience. He thought of his father's words—S *for square*—as he tasted dust in the back of his throat.

"Nothing," he said. "Forget it."

"Can you be serious for just a second?" She took a deep breath. "First, I took out an ad for a roommate this afternoon, on Craigslist. The way I see it, we can rent the spare bedroom out for at least eight hundred dollars a month, which means we only have to come up with another fourteen hundred to cover the mortgage. Plus a few grand to cover the payments we missed already."

Jeremy was nauseated. "A roommate? You want a stranger to live with us?"

Claudia offered him an apologetic look. "It doesn't have to be forever. Just until we get back on our feet."

"But you use that room as your office!"

Claudia jumped up and turned back to the crack. She stood in front of it with her hands on her hips, as if challenging it to break open again, and then attacked the spackle with renewed aggression. "Yeah, about that." Her voice was low and congested. "I think the other thing we have to face is that my career is not going as planned. My film tanked, Carter doesn't return my calls—he's basically dropped me as a client—and, let's be honest, I'm probably not going to get another directing job for a while."

"That's not true," he protested. Her casual self-indictment made him ill. This was not the Claudia he liked the most, the woman who had breathtakingly summoned *Spare Parts* into being by sheer force of will, the woman who stayed up late at night watching the director commentary tracks on Criterion Collection classic film DVDs and reading cinephile magazines with titles like *American Cinematographer* and *Cineaste*. Or maybe—he thought with surprise—it *was;* wasn't this approach to their foreclosure just a variation on the same stubborn nose-to-the-ground determination? Less inspired artistic vision than tortoise-like perseverance? "Of course you're going to make another movie."

"Not unless I take Carter's advice and start writing wedding movies."

Jeremy winced. "You just have to keep trying."

"Actually, for the time being I think I need to *stop* trying. Take a break, for my own sanity." The muscles of Claudia's shoulders flexed and strained as she scraped away the last rough nubs of spackle and then stood back to survey her handiwork. The crack had been erased, leaving just a faint ghost behind as a reminder.

"Take a break?" He couldn't make sense of this. "Claudia, look at me. *You do not take a break from your dreams.*" He knew that sounded like a daytime talk-show cliché—this also, he realized, sounded like something Jillian might say—but in this moment, the sentiment seemed vital. It was of critical importance that she *not* step away from the person he wanted her to be.

She whirled around. The whites of her eyes were veined and with the ashen dust caked in the cracks of her face she looked ten years older. Frazzled and defeated. Frighteningly—and this was the first time he had ever had this thought—she looked kind of like her mother, Ruth, a sweet, sagging woman with a penchant for animal appliqué sweatshirts. "It's not like I'm going to stop trying altogether, but"—she hesitated—"I took a full-time job today, Jeremy. As a high school teacher. At Esme's mom's school. The money's not great but it'll be enough. And I can still write scripts at night. I'll do it for a year and then see where we're at. Or maybe you'll finish your album and be able to pay the mortgage yourself and it will become a non-issue."

Her words flopped onto the floor, a sodden lump. Jeremy stood regarding them balefully. "You did all this without even asking me." His words came out colder than he intended them to; colder than her proposal merited, probably, but he felt compelled to punish her anyway, for some grievance he couldn't quite name. "You just gave up on everything we always said we wanted for ourselves. For four stupid walls— that are crumbling, by the way, despite all your work—and a wooden floor."

"I'm doing this to *save* what we said we wanted for ourselves."

"Are we even talking about the same thing?"

Claudia violently kicked her work clogs off, sending them skittering across the dusty floor to land against the plastic-covered television set. She turned to look at him with fury distorting her face, rendering her unrecognizable. It stopped him cold. "Look, Jeremy. *Someone's* got to step up to the plate." She spat the words at him. "And since you don't seem interested in doing it, I will."

"This whole thing is your fault. You talked me into this house in the first place. It wasn't my idea. We never should have bought it." Jeremy realized he was whining. "I should have trusted my gut!"

Claudia's voice ascended to a pitch he had never heard before, a glass-endangering vibrato. "Your *gut*? Well, Mr. King of Hindsight, your *gut* never spoke up about its concerns when we were house-shopping, so, too late. Your *gut* failed to pay the last two mortgage bills! It's so much easier to blame anyone but yourself, isn't it? Take some responsibility!"

Jeremy sat down heavily on the chair. He would have laughed at the weirdness of this moment—they were *fighting*—if it wasn't so traumatic. He hated the sound of Claudia's raised voice after all, and now the only way he could think to stop it was to play on her sympathies and act the part of the wounded party. "I'm just hurt that you didn't include me in your decision-making," he said, lowering his voice. "You don't care what I think at all. Christ, Claudia, you advertised for a *roommate* without asking me?"

It worked. Claudia stared at him, breathing hard and visibly deflating. "Of course I care. Look, I'm sorry. I just didn't think we had a choice." She sighed and swiped at the dust on her face, leaving long finger marks that revealed dark crescents of exhaustion ringing her eyes. "This whole thing has taken a lot out of me. I think I need a nap. Maybe you do too."

Jeremy wondered if there was an intimation in this statement, but the prickly expression on her face suggested a desert without an oasis. "No," he said, cranky. "I'm going to watch TV."

She disappeared into the bedroom. Jeremy sat down on the couch, translucent plastic sheeting crinkling under his rear. He picked up the remote and turned on the television set, not even bothering to remove the plastic, and watched the watery images that swam through with halfhearted interest. Inside him, fury and guilt engaged in a heated skirmish, one side hating Claudia for popping his bubble and the other reminding him of his old promise to take care of her. Was her proposal really so awful? *Yes;* one side brandished its bayonets. *You'll survive,* parried the other.

After a minute, he snapped the set off. He picked up his guitar, played a few chords, then put it down again. Finally, he tiptoed to the door of the bedroom and stood there, staring at Claudia. She had taken her work clothes off and was asleep, facedown on top of the bedspread, wearing a T-shirt and a faded pair of his boxer shorts. A small puddle of drool darkened the pillow.

Jeremy closed the door and went back to the living room, where he opened his laptop. The computer whirred drowsily; the desktop photograph of a chubby five-year-old Claudia sparked up and spread across the screen. She stared at him curiously from across the years, skeptical of the person looking back, unconcerned about the melted orange popsicle smeared across her face.

It took only a few seconds to locate the e-mail where he'd saved it, in a folder marked PERSONAL. AOKI, he typed quickly:

Good to hear from you. I'd love to see you. When do you get to town?

He clicked SEND before he had a chance to think better of it and then sat and watched as the software churned, sent its feelers across the Internet, and catapulted his message out into the cooling summer night.

Claudia

TO GET TO ENNIS GATES ACADEMY, CLAUDIA HAD TO DRIVE WEST: down the hill, then west over the industrial flats of Glassell Park, across concrete-choked Los Angeles River and through the dismally mis-named Elysian Park. Turning up onto Beverly Boulevard, she contin-ued through lower Hollywood, past the *panaderias* and pet stores with their hand-painted signs and rotting birdcages in the windows, and, to the south, the glassed-in high-rises of Koreatown. Here, she hit the first early morning traffic. Trapped between badly timed lights, the cars gunned forward en masse and then jerked to a stop, swapping lanes in a futile and dangerous dance. In this manner, she inched her way past the grand Spanish villas and SLOW CHILDREN AT PLAY signs of Hancock Park, and through the Fairfax district, where Russian Hasadim in furry flying-saucer hats stalked past designer boutiques. Finally, after almost an hour, she arrived in Beverly Hills. Here sat Ennis Gates Academy, on the end of an otherwise residential street where the mansions girded themselves with high gates and the lollipop palms swayed over empty sidewalks.

Claudia parked her aging Jetta in the half-full teacher's lot. She was an hour early for first bell, and the campus was still quiet. She had half expected a welcoming committee, there to greet her on her first offi-cial day as an Ennis Gates Academy teacher, but the front entry was va-cant save for an elderly registrar who sat at the receptionist desk reading a romance novel, a bowl of sugar-free hard candies placed before her. The registrar raised her head and looked quizzically at Claudia, noted the book bag, and smiled, apparently deciding that Claudia belonged there after all. She licked her thumb and turned a page in her novel, uninterested.

Claudia pushed onward, through the double doors and out into a small courtyard, where a smattering of early students were gathered in clusters around a fountain, comparing summer vacation photographs on each other's iPhones. There, Claudia hesitated, trying to remember her way. The campus of Ennis Gates was mazelike, a quirky scattering of neo-Modern boxes crosshatched with industrial steel beams and painted in creativity-stimulating hues of purple and emerald and turquoise, rising up along the base of a hill. She'd visited the campus four times in the last three weeks, and she still couldn't quite recall the best way to her homeroom.

When she'd called Esme, she'd half expected that the school would already have found a new film teacher. "You're recommending *yourself*?" Esme blurted. "That's not what I was expecting to hear." But she promised to call her mother right away, and indeed, before Claudia even had a chance to step away from the telephone, it was ringing again, with Esme's mother Nancy Friar on the other line.

"I'm sure you've heard from Esme that we're desperate," Nancy began. "Oh, dear, that didn't sound good, did it? Let me rephrase: Ennis Gates Academy would be thrilled to talk to you about the position. I've heard the most lovely things about your film—though I have to confess I haven't had a chance to go see it yet, maybe this weekend . . . Oh, it's not in theaters anymore? Shoot. Well, Esme can't stop talking about it, and I trust my daughter's taste. My point being—any chance we could get you to come in for an interview—well, today? We're really in a bind."

It was as if Claudia was doing them a favor, not the other way around; but she couldn't take any pleasure in this. Just the thought of teaching brought up the unsettling image of her older sister, Danielle, who substitute-taught first grade back in Mantanka. Danielle's home had disappeared entirely underneath a blizzard of children's artwork: Walls, cabinets, appliances, mirrors, all were taped over with gooey finger-painted landscapes, mutated puppies in dripping watercolor, lopsided daisies rendered in flesh-toned crayon. Danielle herself had a tendency to lapse into baby talk not just with her own four children but with her husband ("Aren't you my favorite hubbie-wubbie, hmmm?"), kept a collection of shopworn stuffed animals on the marital bed, and had apparently lost the ability to maintain a conversation without at least one reference to her "little sweeties." Teaching seemed a safe, benign sort of life, one that Claudia had never wanted for herself; the kind of life that had led her to flee the Midwest in the first place.

And yet she saw no other option: They needed money, *immediately*. The phone calls she'd made to her industry contacts had gone unreturned; she couldn't even dredge up any advertising work. And even if she did sit down to write a new, even more commercial script (with vampires or puppies or star-crossed lovers or, ideally, all three), it would take at least six months to finish and then even longer to sell, if it sold at all. She had no job prospects, no skill set other than this one marginal one. She couldn't quite wrap her head around it: If she really was such a good director—and this was what she had always been told; surely, she was at least *competent,* which was more than you could say for a lot of the filmmakers out there—how was it possible to be so summarily dismissed?

"Hollywood has a short memory," RC told her, when Claudia called to talk through her career dilemma. "Produce something new, and they'll forget your failures."

"It's easy for you to say," Claudia said. "You've already made it. No one's going to pay me to write anything new right now, and I still have to cover our mortgage somehow."

RC grew quiet. "I see what you're saying. This industry is a bitch. I wish I had the answer for you."

"It's not your fault." On the other end of the line, she could hear the shrieks of RC's boys. "You know, I always thought there was some sort of natural forward progression to life: one event leading naturally to a better one—a line graph in constant upward motion, you know? Just look at my parents. My father got a sales job in a hardware store after college, and that eventually led to him owning one store and then two.

They traded in their small house for a bigger house, they saved money, and everything just grew steadily upward until now they can retire comfortably."

"Yes, but they didn't take any risks." Something crashed and broke in the background, and RC covered the receiver to yell, "Lucas, go to your room *now*! . . . Filmmaking is a totally different industry," she said, returning. "It's *defined* by setbacks and comebacks. Not neat upward parabolas. I'm sure you're aware of that."

"Of course," Claudia agreed. But the truth was that she'd never imagined that you could be going down your carefully chosen path, taking all the right steps, and suddenly find out that it was a dead end. There was no *logic* to that narrative. Where was the happy ending with the uplifting credit-sequence score?

"I just hope you don't get cynical. Your sincerity is one of your greatest assets. It's refreshing to meet someone nice, in this industry."

"Yeah, well, clearly Hollywood has no interest in *sincere*. What I really need is to be more of a bitch."

"Just hang in there," RC offered. "You'll figure something out eventually."

But Claudia couldn't *just hang in there,* not right now. The past weeks of stunning defeats had drained something vital away, squeezed her heart out like a sponge and left it dry and empty on a shelf. With her career on hold and her home in imminent danger—an intangibly *wrong* feeling in the air—something shifted inside her, so that when she thought of the days ahead she saw not a vista of opportunity but a minefield braced with barbed wire. She *was* growing cynical: There was a germ of anger-fueled pessimism inside her that she'd never really noticed before.

Extreme measures were clearly necessary. So she bit back her reservations about the teaching job and went in for the interview that same day. There she spent two hours talking with Nancy, and then three other members of the school's hiring board, talking uncomfortably about her film's critical accolades; about the short film that won her a student Oscar back at UCLA film school; about her time working in the production offices of the famous director. She emphasized the high school English tutoring she'd done back in her post-college days in

Wisconsin, in the hopes of proving that she really was qualified to teach (what other option did she have?). And when Nancy called her back, that same evening, to offer her the job—"a probationary position, you understand; we'll see how this first semester goes, make sure it's a comfortable fit for both of us, before we talk long-term"—she'd accepted it with resigned gratitude.

Maybe she should have waited to talk it over with Jeremy, but it seemed better to accept quickly, before the pain of her decision sank in. That evening, while she waited for him to come home from work, she sat in the living room and polished off a bottle of shiraz. At first, she tasted defeat in the tannic dregs of her wine, but with a second glass, and then a third, it increasingly seemed like a heroic—and yes, *grown-up*—decision she'd made. Maybe safe and benign *was* the proper response to the days ahead. Maybe it would even be a *relief* not to be battling the film industry for a while. She'd salvaged something important by doing this, she knew: As painful as it was to take a conventional job, homelessness would be worse. *That* felt like a far more permanent fracture, cracking deep into her very foundation.

This job is only temporary, she reminded herself now: She would come up with a new script idea, devote her evenings to writing, wait out their crisis. By next year, she could be living RC's comeback cliché, a plot device that—it was true—was nearly as popular in Hollywood as *alien invasion destroys New York* or *man falls in love with hooker with a heart of gold*. Still, despite the forced optimism, she sensed something ominous hanging in the air, something bigger than her: A global day of reckoning was coming. As she looked around the courtyard of Ennis Gates Academy, a pernicious little voice in her head broke into her reverie: *Brace yourself. This is the rest of your life.*

"You look lost." She turned to see a middle-aged woman standing behind her, kinked to the right from the weight of the bulging hemp book bag hooked over her shoulder. Her cropped gray hair was spiked with gel, offset by red plastic cat's-eye glasses with leopard-print earpieces.

"The teachers' lounge?" Claudia said helplessly.

"Follow me." The woman began a swift lurching gait across the quad, clutching the book bag to her side with one hand while reaching out with the other to shake Claudia's. "Brenda," she said. "Hunter. Philosophy and Ethics. Are you the new Modern Languages?"

"Film." Claudia struggled to keep up with her, aware how slight her own tote—an Amoeba Records freebie bag, half-filled with some handouts and two DVDs—seemed in comparison. "I'm replacing John Lehrmann."

"Oh, yes, John. The handsome fool. I never understood why everyone here loved him, and it turned out I was right, wasn't I? Idiot." Brenda gave Claudia a once-over. "You're a cute young thing, aren't you? I'm surprised they didn't overcompensate by hiring someone repulsive."

"Oh, well, I'm married."

"So was he," Brenda said. She pointed to the left as they passed a two-story glass building, flanked by tennis courts. "Athletic center. Tennis courts are real grass, of course. School built them a few years ago for a student competing at Wimbledon. Cost six million."

"Six *million*? Just for tennis courts?"

"And he came in tenth. Big disappointment. Poor kid." She turned left and up a set of stairs toward the next cluster of buildings, surprisingly quick despite her burden.

Claudia reached the top, panting slightly. From this vantage point, she could see down the hill to the front gate, where the students were starting to arrive. A line of SUVs and Priuses emptied into the student parking lot, windows rolled down and hip-hop blaring from surround-sound stereo systems; another line of luxury sedans triple-parked by the entrance, ejecting younger children who didn't have their driver's licenses yet. A solitary limousine idled in the handicapped zone, regurgitating a tiny girl from its tinted-glass depths.

Brenda followed her gaze. "That would be Clarity Schilling."

"Of . . . ?" Claudia mouthed the name of a pair of famous actors.

"Yes. She's the only kid whose parents are so self-important as to drop her off in a limo. Most celebrity parents here prefer to play it low key. Clarity hates it, of course." They turned into the main quad, past an enormous array of blue solar panels that arced in a decorative curve over the path, and toward the cafeteria. Brenda flicked her hand at the solar display. "The campus went all-green three years ago. First high school in the nation to do so. Water in the toilets is all runoff from the landscaping, if you're wondering why it looks brown."

Teenagers were arriving in droves now, thronging down the paths around them. At Ennis Gates Academy, the students wore a uniform of navy blue: V-neck sweaters worn snug over white polo shirts; pleated skirts of acrylic that hung stiffly around girls' knees; for the boys, unflattering slacks, worn several sizes too big so they flapped around the legs like sails. One teenage boy, with a fedora jammed over two stubby ponytails, stopped as they passed and doffed his hat to Brenda.

"Madam Hunter," he said, speaking from his exaggerated bow. "I do believe I have the honor of being in your Eastern Philosophers course this semester."

"Oh, reeeeally. Well, this should be fun. Wait until I nail you with Berdyayev." Brenda laughed. "And tell your housekeeper I fantasized about those brownies with the marshmallow centers all summer." She turned to Claudia and winked as the boy jammed the hat back on his head and moved off toward the stairs.

They veered right, around the side of the cafeteria and toward a set of glass double doors. Brenda shoved the doors open with one hip, gesturing grandly with her free arm. "And here we are. Home sweet home."

The teacher's lounge was a vast room, as sleek and gleaming as a cruise ship. It boasted a buzzing double refrigerator, a shiny row of stainless steel microwaves, and a half-dozen round lunch tables topped with flowering cactus arrangements. A glass picture window faced out onto the quad, allowing the teachers to view their charges while eating lunch. Stiff couches in bold primary colors faced off at jarring angles. On one of them reclined a lumpy older woman in high-waisted mom slacks and orthopedic shoes. She slurped at brown liquid from a Ritalin promotional mug as she flipped rapidly through a Prentice Hall catalog. She looked up at them. "Hi there, Brenda," she said. "Ready to face the hounds of hell?"

Brenda shook her head at Claudia as they walked toward the kitchenette. "That's Evelyn. Political Systems. Don't mind her, she's all bark. And the kids are great." She extricated a tea bag from her voluminous tote and plunked it in a mug emblazoned with the Ennis Gates logo.

Claudia pulled the coffee pot out of the machine and tentatively sniffed its contents. It smelled fresh enough.

"If you want the good stuff, you have to wait for the cafeteria to open at first break," Brenda said, bobbing her tea bag up and down in the steaming depths of her mug. "There's an espresso machine in there."

Claudia opened her mouth to marvel at this latest revelation and then snapped it shut again, realizing that she was starting to look like a wide-eyed naïf. Instead, she filled a mug and took a tentative sip. "It's OK. My parents raised me on Sanka," she said, "so I have plebeian tastes." This wasn't quite true—living in LA, she'd grown to appreciate a single-source, fair-trade, microbrewed latte—but that didn't mean she couldn't still summon that older Claudia, the one who'd never tasted sushi until she arrived in California and who used to eat her mother's meat loaf and Tater Tot dinners without flinching. The coffee was bearable; anyway, she was still too groggy from getting up at such an unreasonable hour to be picky. Tomorrow she'd look for the espresso machine.

Brenda had wandered over to an enormous bakery box packed tight with croissants. "Who is this courtesy of?" Brenda called to Evelyn.

Evelyn shrugged. "Who knows. The Hoffmans?"

Brenda picked the top layer off a croissant with her fingernail, then gave up and lifted the whole thing to her mouth. "I lost six pounds this summer and I swear it'll all be back on my ass within the week. I don't know what the parents think they're doing to us. Making us all too fat and lazy to chase their kids around, maybe."

"Speaking of—ask her," said Evelyn, sitting up.

"Right!" Brenda leaned in close. "I don't know what you're doing this Thursday night, but some of us—teachers, I mean—get together weekly. There's no union here, of course, so we formed a kind of ad hoc support group. We need to stick together, you know. Us versus them."

"I doubt I'll have time," Claudia said. "I need my evenings to write."

"Write?"

"Screenplays." She lowered her voice. "I'm actually not a teacher. In real life, I'm a filmmaker."

Brenda flinched visibly. *Oh God,* Claudia thought, *I managed to insult her in less than fifteen minutes on the job.* Still, her goal here wasn't to get cozy with the other teachers, but to put in her time and take home a weekly paycheck. "In real life. Right. Of course not. Well, invitation stands," Brenda mumbled. Flakes of pastry clung to the front of her blouse, and she knocked them off with the palm of her hand. "So, Claudia, let's see your roster. I'll tell you about your students."

Claudia pulled the sheaf of paperwork from her bag. She'd spent the previous evening scrutinizing these pages, as if they were in code and she needed to locate a hidden key to unlock their meaning. There were convoluted class schedules, indecipherable campus maps, board meeting agendas, lists of school rules ("Do not fraternize with parents outside of school" and "No sexual contact with students, including hugging or kissing" and "Do not accept gifts of more than $200 in value from any parent," the last of which stopped her cold: Who *were* these people?), and three pages of names that she studied, trying to envision the faces behind them. She handed these over to Brenda, and watched the other woman's twitching face as she scanned the list.

Brenda jabbed her finger at the pages. "It's a good group you've got here," she said, as Claudia peered over her shoulder at the list of tiny type. "Jordan Bigglesby, she's the undisputed social princess of the school, would be our prom queen if the school went for that kind of stuff, which of course we don't. Mom's an actress, you'd recognize her if you watch that sitcom with the monkey. OK, you've also got Theodore Kaplan, who will undoubtedly fail your class because he misses too many tests for rugby practice. He thinks he's going to get into Harvard as a legacy—Dad's an entertainment lawyer over at Mannatt—but he's got another think coming. Lisa Yang is a smooth talker, don't believe a word she says. Her mother's a publicist, reps all the big stars, so she's learned a few tricks. Mary Hernandez—a scholarship kid, extraordinarily bright, always very serious. Doesn't quite fit in here but will probably show up everyone in the end." Her finger traveled farther down the list and then stopped. "Oh. Penelope Evanovich is in your senior seminar." Brenda looked up at Claudia, meaningfully.

Claudia stared back at her, as the name plucked at her memory. "Evanovich, as in Samuel Evanovich?"

Brenda nodded soberly. "Oh, yes. He's on the board here."

Claudia took this in, excitement pistoning in her chest. Samuel Evanovich was one of her film idols, a legendary movie producer with a long list of Oscar-nominated dramas; in the golden days of American cinema, back in the sixties and seventies, he'd put his thumbprint on almost every significant Hollywood movie and at least a dozen Oscar winners. He *was* the Hyperion Collection. Claudia attended his lecture at Sundance last winter, a shambling ursine figure who drank scotch on stage, and yet somehow his expansive memories of wilder times in the industry seemed not drunken or solipsistic but searingly insightful. She seemed to recall that he was currently married to a former soap-opera actress who once held the title of Miss Arizona.

"So? What's Penelope like?" To her own ear, she sounded overeager.

"Too spoiled for her own good," barked Evelyn, from her couch, not bothering to look up from her catalog.

Brenda sighed. "That kid. She is—how shall we say this?—not cute, which has made things rather hard for her here. She's smart, but not always very diligent about doing the work assigned to her. An attitude problem, you could say. Though"—she peered over the top of the red frames—"word is that she wants to be a filmmaker just like her daddy. So that could be interesting for you."

"Interesting how?"

Brenda shrugged and picked up a second croissant. "The kids here are amazing. Really. You're going to have fun. Just don't let them intimidate you. When they smell blood, that's when things get out of hand. Remember—you're the boss."

"That shouldn't be a problem." Claudia proffered a smile that belied the butterflies flapping about in her stomach. "I figure if I can coerce a Vicodin-addled actress out of her trailer or discipline a bunch of middle-aged teamsters, I can probably handle this."

Brenda patted Claudia on the back as she hoisted her tote bag back on her shoulder. "That's the right attitude," she said. "Go knock 'em dead."

As she left the teachers' lounge and began the hunt for her homeroom, Claudia felt her pace quicken. Suddenly she had a clearer picture of the year that lay before her. Stepping around a massive steel curlicue sculpture (either a real Richard Serra or a very good knockoff), she found herself fantasizing that Penelope Evanovich might become her star pupil. There would be a cozy mentorship, after-school hours spent discussing the techniques of French New Wave cinema, perhaps even the occasional invitation for a home-cooked dinner chez Evanovich, where (after watching a classic film in the family's home theater) Claudia could be coaxed to show an appreciative Evanovich *père* her last script—which of course just needed the guidance of an understanding producer to get off the ground. . . .

She stumbled, realizing that she'd somehow tripped over the front steps of her own classroom. The room she was to teach in was a brand-new screening room that seated fifty, with stadium seats canting down to a small stage. It had a high-definition projection system, a DVD library with four hundred titles, Wi-Fi, and an equipment room outfitted with several professional-quality video cameras. Unfortunately, the architect who designed the screening room had neglected to consider the fact that this was also to be a teacher's office, and built a desk in only as an afterthought. This was shoved in back of the stuffy audiovisual closet behind a humming rack of DVD players.

She flipped on the overhead spotlights, illuminating the vintage movie posters she'd hung in previous visits: *Butch Cassidy and the Sundance Kid, Jules et Jim,* and a somewhat shopworn Polish print for *2001: A Space Odyssey.* She threw the windows open to let some warm September air into the dark room. She wrote her name in big letters on the whiteboard, still stained with the blue-inked ghosts of lessons past, and straightened a stack of handouts entitled AMERICAN CINEMA SINCE 1960. And then she sat in a wooden chair on the dais and waited for her students to arrive.

The bullying echoes of the first bell rang through the concrete corridors, where whirlpools of teenagers now swirled and eddied and drifted, carried along by a hormonal tide. Her students began to spill into the room, raucous and giddy from their summer vacations. As the second bell rang, the students shook out their plumage and distributed their backpacks and settled down into studied poses of adolescent ennui. A bespectacled boy with a miniature purple mohawk ran in from the hallway and flung himself into the closest available seat and then smirked, daring her to say something. Twenty-eight eyes stared expectantly at her. She cleared her throat, and her career as a teacher officially began.

Later she would look back at the events of her first day at Ennis Gates and recall very few details. She took attendance, over and over, carefully matching faces to names, attempting mental mnemonics until she finally gave up and just figured she'd remember them all in time. She laid out a three-month curriculum for each of three different classes, and distributed a small forest's worth of handouts. She played the opening sequence from *Dr. Strangelove,* led a slightly halting class discussion on political films, and played the climactic sewer hunt scene of *The Third Man* and lectured on noir lighting techniques. She had each student write a brief in-class essay on the subject "The Best Movie I Saw This Summer" and was surprised, when she flipped through them afterward, how bright these kids really were. Sure, a few offered insights like "Yeah, the action sequences in *Batman* rocked" or "I really liked the lesbian pool scene," but others cited films like *9½ Weeks* and *The Diving Bell and the Butterfly* and *His Girl Friday,* and if they did pick a blockbuster Hollywood flick, they cited it for "cutting-edge animation technique" or "an interesting twist on the genre of comic book adaptation." Perhaps they were just trying to impress her, but as she read the essays, she could see the semester unfolding in a much more promising way than she'd ever imagined. The students were attentive, eager, and intellectually curious, and only tiny details revealed the fact that many of their parents resided in an entirely different tax bracket than Claudia: a $2,000 Chloe purse here, rare Japanese skate shoes there, the widespread use of MacBooks rather than spiral-bound notebooks.

But of all the students she met that day, only one really stuck in her head when she got home that night: Penelope Evanovich.

The girl was in her afternoon senior seminar, and she recognized her right away: In the game of genetic roulette, Penelope had lost her spin, inheriting none of her mother's symmetrical beauty-pageant features.

Instead, she had acquired her father's hyperthyroidism—her eyes protruded in a permanently goggle-eyed expression of vague panic—and his hirsutism—wiry black curls erupted from her head. She had even inherited her father's paunch, which probably wasn't helped by the bag of Cheetos she was eating.

If Penelope hated seeing her furry pop-eyed form reflected in the gazes of her Master-Cleanse-slimmed, vacation-tanned, and professionally highlighted Beverly Hills peers, she hid it well. Instead, she appeared to embrace her own nonconformity. Her legs were housed in defiantly shredded purple tights, her backpack was regulation army surplus, and a faded black T-shirt that read (from what Claudia could see) RST CLASS BITC peeped out from under a button-front shirt. A streak of inartfully applied green hair dye looped through her ponytail before fading out in a bleached end. From her left lobe hung an earring that appeared to be a diamond-studded skull. Claudia could only imagine how the former Miss Arizona felt about all that. She smiled at Penelope as the girl plopped herself into a front-row seat. An encouraging sign.

Claudia began that class with a group viewing of *The Graduate.* Standing on the stage, she guided the students through the magnificent seduction scene between Mrs. Robinson and Benjamin Braddock, thinking to herself as she did that her new job was almost too fun to be real. Just as she was pointing out how the director had used a black-and-white color palette to delineate the character's moral dilemma, Penelope's hand popped up. Cheered—*not even ten minutes in and she's already excited about the class!*—Claudia barely had a chance to acknowledge the hand before the girl abruptly began talking.

"Um, my dad executive-produced *The Graduate?*"

The students in the room sat up to ogle Penelope, who was surrounded by a moat of empty seats. Penelope twisted the green curl of hair around a thumb and tugged it straight.

"Oh, really?" Claudia wasn't quite sure of the proper response to this statement. *Of course he had,* she thought. She should have realized that sooner. "That's wonderful."

"Yeah, and he told me the only reason they used that color palette was because the production budget was cut in half, they had to use the costume designer's house as a set, and that was just the way it looked. So it wasn't actually intentional."

For a moment, Claudia was completely flummoxed. She could feel the eyes of the other students sliding from Penelope to Claudia and back again, eagerly anticipating conflict. "Well," she said, finally, "in this class one of the skills we'll be learning is critical interpretation, which is subjective, depending on the perception of the viewer."

Penelope's eyes grew even rounder—whether from surprise, or skepticism, or stimulus, Claudia wasn't quite sure. "Personally, I think it's pointless to make stuff up that isn't really there," the girl announced.

Claudia shuffled her notes, unmoored. Was this a challenge or an invitation for intellectual debate? "That's something we can discuss in a different class. But today, let's move ahead to this hotel room scene, which we'll see is shot entirely in the dark." She hit PLAY on the remote, cutting off any further conversation.

When the bell rang a half hour later, Penelope didn't head toward the door with the rest of her classmates but worked her way toward the stage. She stood waiting at the bottom of the stairs, scratching one calf with the toe of her sneaker while Claudia chatted with Mary Hernandez.

Mary had brought Claudia some sort of home-baked pastry, a flattened disk filled with quince paste. She offered it shyly to Claudia in a fragrant, butter-stained bag that read Chicken Kitchen. "It's not really from the Chicken Kitchen," she apologized. "I just work there."

"It smells delicious," Claudia said.

"I'm really excited about this class, Mrs. Munger," Mary continued, and tugged at the thick braid that she had pulled over her shoulder. She had a gap between her front teeth that hadn't been fixed by orthodontia and a broad forehead freckled with adolescent acne. "I watched the Film Noir series at the Egyptian this summer to prepare. Though I work most evenings so I missed a few. *Murder, My Sweet* and *The Glass Key.* I read that they aren't considered particularly seminal, though."

Behind Mary, Penelope snorted quietly; perhaps the girl was just clearing her throat.

"We're not really going to be covering classic *noir* in this class," Claudia said, distracted. She watched Penelope out of the corner of her eye, worried that she would grow tired of waiting and flee. "We're looking at American cinema *after* the nineteen sixties."

"Oh." Mary looked distressed, as if mentally counting the paychecks she'd wasted on movie tickets. "I'm sorry."

"No need to apologize. It's never a waste of time to learn more about film," Claudia said.

"I'm applying to UCLA next year," Mary continued. "I was hoping I could talk to you about your experience there? I read your bio on IMDB, and I know you attended. It would be so great if you could write me a recommendation, Mrs. Munger. We could schedule something now, if you have a minute."

Penelope checked her watch and edged back toward the door, losing her patience. Claudia felt opportunity slipping away—this could be her one and only chance to foster a connection with Penelope. "Recommendations already?" Claudia demurred. "Let's wait until we're a little further into the semester, so we can get to know each other. We have plenty of time."

"Actually—"

But Claudia had already beckoned Penelope up the stairs with the one hand, jiggling the paper bag gratefully with the other. "We'll talk soon, Mary. And thanks for the pastry."

Penelope climbed up the stairs toward Claudia, maneuvering around Mary Hernandez as if she were a roadblock planted in her path. She came to a stop directly in front of Claudia, blocking Mary. Mary stared at the back of Penelope's head for a long moment and then quietly melted away. Claudia barely noticed her leave until she heard the classroom door click behind her.

"Mrs. Munger," Penelope began.

"Claudia is fine," Claudia said, eager to slide past their earlier, unsettling encounter. "No need to stand on ceremony. I'm not a formalist."

Penelope scrutinized Claudia. Her fiddling hands had woven her curly hair into a knotty-looking beehive, and it flapped over the girl's eyes. "What was the name of the last film you made?" she asked, pushing the hair aside.

Claudia smiled. *This was more like it.* "*Spare Parts.*"

"Oh." Penelope snapped a piece of fluorescent pink gum between her teeth. "I never heard of it?"

Claudia tried to prevent a grimace from rippling across her face. "It's a love triangle, between two girls and a guy. It takes place in the organ transplant ward of a hospital. It's an homage to Howard Hawks, and the snappy dialogue that was popular in prewar cinema."

"Did it go, like, straight to video or something?"

"No. It was in movie theaters."

"Oh? When did it come out?" Penelope tilted her head to assess her teacher. Claudia could sense the girl sizing her up but couldn't quite interpret the conclusion Penelope had come to.

Claudia smiled warmly, determined to be the one person at Ennis Gates that could break through Penelope's armor. "The end of July."

Penelope looked surprised. "And it's already not in theaters anymore?"

Claudia picked up the whiteboard eraser, feeling defensive. "No, but I could bring you a screener, if you'd like to watch it."

"Yeah, great, thanks," said Penelope. She slung her backpack over one shoulder and began to make her way toward the door.

"By the way," Claudia called after her, "I love the hair. I used to dye mine too. Black."

Penelope turned back, blatantly assessing her. After a moment, she offered a fleeting, heartbreaking smile that belied the RST CLASS BITC slogan on her shirt. "Thanks," she said.

Claudia watched Penelope leave, sensing that they'd made some sort of breakthrough. She imagined Penelope and Samuel watching the screener together, perhaps discussing its artistic merits, and felt her body tingle, bristling with life for the first time in weeks. She stood there at the front of the empty classroom and found herself smiling as she listened to the last reverberations of the students vanishing from the corridors. *I can do this,* she thought. *I might even like this.* She packed essays into her Amoeba tote, flipped off the lights and locked the door, and ventured back out into the purple maze to try to locate her car.

Lucy Fitzer was what Claudia's mother would have called a "fireplug." She was certainly as compact and squat as a hydrant, with the only protuberance being a pair of enormous breasts that strained at her tank top and tipped her slightly forward when she walked. She marched through their house, flipping open closet doors, peering behind curtains, and firing questions like buckshot, while Jeremy and Claudia—slightly stunned—followed a few steps behind. It was almost as if Lucy were giving the house tour instead of them.

"Oh my God, what a gorgeous view," Lucy marveled. "Can you see it from the bed—look at that, you can! How wonderful. It's quite a good-sized room, isn't it. Oh, it's where *you* sleep? I see. Love your quilt—did one of your grandparents make that? A thrift store! Don't you worry about germs? No? I guess I'm just germphobic, comes with my job. Oh, a claw-foot bathtub! Heaven. I adore bubble baths. OK, so *this* would be my room. Well, it's certainly cozy. Does it have a walk-in closet? Oh. I guess none of these old houses do. And here we have the kitchen. . . . Does that old stove actually *work*? Really? Wow. Well, I have a brand-new toaster oven I can contribute. My mom gave it to me for my birthday last month; she said it was a hint that it was about time for me to get the heck out of her house and find a place of my own. God, *mothers*. This looks like a comfortable living room, does the fire-place work? I do love a nice cozy fire in the winter! And that's. . . . quite a painting. Very *modern*. I prefer landscapes myself—in fact, I sometimes even dabble with watercolors. Not that I have any *talent* for art . . . not like you guys, I'm sure."

By the time they sat down in the living room for an interview, Claudia was depleted, as if Lucy's soliloquy had drained her of speech too. They squared off across from each other, Lucy in the armchair and Claudia and Jeremy seated on the couch. Lucy tugged at the knees of her jeans, trying with little success to smooth out the wrinkles that strained across her thighs. Her breasts bubbled over the top of her tank top, softly rippling when she breathed like currents in a waterbed.

"So, Lucy, why don't you tell us about yourself?" Claudia tried to show some genuine enthusiasm for Lucy's answer, but mentally, she'd already moved past the woman sitting before them to worry over the other potential roommates that were left on their list. There were only two, and neither sounded particularly promising. One was a forty-four-year-old divorcé who mentioned in his e-mail that he was on step eleven of his AA plan and hoped to enter a "Christian household that would support his ongoing commitment to clean living." The other was a nineteen-year-old girl, barely older than Claudia's students at Ennis Gates, and that just seemed wrong.

Their ad had received a dismal response. Perhaps it was the unrecognizable Mount Washington address, or perhaps no one wanted to live with a married couple, but in the three weeks that the ad had been posted online, they'd received only eight responses. Already, they'd met and dismissed a twenty-five-year-old secretary who showed up with a six-week-old infant strapped to her chest, a comic-book-store clerk who spent most of the interview talking about his passion for squirrel hunting, and a skeletal man with no discernable profession who shut himself in the bathroom three times, each time coming out suspiciously red-eyed and runny-nosed. Two of the most promising candidates—a musician in a band that Jeremy was familiar with and a grad student at the Culinary Institute—had bailed on their interviews at the last minute, saying they'd already found other places to live. Lucy was third-to-last on the list.

Claudia was choking down the idea of a roommate as if it were a dose of cherry-flavored Robitussin: something to be tolerated only because it would be better for her in the long run. It's not that she was a tremendously private person—she'd lived happily in dorms and group apartments all her life, had no compunction about sharing soap or being seen in her pajamas—but she believed in the sanctity of their lifestyle. This was Jeremy-and-Claudia's world, and—barring a roommate who magically paid for a room but never used it—she was holding out for someone who would fit unobtrusively into what they'd already begun. Someone creative and low-key like them who might even serve as a kind of sidekick, a Victor Lazslo to their Rick and Ilsa. But frankly, by this point, they were too desperate to be picky. They'd managed to pay this month's mortgage by selling off two of Jeremy's extra guitars and taking out a cash advance on their credit card, but next month's was looming, and they still owed the bank nearly $7,500 in back payments. Claudia's Ennis Gates paycheck would take up much of the slack, but it wasn't like teaching was a high-profit position. Judging by the budgets they'd worked up, they were still going to fall hundreds of dollars short every month, even after they canceled cable and the home phone line.

"I'm a nurse," Lucy was saying. "I work in trauma at Good Samaritan downtown. Did you ever watch *ER*? That's me! Not the George Clooney doctor, but the—you know—the Julianna Margulies."

Claudia sat up straight and tried to look interested. *Open your mind,* she thought to herself. *So maybe she seems a bit . . . overeager, but perhaps that's just nervousness? Which could be seen as an endearing trait, really.* She glanced over at Jeremy, slumped on the couch beside her, an ironic smile flickering across his lips. He did not appear to be charmed. She kicked his ankle under the coffee table and, when he looked at her, pinched her eyebrows together in disapproval. He flared his nostrils and crossed his eyes back at her.

"A nurse," said Claudia. "Well, I guess we'll know where to go if we have a splinter, then."

"Or a self-inflicted gunshot wound," Jeremy added brightly.

"God!" Lucy looked appalled. "I certainly hope not. You don't keep a gun in the house, do you?"

Claudia nudged Jeremy's ankle again. "He was just joking."

"Whew!" Lucy breathed a sigh of relief and fanned her face, which set off a tidal wave of bosom that threatened to spill out of her top entirely.

"I take it you grew up around here somewhere?"

"In the Valley, near Van Nuys. Yes, I know, I'm a Valley girl! *Like, omigod!* Ha-ha. Joking. I've been living with my parents since I got out of nursing school. I had a lot of debt to pay back, you know how it is. But we're all settled up now." She smiled warmly at Claudia, scanning her face. "You know," she said, "you might want to get that mole on your neck looked at. We had someone in the ER the other day who was half dead from a malignant tumor that started as a sunspot. Just saying—"

Taken aback, Claudia lifted her hand to her neck, feeling the mole. Jeremy chose this moment to pipe up. "What kind of music do you listen to?"

"Oh, I don't know," Lucy said. She seemed taken aback by the question. "Mostly country western, I guess. You know, like Garth Brooks?"

Claudia watched Jeremy's face convulse with ill-concealed horror. "Jeremy's a musician in a rock band," Claudia offered quickly. "So he plays his guitar a lot. Would that be all right with you?"

"How wonderful!" Lucy's face lit up. "I used to play the ukulele, back in high school. I know, dorky, right? Maybe I'll drag it out and you can teach me a few things. I'm always looking for a reason to take it up again. . . ."

Jeremy looked at Claudia with silent pleading in his eyes, the wide-eyed disbelief of a puppy that can't believe you're making him go outside in the rain. He shook his head imperceptibly; *no, we can't do this.* Claudia looked down at her lap, trying to imagine Jeremy and Lucy sitting side by side at the breakfast table, battling for the TV remote, waiting in line for the shower. He was right: Inconceivable. She reluctantly nodded in agreement. *We'll post another ad, maybe put up flyers on the community bulletin board by the school,* she thought.

"Lucy, we really appreciate—" she began, but Lucy was still talking.

". . . . although really it's not very likely that we'll find the time. I'm actually on the night shift at the hospital. Did I mention that? No? Well, I work seven P.M. to seven A.M., and we're on six-day shifts, so I'll probably be leaving the house about the time you get home from work and I'll get back when you're leaving. It'll be like I don't even live here." She jutted out a moist lower lip and twisted it wryly.

Claudia and Jeremy looked at each other as they took in this promising new piece of information. They held a mute conversation with their twitching eyebrows. *She'll never be here; we can't do better than an invisible roommate,* Claudia said to Jeremy with one raised brow. *Yes, but she's not like us at all,* Jeremy retorted with a double blink. *We have no choice, we need to pick* someone *and she's not so bad, considering,* Claudia blinked back. Finally, Jeremy rolled his eyes, crossed his arms, and sighed.

"We want eight hundred, plus shared utilities," he said. "And first and last month's rent as a deposit. Could you handle that?"

Lucy pursed her lips. "Yeah, I wanted to talk to you about that," she said. "If I can have the other bedroom, the bigger one with the view, I'll pay a thousand."

A long silence passed over the room. Claudia crab-walked her hand across the pebbled leather surface of the couch and located Jeremy's. She wormed her fingers under his, rubbed the thick guitar callus on the pad of his thumb. His hand swallowed hers, gripping it hard, a desperate sea anemone in a dying tide pool. *We'll survive this,* Claudia tried to tell him with her palm. *We love each other. People have survived much, much worse. All this is only temporary.*

"How soon can you move in?" she said.

Jeremy

Jeremy,

Four years. Really, it seems longer. Isn't it curious how as time passes memory begins to smear and blur and becomes somehow less about fact *or* event *and more about* visceral impression, *like a vaguely accelerated pulse or a dark twist in the back of the throat? You are to me a stomachache, the thought of you evokes a pang in my upper intestine. I should paint that.*

I heard Jillian died. So very sorry. I liked her.

I'm in Paris doing an installation right now (what an odd city, really— the French, and their strange anal fixation!), but will arrive in Los Angeles in October. I'm glad you'll see me when I'm in town. I think it will be restorative, truly. What have you made of your life? I can barely imagine what living in LA is like—are you really happy out there? I could hardly stand so much sunshine.

I hold no grudges—tell me everything.

aoki

Aoki—

So I'm a stomachache, huh? Not like, an itchy feeling under your armpit or a burning sensation in your left nasal passage? I'm a little bit offended to be such a pedestrian ailment.

Honestly, though, it's good to hear you're still tripping the light fantastic. I would expect no less. Here's the rundown of my world: I'm in a new band (with Daniel, remember him?). We're just finishing off our first album—I think you'd like it. Claudia is great; her film came out this summer and now she's teaching. This dismal economy's taking its toll, but overall, things are great.

And as for LA—well, I was born here, don't forget, so it's home turf. Rain is overrated anyway.

Thanks for the nice words about Jillian. I still miss her.

Take care,
Jeremy

Jeremy—

So, was that e-mail supposed to be a kind of virtual spanking (and by that I mean not the good kind)?? Obviously things ended rather badly between us, and I also know you weren't ever a big written-word sort of man, but really, I've gotten more thoughtful e-mails from my senile great-uncle Hiroyuki back in the old country. Everything's "great." Could you be slightly more specific? I'm not asking you to tear your soul out and send it to me in a box wrapped with silk ribbons, but I wouldn't object to just a bit of heartfelt detail. I know what your penis looks like. I know what it tastes like, so don't pretend I'm a stranger.

Or are you really so complacent now that you have nothing left to say? I've heard that this is what domestication does to men, sometimes.

So Claudia's a teacher? Well, now, isn't that a respectable job!

"Take care" (I mean, really, Jeremy!)

aoki

Aoki—

You think I'm domesticated? Coming from you, I suspect that's an insult. Trust me, underneath the happy-husband exterior I'm still the spontaneous guy who went train jumping with you across East Germany; the same guy who took peyote and then went camping in Central Park in a hailstorm. OK, so maybe I haven't gotten arrested for streaking through Union Square in a while, but just last week I had ice cream for breakfast!

Anyway. Sorry if I'm acting a little gun-shy, but . . . well, it's been a long time, and I am.

Jeremy

J—

Why? Are you still hung up on me?

a

Even now, some twenty years after the fact, Jeremy could still viscerally recall the first moment he stepped on a stage. His seventh-grade talent show was perhaps not an epic event in anyone's memory but his own, but still, it was the night from which the rest of his life seemed to stem. All the other musical numbers that evening had involved lip syncing and dance routines—1987 was all about "Papa Don't Preach" and neon-pink spandex—or else mediocre renderings of Beethoven on flute or piano. But not Jeremy's. He and his new friend, Daniel, had stepped onstage with a song Jeremy had written himself to a tune that borrowed heavily from the Beastie Boys, dressed in a costume of Billy Idol-esque gel-spiked hair and shredded jeans that Daniel's mother had gamely distressed for them. They were, of course, ridiculous, but Jeremy didn't know that at the time. All he knew was that when he stepped out there and the spotlight fell upon his face, nearly blinding him, something clicked internally. Daniel was petrified, his hands fumbling at the strings of his brand-new guitar, but Jeremy strode straight to the front of the auditorium stage as if it were the place he most belonged in the world and belted out his song with the confidence of a veteran rock star. Banging away at his guitar, screeching vaguely off-key—his voice had just started the process of changing from soprano to mild baritone—he no longer noticed the school jocks chewing spitballs in the back row, the crackle of the ancient speaker system, or the unfortunate smell of pea soup and stale grease left over from the lunch period. After years of itinerant living with his mother, feeling slightly lost in every new place they landed, he'd finally found a place where he belonged. Up there, onstage, he was someone entirely new, someone *electric,* someone *extraordinary.* And he had power over his audience: He could seduce them, he could make them adore him, he could make them *sing.*

It was true. The kids in the audience loved the song, even if the panel of adult judges awarded the top prize to a Japanese girl who played "The Flight of the Bumblebee" on her grandfather's violin. In just three and a half glorious minutes, Jeremy's position at Martin Luther Middle School was elevated to something close to a rock god. Throughout the rest of junior high and high school, Jeremy and Daniel's band—which eventually traded in Daniel's synthesizer for a real, if spectacularly untalented, drummer, and picked up the rather uninspired name Purple Voodoo Smoke—was the school's go-to group for parties and class events. No longer was Jeremy just a misfit kid whose mother dressed him in weird cotton clothes she'd picked up in India, he was a heartthrob, sensitive and artsy and just feminine enough not to be scary to the girls in his class. He lost his virginity by ninth grade.

In some ways, the rest of Jeremy's life had been an attempt to recapture that first transcendent moment onstage. Each time the lights came up and he found himself there, with twenty or a hundred or a thousand eyes trained on him, he felt himself on the verge of some sort of discovery, as if each new song that he delivered to the people below might sanctify him, renew him, reveal something about himself that he'd never known before. Often, he was disappointed: Even during the height of This Invisible Spot, when the band was playing to enormous crowds in Tokyo, he'd never quite experienced that same epiphany, the same giddy high of self-knowledge that he'd experienced in the seventh grade. Sometimes he was just up there, hot and self-conscious, wasting his beloved songs on an indifferent crowd. There were even periods of time—during the year that his mother died, for example—when he didn't play music at all. Still, he always eventually came back to the same place: the front of the stage, the guitar slung around his neck, microphone poised inches away, in search of a long-lost feeling.

And *this,* this moment right now was very close indeed. The darkly cavernous club was packed to capacity, standing room only—which was really incredible for a new band showcase on a Monday night in

September—and Audiophone had never played better. Two songs into their set, and already Jeremy knew that something extraordinary was taking place. Daniel, as lead guitarist, still tended to grow shy when performing, turning sideways to face Jeremy as if by doing so he might somehow deflect attention from himself. But tonight he was playing to the crowd, with a foot casually up on a speaker, his shoulders rising and falling in a dramatic flourish that underscored each new utterance from his guitar. Behind him, Ben was whaling away at the snare drum with an intense fury that was, Jeremy suspected, fueled by a line of cocaine, probably ingested when Ben vanished to the bathroom two minutes before they went onstage. But if cocaine always made Ben's drums sound this sharp, this brutal—well, hell, Jeremy would pay for his next eight-ball himself.

But the real epiphany tonight was Emerson. Emerson had always been the most unlikely member of Audiophone. He worked at one of those three-name financial firms downtown, doing mergers and acquisitions; he drove a BMW 5 series sedan and wore suits to work and had a special rate at the Four Seasons because he stayed there so often on business trips. Even in jeans and a T-shirt he somehow looked less like an aspiring musician than a slumming yuppie. He was the weak link, the least experienced among them, and the band member most likely to forget a critical bridge or boff the tempo when they played live. Still, he played the bass with moderate skill and extreme enthusiasm, and he'd adopted the mantle of band sugar daddy with such cheerful generosity that Jeremy didn't have the heart to tell him that his haircut was objectionably short or that basketball shoes weren't really appropriate footwear on stage. (*They'd work on that before the band went on tour,* he thought.)

Tonight, Emerson had shown up a half hour late to sound check smelling suspiciously like whiskey and tacos. He'd barely spoken a word as they'd raced through setup, his face set with a panic that made Jeremy's heart sink: Emerson was going to seize up again. But his fears were unfounded, because here Emerson was, improvising a new turn on the opening to "Super Special"—something he'd never done before—and doing it remarkably well. He played with his eyes closed and a blissful smile on his face, seemingly lost in a beautiful world of his own making where quarterly earnings didn't matter and the only merging taking place was of bass with guitar.

Emerson opened his eyes and caught Jeremy looking at him. He offered an abashed smile, almost as if he felt guilty for enjoying himself so much, as Jeremy stepped forward and grabbed the microphone:

> *"I don't know why you think you're super special,*
> *Yes, you're special-looking*
> *But you're not especially deep."*

The first few words were rough, as he fought with a burr in his throat, but then his voice opened up and the rest of the lyrics poured out in a happy growl. Singing had never been Jeremy's true forte—his real skill lay in his one-on-one communion with his guitar—but he had a decent baritone and could sing consistently on key and had been told his voice was "arresting" by more than one critic. And he secretly enjoyed being the fulcrum around which the rest of the band rotated; enjoyed serving as a kind of medium through which everyone else onstage spoke directly to the audience; enjoyed, of course, the extra attention granted to the lead singer.

> *"You know what would be*
> *Really super special to see?*
> *The day when you wake up and realize*
> *You're as ordinary as me."*

He wasn't sure who this song was about, specifically—a bitter diatribe about one of Daniel's unrequited crushes, probably. Audiophone's lyrics had always had a cynical bent, a result of Daniel's chronic relationship frustration, but Jeremy liked that their music had a certain bite. He matched the melancholy of Daniel's lovelorn words by composing haunting tunes in minor keys, but often gave them a final upward twist and an exultant journey to the finish so that the audience would be left with an indeterminate sense of victory over adversity. He didn't want their music to be a bummer.

The band maneuvered through the tricky bridge and launched into the chorus. Stepping forward to bark out the call and response, Jeremy peered out at the audience and realized that they were dancing. That had never happened at a show before. Crowds at these kinds of showcases tended to be jaded hipsters who stayed planted in one position throughout the entire set, too concerned about appearing sincerely enthusiastic to do anything but bob their heads in time. Not tonight. These kids were *really* dancing: pogoing up and down, waving their hands above their heads, ricocheting off one another like waxed pinballs in a vintage arcade game. The room smelled like spilled beer and fresh sweat.

And there was Claudia, in the very front. She looked especially pretty tonight, with her curls all twisted up on the top of her head, wearing a pair of dark jeans that hugged her soft rear in a loving denim embrace. She smiled up at him, her lips mirroring the lyrics coming from his own mouth—*You know you're super special*—and for a moment it seemed like he was playing to her and her alone. He liked the way she always wanted to be right at the very front of the stage, as if publicly declaring herself his biggest fan. There was something so unself-conscious about this, such a pure, unadulterated enthusiasm for the music; and such a contrast to the studied cool of Aoki, who had always watched him from backstage, safely removed from the hoi polloi.

He closed his eyes as he played, forgetting momentarily the foreclosure notice, the appalling new roommate who had moved her trunks in just that afternoon, the negative bank balance, and Claudia's upsetting recent behavior. He could hear his own music clearly, as if he were one of the kids dancing in the audience; he fell in love with the notes that were spinning, almost on their own volition, off his guitar strings. The stage spotlights burned starbursts into the back of his eyelids, exploding in time to the music.

And then their set was over, just a quick encore song to squeeze in before the next band was up. As his fingers picked out the virtuosic last solo, a show-offy little line that he'd composed just the day before, he wished Audiophone had enough material to extend their time onstage forever. He reached for the microphone once more.

"No Assembly Required
That's what you promised me
It was always 'Buy one, get one free.'
But now I've got this flat-pack box
That came at an incredible cost
And the instructions nowhere to be seen."

At one point, he'd thought he might never play in a band again. After moving back to Los Angeles, Jeremy couldn't even *look* at his guitar without experiencing a wave of physical repulsion: This was the lingering damage from the ugly implosion of This Invisible Spot and the death of his mother. For almost two years, he stoically ignored advances from former music industry acquaintances, let his copy of *Pro Tools* grow dusty, and threw all his creative energy into his relationship with Claudia instead. It was his old friend Daniel—now a technology journalist at a daily newspaper but still nostalgic for his glory days onstage—who forced him pick up his guitar again. At first, it had just been the two of them, noodling on their instruments in Jeremy's living room, but then Jeremy ran into Ben—the former drummer from a group he'd known in New York—and after that Daniel had invited his friend Emerson to jam with them, and suddenly there they were: a band.

Jeremy had heard their potential right away—the natural swing in Emerson's bass lines, the quirky charm of Ben's slightly off-tempo drumming, Daniel's transformation from self-conscious geek to virtuoso when parked behind the safety of a guitar. Under Jeremy's tutelage, Daniel began showing up to night practices with notebooks full of surprisingly catchy lyrics, and Emerson cemented the deal by renting a studio space in an industrial neighborhood in the Valley and promising to pay for the expenses of recording the album. It turned out that Audiophone had an easy chemistry in the studio—they were potentially even better, Jeremy thought, than This Invisible Spot had ever been. Less *gimmick* and more *groove*. Which was a good thing, especially now that so much was riding on the success of their album. If only they could finish the damn thing.

It wasn't like the band was stagnating. They'd played a few shows at prestigiously grungy east-side venues and local music festivals, signed with a good manager, received strong write-ups on music blogs. All spring, the songs were materializing out of them like some kind of collective mystical ritual—their practices so intense that Jeremy would come home depleted and sleep for ten hours—but at some critical point this summer they had lost steam. First, it was a business trip that took Emerson to Malaysia for two months, and then Ben the drummer's epic hangovers took their toll, and now it was Daniel who had canceled their last three practices for suspicious-sounding "personal reasons." At this rate, it would take another six months to complete the album. Jeremy didn't have that kind of time; his problems were much more urgent than that.

Isn't that a respectable job? He thought of Aoki's e-mail for the hundredth time this week, and could practically see the snide curl of Aoki's lip as she typed that line. His first instinct had been to avoid mentioning Claudia entirely in his correspondence with Aoki, as if that might somehow protect her from his ex-girlfriend's cutting opinions—but then he thought it might appear to Aoki that he was disavowing his wife. So he'd dropped in a careful mention of her, and sure enough, Aoki had managed with one word to dismiss her. *What Would Aoki Think?* Not much, clearly. But that wasn't the worst of it. The worst was that when he read Aoki's dismissive response—*Isn't that respectable?*—his lurching first reaction had been an involuntary nod of agreement.

He didn't even recognize his wife anymore, this grimly focused woman who put on pumps in the morning and left for work before he'd even woken up and then spent her evenings grading papers instead of drinking margaritas at El Compadre or going to see bands with him or working on the screenplay she'd promised to write. They hadn't even had sex in weeks—she fell asleep early now, thanks to her 5:30 A.M. wake-up time. Even though he understood that the House Problem had forced this situation; even though he could relate to how defeated she felt by her stalled career; and even though he respected teachers, on principle, for taking on such an important task (educating the leaders of tomorrow and all that)—despite all this, he still couldn't quite reconcile the fact that the inspiring director he'd married had been replaced seemingly overnight by a home-obsessed, depressingly bourgeois, constantly stressed-out schoolteacher. He watched this strange new Claudia, fussing over curricula and grading systems and mortgage balances and Excel spreadsheets, and couldn't help thinking that she had overreacted and let go of something critical. Maybe Claudia was saving their house, but her transformation into this new person felt like a different kind of betrayal.

But Audiophone's success could save Claudia. Could save *both* of them. A finished record might set an inspirational example for Claudia, yes, but it might also net them enough cash to let her quit that job and boot out Lucy. Like turning in the pawn ticket to get their lives out of hock. Getting rich off his music had never been the goal, exactly—you were stupid if you thought you'd do that as a musician these days—but it wasn't unrealistic to think it might make *some* money. If Audiophone knocked out the album in the next month or two, by the end of the year they'd have something to sell. And who knows? They could get a record deal, go on tour, have a radio hit, lay claim to a miracle. Life could return to the way it used to be, only *better.*

Judging by the enthusiastic response of the audience tonight, maybe it wasn't such a wild fantasy after all. As the crowd's cheers crescendoed into a frenzied climax, Jeremy lifted the last crowing notes of "No Assembly Required" out over the heads of the audience and then dropped the song, crashing, to a finish. The house lights came up and the DJ put on a Prince song and the audience began to drift away, back toward the bar. The band broke down their instruments in the dark, invisible except to a clutch of friends and acquaintances who lingered near the steps, waiting to greet them. Claudia pushed through the throng and met him at the edge of the stage.

"You were amazing tonight," she said. "The best you've ever played." She reached up to grip his hand possessively.

He jumped down off the stage and grabbed her close to kiss her: He was wound up, flush with adrenaline and a little bit horny. She pressed herself against his sweat-drenched shirt and kissed him back, hard. "And did I mention how devastatingly cute you are up there?"

"I nominate you president of my fan club," he murmured, happy to see that the old Claudia had returned.

"Does that come with special privileges?" She looped her fingers through the belt loop of his jeans and tugged him in toward her.

He bit his lip in mock consternation. "I could offer you an auto-graphed fan photo?"

"I had something more personal in mind." Her hands slipped down into the rear pockets of his jeans, and he wrapped his arms around her waist, locking their pelvises together. She muttered in his ear: "How soon can you get out of here?"

Jeremy glanced back up at the stage, where the rest of the band was untangling cords and bundling Ben's drum set away. A rotund middle-aged guy in a faded Velvet Underground T-shirt and baseball hat was lingering a few feet away, watching Claudia and Jeremy hawkishly. "I've got to break down," Jeremy said. "And maybe the guys will want to get a drink afterward. What do you think?"

Claudia leaned back and pulled her arm around him in order to check her watch. She grimaced. "I shouldn't. It's already way past my bedtime for a school night. I need to get up early and correct papers, anyway. But you should go."

"You sure?"

She placed her hand on his chest, pushing him backward. "Go, cele-brate. I'll always be there tomorrow."

Velvet Underground moved in closer, breaching their privacy. Jer-emy released Claudia reluctantly. "You promise?"

"I promise." She kissed him again and moved away, offering Velvet Underground an annoyed glance as she passed by him.

Velvet Underground immediately stepped forward into the breach, thrusting his hand so close to Jeremy's sternum that he had no choice but to reach out and instinctively grab it, if only to prevent it from jab-bing him in the chest. There was something scratchy and sharp in the man's palm, and when Jeremy pulled his hand away he realized that he was holding a slightly worn business card. *Julian Bragg* it said. There was no title below it, no company name, no phone number, just an e-mail address.

"I've been wondering what the hell happened to you," Julian began. His voice was raspy from too many late nights at loud clubs; bloodshot eyes peered out from below the brim of his faded baseball cap. Julian could use a shower and shave—the bristles growing in uneven patches across his chin were silver—but somehow despite all these handicaps he was a commanding presence in the room. It was something about the way he stood firmly upright, not in the least bit abashed by his graceless physical presence, and Jeremy thought, as he stared at this man, that bothering to look cool was something that only uncool people needed to do. "Jeremy fucking Munger. This Invisible Spot was completely screwed when you left; you were the real talent in that lot. What took you so goddamn long to start something new?"

Jeremy cleared his throat and glanced up at his bandmates, who had finished breaking down their instruments and were lugging them toward the green room. "Personal issues," he said.

"Well, it's about fucking time. Nothing more depressing than genius going to waste."

Jeremy glanced at the card again, the name—*Julian Bragg*—ringing soft bells somewhere in the back of his hippocampus. "I'm sorry, but do I know you?"

Julian peered down, looking at his own card as if he were double-checking what was written there. "*Julian Bragg. Braggadocio Entertainment,*" he repeated. "I do music-licensing deals. That's where the money is these days, you know."

Jeremy smiled, suddenly realizing why he'd recognized this guy's name. "You license music for all the iPod ads."

Julian winked and stepped backward, tugging his cap down. "Indeed I do. Also Nike, Volkswagen, those teenybopper shows on Fox. You want to start making real money, I'm your man. That "Super Special" song, it had *laptop commercial* written all over it. You have a rep yet?" Jeremy shook his head. "Well, now you do."

"We haven't finished the album yet," Jeremy said. "We don't even have a record deal."

Julian shrugged. "I'll get you one. How close are you to being done?"

The next band had arrived on stage and were knocking about in the dark, plugging in their amps. The audience surged forward in anticipation, jostling Jeremy and Julian up against the steps. Jeremy drew in closer and spoke quickly. "Two or three more songs. Plus we have to master the album," he paused. "Maybe six weeks if we really bust our asses."

"Well, bustamove, buster," Julian said, and knocked Jeremy's shoulder with the edge of his hand. "I'll be in touch. *Audiofuckingphone.* Brilliant, really." He raised a beer—nonalcoholic, judging by the smell of it—in a one-man toast and meandered away. The audience edged aside to let him through as the band onstage slammed into the first song of their set with a squeal of eardrum-popping static. Jeremy raised his own invisible toast to Julian's disappearing back and turned to go locate his bandmates.

He found them in the green room backstage, drinking warm Coors Light and sharing Zesty Taco Chipotle Ranch Doritos out of a crumpled bag that looked like it might have been left there for the last decade. The sweat was drying on their faces and their salty foreheads sparkled in the light of the bare bulbs overhead. The dull thump of a bass line from the band onstage pulsed through the floor. The ceiling fan whizzed overhead, spinning hot gusts of air around them. A giant graffiti penis was scrawled on the far wall, just below a panel of chipped soundproofing.

Jeremy planted himself before them, flush with determination. "We were amazing tonight," he announced. "Emerson—that opening line you improvised on *Super Special*? Remember it. Daniel—way to engage the audience, friend. Ben—nice work with that last solo. We should all be proud." He paused, for dramatic flourish. "We are getting so tight. But guys, we've got a lot more work to do, and we have to do it pronto. No more screwing around anymore."

Ben flopped down in a battered armchair: "Good playing with you too, killjoy." He rolled his drumsticks compulsively back and forth in his lap. Ben's jeans gripped his legs like sausage casings, and his blond hair and beard flowed Jesus-like across his tattooed shoulders; an extreme look that Jeremy knew he should probably be adopting himself if he wanted to fit in with the hipster rock crowd but couldn't really bear the idea. The amazing thing was how much time and effort Ben spent on looking like he'd made no effort at all.

"Have we been screwing around? I thought we were doing pretty well, actually," Emerson said. He licked his thumb and scrubbed at a black smear on the side of his tennis shoe.

Jeremy turned to Daniel, expectantly. Daniel had always backed him up, ever since they first met in sixth grade, when Jeremy returned to the States after a two-year stay on an Indian ashram with Jillian. When the kids at school made fun of Jeremy's macrobiotic lunchboxes, Daniel would punch them; when Jeremy wanted to cut school in order to feel up Maggie Bond, Daniel would forge a doctor's excuse; when Jeremy returned home from New York and couldn't handle staying in Jillian's cancer-ward bungalow, Daniel let him sleep on his couch; when Jeremy got married, Daniel stood up as his best man. Daniel attended Jillian's memorial service, and hadn't cringed or made a funny face when the shaman pressed Jillian's ashes into his forehead and waved sage under his nose. But now Daniel just fidgeted with his watch, as if he hadn't heard a word Jeremy said.

"Look." Jeremy hated being the bad guy. He'd managed to skate through most of his life without ever being forced into this position—the guy in charge, the guy laying down the rules—and it made him uncomfortable to have to be the band leader. He smiled, softened his voice. "We have to pull it together and finish the album. Otherwise, why are we doing this?"

Ben's cellphone chimed out the arrival of a text message, which he examined intently. "Because chicks dig it?"

"Because we love the music," Emerson said, sincere.

"Yes," Jeremy agreed. "Because we love the music. Of course. But *also* because we want to put out a really great album, get a six-figure licensing deal for a commercial, receive critical acclaim, and headline the Hollywood Bowl. This is what I propose: Let's recommit to practices. Let's agree to get together every night—don't roll your eyes, Ben, I'm serious—every night until we have the album knocked together. I bet we could finish it in, like, a month. Maybe two."

Ben looked like he'd been handed a lemon and told it was a cupcake. "Dude, you're married. You have no social life. How am I supposed to get laid if I'm holed up in the studio with you tools every night?"

"We all know you aren't getting any and you won't get any until you're a rock star—at which point you can have all the cheap, regrettable sex you ever dreamed of. But we need to finish the album before that'll happen. So, how about it? Every night, starting tomorrow?"

"Not tomorrow," said Emerson. "I've got a client dinner. I'd cancel if I could, but things are a little dicey at work right now."

"OK," Jeremy said. "Wednesday, then, and every night thereafter."

Ben shrugged. "I can't do Wednesdays or Saturday afternoon, because that's when my other band practices. But I'll do my best on the other nights."

"Deal. And we should map out a plan of attack, set some deadlines." He turned to Daniel expectantly. But Daniel's gaze remained firmly on the floor, just above a cigarette burn in the industrial carpet, with a persistent little smile flickering across his pink chafed lips. There was something strange about Daniel's behavior tonight—not just his newly discovered onstage confidence, or the way he'd cradled his guitar close to his groin, fingering the frets with an absentminded caress. It was the way he just stood there in the corner now, bruised-looking eyelids swagged across his cheekbones, smiling shyly at the toes of his sneakers. Jeremy had known Daniel since fifth grade, and the only time he'd ever seen his friend look like this was when Riva Richards let him deflower her in their junior year of high school. Was Daniel in *love*?

Daniel swayed with apparent exhaustion. "Sure, that all sounds fine, Jeremy, but . . . can we talk about all this at our next practice? I've gotta be somewhere."

"Now?" Jeremy glanced at the clock; it was eleven-thirty. "I thought we could all go out for drinks. Celebrate." But Daniel's words were like a recess bell, springing everyone into action. Ben tumbled off his chair and raced for the door, already dialing his cellphone. Emerson kicked at the nest of extension cords that had coiled around his feet, releasing himself. "Maybe next week," he said, apologetically. "Things are kind of imploding at work, and I've got to be in the office early tomorrow."

Jeremy watched them collect their bags with dismay. "Fine," he said. "We'll make a schedule on Thursday. Just remember, guys: priorities. OK?" He smiled encouragingly, and then pitched his guitar pick across the room toward his open guitar case. He meant it to be a gentle lob, a gesture of casual confidence, but he threw it a little too hard and it skittered across the top of a box of concert posters, bounced across the industrial carpet, and landed in a forlorn cluster of dust bunnies in the corner.

Daniel followed Jeremy out to his car, watching Jeremy heave his guitar into the backseat of the convertible. A police helicopter flew by overhead, stirring up a vortex of refuse along the wall of the nightclub. The storefronts were dark, only the red blinking eyes of their alarms keeping watch in the windows. It was mid-September and the nights had already grown heavy with dew; soon, he'd have to put the car's top up at night.

Daniel and Jeremy shuffled around the car, keeping its steel bulk between them. They shared that twinned quality that comes from too many years of shared taste: They cut their flyaway hair the same way, curling a bit too long around the ears; and were nearly the same height and weight, with loose spaghetti arms and sinewy legs and stomachs a little too soft from beer; and they both owned wardrobes of faded T-shirts and tenderized jeans and unshowy Converse sneakers. It was unspoken that Jeremy had always been the handsome one—he had a delicate symmetry to his face, and women had responded to his high cheekbones and blue eyes and long lashes as early as junior high, whereas Daniel's jaw was square-boned and his ears vaguely simian. From a distance, though, they could be mistaken for each other. Seeing himself in Daniel was reassuring, proof that Jeremy hadn't veered too far from an acceptable mean. But tonight, as he looked at Daniel, he saw that his friend was different: He had cut his hair shorter, used gel, changed into a button-front shirt, shaved.

Daniel leaned against the hood of Jeremy's car, bracing himself with sneakered feet. "It was a great show," he repeated.

"A licensing rep came up to me afterward. He wants to see our album when we're finished," Jeremy said. He sat on the hood next to Daniel, letting the metal dimple slightly under their combined weight. "So I need you to finish those lyrics soon, OK? We've got a good opportunity here, and I don't want to screw it up. I really need this."

This didn't have the impact on Daniel that Jeremy expected. Daniel still looked distracted, half a world away. "Sometimes I wonder, who do we think we're kidding?" Daniel mused. "You and I, we're both thirty-four; Emerson is thirty-five. The only person still in his twenties is Ben, though God knows he seems to be trying to make up for all of us. But rock and roll is a business for kids, and we're really pushing it." He prodded his gut with an index finger. "I mean, it's not like we're going to make the cover of *Rolling Stone* with these bodies."

"Speak for yourself. We have a *real shot,* Daniel. Trust me. I've done this before." He paused. "I don't have anything else *but* this."

Daniel threw him a strange look. "Fine, I'll get on it." He fixed his gaze at the ground, his head bobbing slightly, as if holding a conversation in his own head. He kicked a stone and sent it skittering across the parking lot. "Where is all this coming from tonight, Jer? Did something happen?"

Jeremy picked at a pink bougainvillea blossom that had glued itself to the hood, while he tried to figure out how to answer this. He'd already roughly sketched out the facts of the situation to Daniel—the impending foreclosure, the mortgage hike, the money crunch, Claudia's job—and he suspected that Daniel wanted more details, a more emotional catharsis that Jeremy didn't feel ready to give. "Oh, you know, it's the same stuff," he said, noncommittally. "We had to take in a roommate."

"No shit." Daniel's shoe sent another stone skittering. "That's got to be weird."

Jeremy shrugged. "It's only temporary, I hope."

"Guy or girl?"

"A nurse, named Lucy." Lucy. Oh, God, just intoning her name made him want a drink. She'd moved into their vacated bedroom that evening. It broke his heart. Waking up every morning to that view over downtown had always been his favorite thing about living in Mount Washington; it somehow made up for the isolation of living on a cul de sac on the top of a hill. The fact that he could see that little sliver of skyline from their bed—the lights of downtown, winking at him in the dark—had always given him a reassuring sense of connection with the rest of the city. For just two hundred bucks a month, he had sold out;

they had shoehorned their king-size bed into the spare bedroom, whose one window looked out at a concrete retaining wall.

He'd just been leaving that evening when Lucy arrived with her big wooden trunk in tow. She stood in the doorway of the house with a key—their key!—in one hand, an overflowing Hello Kitty duffel in the other. When they first met, he had pegged her as an average-looking girl who'd lucked out with those spectacular breasts; today, even those were hidden under floral acrylic nurse's scrubs. She looked pleasantly forgettable, like someone's kid cousin who worked the checkout line at the supermarket.

"Hello there!" she said, as he tried to brush past her to the door.

"Hello goodbye," he mumbled. "I'm on my way out."

"That's too bad. I brought a bottle of wine. I thought we could make dinner or something, get to know each other." Big, damp brown eyes wheedled and begged behind fluttering lashes. Was she flirting with him?

"Got a show, sorry. Maybe another time." He barely managed to keep a straight face.

She smiled, unperturbed, and then threw her arms around him in a hug. "I'm so happy to be here," she offered. "There's such a great vibe in this house. I'm really flattered to have made the cut."

He'd mumbled something affirming and extricated himself from her embrace and fled, his behavior just this side of rude. *I'm not a very nice person,* he thought now. *I should be friendly to her, if I'm going to live with her.* Yes. He'd work harder at being tolerant and focus his energy on getting the album done instead: It was the wiser tactic to getting her out of the house. He flicked the bougainvillea bloom off his finger. "She's all right," he told Daniel now. "Bearable."

The police helicopter was back. It hovered overhead and skipped its spotlight across their faces. They looked up and covered their eyes with their forearms, staring up into the accusing light, until the helicopter swung south, toward downtown. Jeremy watched Daniel wipe dust from his face, smooth back his ruffled hair, tuck his shirt in.

"So, are you going to tell me about the mystery woman?"

Daniel flushed, a bright unseemly pink. "How did you know?"

Jeremy arched an eyebrow. "You smell like a drugstore counter. Is that Aqua Velva?"

Daniel stared down at his lap, looking for the answer to Jeremy's questions in the crotch of his jeans. "She's. . . . she's great," he stuttered. "Cristina Villareal. She works at a museum. Downtown. We met last month, at a dinner party. Cristina, she's—well, she's thirty-six. Incredibly smart. Pretty, but not the scary sort of pretty." Jeremy watched Daniel struggle to regurgitate these details, trying to make them add up to something that he couldn't quite articulate.

"You're in love."

Daniel's nose flared. He looked like he might melt down entirely. Daniel had never really been in love before, not that Jeremy knew about anyway; instead, he pined after girls who had already relegated him to just-a-friend status or dated surly women who treated him like their personal assistant. His one long-term relationship—with a mousy, needy girl who was too scared to drive a car—had happened mostly out of desperation, at a point in his twenties when Daniel had been insistent on finding a girlfriend, any girlfriend. Truth was, Daniel didn't know how to stand up for himself or how to recognize his equal in a woman. Sometimes, Jeremy thought his friend would be single forever, living in his musky bachelor pad with only a dog for company, clumsily hitting on waitresses at restaurants, eventually dying in his La-Z-Boy while a Dodgers game played on mute.

"Yeah," Daniel said finally. He stared at a bum down the street, who was erecting a shelter out of flattened cartons. "Yeah, it's definitely love."

Jeremy considered this, circumspect. "I'm happy for you," he said. He put his hand out and rubbed his friend's back through the T-shirt, until the moment began to feel too loaded. "How'd you get her to date you? Club her over the head and drag her back to your lair? No, you must have taken her to a hotel. Your apartment would have scared her off by now."

But Daniel didn't laugh. He just shook his head, again and again. "Jeremy—she's pregnant." His voice cracked on the last word, and he said it again: "We're pregnant."

Daniel's back, under his palm, was slack and hot. Jeremy pulled his hand away, trying to read the cryptic expression on his friend's face. He couldn't remember ever hearing Daniel use the word *we* regarding a relationship before; certainly he'd never used it like this, paired with that other terrifying word, *pregnant*. "This is—a good thing?" he asked carefully.

Daniel's eyes were luminous under the fluorescent streetlights. "It's a great thing," he said, and his voice was grave and serious. "I bet you think I'm insane, but I'm not. We just knew. Right away, from the second we met, we knew. It's not like we intended to get pregnant, but it's not like we really tried *not* to either. It just felt . . . right." That word again—*we*—kept tumbling from his mouth, and Jeremy wanted to tell him to stop it, to stop acting as if he'd managed, in the space of less than a month, to merge himself completely with a stranger Jeremy had never met.

Daniel was staring at him, and Jeremy realized he'd been silent for far too long. "I don't think you're insane," he said. "I figure you're just trying to beat Claudia and me. Remember, we got engaged in less than six months? So, see, I'm all for crazy love."

But he knew, from the stunned expression on Daniel's face, that this wasn't the same as that. Not at all. His relationship with Claudia hadn't been a grand combustion, the kind of crazy love that devours you alive, the way it had been with Aoki, and the way it apparently was with this Cristina person; it had been a mild simmer, something gentle and protective and kind. If Jillian hadn't been dying, he probably would have dated Claudia for years before finally making the big leap. But Jillian *was* dying, her lungs were ejecting thick black clots of metastasized death as she shriveled away, week by week in her sari-covered bed; and the thought of being without a family once she died (his itinerant father hardly counted) made him go cold all over. It seemed like a last gift he could give Jillian—the chance to know her son was going to be OK once she was gone, that he had this sweet, smart, loving girl who would take care of him.

He had let himself sink into Claudia as if she were a soft velvet cushion, let her cosset him in a way Aoki never had and, frankly, never could have. He felt at peace in Claudia's arms, even when he was in tears—he couldn't remember the last time that a relationship had felt like that. And maybe he did hastily ask her to marry him for a lot of the wrong reasons—because he felt indebted to her, or because of the selfish impulse to be nurtured like this for the rest of his life, or to get engaged before Jillian died—but there were a lot of the right reasons too. There was also love. Yes, a different kind of love than Aoki, but that didn't mean it was any less real.

"Aoki e-mailed me," he blurted out.

Daniel snapped sideways. "You're kidding. What did she want?"

"Just to say hi, I think. She's going to be in town next month. We might have a coffee." He didn't mention the rest of their correspondence, or the way he'd started to check his e-mail compulsively, anticipating the electric thrill of seeing Aoki's name in his in-box. Their communication had slipped quickly into something more than he'd intended, with his first, carefully worded responses; it had become dangerous, and he knew it. He felt like an alcoholic must when they finally fall off the wagon, when they take that first burning slug of whiskey and taste the memory of joyful obliteration.

But he couldn't tell Daniel this. Daniel adored Claudia, had always treated her with such doting respect—bringing her flowers for her movie premiere, calling her for "girl advice"—that Jeremy had sometimes wondered whether his friend had a crush on his wife. Already, Jeremy could feel the cold front of Daniel's disapproval, a frozen restraint in his friend's voice. "Does Claudia know about this?"

"Not yet. But I'm going to tell her."

"Do you really think it's a good idea, seeing Aoki? I mean—I was there when you got back to LA. She tore you apart."

"It'll be fine," he said. "It's not a big deal. I'm married now, remember? Model husband."

"Whatever you say, man. Just be careful." Daniel stood up, fishing his keys from his pocket. "I gotta go. Cristina's waiting for me at home."

"Moving so fast." Jeremy slid off the hood. "When do I get to meet her?"

"I don't know. Soon?"

"You should come over to the house for cocktails."

"That'll mean bailing on practice that night, though. Right?" Daniel winked, and began to jog down the street to his car.

Jeremy watched him go. "Hey, Daniel," he called. Daniel turned, kept jogging backward. "Congratulations. It's really great news." Daniel flashed a grin and waved a hand and then vanished.

Jeremy climbed into his convertible. The engine rumbled to life under his feet and he drove off down the street, turning right and then left, until he merged onto Sunset Boulevard. The cooling night air crisped his face as his triumphal mood began to wane in the face of Daniel's announcement. *I shouldn't tell Claudia about the pregnancy,* he caught himself thinking, *because then she'll want a baby too.* He wasn't ready for a kid yet, not by a long shot. A baby would tether them forever to a life without risks or spontaneity, and God knows they were already trapped enough these days. Against his will, he found himself thinking again of Aoki, jet-setting around in the world on impulse, lunching in French cafés and putting on shows in Tel Aviv. As he shot eastward through the deserted streets, he decided that it was time to e-mail Aoki and nail down a date.

Claudia

THE CLOCK SAID IT WAS FIVE IN THE MORNING. CLAUDIA HAD TO prop herself up on the pillow and peer over Jeremy in order to read the time; thanks to the cramped nature of their new sleeping quarters, which allotted no room for a bedside table, the alarm clock's new home was on the floor. She flopped onto her back, tugging her half of the blanket back from its incarceration between Jeremy's twisted legs. Whatever had disturbed her—a raccoon in the driveway? A coyote howling in the canyon?—clearly had not bothered him. He was motionless, except for the gentle fibrillations of his nose as he snored.

She lay in the dark, listening hard, waiting for the noise to come again. As her eyes adjusted to the light, she surveyed the blurred, dusky surfaces of their new makeshift bedroom. Sometimes it felt like they'd eaten Alice in Wonderland's cake and grown three sizes too big: The possessions that had fit so comfortably into the master bedroom—the big oak chest of drawers, the television cabinet, the Queen Anne armchair she'd found in the street and repainted white—were completely out of proportion in here. For lack of space, they'd relinquished the chair completely: It was in Lucy's bedroom now, and Claudia mourned its absence. But there was no room in here, really, for anything but the king-size bed. This nearly touched the walls on either side, which made getting dressed in the morning a hazard. Claudia had gotten in the habit of dressing in the hallway, furtively yanking up her pants in the dark in case Lucy came home and caught her.

Lucy. The noise had begun again, and now that Claudia was fully awake it was clear that the sound wasn't animal at all. It was human: a high-pitched squeal, amplified through the grated vent in the wall. The metallic scraping that in a semiconscious state sounded plausibly like a garbage can being looted by the local wildlife was actually the damage caused by a cast-iron four-poster bed rubbing rhythmically against a wall. Lucy was having sex. Claudia listened intently, curious and repelled.

She poked Jeremy in the side. "Listen," she said. "Lucy's getting some action."

Jeremy grunted and rolled over, taking the blanket back with him. He muttered something inaudible and resumed snoring.

There was no point in trying to go back to sleep; she had to get up in half an hour anyway, in order to make it to work by seven. Instead, she clambered over Jeremy's legs, grabbed her bathrobe from the hook on the back of the door, and tiptoed past Lucy's room to the kitchen. She stood groggily there in the dark, waiting for the coffee to percolate as the gurgling of the coffeemaker mingled with the fainter groans and muffled giggles coming from the other side of the house.

So far, Lucy had been, as promised, an invisible roommate. Claudia was usually gone by the time Lucy returned home from work, and during Lucy's days off—which, as far as Claudia could tell, came intermittently and often during the middle of the week—she vanished to Van Nuys to visit her mother. But there were signs of their new roommate everywhere. Baroque underwear—frilly lace garments, which Lucy hand-washed in the sink—hung from a line in her bathroom. The refrigerator was packed with mysterious items only barely recognizable as food: Jello-lite strawberry pudding cups, vanilla Chug, toasted-coconut-covered marshmallows. Six unappealing watercolor landscapes, as unskilled as Lucy had promised they would be, now hung on the wall in the hallway, and a mumsy chintz love seat that Lucy had inherited from her grandmother was plopped right into the center of their otherwise carefully curated living room. Lucy had made herself right at home, and of course Claudia didn't fault her for that; but she couldn't help feeling that an enemy encircling their encampment was about to close in. *It's better than the alternative,* she told herself. *It's better than foreclosure.* From the bedroom, she heard a garbled moan and then silence.

A cup of coffee in hand, Claudia flipped through the morning paper, skipping past the graph on the front page, depicting the plummeting New York Stock Exchange, and the business section, bemoaning the government seizure of Claudia and Jeremy's bank, and over to Real Estate. Here she found a four-page photo essay documenting the foreclosure epidemic in the Inland Empire. In the pictures, empty houses sat like tombstones, marking the death of an era. Faded FOR SALE signs hung limply in the hot desert sun, as the desolate peaks of the San Bernardino mountains loomed overhead. Black algae blanketed the bottom of never-used swimming pools; abandoned swing sets sported rust and graffiti tags from the local delinquents. At the entrance to a half-built planned development—where the rotting houses lined the horizon, their wooden skeletons exposed to the elements—a sagging banner begged passing drivers: PARADISE VALLEY HOMES, $399,000 AND UP! LIVE HERE NOW.

"Why don't you sell your house for a loss and just move somewhere cheaper?" That's what Claudia's mother had said to her last week, when Claudia called to cry about the outrageous mortgage, the unwanted roommate, the money she was pouring into four-dollar-a-gallon gasoline for her crosstown commute. "You don't have to live in the middle of Los Angeles, honey. You could move out to the suburbs. It's safer there anyway, and you could still commute to work." Thinking of Ruth's words, Claudia stared at the tract homes in the photographs and shuddered. Was that what it was going to come to? Sure, for an hour-and-a-half drive on the Interstate (if traffic was good, which it never was), anyone could have their pick of these foreclosed homes at cut-rate prices. This was the "golden opportunity" left behind in the sludge of America's waning economy. But Claudia wanted to be here, in the middle of the city, among the living. Wasn't that why she had left Wisconsin in the first place? It didn't seem fair: According to the news, the world was collapsing around them: investment banks shutting their doors daily, unemployment at six percent and rising, oil topping $100 a barrel, the stock market in free fall, and the second Depression barreling down on them. But in urban Los Angeles, a shoebox-sized starter home in a not-great neighborhood cost over half a million dollars, minimum, even now. "Why don't you move somewhere cheaper?" She wished she had a more logical answer for her mother, one that made sense even to her.

She closed the newspaper and began going over her notes for today's "open dialogue hours." This was the Ennis Gates version of parent-teacher conferences; it lasted almost a month and involved lengthy one-on-one sessions with each student's parents. Claudia felt as if she had gone on trial, with a never-ending parade of overprotective parents serving as a host of inquisitors testing her faith. "I want to make sure that you understand Robin's special test-taking needs." "Theodore mentioned that you assign much more *homework* than his last film teacher." "I noticed that Jordan was writing an essay about *Taxi Driver* last week. Do you really think that's an appropriate movie for a sixteen-year-old?" "Can you possibly check to see that Kelsey is taking her Adderall after lunch?"

After only a week of meetings, Claudia's head was reeling with the details she needed to remember, the land mines she had to avoid in coming months. This afternoon, she had three sets of parents coming in—the parents of Mary Hernandez, Lisa Yang, and, most promising and problematic of all, Penelope Evanovich.

Claudia's first weeks at Ennis Gates Academy had passed in a pleasant ego-affirming haze. Classes were *fun*. Her students were eager (eager!) to discuss the stylized sets of German Expressionist film and how the chiaroscuro in *Touch of Evil* reflected themes of moral ambiguity. They asked her for movie and (after learning that her husband was in a band) music recommendations. They brought her *rugelach* and brownies that their Peruvian housekeepers had baked. When she walked through the Academy's campus, they would call out at her from across the quad. *Hey, Munger! Yo, Munger, what's up?* Even though she probably shouldn't have encouraged such informal intimacy with her students, she couldn't help but love it. Here, finally, was her captive audience, an audience that spent every day staring at her attentively and (when they weren't sending surreptitious text messages or examining their split ends or inking elaborate designs on their canvas Chuck Taylors) *listening*. They jotted down her words as if they held real value. When she graded essay tests, she was startled to recognize exact phrases that had come from her mouth, dutifully recorded and memorized and

then regurgitated in smudged ballpoint pen. This was definitely the upside of teaching, she thought; no studio executive would ever look at
her with the kind of trusting adoration these students offered.

But then there was Penelope. The senior was proving to be a
headache, despite Claudia's attempts to coax her out of her aggressive
armor. Penelope had taken possession of a seat on the far side of the
classroom, and sat there every day, slumped sideways in her chair, barely
lifting her pencil, and regarding Claudia with undisguised skepticism.
Rather than raise her hand now, she just blurted out her reaction to
Claudia's lectures, often before Claudia had even finished a sentence.
She prefaced almost every utterance with "My dad told me that" òr "I
visited Redford's set once and" or "We have an original print of that
movie at home, and I'm pretty sure that" and brought almost every discussion to a dead halt.

Although the other students, themselves a fairly jaded and experienced bunch, usually rolled their eyes at Penelope, Claudia had noticed
that they were beginning to be affected by her behavior. More than
once, a student had unthinkingly directed a question directly to Penelope rather than Claudia. Perhaps this wasn't so surprising, considering
that Penelope's inside knowledge of late-twentieth-century cinema,
culled from her father's filmography, occasionally seemed greater than
Claudia's own. (One evening, Claudia cross-referenced her curriculum
with Samuel Evanovich's IMDB profile, only to discover that he was
linked to almost half the movies in her lesson plan.) Still, Penelope's
presence in the classroom was like a black hole, draining Claudia of energy and enthusiasm.

To make matters worse, Penelope wasn't exactly turning out to be
the star pupil that Claudia had once envisioned. (That role belonged
unequivocally to Mary Hernandez: the deadly serious student hadn't
received anything lower than an A minus). Penelope offered up half-
written essays, failing to complete them even when Claudia cut her a
break and gave her extra time. She turned in quizzes with more doo-
dles on them than answers. It wasn't that Penelope didn't know anything about film; that was abundantly clear. Was there some kind of
learning disability that had yet to be diagnosed? Fear of test-taking?
ADD? Dyslexia? Claudia didn't want to consider the alternative: that

Penelope had taken a dislike to her for some reason, and this was a deliberate gesture, a middle finger extended straight at her. After all, she'd borrowed that screener of *Spare Parts* and not only never gave Claudia any feedback, she never even returned it. The vision of that cozy evening chez Evanovich was fading, week by week, no matter how hard she tried to overlook Penelope's antics and encourage some sort of camaraderie in their place.

This afternoon she would have to address these problems with the Evanoviches. It was a conversation she'd been dreading for weeks: *Hi, Mr. Evanovich, so nice to meet you, I'm a huge fan of your work. Will you please autograph my copy of* The Manchurian Candidate, *which we're discussing in class next week? By the way, your daughter is a know-it-all who needs an attitude adjustment. Yes, I know she's gotten this far at Ennis Gates without anyone else making a stink, but I'm just that kind of teacher. Also, I know she worships you, but can you tell her to stop mentioning you when I'm lecturing?* She could not imagine this going over well.

Her plan was to draft out her thoughts in advance, leaving no room for blurted annoyance or unintentional obsequiousness. She sat with a pencil in hand, thankful for the stillness of these dark moments before dawn, as she mulled over the most politic way to present her case. *I think we need to discuss your daughter's motivation issues,* she wrote, then scratched it out. *Penelope is a winning kid but . . .* No, too pandering. *I wonder whether a consultation with a learning capabilities tutor would be useful,* she finally began, just as she heard a rustling in the hallway, footsteps approaching. A male figure appeared in the doorway, tripped over the threshold, and toppled forward into the kitchen, landing almost in Claudia's lap. She pulled her bathrobe closed with one hand as she tried to steady him with the other.

The man was wearing nothing except for a pair of tight white cotton briefs. He was also, by Claudia's measure, about twice Lucy's age: A thin ruffle of hair encircled a bald patch on the top of his head, gray curls erupted off his bare barrel chest, and his fleshy face drooped, as if someone had tugged his skin loose from the bones. When she reached out to grab his hand—soft, like a baby's—and heaved him upright, she noticed that he was wearing a wedding ring.

"Thanks," he muttered, clearly embarrassed by her presence. "Didn't think anyone'd be up at this hour." He turned to flee, and bumped straight into Lucy, who had appeared in the doorway behind him. Lucy wore an astonishing garment: a floor-length silk nightgown in pink, trimmed with marabou feathers, like something the femme fatale would wear in a 1930s film noir.

"Claudia, you're awake! I hope we didn't wake you up?" Her face revealed none of her partner's mortification; if anything, she looked pleased to have been caught. "I see you've met Pete. Pete, this is my roommate, Claudia."

"You're home . . . early," Claudia said faintly. "I thought you got off work at seven A.M.?"

Lucy walked to the fridge and opened it. She fished around inside, retrieving a Heineken—one of Jeremy's, Claudia noted to herself, but said nothing—and handed it to Pete, who inched toward the doorway, clearly itching to leave. But Lucy plopped down at the kitchen table, across from Claudia. "Oh, they're fiddling with our schedules at the hospital," she said. "I got off early and Pete gave me a ride home. Pete's a surgeon at Good Samaritan. Thoracic."

"Thoracic. Is that the—the throat?" They were all smiling at each other, but only Lucy's grin seemed genuine.

"Actually, lungs and diaphragm. . . . You know, Lucy, I should probably get going," Pete muttered, putting the beer bottle down on the counter.

"Oh!" Lucy popped up from her seat. "Don't go yet! I'm sure Claudia doesn't mind us being here, do you?"

"Of course not," Claudia lied, eyeing the scratch paper under her hand, the clock ticking away the minutes until she had to leave.

But Pete was already out the door. Lucy sighed and rolled her eyes, as if he were a rogue child who must be humored. "Don't mind him, he's just tired," she whispered. "Surgeons put in such long hours and the late nights really start to mess with your head after a while. Oh, by the way! They're changing my schedule at the hospital. I'm back on day shift starting tomorrow, so, back to real life for me! Maybe we can all go to see a movie together this weekend?"

Claudia felt her smile ossifying across her face. Day shifts? Movies together? What happened to invisibility? "I'm not sure about our plans," she said carefully. "But I'll talk to Jeremy about it."

"Fabulous." Lucy turned to pursue Dr. Pete back to her bedroom. The dawn was starting to break outside, with gray morning light washing in from the east. Claudia rose from her chair and went to the sink to pour out the cold remains of her coffee, before heading down the hall to break the bad news to Jeremy.

Lisa Yang's parents were the first of the afternoon—a brash movie publicist and her real estate magnate husband who peppered Claudia with concerns about their daughter's GPA, argued that a B-plus on an essay should have been an A-minus, wondered aloud whether Lisa's extensive extracurricular activities (soccer, debate, student council) merited more grading leniency, and generally made it clear that Claudia's primary concern should be helping their daughter get into Yale. By the time Luz Hernandez marched through the classroom door, fifteen minutes late for her meeting, Claudia was already exhausted.

Luz was a stout woman in unfashionable high-waisted jeans and generic white basketball shoes, toting an overstuffed fake Chanel purse in one hand and the now-familiar Chicken Kitchen bag in the other. As the woman came closer, Claudia was shocked to realize that Mary's mother was roughly her own age. Her brow was etched with exhaustion, but her black hair—braided, just like Mary's—was still free of stray grays. Unlike Mrs. Yang, and most of the other Ennis Gates mothers, who painted their faces with an artful rainbow of age-defying concealers and neutral eyeshadows and smoothing creams and self-tanners, Luz Hernandez wore no makeup at all. Somehow this made her look even younger. *She must have been in high school when she had Mary,* Claudia realized.

"Quince pie, I assume?" Claudia said, masking her surprise by reaching out for the bag.

"*Pastelitos de membrillo,*" Luz corrected her, rolling her *r* with pointed brio. "My mother's recipe."

"I always enjoy the treats Mary brings. It's very generous of you."

"Mary says all the students bring food," Luz said flatly.

"Yes, but—" Claudia said, and stopped without finishing the rest of her sentence—*Yes, but most of them bring things their housekeepers bake*—as she recalled that Luz was, in fact, a single mother who made her living as a housekeeper and nanny to Hollywood-type families living up in the hills. Her quince pies were undoubtedly being delivered to other teachers at other private schools at that very moment. Although probably not in Chicken Kitchen take-out bags.

Claudia gestured toward the chairs that she'd set up in a triangle on the stage, and Luz settled uncomfortably in one of the plastic bucket seats across from her. She didn't bother examining the room as the other parents did; it was as if the physical trappings of Ennis Gates were of no concern to her whatsoever. She wondered if Luz resented the very existence of Ennis Gates in all its sanctified bourgeois privilege, or whether she saw it as her daughter's golden ticket out of an economic sinkhole. *Probably some combination of the two,* she thought.

"My daughter is a good student," Luz announced, out of the blue.

"Yes," Claudia agreed. "My top student."

Luz smiled, revealing coffee-stained teeth. It wasn't a smile of pleasure; it was the smile of a woman who already knew. "She's going to go to UCLA."

"Yes, she mentioned that was her goal," Claudia said, sensing that she was not the one running this meeting. She glanced at the clock—the allotted half hour was nearly gone already, and the Evanoviches would arrive in a few minutes. "With her grades she can go anywhere she wants. Ivy League, even."

"State school is cheaper than Ivy League," Luz said. She scrutinized Claudia. "Better financial aid. And she can live at home. You're writing her recommendation, right?"

Claudia's chest lurched uncomfortably as she remembered this long-forgotten promise; she hadn't even set up the meeting that Mary requested. Apparently Mary had been too shy to ask twice. "Soon," she apologized.

"Well, she needs it next month for early admission, so don't wait too long, OK?" Luz said, vague confrontation larding her words. "October thirty."

"Of course." Claudia scribbled this down in the margin of her note-book, page fifty-six of the must-remember items that had been con-veyed to her over the last few days.

"You have anything bad to say about my daughter?" Luz continued.

"No," Claudia said, truthfully. She didn't have much to say about Mary that hadn't just been acknowledged. Mary was a great student; she never missed class; she sat quietly in the front of the classroom and always raised her hand instead of blurting out the answer. She was sincere—annoyingly sincere, with her perpetual supply of quince pas-tries in Chicken Kitchen bags. Watching inoffensive little Mary sitting quietly on her own, earnestly scribbling down every word Claudia spoke—a clear outsider at Ennis Gates—Claudia occasionally glimpsed echoes of herself: the orthodontic headgear–wearing adolescent who, at five foot eight by her freshman year of high school, had been a gan-gling, shy Architeuthis doomed to attend the homecoming ball stag and dance only one slow song with a pitying member of the boy's bas-ketball team. For some reason, this didn't endear Mary to her. Instead, she wanted to look quickly away, as if Mary represented a familiar overeagerness and yearning intention that Claudia had once shared but now wanted to shed entirely. (*Nice girls like you are devoured as an* amuse-bouche *before the main course,* she'd remember RC's words, looking at her.) So she let her attention be dominated instead by the brattish Evanovich scion sitting behind her, the brutal RST CLASS BITC who knew how the game of life was played. Somehow, in that process, she'd managed to block Mary's request from her mind entirely. *Write the rec-ommendation,* she told herself. *She needs it more than anyone else here.*

"She works too hard," Luz continued. "I don't think it's healthy. I thought she'd go to this fancy school and get more personal attention, but the teachers here only care about the rich kids whose parents are on the board. All they do for my daughter is assign homework."

"I'm sure that's not true," Claudia said. "Anyway, I'll write that rec-ommendation. Promise."

Luz stood. "Well, I'll go now," she said. "I'm supposed to be in Los Feliz by five."

"Thanks for coming in," Claudia said. From the hallway, she could hear heavy footsteps approaching, the lumber of a lazy self-satisfied bear. A woman murmured, and a man's sonorous voice answered her, setting the windows vibrating in their sills. *The Evanoviches,* Claudia thought, and smoothed her hair instinctively.

Luz set her jaw with a forward thrust. "These things are a waste of time," she complained. "No one ever says anything I don't know." She snatched up her purse and scurried out of the room, giving Claudia only a few seconds to mentally prepare for the grand finale of her afternoon. She tucked the Chicken Kitchen bag into her tote, shook out the wrinkles in her shirt, and raced toward the door, her palms sweating, just as Samuel Evanovich's heavy tread came to a stop outside her classroom.

"You must be Mizz Munger?" Samuel Evanovich's hand was enormous, a thick fleshy paw that swallowed Claudia's hand, mangled it in a moist embrace, and then spat it out, flattened and sore. "We've been very curious to meet the new film teacher."

Samuel looked just like Claudia remembered him from Sundance, an imposing wreck of a man. His rolled-up shirtsleeves strained against meaty forearms, and the waistband of his khaki pants strained against a formidable belly. The black hair of his chest grew straight up out of his collar to merge seamlessly with the beard that grew down from his chin. He stood in the doorway to the classroom, blotting out the late-afternoon sun.

Dwarfed by her husband, Bunny Evanovich looked like a surprised deer—a frail blonde with a shiny forehead that had been surgically pinned back toward her temples and an upper lip that looked like it had been inflated with a bicycle pump. She stood beside Samuel, flexing her wrists in small agitated circles. "Charmed," Bunny offered blandly, but didn't extend a hand.

"Please, sit." Claudia gestured them toward the stage. She tried not to stare at Samuel as he settled down across from her, his bulk drooping over the edge of the diminutive chair. She smiled at him, hoping her idolization wasn't as transparent as it felt. "So," Samuel said. "Tell us about Penelope. Tell us everything we need to know."

Claudia shuffled the papers on her lap. The paper containing her prewritten speech grew damp in her hands: Now that he was in front of her—*Samuel Evanovich!*—she'd completely forgotten the opening she'd memorized. "Well. It's very clear that Penelope has a passion for film," she began weakly, as she surreptitiously opened up the paper to remind herself of her lines.

"Of course." Samuel grimaced impatiently. He fixed his gaze around the room, taking in the movie posters, the stacks of scripts, the banks of DVD players buzzing in the closet. "She's been making her own movies since she was three."

"She has?" Claudia had not expected that; it gave her a quick flush of admiration for the girl. Perhaps there was something still to be extracted from her; it would just take the right finessing touch to break through that prickly wall. "I'd love to see them. I'll encourage her to bring them in and show me."

"She's very private," Bunny offered, in a voice pulled as tight as her skin. "She only shows her daddy. Not even me."

"Genius often expresses itself through introversion." Samuel stood up and ambled over to the podium, where Claudia had lined up a stack of movies to screen for her students.

"Introversion," she said, trying again. She glanced down at her notes, but couldn't find her place. "Well, I'm not sure that that's exactly the word I would use to describe Penelope's—"

Samuel cut her off. "Altman was one of the shyest people I ever met. Except when you got some tequila in him. Christ, then he'd never shut up. You'd have to distract him with a hooker or something to get him to leave you alone." He ran a finger along the spines of her DVDs. "Good grief, are you really going to show them *Star Wars*? Lucas is such a hack."

Claudia nodded as neutrally as she could. She longed desperately to banish the distracting Bunny, put Penelope aside altogether, and engage Samuel in a spirited debate about the history of American cinema. *I'm one of you,* she wanted to tell him. *I'm not just a schoolteacher.* "Well, I do think that the film offers an interesting study of the dialectic between chance and order. By the way, Mr. Evanovich—"

"Samuel, please."

"Samuel, yes. I should confess that I attended your lecture at this last Sundance and found it very inspiring. Really, I'm quite an admirer, having directed myself"—she hated herself for blathering on like a hormonal fanboy but she couldn't quite stop herself; it took all the effort she could muster to reel the conversation back to the appropriate topic: Penelope—"so I can only imagine the influence that your knowledge must have on your own daughter. Maybe you might try to use some of that influence to encourage her to be more—how should I put this—" She stuttered to a stop here, because Samuel had wandered back over and was pushing a finger under her chin, directing her face up toward him. He stared down at her, examining her intently.

"You," he said. "I know you."

"You do?" She looked over at Bunny, hoping her smile might defuse the awkwardness of this intimacy. Bunny was rotating her hands again, apparently more fascinated by the inner workings of her wrists than her husband's sudden interest in her daughter's teacher.

"Yes." He released her face and sat down heavily across from her. "You made that quirky little romantic comedy, am I right?"

Claudia felt her heart hiccup in surprise. "That's right," she said. *"Spare Parts."*

"I saw it at Sundance. You did a Q-and-A afterward. You were rather . . . passionate, I recall. Talked a lot about cinema-verité techniques, the credible narrative." His gaze was intense. She noticed, for the first time, how piercingly black his eyes were, like obsidian caves. Her cheeks were warm—was she blushing? She hoped not.

"I'm flattered you stuck around," she murmured. "I wish the rest of the moviegoing public had."

"Didn't perform well at the box office, eh?"

"That's a bit of an understatement."

He reached up and wove a finger into the tangle of his beard, tugging it down toward his paunch. "I could have told you that."

"Oh." Her stomach lurched unhappily. Was she the only person in the world who had been so blind to her own mistakes? "A few people liked it, at least. It got good reviews."

"It's not that it wasn't good," he said. "It had lots of promise. You're clearly an actor's director; you really got that TV actress to work hard. No, it's that it had no marketing hook. I would've played up the lesbian angle, myself. Reedited it to focus on that: a new American love story. Homo marriage is very on trend right now."

"Ah," she said, not sure how to take this. "Well, I guess, all things in hindsight."

He threw his palms up in agreement and sat back. "So what are you working on now?"

Claudia's mind raced in circles; she wished she'd written something new besides a script that had already been rejected by every studio in town, but how was she supposed to find the time to write new material when this teaching job was taking up every odd minute of her waking hours? "Well, my most recent script is about human trafficking on the Mexican border," she began. "It's kind of a work-in-progress—"

"Toughen up, cookie," he interrupted her. "Never apologize for your own work. Why don't you send it over to me, and I'll take a look at it. I'm always looking for new material."

At first she wasn't sure that she'd heard him correctly; his words hewed so closely to the imaginary conversation she'd conducted in her head that she assumed she must have misheard. "Send it over?" she repeated helplessly.

"Unless you have a copy with you?"

Her hand rocketed instinctively toward the tote bag at her feet, as if her screenplay might be waiting there at the ready. Why hadn't she thought to keep a fresh copy on hand? A small furry animal was clattering about in her rib cage, threatening to break free. "I don't have it with me," she said. "But I can messenger one over tomorrow."

"Penelope." Bunny's voice drifted faintly in. "We're here to talk about Penelope, honey."

Samuel turned to Bunny, a surprised look on his face, as if just remembering her presence beside him. "Yes, Penelope. Of course, *golubushka*. Sorry, Mizz Munger—what were you about to say before I interrupted you?"

Looking back, she would blame the giddy possibility in the air—the first true jolt of hope she'd felt since the day her film tanked, two months earlier—for shaping the response that came out of her mouth. It wasn't that she was kissing Samuel's ass, per se, or trying to make sure that she was in his good graces before he read her script: It was, simply, a case of unanticipated optimism gone awry. She was simply too dizzy with excitement to frame a negative thought about even her most problematic student. At least, that's what she told herself in order to quiet her guilty conscience.

"Right," she said. "About Penelope: Really, she's a rising star."

"Cheers." Jeremy was holding his wineglass out to her. "To Samuel Evanovich's new protégée."

Celebrating with a dinner out had been Jeremy's idea. Restaurants weren't really in their budget anymore, but Jeremy knew of a new no-frills BYOB Italian place in Los Feliz that was supposed to be cheap. Maybe it was, comparatively, and the setting certainly didn't evoke a splurge—they sat at picnic tables bolted to a concrete patio, with a few strands of Christmas lights strung overhead for ambiance—but a $15 bowl of spaghetti certainly didn't feel like a bargain. When had life become so expensive? It had snuck up on them, waited until they weren't paying attention, and then walloped them with $12 beers and $120 tennis shoes and $350 traffic tickets. She felt like her grandpa Bernie, sometimes, who nattered on constantly about the days of nickel pickles and houses that could be bought for a few thousand bucks; but seriously, it wasn't that long ago that she paid for her coffee with pocket change, and now it wasn't unusual in the least to drop a five-dollar bill on a cup of aged Sumatra. It was as if the desire to live in a city, in close proximity to arts and culture, had become a punishable offense, your sentence being a lifetime of penury. What was the driving force that had pushed the cost of urban life so high? Was it the outrageously wealthy few who insisted on only the most expensive things, blithely flinging their money so far and wide that prices everywhere had risen to accommodate this indulgent minority's whims? Or was it the inflated cost of essentials—the gas, the corn, the real estate—that forced businesses to jack their prices up in order to just barely survive? Was it flat-out greed or was it desperation? She wished she'd studied economics, because sometimes, without knowing any better, it felt like she was a dupe who was being played by a conspiracy of shop owners and restaurateurs.

Still, she smiled and proffered her glass for Jeremy to clink. "No—to Penelope Evanovich, the best worst student a teacher could wish for.

Let's just hope Samuel reads my script before her midterm report card arrives in the mail." She took a gulp of the four-dollar cabernet they'd picked up at the liquor store across the street. It tasted like rubber cement, but she wasn't about to complain. There was no room in her life anymore for luxuries like wine that came with actual corks.

"I'm sure he can look beyond that," Jeremy said. He tasted his wine, made a face, and sat back with a smug expression on his face. "See? I *said* you were giving up too fast."

"I don't want to get ahead of myself, though," she worried aloud. "He reads a hundred scripts a week. He may never read mine. He could read it and hate it. He could read it and like it but not care enough to do anything about it. And it's so *serious*. Really, I should have written something new—something with more commercial appeal—to show him. . . ."

"Stop it." Jeremy shoveled a forkful of spaghetti in his mouth. "I've read the script. It's fucking brilliant. It's a piece of *art*."

She shrugged. "I'm not sure I believe in art anymore."

Jeremy lifted an eyebrow. "You don't believe in art."

"Everyone we know thought they were going to be artists. Painters or musicians or filmmakers or writers, somehow more *authentic* than everyone else, right? But really, how many have done what they thought they would? We were all so naïve. We live in an information age, not a truth age; the only way to really make it now is to sell out to the biggest distributor, pander to the broadest audience. So that means you direct a schlocky thriller for a movie studio instead of working on a little jewel of a film that no one will ever make, or else you go on a reality TV show or something—come on, Jeremy, that's what it's all about. Especially now. No one cares about *art* anymore. I mean, four people in the country saw my film, and it wasn't even *that* edgy, comparatively speaking."

Jeremy stared at her, uncomprehending. "When did you become such a cynic?"

"I'm not being cynical, I'm just being sensible. Point is, I'm not sure I should be pursuing a depressing drama right now. Maybe it's not the best way to jump-start my career again. I need to play by Hollywood's rules."

"Well, *I* think that Samuel Evanovich is going to decide you're a genius and help you make your movie. And then you'll change your tune. God, Claude, aren't you excited at all?"

"Of course I'm excited. But I've been pretty burned lately."

Jeremy smiled and reached across the table to grab her hand. She squeezed it back, letting his faith in her inflate her like a balloon, despite her better instincts. She smiled and drank her wine as a suicidal moth flung itself against the hurricane lamp on their table, trying futilely to immolate itself in the flame within. After a moment, the chattering self-doubt returned. "Before I send it in to Evanovich, I might just do a quick revise on the script to make it more palatable—maybe lose the Spanish subtitles or set it in Florida instead of Mexico. Add a more upbeat ending. Even then, it's still a really, really long shot. Maybe I should just write something new, really quickly—"

"You should be doing that anyway," Jeremy observed, withdrawing his hand. "No matter what Evanovich says about this script. Wasn't that supposed to be the plan in the first place when you took this job?"

Claudia picked apart a meatball, found raw meat in its center and pushed it aside. "I know. It's just—teaching takes up so much time. I had no idea. Really, these kids are so smart, I can barely keep up with them. Listen to this." She reached into her tote and fished out a paper that Mary had just turned in. "*Derrida insists upon the temporality of meaning in signification, extending to the cinema his notion of ecriture.* What does that even mean?"

Jeremy shuddered. "She probably stole it off the Internet. That's what I would have done."

"Not Mary. It would never occur to her. Type-A overachiever. Do you know the difference between *diachronic* and *synchronic*? I had to look that one up too. No wonder I have no time to write a new script."

"Then quit," Jeremy said. "Reprioritize. I hate that you're working so much, anyway."

"You know that's not an option for us right now."

Jeremy grunted, clearly regretting having started down this path. He leaned over and stuck his fork in her ruined spaghetti, and then looked up at her, waiting for her approval. She nodded, and he ferried a dripping strand back across the table into his mouth. They sat in awkward silence for a moment, ignoring the issues now sitting at the center of the table alongside the bread basket and red pepper flakes.

"So," Jeremy began, wiping tomato sauce off his chin. "I've been meaning to tell you something. Aoki's coming to town for a show next month, and she wanted to meet me for coffee, just a friendly catch-up, nothing big, and I said I would." He paused. "If that's OK with you."

It took Claudia a minute to respond. She picked through the content of this statement to arrive, finally, at the unspoken subtext. "So wait—since when are you talking to Aoki?"

"Not talking! She e-mailed me, a week ago. Maybe two."

"And you took this long to tell me?"

"I wasn't sure how you'd react. I didn't want to risk upsetting you." He furrowed his eyebrows at her. "Are you upset? Please tell me you're not. I really don't want you to think it's a big deal. I should have said something sooner."

"I'm not upset." Was she? She had always prided herself on not being the jealous and demanding sort of girlfriend. It was one of the things she liked about herself, that she was the easygoing type, the kind of person who encouraged her boyfriends to stay in touch with their ex-girlfriends (even if, as in the case of Aoki, the thought of those ex-girlfriends gave her hives) and didn't blink an eye when they made friends with other women. She'd always liked to imagine that the men she dated would say this about her—"Yeah, she's totally cool"—and fantasized even further that perhaps her trust in them would, if the situation ever arose, be the reason why they would resist temptation. Also, she knew Aoki was insane. When Jeremy talked about her, his eyes grew haunted and seemed to sink back into his head: His ex was a demon whose exorcism had nearly killed him. She knew he knew better than to do anything stupid with her. So why, now, did his revelation make her feel like she'd swallowed a spoonful of vinegar?

"Honestly, I'm not upset," she repeated. She reached for the wine again and filled her glass and then his. "But are you sure you really want to see her?"

"No," he said. He focused his attention on the Parmesan cheese shreds that had melted on the edge of his plate, scraping at them with his fork. Husband and wife both studiously avoided looking at each other. "But I think she's trying to apologize. Maybe it's part of some twelve-step plan? And since she reached out and made an effort, I feel I should reciprocate. But look—if you say no, I'll tell her I'm just not up for it."

She took a long swallow from the wineglass and let the acid alcohol warmth spring upward to her head. The moth flapped against the lamp a few more times and gave up. "Well, I'm fine with it as long as you are."

Jeremy's stood up, leaned across the table, and pressed oily lips against hers. "I am so lucky," he said. "I don't deserve you." His words were thin and cracked—was that a burr of disappointment she was detecting? But he grinned and then nibbled his way down her ear and neck to the electric place near her clavicle and let his lips flutter there, tickling her. His T-shirt was in danger of being soaked by the bloody remnants of her spaghetti.

"You're right, you don't deserve me," she said, as she whinnied and gasped for air, finally pressing him away with the flat of her palm. "Can we order dessert now, please?"

"Yes, ma'am," he said. "We will spend the last of our children's inheritance on a slab of premade tiramisu. And we will love it."

She smiled back at Jeremy as he flagged down the waiter, but the truth was that she had lost her appetite for dessert. Surely, she'd done the right thing—so why did it feel like such a mistake?

Jeremy

THEY WERE THE OLDEST PEOPLE AT THE BAR. THE BAND MEMBERS had collectively decided that Ben should pick a place to drink, correctly assuming that he was more plugged into LA nightlife than they were, and he'd brought them here, a tiki bar sardined full of tiny girls with interesting hair and boys wearing T-shirts for bands that had broken up before they were born. Velvet paintings of Mexican wrestlers hung askew over red Naugahyde booths. Kanye West blasted from overhead speakers, drowning out any possibility of meaningful conversation. The palm fronds that canopied the bar were limp with age.

Going out for drinks had been Daniel's idea. "Let's take a break from the practice grind and just hang out and talk," he'd suggested that afternoon. Jeremy had been about to object, but really, didn't they deserve a night out? Yes, the band still had work to do—they needed two more songs before they had a complete album—but look how far they'd come, in just a few weeks! Over the last half-dozen practice sessions, Audiophone had nailed down the chorus of "Mysterious Mrs. X" and finished a new and as yet untitled song with an addictive hook. Practices were happening on schedule, three times a week—not the daily practice Jeremy had initially hoped for, but a vast improvement nonetheless—and Ben had only failed to show up once. Some threshold had finally been crossed: The finish line loomed just ahead, only a short sprint away. He'd sent an e-mail to Julian Bragg earlier that week: A FEW MORE WEEKS UNTIL ALBUM IS FINISHED. STAY TUNED.

Emerson—still wearing his suit from work, woefully out of place

even with his tie half undone—staggered back to the table with four
tequila shots braced between his fingers, narrowly averting disaster on
a step by the foosball table. He landed heavily in the booth next to Jeremy and slid sideways so that his mouth was just a few inches from Jeremy's ear. Judging by his alarming breath, Emerson was already drunk.

"Drink up," Emerson said, nudging a tequila shot toward Jeremy
with the tip of his finger. Jeremy took a tiny sip and put it down again,
ignoring Emerson's look of aggrieved disbelief. He didn't want to
drink too much tonight. He was seeing Aoki in the morning, and it was
going to be challenging enough to see her *without* a hangover. Aoki.
Just thinking of her caused his nerves to jangle like a pocket full of
spare change.

Claudia was being extremely accommodating about Aoki. He'd half
expected her to get upset when he finally screwed up the courage to
tell her, but he should have known that Claudia would be nothing but
supportive. She had even *encouraged* him to get together with Aoki—
said it would give him "closure"—although he sensed, in the clipped
tightness of her words, a concern that contradicted her supposed indif-
ference. Anyway, there was no reason for her to be jealous, was there?
A friendly coffee with an ex-girlfriend: That's all it was in the end, he
wasn't really doing anything wrong, so why did he feel like he was getting away with something? He'd spent the last few days being particularly attentive: bringing Claudia coffee in bed, massaging her feet when
she complained about standing all day, even performing an act of sexual gratification of which he wasn't usually very fond. Was he bribing
her or thanking her? He wasn't quite sure. Anyway, he wasn't going to
do anything stupid; certainly, not anything that would endanger his
marriage. He would go tomorrow, have what was probably going to
prove a benign, disappointing coffee with Aoki, and officially move on.
Closure. Frankly, it would be a relief.

He looked around the room, noticing a clutch of black-haired girls
in obscenely tight metallic leggings and vertiginous footwear who
were posing with their cocktails in the middle of the room. They tossed
their hair back over their shoulders and jutted their pelvic bones forward as they preened for an audience they refused to otherwise acknowledge. They had to be nineteen, at best. A decade and a half

younger than he. Was he too old to be of interest to them anymore? He wasn't quite sure how he'd landed here, age thirty-four, a married man, with a soft band of flesh permanently affixing itself around his waist and bruised-looking pouches forming under his eyes. His grip on the privileges of youth was tenuous these days, but he wasn't ready to let go yet. He thought of the words of his father, Max—*You are only as old as you think you are*—and smiled at the girls. Just a test. They turned away, ignoring him.

Jeremy caught Daniel's eye. "Do you think they're even legal yet?"

Daniel shook his head. "Girls sure didn't look like that when I was their age. I'm not sure I approve."

"Jesus, Grandpa," Jeremy said, cuffing Daniel on the shoulder, "come on. You make it sound like we're half dead."

"I don't know why Daniel's complaining." Ben tilted his head to get a better angle on the Lycra-clad rears.

"They're kind of like transvestites, parroting some weird idea of womanhood but getting it all wrong." Daniel continued. "What ever happened to age-appropriate clothing? It's sad, really. No one wants to just be a kid anymore. It's the acceleration of youth. They go straight from birth to adulthood and skip adolescence entirely. They start prepping for college applications in nursery school. No wonder they're all so jaded."

"If they knew how much it sucks to be an adult, they wouldn't be in such a rush to grow up," Emerson said, his voice dark. He spun his shot glass like a top. It skittered off the edge of the table and landed in his lap, spilling tequila on his suit. He stared down at his legs. "Dammit."

Jeremy offered a handful of damp napkins to wipe up the mess, but Emerson pushed them away. He swiped at his trousers with the side of his hand and then licked tequila off his palm. "It doesn't matter. I'm not going to be wearing this again anytime soon."

The expression on Emerson's face stopped Jeremy cold. "Hey, is something up?"

Emerson looked past him to Daniel. Daniel looked down at his own tequila shot as Jeremy swiveled his head back and forth, trying to figure out what was going unsaid.

"We need to talk," Emerson said. His breath hissed out of him in a long resigned sigh. "OK. First off, I was let go today. They closed our entire office. Two weeks' severance. I didn't even get to keep my laptop."

Was it selfish of Jeremy that his first thought was *I guess that means he'll have more time to practice now*? "Oh, wow. I'm really sorry," he said.

Emerson slumped more, until his chin was nearly parallel with the top of the table. "It's not that I couldn't see it coming. I mean, you had to be blind not to see that we were a bunch of deluded optimists. The whole fucking country. There was no way reality would ever line up with our projections. My entire job consisted of shuffling imaginary money from one location to another, and making sure that the numbers only ever went one direction, but really, where did everyone think it was going to end, infinity?" Emerson picked up his shot glass, remembered it was empty, and put it down again.

"You'll find another job," said Jeremy. He softly patted Emerson's shoulder. "You're too smart not to. Things always end up all right in the end, especially for people like us. You just have to think positive."

"You're missing my point," Emerson said. "That kind of wishful thinking doesn't work anymore. I don't think it ever worked in the first place. You can't just *hope* things into being, it's ridiculous. *People like us*? We're just like everyone else, Jeremy. I mean, who's going to hire me, with what money? There *is* no money, anywhere. It's gone. It never really existed in the first place. It was just a mass hallucination. Seriously, we've all been living in some sort of fantasy world where everyone thought they were entitled to get everything they wanted without making any sacrifices, and no one would ever lose. Well, guess what: It's over. And now we're all fucked."

Jeremy hated this line of thinking: Even over the last few months, as it had become clear that something radical had shifted in the American economy, even as his own mortgage situation blew up in his face, he had been able to convince himself that the bigger world crisis that he kept reading about in the newspaper didn't apply specifically to *him*. After all, he hadn't had a chance to cash in yet! He'd spent the last decade, the boom years, feeling entirely apart from the windfall that everyone else seemed to be participating in. Even when This Invisible Spot had been at the peak of its popularity, the money had paid the rent on a nice flat in the East Village and kept him comfortably in beer and organic apples but never made him rich—certainly, not if judged by the inflated cultural standards of wealth. He and Claudia had bought the cheapest house they could find, and they still couldn't really afford it. No, the *real* money always lurked on the fringe of his existence—the modernist houses in the hills, the German cars, the designer sneakers, the front-row tickets to Lakers games. But he'd always assumed he'd catch up someday—that if monetary success was the implied birthright of his generation, he'd eventually get his percentage. And, yes, the economic reality of the new millennium was clearly Winner Takes All—you were either rich or broke, with an ever-widening gap in between—but he'd never considered the possibility that he would permanently end up in the latter category. Now Emerson was making it sound like Jeremy had missed his window entirely and was about to be handed the credit card bill for everyone else's dream vacation instead. Jeremy refused to believe it.

"Look, I know you're upset, and rightfully so, but don't you think you're being a little extreme? What goes down must go up eventually. Oh, wait. I guess it's the other way around. Forget it. Anyway, you've got other things to focus on now, anyway. The band, for example. We're so close! I mean, I can't promise you a banker's salary, but I bet we can be making a pretty decent living by the new year if we work it right. A good licensing deal could get us fifty thousand, even more, and there's this guy, Julian Bragg—"

Emerson shook his head. "Yeah, the band. That's the other thing. I can't bankroll the band anymore. That studio space costs almost a grand a month, and I don't even know where I'm going to get the cash to pay my own rent."

The music on the jukebox changed; Jeremy recognized the thrashing, drum-heavy tune as belonging to a popular faux-ska band that This Invisible Spot had opened for back in 2002. They were a bunch of college-age twits who drank Red Bull and vodka and thought it was funny to try to set their farts on fire; they wrote songs with titles like "Blue Balls 4 U" and bragged about the blow jobs they got from their groupies. Those four shows were the worst of This Invisible Spot's career; by the end, the two bands weren't even speaking to each other.

But the twits had gone on to heavy rotation on MTV *Total Request Live* and released two triple-platinum albums. They now traveled by private jet and dated Disney TV starlets.

"We can probably practice in my garage," Ben offered. He showily scraped his hair back into a ponytail and glowered meaningfully at a girl walking past their table. "My roommates will hate me for it but I don't like them anyway."

Jeremy's mind raced ahead, detecting new roadblocks. Moving the band's practice location would set them back at least a week or two, and if Emerson couldn't even afford studio rent, how was he going to afford the ten grand necessary to mix and master the album? "So it's Ben's garage, then," he said, trying to sound upbeat even as he sensed the fractures opening around him, doubt flooding in. Daniel and Emerson looked like the end of the world had arrived, and Gabriel had just personally delivered the bad news. "I take it this also means we'll need to start thinking about how we'll pay to finish our album, right? That's OK. We'll just get creative about money, throw a fundraiser or something. We could put on a show, all proceeds going to the album." He turned to Daniel. "Didn't you have a friend who did something like that, to pay off a hospital bill?"

But Daniel was staring at the table, tearing his cocktail napkin, his mouth forming words that Jeremy could barely hear. The music was really far too loud, because through the static distortion of that lumpy bass line it sounded like Daniel had just said, "I think it's time for the band to break up." Surely, Jeremy had misheard. But the rest of his bandmates were all nodding soberly, or maybe bobbing their heads in time to music that Jeremy couldn't hear.

"God, you guys really give up easily, don't you?" Jeremy spoke quickly. "That's just idiotic. We don't have to spend a fortune on the album. We'll do it on the cheap. I'll call in some favors." By now Jeremy was shouting to be heard over the music, which grew louder by the minute. *"This is what the musician's life is all about, you pussies! It's supposed to be hard! If it was easy everyone would do it!"*

Emerson shook his head. "I'm too old for it to be cool to be broke."

A group of girls had clambered up on the banquette next to them and were dancing barefoot on the Naugahyde. They waggled their limbs in exaggerated freedom, not concerned in the least about the fact that their drinks were sloshing on the heads of the people sitting below. Jeremy desperately wanted to climb up there with them, get deliriously drunk without worrying about the hangover, dance on the furniture without thinking of the security guards who would come over and tell them to get down, kiss a stranger and never ask her name. He couldn't remember the last time he had done that. This realization, more than the news that the band was about to break up, triggered a wave of panic that made him want to vomit.

"It's not just the money," Daniel was saying. "I was already thinking it was time for me to quit the band. I can't make it a priority anymore. Because of the baby, you know? I need to use any spare time I have to get extra freelance work—the newspaper's talking about layoffs and I figure, just in case. I have an offer to ghost-write a celebrity memoir, and I think I should take it." He looked at Jeremy with pleading, bovine eyes: "The whole life-of-a-musician thing is just not really feasible for me anymore. How am I going to go on tour with a wife and a baby?"

"Wait—a wife?" Ben echoed. "You got engaged too?"

Daniel nodded. "It's kind of a rush job, because of the baby. We're doing it over the Christmas holiday. You're all invited."

"Great," said Jeremy. "Just fucking great."

Daniel looked pained. "You could at least be happy for me."

"I am happy for you. I just wish it didn't have to be at the expense of the band. *Our* band. Don't you *care* about music?"

Daniel's fingers worried at the shreds of damp napkin. "Of course I care. But right now, other things matter more to me. Family, you know?" He stuffed the paper into his shot glass. "Maybe you need to find another band, Jeremy, one that wants it as badly as you do. Truth is—we've never really been able to keep up with you. Emerson and I are just not in a position to pursue this the way you want to. We never imagined this as our entire *lives.* "

Jeremy realized what Daniel was suggesting. "Wait. You two talked about this in advance? You already agreed to break up the band?" Daniel and Emerson stared at each other guiltily, clearly complicit. "So the whole *let's get a drink thing* tonight, that was just some kind of booby trap?" He thought back to their live show, realizing suddenly that his bandmates had been playing so well that night not because of some creative breakthrough but because they already knew they had nothing left to lose.

He picked up his neglected tequila shot, finished it with one shuddering gulp, and turned to Ben.

"What about you? Are you bailing out too?"

"Whatever." Ben stood up, his eyes fixed on a girl across the room. "This isn't the first band that's ever broken up on me. It looks like the other band I'm in is getting a record deal, anyway."

"I feel bad, Jeremy," Daniel said, "I really do. But you're better off without us. Take the material and start another band. You composed the music anyway. You can use the lyrics, if you want."

Jeremy wouldn't look at him, refusing to grace his best friend's betrayal with even a smile or a nod of forgiveness. He could barely see Daniel anyway, blinded by the sudden flash of light that was his life going into supernova. *It was all just a mass hallucination.* Was it possible? Had everything around him been a fantasy, born from false hope and sustained by delusion? Emerson was saying something but Jeremy couldn't hear him through the high-pitched ringing in his ears. He suddenly, desperately, missed his mother.

"Don't ever compromise." That's what Jillian told him on the day, fifteen years ago, when he moved to New York. Jillian was driving him to the airport to catch the red-eye—he still remembered that stuttering old diesel Volvo, the backseat piled so high with Jillian's patient files that no one had sat back there in years—and as they putted along Lincoln Boulevard in the dark it had struck Jeremy for the first time that he was leaving his mother all by herself. For years, it had been the just two of them: Jillian and Jeremy, the two J's, an impregnable unit. Puberty had exposed the claustrophobia in that intimate equation: It wasn't easy being the sole outlet for his mother's endless outpouring of attention, especially when all he really wanted to do was hide in his room to play guitar and memorize the one tattered copy of *Playboy* he'd stolen from Daniel. He'd been desperately looking forward to college and New York, the chance to be Jeremy without the Jillian. But now that he was about to climb on a plane, it suddenly occurred to him that his mother might not survive without *him*. She'd never been on her own, didn't have anyone but him! How could he leave her?

"Mom, are you going to be OK?" he'd asked her, examining the side of her face, where furrows had taken up permanent residence in the translucent skin around her eyes. Gray strands sprang free of the batik scarf that she used to fasten her ponytail. She looked drawn, frail. "On your own, I mean?"

"What kind of question is that?" She took her foot off the gas and the car slowed, choking, to a crawl. Behind them, a Mercedes honked and then swerved to pass.

"Just—I feel like I'm abandoning you. Maybe I shouldn't go."

Jillian yanked the wheel to the right, veering over to the side of the road. She pulled to a stop before a shuttered liquor store and sat there, the idling Volvo shuddering in protest.

"So if I said I needed you to stay here with me, you'd stay? Is that what you're telling me?"

He hesitated, unsure. "Maybe."

Jillian grabbed his hand, squeezing it so hard he thought she might crush his fingers. He wondered whether she was about to cry, to tell him that yes, he should stay, and in an instant he saw his life in New York vanishing. But then he saw the flinty, hot fury in his mother's face.

"Don't *ever* say that again," she hissed.

He shrank away, his back pressing into handle of the passenger side door, but she tugged on his hand, reeling him in. With the other hand, she gripped his chin, pulling it toward her face.

"You are not to compromise your dreams. *Ever.* Do not give up on what you want just to please someone else. And by that I mean, do not take a job you hate just to pay the bills, do not stay with someone you don't love just so they don't feel bad, do not let anyone tell you what you should and shouldn't do or what you are or are not capable of. That's the only rule I've ever lived by. You're empathetic, Jeremy—you want to please people, you don't want to upset the balance, and if you're not careful that will get in the way of the things you want. But I believe, Jeremy"—and here she paused, a hitch in her throat, the intimation of tears—"I believe you really can have it all. My beautiful, talented boy. You can. Anything your heart desires."

He'd gotten on the plane, of course. And even though he'd never really bought into all his mother's New Age mysticism—the energy healing, the chakra readings, the Ganeshes cluttering their coffee table—this lecture had stuck with him throughout his eleven years in New York, throughout the rise (and collapse) of This Invisible Spot and his relationship with Aoki. But now, with his disloyal bandmates sitting in front of him looking glum, having finally come to some kind of dead end in his life, Jillian's words returned to him with a new, cruel edge. *But what if you have nothing left to compromise?* he asked his mother, mutely.

He rose from his seat, stumbling blindly out of the booth with no particular destination in mind. He found himself standing just below one of the dancing girls, a pretty blonde in a spangled silver minidress, devastatingly young. She glanced down at him just as she flung her arms up over her head, in jubilant answer to the rising call of the pop tune on the jukebox, and then bestowed a fairy-tale smile on him, a smile of such pure beatific joy that Jeremy wanted to cry.

"I'm still here," he said out loud, unsure whether he was addressing the girl or the former members of Audiophone or himself. "I'm still here."

He arrived home drunk and furious. The street was quiet, the houses all locked down for the night, only the motion-detecting security lights illuminating his path as he made his way toward his front door. He slammed the door closed behind him, not thinking about whether it might wake up the tenants of the house until it was too late.

In the living room, he could hear the buzz of the television set—was Claudia still awake?—and stumbled toward the sound, stopping first in the kitchen to raid the fridge. His beer was gone—again. He was pretty sure that Lucy was giving it to her doctor boyfriend, which just pissed him off even more. In a petulant act of minor revenge, he helped himself to her bag of toasted coconut marshmallows and popped one in his mouth, then crammed another one in and another until his mouth was stuffed full. He was still chewing his way through the toxic fluff when he arrived in the living room to find the marshmallows' rightful owner sitting there, much to his dismay.

Lucy sat in her floral chaise in front of the television, wrapped in a silky pink robe with some sort of feathery trim. The overhead lights were off but she'd lit a cluster of candles that sat in the center of the coffee table, releasing a faint scent of carbon and vanilla. SpongeBob SquarePants flickered on the screen.

"Hail to the conquerer." Jeremy intended this to be funny but he couldn't stop the bitterness from slurring his words. "She gains mastery of the remote."

Lucy flinched. Her eyes flickered to the bag of marshmallows in Jeremy's hand. He held the bag out to her and she opened her mouth to say something, but then shut it and shook her head instead.

Jeremy sat down heavily beside her on the chaise. "Why are you watching a children's television show?"

Lucy shrugged. "There's nothing in cartoons that will make me feel bad," she said. "There's enough horrid stuff in the world that I have to deal with every day at the hospital, so I don't really want to watch it on TV when I come home. No one ever dies in these kinds of shows unless they're really bad guys."

Jeremy was struck silent by this; in his drunken state it seemed like a rather profound thought. He examined his roommate with a new respect. Lucy sat up against the cushions, pulling the robe tighter around her. He could see the ridged outlines of her nipples under the straining satin, the drape of her fleshy thighs. He found himself getting a minor hard-on despite himself and shifted his attention to the television, where SpongeBob SquarePants was having his temperature taken by a blobby pink creature that appeared to be an obese starfish.

Next to him, Lucy shifted away slightly, tilting her torso to maximize the space between them. She seemed vaguely frightened: Was he really that scary? Had he been too obvious about his contempt for her? He wasn't a bad guy, was he? He was suddenly desperate to know what he looked like to her. Maybe someone who was a complete outsider could look at him objectively and tell him what everything was all about. The last of his anger fizzled away, replaced by a deep, shamed sadness.

"I'm sorry if I haven't been very friendly to you," he said to the television. "I'm just a little protective of my personal space."

Lucy turned to study him. "I'm not that bad," she said. "Even if I'm not as interesting as you guys."

"I know. You're right. I'm sorry." He paused. "My band broke up tonight."

Lucy looked surprised, and he wondered whether she was surprised that the band had broken up or that Jeremy was revealing this to her in the first place. "Oh. That must be terrible."

"I'm the last man standing," he continued, realizing that he really was *quite* intoxicated. The cartoon creatures on the television multiplied in front of his eyes, and he had to put his foot on the floor to stop the room's wobbly spin around him. "I've been abandoned in limbo land, Lucy," he said. He looked imploringly at Lucy, his newfound compatriot, waiting for whatever words of wisdom she had to offer him.

"I'm not sure I get what you mean," she said.

"Help me," he croaked.

She looked at him with a swift, assessing gaze. "Sure, I'll help you," She stood up. "First of all, you really should go to bed because it sounds like you're pretty drunk. Try taking some vitamin B-Twelve with two Advil. Or drink some pickle juice. That's my mom's cure. It's nasty but it works."

"I don't think we have any pickles."

"You can have mine, they're in the fridge. " She turned off the television. "I'm headed to bed, OK? Feel better!" She swished off toward her bedroom—*their bedroom*—with the satin robe slapping around her calves, bare pink toes gripping the wooden floor.

Jeremy lay back in the dark, disappointed, and watched the candles on the table cast flickering haloes across the ceiling. But this just made the room spin again, so he leaned over and blew them out and then lurched his way back toward the bedroom, where he found Claudia dead asleep. He located a glass of stale water on the floor and drank it greedily, then stripped his clothes off and climbed into bed beside her. He wormed his way toward the warm depression on her side of the bed and then pressed his lingering hard-on against the comforting warm cleft of her rear. She murmured something incoherent and moved away.

"Come on," he said, nudging her. "Wake up."

"Nnnnnnnnnuh," she murmured blearily. "Time'sit?"

"Not that late," he said. He scooted in closer and prodded her again. "Please? I had a shitty night."

He waited for her to notice the intimation of disaster in his words, to roll over and reach out to him in consolation. But she had already fallen back to sleep. He flopped onto his back, listening to her breath fill the room—quick and shallow and regular—while he helplessly rode the loose circles of his inebriation, a feather circling the drain, until the metronome of his wife's breath finally lulled him to sleep.

Jeremy arrived at the Silver Lake café where he had arranged to meet Aoki still feeling nauseated. He'd woken up late, long after Claudia had left for work, with curdled froth in his mouth and the sensation that his brain had spent the night wedged in a car door. When he looked in the mirror, he saw bloodshot pupils and puffy crescents under his eyes. This was not the impression he'd wanted to make.

He hadn't bothered going in to work—Edgar was in Japan, anyway—and instead spent the early part of the morning showering and drinking cup after cup of strong coffee. He shaved, and then regretted it: It would look like he was trying too hard. He put on a T-shirt of his own design, then decided it might seem self-conscious or narcissistic and changed into a button-down shirt. Too stuffy. By the time he finally left to meet Aoki, he'd put on his usual uniform of jeans-and-T-with-cool-jacket and managed to conceal most of the damage of the night before with some of Claudia's under-eye cream and a glass of tomato juice fortified with just a splash of vodka to settle his nerves.

The café was packed, and a line snaked out the door across the patio. It was the kind of place where they brewed socially responsible coffee by the cup for five dollars a pop, and Jeremy could imagine Claudia cringing at this unnecessary splurge. But he'd chosen the place because he knew it was the kind of place Aoki would like, somewhere new and progressive in a neighborhood that still retained a little bit of grit. He stood in line, waiting with all the other supplicants for his moment with the award-winning barista, listening to the tattooed couple in front of him discuss global warming with heated liberal self-righteousness. By the time he reached the barista, ten minutes later, Aoki still wasn't there. He looked at the line behind him, which now reached out to the curb, and made an impulsive decision. "An iced Guatemalan," he said. "And a double cappuccino, nonfat milk."

He took the drinks out front, to a tiled patio with a view of the street, and settled in at a table between two screenwriters working on laptops. A giant abstract collage made from dried ferns and flattened bottle caps loomed above him, part of an art installation. *Hope for Future,* its placard said. *$850.* He looked at it for a minute, appalled, then switched seats so it wouldn't be in Aoki's line of vision. To make the minutes pass, he flicked through the messages on his BlackBerry, noting two e-mails from Daniel that he didn't open, and one from Claudia that he did.

Sorry about last night, but I'd taken an Ambien and was dead to the world. What happened that was so awful? I'll have a break around noon—I assume by then you'll be done with your coffee with Aoki? Please call to let me know how it went? Have fun, but not too much, OK?

The e-mail was a giant pointed question mark. He could feel the strain in her words, the effort it took to hide her anxiety and pretend she wasn't concerned; probably he was supposed to reply with some sort of reassurance, but honestly he wasn't in the mood. He closed the e-mail without responding.

He noticed that the barista had drawn a heart in the foam of Aoki's cappuccino and worried that she might think he asked to put it there. Then he thought she wasn't that stupid. He wished she'd just show up so he wouldn't look so idiotic sitting by himself with two drinks. Why was he here anyway? What did he want? He hoped maybe she wouldn't show up at all and he could just go home and return to his regular life, or what remained of it. His coffee was getting watery but he didn't touch it.

"This much hasn't changed," he heard. "I am still always late."

Aoki stood before him, somehow both smaller and larger than he remembered. She wore all white, a strange deconstructed skirt and a tight ribbed top that buckled across the chest, with flat purple sandals. Her hair was long now, and she had it up in an elaborate topknot, so shiny it looked lacquered. She smiled through parted lips painted with bright red lipstick. She looked . . . angelic, arty, beautiful, supremely self-confident, by far the most unique woman in the whole café. She looked exactly like Aoki.

He stood up, knocking the table askew as he tried to squeeze past the screenwriters to get to her. She stepped forward and there was an awkward moment—would there be physical contact, a hug?—which ended when Aoki leaned in and gave him a kiss on each cheek, European style.

"I ordered for you," he said. "So you wouldn't have to wait in line. Still drinking nonfat cappuccinos?"

"You remembered," Aoki said. She sat down and drew the cappuccino toward her. "And here I thought I'd nurtured such an aura of unpredictability."

"Some things never change."

"It's true," she said, and looked down at her cup. "A heart. How cute."

"They'll also do a little smiley face, if you prefer."

Aoki laughed and took a sip, mutilating the heart. She sat back and examined him. "You look exactly the same. I knew you would."

"And here I thought I'd nurtured such an aura of unpredictability," he said wryly. It was odd to be joking like this, to be so light with her, when so many memories of their time together were painted over in apocalyptic blacks and purples. He'd spent so much time remembering the unhinged woman who slit her wrists in the bathtub, who shot up heroin, who slept with his bandmate, that he'd almost forgotten how quickly he could be drawn in by this Aoki—witty, flirtatious, compelling.

"That was a compliment. You were always too handsome to bear."

He flushed, incapable of resisting the flattery, thrilled that she still found him attractive, conscious of the danger in this knowledge. He didn't think Claude would like the direction this conversation had gone already. "In that case, I'm sorry to have pained you."

"I don't think you are sorry," Aoki said. "Otherwise you wouldn't have dumped me so cruelly."

The words sat there between them, waiting to be acknowledged. He was disoriented, although he should have expected this. These had always been Aoki's favorite conversational gambits: Disrupt, destabilize, disarm. *But that isn't how it happened,* he thought to himself, and wondered whether she had rewritten their whole relationship as a grand betrayal. Jeremy looked at her closely to see if he could locate the hysterical Aoki, the one he'd left crying on the floor of her studio four years ago. Was her e-mail promise—*I hold no grudges*—an empty one? Was this an ambush after all, or a step on her twelve-point recovery plan?

"Do you want talk about that?" he offered, carefully. "Are we supposed to rehash our relationship now and figure out what went wrong?"

"God, no," Aoki said, pursing cherry-red lips in pretty distaste. "I did all that in rehab already. I've spent far too much time as a victim to the tyranny of nostalgia already. Regrets take up too much room. Let's just say, then was then. I wasn't healthy. Your reasons for going weren't unreasonable. And leave it at that."

"Fine with me," Jeremy said, relieved. Maybe she was just pretending to be so unperturbed; either way, he'd accept it. "So we're friends?"

Aoki laughed. "Of course. Actually, you've been on my mind a lot lately—in a good way. I get a bit lonely, sometimes, with so many strangers tugging at me all the time that I never have time for the people who are *real* to me. So I've been spending a lot of time thinking about the people who really understand me. Who knew me—before all *this.*" She flicked a hand abstractly, gathering the entire café and the world beyond into the circumference of her personal fame, and then gazed up at him through stubby black eyelashes. "That's why I contacted you."

He watched her watching him. Years of history seemed to flash between them, unspoken. It was as if they were veterans from a war that only the two of them had fought, sharing scars from battles that no one else could possibly comprehend. He had let himself forget so much. "I'm glad you did."

She sat back, pleased. "I knew you would feel that way."

A diesel bus groaned past, just a few feet away, bringing conversation briefly to a halt. Aoki pinched her nose to block the smell of car exhaust, and Jeremy leaned in to fill the gap of sudden silence: "Well, if we don't want to talk about the past, what should we talk about instead?"

"Oh, you pick," she said.

"OK. Tell me what it's like to be a superstar artist."

"You really want to know?" She made an exasperated face. "It's bloody awful. Everyone wants to talk about my *myth.* The critics, they say anything they want about me, invent meanings for my work that I never imagined, deconstruct my life and then label it *me,* and I can't do anything about it. Remember how I used to enjoy screwing with the public? Making up stories about my *time spent living with Nepalese yak herders* or my *hermaphrodite birth* and seeing how they scrambled over fictitious crumbs? But now they don't believe me anymore and instead this whole *myth* thing has emerged. You know what some critic wrote about me the other day? 'Aoki exemplifies the fractured soul of the post-modern media age, her constantly reinvented personae externalizing the root of human disconnection.' It's like I'm not a human being at all anymore."

"Strange," he said, surprised by the force of her diatribe. "I thought you would like that sort of thing. You used to live for it."

She looked momentarily abashed. "I know. But that was before I knew it would become such a monumental bore."

"So are you unhappy?"

She ran a finger along the rim of her cappuccino cup, scraping off brown froth with the raw edge of a bitten fingernail. "No. It's very nice to be rich and respected. I get to do whatever I want whenever I want it. I keep apartments in three cities. And I love the art, of course."

"Sounds awful," he said, pulsing with jealousy. *That would have been my life if I stayed with her,* he thought to himself; and then, before he could stop himself, *Did I make a mistake?*

"You'd love it," she said. She smiled, and an understanding seemed to pass between them. "OK. Now you," she said. "I'm desperately curious about who you've become."

Aoki was looking at him with her head tilted to one side, her eyes narrowed in thoughtful contemplation. It stirred in him a bright shock of recognition: He remembered this look, the one that made you feel like you were the most fascinating person on the face of the planet, a person of infinite depth and undiscovered capabilities. It was the look she'd seduced him with in the first place. Was she trying to seduce him again? Did he *want* to be seduced? "I should tell you about Claudia," he said stiffly.

Aoki shook her head vigorously. "I don't want to hear about *her* yet. Tell me about *you*. Let's start with your music."

"That's a sore subject," he said, hoping he could stop this line of questioning, reluctant to reveal the mundane details of his life. "My band is no more."

"I thought you were about to finish an album?"

"So did I. Events conspired against me. My bandmates bailed out. Just yesterday, in fact."

"Daniel," she said. "Your friend the journalist?"

"Yes, he's having a kid and he had to quit. But he wasn't the only one."

Aoki made a face. "He was always too mild for my taste. Anyway, you shouldn't have been playing with amateurs. You're better than that."

"They were actually quite good," he objected. "We had a lot of potential. People were eagerly awaiting our album."

She seemed not to have heard this. "You want to know what I would have done, if I were you? I would have set up meetings with managers the minute I got to Los Angeles, used all those contacts from your This Invisible Spot days. You could have found *professionals,* other high-profile veterans like yourself—like that guy who played guitar for The Villains, remember? He's out here; he started a kind of—what's that hokey word they use now?—superband. LA is the music capital of the world, even if it doesn't have much else going for it, and I'm sure people would have died to work with you. You could have gone solo, even. Honestly, you missed an opportunity."

Jeremy took a sip of cold coffee, registering this truth for the first time. He saw the last two years with Audiophone reflected in a whole new and far less flattering light. She was right; he hadn't ever tried to succeed on his own, not in any kind of significant way. He'd just let his music career proceed in the easiest way possible, had succumbed to complacency and the comfort of friendship. Only now did he realize that he'd completely failed to think strategically; had failed to realize that was even a concern.

"I was distracted, I guess," he said. "By—other things."

"Right. Claudia," she stated flatly.

Claudia's name on Aoki's tongue made him cringe. Shame tugged at his sleeve, reminding him who he was now. "Not just Claudia. It's also . . . well, we own a house, which is a time and money suck, particularly now with the economy the way it is." Aoki arched an eyebrow, which Jeremy ignored. "And I've got a day job, of course."

"Yes. Designing T-shirts. A lifelong ambition of yours, I remember."

He retreated from her, falling back in his seat. "What's your point?"

She leaned in and—another shock—put her hand on top of his. Her palm was cool and soft, and he looked down at it there, a pale starfish impaled on his fist. He suddenly recalled a hundred vivid moments with that hand, paint-speckled and tiny and always so cold. When she used to grip his body it tingled and burned, as if he were naked in a snowstorm. Claudia's hands were much bigger and warmer but somehow less possessive. He thought of pulling his hand away from Aoki but he couldn't quite do it. His heart flopped and thudded as the years of pent-up emotional memory flickered back and forth between them, an electric current.

"You could be so much bigger than you are," she said.

"Being rich and successful isn't the only way to be happy." He said it instinctively, the old cliché falling from his lips before he had a chance to really decide whether or not he believed this. Of course he did. But it might make you *happier.*

"It's not just about that. It's about fulfilling your potential." She shook her head. "And so? *Are* you happy?"

He paused, too long, to ask himself a question he hadn't really asked before. He waded through the quagmire of the last few months—the career failures, the money troubles, the disaster of their home, and the quickening fear that he was headed toward a life of mediocrity—and then clambered out again, ticking off items in the plus column: his marriage to a lovely woman, old friends, a pleasant enough lifestyle. It was depressing that he had to work to list these things at all, though, and by the time he'd readied himself to answer in the affirmative—*happy enough*—Aoki was already shaking her head. "I refuse to let this happen, Jeremy."

"I don't think you have much say in the matter."

"I'm sure I can do *something*. I know so many people. I'll make some calls." She was so familiar, this Aoki; he used to admire her blithe self-confidence, the way she believed she could make almost anything happen just with the force of her desire. But suddenly he didn't like this aspect of Aoki at all: Who was she to march in after all this time and tell him what to do? He didn't want to be her pet project. *I'm perfectly capable of running my own life,* he told himself, despite the evidence suggesting otherwise.

"Thanks for your support, anyway," he said, halfheartedly.

"Not at all. If anything, I owe it to you. After all, you left This Invisible Spot because of me, so really all *this*"—she held up her free palm and once again described a semicircle that encompassed the entire city; did everyone else's world belong to her, too?—"is my fault." Aoki smiled apologetically; and as she did something seemed to shift, so that once again she was the woman he'd always known—beautiful and compelling and slightly unstable but, still, someone who believed in him right from the start. She wanted to throw him a lifeline, and he should be grateful for that even if he hated the fact that she saw him as a cause to be saved. He knew he could never turn down her offer of help. Maybe she knew that too. He felt himself slipping into a neat little web that Aoki had woven, wondering whether she had planned this all along and hating himself for being so willing to get trapped in it. *In order not to be a failure,* he realized, *I may have to become a bad person.*

Out of the blue he wanted, very badly, to lurch across the table and kiss her, just to see how it felt, what might happen to him, whether things would change forever.

He should go home, now, to Claudia, before it was too late.

Looking down, he noticed that they were still holding hands and quickly withdrew his, masquerading his desertion by lifting his coffee cup and draining the last milky drops. "I need to go now," he said, afraid to sit there any longer. "I've got to get in to work. But it was really great to see you."

"You'll see me again, of course," she said. "You're coming to my opening, yes? All my sycophants are sure to be there—so I'm sure you won't *enjoy* it, exactly, but at least you'll get to see what I'm talking about. I did send you an invitation, didn't I?"

"No," he said, his chest tightening. "You didn't."

"Well, consider yourself invited." She flashed a wicked smile, revealing a snatch of bright white teeth and pink tongue. "Bring Claudia," she said.

Claudia

THE APOCALYPSE HAD ARRIVED IN LOS ANGELES, AND A YELLOW scrim of haze shimmered low on the horizon for days on end, as if something were perpetually on fire in the distance. Still two weeks out from Halloween, the weatherman was reporting temperatures topping 100 degrees, an unseasonable inferno.

At Ennis Gates Academy, the air-conditioning system had gone down in a very untimely fashion, and with the doors and windows closed against the light, Claudia's classroom was a stifling coffin. The heat liquefied her students' brains. The teens melted across their seats like softening ice cream, torpid limbs dangling loosely in the dark. Succumbing to their inertia, Claudia had chosen a ringer of a movie today. *Close Encounters of the Third Kind,* not exactly art cinema but at least a classic with some interesting film technique and a strong example of the cultural motifs of 1970s pop cinema. She sat on the stage on her stool, sweaty and agitated, as the movie playing on the screen behind her haloed her with pixilated interference.

From the back of the classroom came a rumbling gurgle that sounded suspiciously like a snore. She paused the movie with her remote and used the laser pointer in her other hand to circle a face on the screen above her.

"Wake up, people. I know it's hot out but let's focus, OK? Extra credit question for whoever answers first: Who's the director playing the French researcher here?"

Another snore sent a wave of muted giggles rippling toward the front of the classroom, where it broke and crashed gently at her sandal-clad toes. Annoyed, Claudia squinted into the gloom, trying to discern which of the inert lumps out there was asleep. She simply did not have the patience, not today.

"Come on, you know who he is. We did a whole section on his films earlier this semester. You're too young to have senile dementia yet."

From the dark Jordan Bigglesby's high-pitched voice rang out. "Gus Van Sant?"

"This movie was made thirty years ago, Jordan. Nice try, but think *French*. Think *dead*."

Mary Hernandez raised her hand, as usual. The stub of a well-gnawed pencil was wedged in her fist, and she waved this back and forth as if she were trying to stab the question with its point. She waited, patiently, until Claudia acknowledged her with a nod. "I was thinking, Krzysztof Kieslowski?" she said, wrinkling her forehead intently. "But I don't know if you'd call him French, really, since wasn't he actually Polish? Although all his most critical works were produced in French, unless you count *The Decalogue*—"

Claudia cut her off. "A good guess, Mary, but no." *Must the girl always go on and on? Who does she think she's impressing?* "Anyone else want to give it a try?"

Nothing, just another sonorous snore, so exaggerated it almost sounded like a parody of a snore.

Claudia sprang from her stool and made for the wall, snapping on the overhead lights. Eighteen pairs of dilated pupils blinked blearily back at her, wounded by the fluorescent assault. There, in the second-to-last row, sat Penelope, her head tipped backward over her seat. Her eyes were winched closed, her mouth hung agape. As Claudia watched, Penelope released another snore. The rest of her students erupted in laughter.

"Penelope?" Claudia bit the inside of her cheek to prevent herself from yelling. "Would you care to answer the question? Or would I be interrupting your nap?"

"François Truffaut," Penelope said, with her eyes still closed, her head still limp over the back of her chair. "*Everyone* knows that."

"And tell me the significance of his presence in this film?"

Penelope let loose an aggrieved sigh. She slid down in her seat until her head was propped upright and looked accusingly at Claudia. "I don't know. He was friends with Spielberg, probably. That's the way it usually works."

"Is it, now. Aren't we lucky we have such an expert here to share with us how the film industry works!" Her response was maybe a touch too bitchy, but she had the right to be short-fused once in a while, didn't she? It had not been a very good month. All the gains of September—the new job, the roommate, and subsequent apparent relief of their foreclosure crisis; the near-completion of Audiophone's album and Samuel Evanovich's unexpected interest in her script—had been obliterated by the disappointments of October. She felt like a bricklayer who has just completed a dam, only to watch the mortar crumble and water come pouring through the chinks.

Jeremy had been moody and irritable all week, perhaps a symptom of Aoki's unsettling appearance in Los Angeles but more likely just the fallout from Audiophone's sudden disintegration. Claudia knew how much that must have hurt. She could still feel it herself, that gnawing ache of creative failure. It was a loss, a huge loss—although, truth be told, she was starting to grow just a little impatient with his defeatist moping. He'd skipped out on work three days in a row, instead spending his time sleeping and watching hours of music videos on YouTube. He was acting as if he'd lost a *child,* not just a band.

Really, what he needed was to pick himself up and move on. There was no room for self-indulgent pouting, not with the economy crashing around them and the few remaining opportunities winking out one by one. As much as she knew she should encourage him to go start another band, she couldn't quite put her heart into it. And she was too cowardly to tell him what she really thought: That what they needed, instead of embarking on yet another risky new endeavor, was a nice safe trench to huddle in while they waited out the storm. Solid jobs, practical expectations. In just a few brief months, the worldview that they and all their friends had grown so accustomed to—a heady mix of recklessness and optimism and self-entitlement—had become completely obsolete. As if disapproving parents had just returned from a long vacation and grounded the world for the wild party that had taken place while they were gone. Dreams of rock stardom—they were a relic of the time before. But she hadn't told Jeremy any of this. No, her role here was to be the sympathetic shoulder, to rub his back and empathize with the vast unjustness of life. She hoped that with just a little encouragement, he'd come to the same conclusion she had.

But in the meantime, Jeremy was so preoccupied with the failure of his band that he hadn't once asked about the status of Claudia's script. Not that there was much to tell him. Claudia had spent a week blowing off all other school deadlines—grading essays, writing college recommendations—as she conjured up some hasty revisions to make the script more appealing to Samuel Evanovich, and then sent the package off by courier with signature required. Since then, nothing. Her e-mail address was right there on the title page—along with her phone number and home address and the contact information for her agent Carter Curtis (more truthfully her former agent, considering that he hadn't returned a call since August)—so it certainly wasn't that he didn't know how to find her. *Hollywood executives never do anything quickly,* she reminded herself. Yet it still required superhuman effort not to look up Samuel Evanovich's home number in the student directory and call him, even if the news was bad, just to end this miserable limbo.

She said nothing to Penelope, of course, about the possibility that she might be working with her father. And Penelope, in turn, continued to cultivate her aggressively indifferent façade. Last week, she'd failed to turn in a single homework assignment. Was that fake snoring a feint intended to provoke her? Claudia shouldn't let it bother her, but it did; she couldn't help seeing Penelope as a proxy for her father, wondering what—if anything—she should read into Penelope's behavior.

"OK," she said curtly. "Since you all seem so uninterested in the film today, I'm going to switch things up. Pop quiz!"

The room erupted in groans as Claudia distributed the quiz sheet that she'd originally planned to spring on them later that week. Maybe it was unfair to do this on the hottest day of the school year, but she was feeling punitive. She sat in front of the classroom grading homework to a soundtrack of operatic sighs and dulled pencils scritching across paper.

She collected the quizzes as class ended and shuffled through them while her students gathered up their backpacks and snack wrappers.

They sat poised on the edge of their seats, feet edging forward, ready to spring forth at the first sound of the bell. The oppressive temperature in the room silenced any end-of-class chatter, leaving only a mute détente. Claudia flipped to the last test in the pile and stopped. It was completely blank, except for a doodle in the corner—a series of concentric stars—and the name YOURS TRULY scrawled at the top in Penelope's unmistakable all-caps handwriting. The girl hadn't even *tried*.

The electronic drone of the first bell burst through the silence and the students leaped as one toward the door. She hesitated and then called after the receding herd, "Penelope, will you come see me up here, please?"

Penelope turned, separating herself from the pack. She walked slowly toward the stage, her regulation plaid skirt swinging around bare thighs, the laces of her combat boots flopping against the carpeted aisle. The teen twirled a lock of hair with stubby fingers frosted in black lacquer and then tugged it to her mouth to gum its end.

Claudia held up the blank test and let it dangle in the air between them. "Want to tell me what this is about? Why didn't you answer any questions?"

Penelope shrugged. "I didn't feel like it."

Claudia stared at Penelope, astonished by her chutzpah: She herself would never have had the guts to say something like that to a teacher. No, she'd spent her life diligently answering questions, doing all the extra credit she could, sucking up to whomever was in charge. For a moment, she almost admired her student, but she quelled this, and forged ahead. "I know you can answer these questions—even if you haven't been doing any of the homework I've assigned you. You're a smart girl, and you already know a lot about film. I just don't understand why you're doing this." She flapped the paper in frustration. Why couldn't she break through to this girl? Claudia was a nice enough person, a pretty decent teacher by all accounts; why did Penelope—and this had become unmistakable—*dislike* her so much? "You realize I'm going to have to give you an F on this test, don't you? And, honestly, that's something you can't really afford, considering your grades in this class so far. If you keep this up, you're not going to pass."

Penelope released the curl from her mouth. It sprang back to her shoulder, drawing a spidery silver thread of saliva with it. "Yes, I am."

Claudia paused, confused. "*Yes, I am,* as in 'Yes, I am going to do the work?' "

"No," Penelope said. She pulled a pack of gum from her backpack and extricated a neon-green rectangle from its paper nest. She popped it in her mouth and began smacking it between her teeth. "As in, 'Yes, I am going to pass the class.' "

The heat was choking; Claudia couldn't take a satisfying breath at all. "What are you trying to say, Penelope?"

Penelope looked at the blank test for a long minute and then back at Claudia. "We both know you're going to have to give me an A. It's really only fair. If you want to work with my dad, I mean."

Claudia's hand hung in the air, frozen and quivering. Silence fell between them, a static sheet separating teacher and student. Outside, Claudia could hear the thump of the girls' basketball team, taking up position on the court behind her classroom. She lowered her arm, letting the paper fall to her side. "I'm going to pretend that I didn't just hear that," she said, her quavering voice betraying her shock. Then she turned on her heel and fled like a coward, away from Penelope and into the A/V closet.

She fussed with the DVD players, trying to slow the heartbeat that rattled in her chest like an oncoming train on a wooden trestle bridge. She should go straight to the principal and report this; and yet couldn't she also be culpable here? Would Nancy Friar, perhaps, be less than pleased that Claudia was attempting to find outside employment with a school board member? (She recalled rule number one on the orientation sheet: *Do not fraternize with parents outside of school.*) She was stopped cold by yet another epiphany—didn't this also mean that Samuel Evanovich had read her script, perhaps even discussed his intentions for it with his daughter, because why would Penelope be bothering to try to use this as leverage if Samuel didn't plan to work with Claudia in the first place? And yet—perhaps Samuel had only pretended to be interested in the script in the first place and was in fact colluding with Penelope, using Claudia's career desperation as leverage

for a better grade for his daughter! Her cranium throbbed as she tried
to parse through the possibilities.

Behind her, she heard Penelope's footsteps, then the squeak of the
girl's gum. Penelope's rasped voice drifted from the doorway of the
closet. "Honestly, Mrs. Munger, do you *really* think you have that much
to teach *me?*"

Shocked, Claudia turned to face her student, trying to frame a measured, teacherly response: something about true knowledge coming
from experience, or work being its own reward. But she hesitated for a
crucial second too long—combating, in that brief moment, an old familiar self-doubt (*a pathetic $39,000 box office in its opening weekend*)—
and in the void that this pause left, Penelope saw her opportunity. She
took a step into the closet, boxing Claudia in next to the whirring
DVD players, and gazed up at her teacher with a sympathetic—
sympathetic?—expression. "Look, Mrs. Munger, I took your class because I need it to qualify for the summer scholar program at USC film
school; but if I already know all the stuff you're telling us, why should
I waste my time with all these stupid assignments? Especially when I
know you have to give me the A anyway."

The electronics were hot against Claudia's back. She felt the knob of
a DVD player pressing into her spine and wondered how on earth she'd
ended up here, in an airless school closet, being bullied by a teenager.
She was a Sundance-annointed director, for chrissakes, with more than
a decade of industry experience: Of course she had plenty to teach the
world. *Claudia* was the one in charge here, not this self-important brat.
It was her classroom, her script, her life.

She summoned a shred of moral righteousness. "I don't think I *have*
to do anything. Now, *excuse me.*" She squeezed past Penelope back into
the classroom and then swung the closet door shut, so abruptly that
Penelope had to jump sideways to avoid being beaned in the forehead
or locked in the closet.

Penelope was silent. She crumpled the gum wrapper in her hand and
shoved it back in her bag. Then she narrowed her eyes and glared hard
at Claudia from beneath her mascara-clotted lashes. "*Fine.* If that's what
you want. But you should know: My dad really, *really* cares about how
I'm doing in this class. And if I'm failing, he's not going to blame *me.*"

Penelope twirled and marched off, her skirt flaring so pertly with her spin that Claudia could see the girl's purple cotton panties gripping the tops of her thighs. Claudia stood frozen on the stage, the blank test in hand, as her student disappeared out the door. Sweat dripped from her cleavage, where her bra trapped the heat in close to her body, drenching the sides of her blouse and pooling in a puddle at her navel. For a moment, she thought she might faint.

Claudia had expected that the person who swept Daniel so completely off his feet would be an overgrown nerd, like him, but the young woman who arrived on their doorstep with a bottle of Malbec in hand was charmingly exotic. It's not that she was pretty, exactly—she had unruly dark hair and was a touch wide across the rear, and her face was dominated by a soft marshmallow nose and bushy Frida Kahlo-esque eyebrows that slashed across her forehead. But she held herself erect with balletic poise in her long peasant skirt and spoke rapid English that was tinted with some sort of Latin accent and smiled, frequently: the toothy, contagious smile of a woman who has yet to find anything to hate about the world.

Earlier this week, it had looked like tonight's meet-the-pregnant-fiancée gathering would be canceled. Jeremy hadn't spoken to Daniel since the band's breakup, and when Claudia suggested that they go ahead with the long-planned get-together anyway, Jeremy had stuck out his lower lip like a pouting child. "Whatever," he said. "I don't know if I can look him in the face right now." But he hadn't said anything specific about canceling either, so at 6 P.M. the house had filled with the sound of onions being chopped, and then the scent of home-made pear-prosciutto pizza wafted into the living room, and at 7 P.M. the doorbell rang on cue.

Daniel and Jeremy knocked each other stiffly on the shoulders with clenched fists—with aggression, or affection, or both, it wasn't quite clear—and then disappeared to the kitchen to mix drinks. Claudia led Cristina on a short house tour, as they exchanged pleasantries about the remarkable heat. Claudia wanted to pay attention to the conversation, sensing that there was a crucial first impression to be made, but she was distracted. Every time Cristina paused to smile, Claudia would flash back to the same sickening visual: herself, sitting at her desk in the stuffy A/V closet, carefully inscribing an *A* into the little square next to Penelope's name on the grade sheet. At first she'd made it a B, as if this equivocation would somehow mitigate her transgression, before deciding that this was pointless. After all, Penelope was demanding an A; a cowardly B would neither solve Claudia's problem nor absolve her of guilt. One couldn't just partially sell out—you either sold, or you didn't sell, and really, was there any question that at this moment in time it was in her own best interest to put her ethical objections up on the auction block? No. No, there was not. So she changed the grade to an A, although she'd written the letter in pencil, as if giving herself permission to go back and erase her mistake. But she knew she wouldn't, not after seeing the threat in Penelope's eyes. Was she stupid to be putting her new career in jeopardy—the *stable* job, the one keeping them afloat—for some wild fantasy she knew was a long shot anyway? But the undeniable truth was that Claudia did long for that movie career; she still lay in bed at night, imagining her movie title in capital letters on the Arclight Cinema marquee, the credits rolling past as the weeping audiences stayed glued to their seats, immobilized by emotion. Compared to that, her transgression today seemed so minor. It was just one little A. And it was probably true anyway that Penelope knew the answers to the test even if she didn't bother to write them down. She *would* have gotten the A, if she'd just tried. Besides, if Claudia really did get her film going with Samuel Evanovich, she'd soon be quitting her teaching job. No one would ever need to know.

She led her guest toward the living room, as Cristina prattled on about something related to the baby. "You wouldn't believe how much a crib costs, especially if you want one that's made with nontoxic materials. Same price as a used car! You'd think with all these recession sales everywhere, things would be cheaper, but not baby gear. But luckily we're getting hand-me-downs from my sister." Cristina smiled with the bland complacency of the newly knocked-up, then turned to look out the window, one palm placed absently on her slightly bulbous belly. "You know, your house is lovely. It's really very cozy up here, isn't it? Like a little nest."

Claudia led Cristina toward the window and they gazed out at the lights of the houses on the ridge across the way, bright beacons in the dark. "It's our oasis."

"I might feel a little isolated, though."

"Maybe, a little."

"You own?"

"Technically, the bank owns," Claudia said, more breezily than she felt. "We're just doing our best to keep them off our backs." She thought of Lucy, who had agreed to stay out of the house tonight, and offered a quick prayer of gratitude that she wasn't around—Cristina didn't strike her as the type of person who would ever get herself in such a financial mess that she'd need to take on a roommate. Lucy would be too embarrassing to explain.

Cristina nodded. "We're thinking of buying soon, maybe after the wedding. Real estate prices are plummeting. Did you read that story today—twenty-seven percent this year so far?"

"At least the crash is working out for someone." Claudia couldn't quite force a convincing smile. "So, tell me about the wedding."

"We're going to hold the ceremony in the courtyard of the museum where I work and then have dinner afterward at a Cuban restaurant. It'll be casual." Cristina spun around and studied the rest of the living room, an assessor doing an impromptu survey. Her gaze snagged briefly on the unfortunate floral chaise, before abruptly snapping to focus on *Beautiful Boy*. "Oh, my God!" she exclaimed. "Is that an Aoki Hamasaku?"

Claudia gazed up at Jeremy's painting, surprised by Cristina's outburst. "Yeah," she said. "You've heard of her?"

Cristina closed in on the painting, bringing her nose just inches from the divots and claw marks in the thick green paint. "Of course. The museum has three pieces by her in its collection. God, this is gorgeous! Why do *you* have it?" She turned quickly and looked at Claudia. "Did that sound bad? I didn't mean it in a bad way. Just . . . it's a surprise to see one hanging in . . . a normal person's house."

Claudia could feel something unpleasant breaking loose inside her. Yes, Aoki was successful, but a *museum collection*? This was an unfortunate revelation. "She used to go out with Jeremy, years ago."

Cristina's mouth shaped itself into a little O of surprise, revealing the pink flesh inside her lips. "Oh, my God, of course. Jeremy is *that* Jeremy! *The Jeremy Series* Jeremy!"

"Well, yes. She used to paint him a lot," Claudia said. This particular moniker—*The Jeremy Series*—was one she hadn't heard before, and she wished she still hadn't. It solidified Aoki's hold on Jeremy's past, consecrating their connection not just as a failed relationship but as a bona fide *movement*. Like Picasso's Blue Period.

"I *know*! There must be at least three dozen paintings of him out there! Do you also own the one that was on the cover of *ArtForum*? That was my favorite. Oh, no, wait, I think I read that Oprah bought that one." Cristina moved her hand across the surface of the painting, her palm hovering above the whorls and divots.

"This is the only one we own." Claudia said, wondering how she could change the subject without being obvious about it. She hated that Cristina knew there was a *that* Jeremy; hated, even more, the fact that Aoki's existence was so prominent in her life again. Somehow, despite her best efforts to blot out Aoki's presence in the world, the woman had managed to slip back into their lives, a development for which Claudia was emotionally unprepared.

Not that there was a specific reason she should feel so ill-at-ease. When Jeremy came home after his coffee with Aoki earlier that week, Claudia had examined him closely for signs of . . . exactly what, she wasn't sure, but *something*. He was flushed, edgy, but that could be the fallout from Audiophone's demise the previous evening rather than any residual excitement from seeing his ex-girlfriend. He'd called their reunion *weird* but *uneventful* and said Aoki seemed *much healthier, but still pretty destabilizing,* which Claudia assumed meant *unpredictable* and *just as crazy as I remembered her.* As least, she hoped that's what he meant. He'd mentioned an upcoming opening they were both invited to, an apparent gesture of détente that had assuaged some of that residual paranoia she couldn't quite rid herself of. There *was* a tinge of sadness in his voice, a hiccup of loss and remorse than brought to mind all of her own ex-boyfriends—a depressive poet from her post-college years who'd broken up with her in order to "find room for his writing" and then married another woman three months later; the year-long affair with a French carpenter with whom she had little in common but sex; the very sweet but slightly dull software engineer whom she'd heartlessly dumped not long after meeting Jeremy. She'd lost touch with all of them, but if they showed up in her life now, wouldn't she feel the same sheen of nostalgia, the lure of what-might-have-been? In that context, Jeremy's coffee with Aoki seemed unworthy of her concern. It was ridiculous of her to be jealous. She'd tried to put it out of her mind: There were just so many other, more important things to worry about right now than a shared cappuccino with an ex-girlfriend.

Except that here Aoki was yet again, somehow impossible to shake: It was almost as if the artist herself had materialized in the flesh, making herself at home in their living room. Cristina moved backward to get a better view of the painting, tripping against the edge of the couch. "Wow," she said. "Have you met her? I've heard so many stories. . . ."

"No. But Jeremy always said she was kind of nuts," Claudia said pointedly.

"That's her reputation." Cristina pulled her cellphone out of her pocket and held it up with a stiff arm, framing a picture. She raised an eyebrow at Claudia, as if asking permission, and then snapped a photo before Claudia had a chance to decide how she felt about this. Violated, a little bit, maybe. Overshadowed, yet again. Cristina examined the photo on her phone, and then snapped it closed and tossed it in her purse. "I hope you have it insured."

Claudia swung to stare at the ugly painting. "Insured? Really?"

Cristina had pulled out a notepad and was taking notes. "It's got to be worth a fortune. The MoMA already owns two of them. One from this series sold at Sotheby's last May for about four hundred, but it was smaller and not nearly as good."

Claudia wobbled slightly, threatening to tip to the right into Lucy's chaise or to the left and capsize the coffee table. She put a hand up to the wall and stabilized herself, certain that the figure she had just heard was implausible, a faulty synapse sending incorrect auditory signals to her ear. *"Four hundred thousand?"*

"I'm not an expert . . . ." Cristina's voice trailed off. "You should really have an appraiser take a look at it."

"Jesus." The wall had begun to tip alarmingly, and in search of a more stable surface Claudia slipped carefully down into the chaise. Once seated, she still felt in danger of passing out, so she leaned forward and rested her head between her legs. Her voice came out muffled from between her knees. "I didn't realize. I thought maybe . . . twenty or thirty thousand."

"God, not in ages." Cristina's voice approached and then descended, hovering above Claudia's bent back. "After she won the Venice Biennale two years ago, her prices really skyrocketed. And you know how the art market exploded."

She won the Venice Biennale? Claudia digested this fact unhappily. What else didn't she know? But it was her own fault. She'd prided herself on the fact that she hadn't Googled Aoki since her engagement, but what once felt like princely self-control now looked like willful blindness. Somehow, Aoki had become downright famous while Claudia wasn't paying attention. *Does Jeremy know all this?* she wondered. *Does he know how much the painting is worth?* She suspected that the answer was yes. If that was the case, why had he been hiding this truth from her?

Suddenly, she wasn't jealous anymore. She was, simply, furious.

"European collectors love her," Cristina continued, unaware of Claudia's silent meltdown. "Are you going to her opening at the end of the month?"

"The opening." Claudia grasped at this, finally connecting back to the present that she knew. She sat upright, feeling slightly more grounded. "I think we're going. Yes."

"I'm jealous. Our head curator's invited, and I'm begging her to take me as her plus one."

"Who wants a *mojito*?" Jeremy called. The two women turned as Daniel and Jeremy crashed into the living room from the kitchen, cocktails splashing across their wrists. Jeremy smiled at Claudia, more animated than she'd seen him in days, as she took the sweating cocktail from his hands.

"So—I had no idea you were *Aoki's* Jeremy!" Cristina lurched toward Jeremy, as if about to flop down at his feet. "Tell me all about her!"

Jeremy flinched. "I'm not exactly *Aoki's,*" he said quickly, and then cast his eyes toward Claudia with silent apology, his loose grin clearly intended as some kind of peace offering: *Really, it's no big deal, honey! Don't pay attention to her!* But the damage was done. Claudia smiled tightly as she stared down at her drink, examining the pulped mint, the bubbles clinging desperately to melting ice cubes, as if these—rather than the painting or her notorious, duplicitous husband—were the most interesting things in the room.

She waited. Waited until the pizza squares were gone, and Daniel and Cristina had finally climbed into Daniel's old Saab to drive cautiously back down the rutted hill; waited until the quiet house was a drained fishbowl, emptied of life; waited until they were mutely shuttling emptied glasses and smeary plates to the kitchen sink, to be washed in the morning. It was then that Claudia finally turned to Jeremy and revealed the inferno of emotion she had been stoking all night.

"Did you know?" she stuttered at her surprised husband, who stood at the stove munching on an abandoned pizza crust. "Did you know that Aoki's painting is worth over *half a million dollars?*"

Jeremy stopped chewing. Crumbs clung to his half-open lips. "Did Cristina tell you that?"

"Is it true?"

Jeremy shook his head. "Jesus. I mean, I knew it was probably worth a lot, but that's a lot more than I imagined."

"What *did* you imagine?"

He ducked his chin, spotting a tomato sauce splotch on the front of his button-down shirt. He swiped at it uselessly, avoiding her glare. "I dunno, maybe high five or low six figures," he said quickly.

"And you didn't *tell* me? You didn't think it was worth mentioning to your wife that we were in possession of something that could alleviate our financial troubles? When we were at the bank, and I brought it up—and you didn't say a *word.* . . ." She dropped the plates in the sink, where they landed with an ominous crack. "We are *this close* to losing our goddamn home! I had to get a *teaching job,* Jeremy. We took in a *roommate!* And all this time we had the money just hanging there on the wall?"

"I guess I didn't think about it like that." His voice was low.

"Well, think about this: If we sold that painting we'd be able to pay off almost our entire mortgage. We could own the house free and clear. Or even if we just pay off half the house—think of everything we could use the rest of the money for. It could let me try my hand at film again, or finance your next album—or, if we wanted to be responsible, we could invest some of it, use it for retirement savings, or—I don't know—put it away for college for our kids. We could set ourselves up for the rest of our lives!"

Jeremy looked like a cornered animal. "Maybe I don't want to sell it."

"You don't want to sell it?" She repeated his sentence slowly.

"Not really, no." He leaned up against the hulking antique stove and fiddled with the cuff of his sleeve.

"It's just a painting, Jeremy. How could a painting possibly be more important than—oh, say, our *future*?"

Jeremy shook his head at the linoleum floor. Before she could stop herself, Claudia finally blurted out the fear that had been haunting her for longer than she cared to admit. "Is it that you're still in love with Aoki?"

"That's not it." A strangled sound came out of Jeremy's throat.

"Then what *is* it?"

"I don't think you'd understand," he said. His words were slurred from the *mojitos* he'd drunk. "You're so *pragmatic* these days."

She leaned back against the sink, wounded by his distaste. "Try me," she said.

"First of all, I don't really think of that painting in terms of what it's worth," he began, slowly. "Its value to me is more abstract than that. I figure, it's a piece of my past, something special—a famous painting, of *me*—that I could never own again. And that makes it kind of—priceless, I guess."

"It's not priceless," Claudia said, unable to bite her tongue. "It's worth more than half a million dollars."

Jeremy gave her a baleful look. "Why do you always have to be so literal? Don't you understand that I'm talking about things that are intangible?"

She hated the picture he was painting of her—a ruthlessly efficient harpy, joyless and practical to a fault. She wasn't that person, was she? "Of course I understand," she said. "I'm sorry. Go on."

Jeremy looked away from her, as if he were staring at something fascinating just outside the kitchen window, but the only image visible in the glass was their own reflection: two blurred bodies, standing at right angles to each other. "Listen, Claude. I can't sell the painting right now. I just feel kind of, I don't know—confused. And that painting's the only center I have. It's . . . who I'm supposed to be. It would be like selling a piece of myself."

"But it's just a picture. It isn't *you*. You're all caught up in some romantic fantasy of a life that doesn't exist anymore, that maybe even *never* existed. It has nothing to do with the reality we live in."

Jeremy turned and stared at her. His eyes were cool and measured. "Frankly, I think your *reality* is pretty fucking boring these days," he said.

Claudia snatched up a highball glass from the counter. Before her brain could register what her hand had in the works, she had flung the glass to the floor, a point just a few inches west of Jeremy's foot. The glass shattered into a hundred tiny slivers, dangerous shards skittering across the linoleum in every direction and lodging themselves invisibly underneath cabinets and appliances. Jeremy jumped back, staring at her with the wounded expression of a child who can't understand what he's done to deserve a spanking.

"Well, how about this reality, then," she barked. "If you don't want to sell that painting, you need to find yourself a new career. No more making your band the center of your life anymore, no more messing around in a pointless day job with crappy pay, because times have changed and that's a luxury we can no longer afford. We've been traveling blindly down this road for years and we've finally hit a dead end and that's reality, as much as you may hate it." The words fell fast and furious from her mouth. "Give it up, Jeremy. You're not a rock star. Not now."

Jeremy nudged a curve of glass with his toe, and then pressed his sneaker down on it. She heard it snap under his foot and flinched. "You haven't given up," he said, petulant. "You're still trying to get a movie made, even if it's in a half-assed kind of way."

She bristled. "What do you mean, half-assed?"

"Honestly? I think you're just using everything that's happened lately as an excuse to quit trying to make *real* movies because you're scared," he said accusingly. "You're scared of failing again."

His words pierced her, an arrow with deadly accurate aim, and she twisted away instinctively. It wasn't fair: of course she was trying! Just think of Penelope and that penciled A, of everything she was putting on the line to get a film made. "That's not the point," she said. "This isn't about me, it's about you. It's about the fact that it's time for you to *grow up* and rethink your priorities. You're almost thirty-five, and you've got a house and a family—and someday soon, we're going to have kids. And yes, I know you wanted the band to work out, so did I, and it really really stinks that it didn't, but Jeremy, it's not the *only thing* for you."

Jeremy was finally looking straight at her. "So you think I should just give up playing music?"

She was being unfair, too extreme, and she knew it; but she couldn't stop herself. The months of frustration poured out of her, a violent torrent directed straight at her husband. "*You're* the one who doesn't want to sell the painting. Apparently you think there are other, more important, *intangible* things than actually, you know, having money in our pockets. Well, you can't have it all, Jeremy. So you better choose."

Jeremy's face distorted with ghoulish hate. He shook his head. "Who *are* you?"

"Who am *I*? Who are *you*? Why don't we discuss the fact your picture is hanging in the MoMA and you didn't even bother to tell me!"

"I didn't want you to be jealous," Jeremy muttered darkly.

"*Should* I be jealous?"

The front door slammed shut right then, and Claudia and Jeremy looked at each other in wounded silence as footsteps approached, two sets. With depressing inevitability, Lucy appeared in the doorway, her married paramour in tow. She barreled toward the refrigerator in a tight pink cocktail dress, oblivious of the fog of tension that hung in the air.

"Hi, guys! You remember Pete?" Lucy flapped a hand at the doctor, hanging back in the doorway. Pete nodded at Claudia and glanced at his watch. Jeremy resumed staring at the floor.

"Can you believe it's ten-thirty and still eighty degrees out?" Lucy spoke into the depths of the refrigerator, her rump hanging in midair, a ripe plum ready to be picked. She withdrew a bottle of chardonnay and turned to smile at them. "I know it's kind of late, but are you two interested in joining us for a glass of white wine? Oh—is that broken glass on the floor?"

Neither Jeremy or Claudia answered. From the doorway Pete coughed twice, a soft cry of distress.

Lucy hesitated. "Oh, no, did I interrupt something?"

"I was just getting lectured by Claudia here about my inadequacy as a human being." Jeremy's voice was black.

Claudia's fists curled into tight coils of fury. "Can it, Jeremy."

"What?" He offered a faux-innocent grin. "I'm sure our roommate would love to hear what you have to say on the subject."

Lucy sagged, the wine bottle drooping in her grip. "Maybe Pete and I should get out of your hair—"

"Oh, no! Don't! We love the company." Jeremy smiled darkly. "We could build a campfire and make s'mores with some of your coconut marshmallows."

Claudia didn't recognize this man, this one who suddenly sounded more like the bullies of her youth than the genial boy she'd married. "Stop it, stop it *now*," she hissed. "It's not Lucy's fault that we needed to find a roommate. Besides, this is what you want, isn't it? You'd rather live like *this*"—she nodded her head at Lucy—"than sell your precious painting, isn't that what you decided?"

"I didn't choose *this* in the first place, remember? All this was *your* idea. You seemed to believe that buying a house would affirm the fact that you were—I don't know, *all growed up* or something—as if home ownership were just something we were *required to do* at a certain point in our lives, God knows why, and I just went along with it, even though it was insanely expensive. I should have known better. And now I'm supposed to give up everything else that's important or interesting in order to keep it?"

Claudia stared at him, willfully blocking out the awkward presence of the other two people in the room. "It's better than avoiding responsibility, which is what you seem to spend your life doing."

Pete cleared his throat. "Lucy, I'm going to head home. Maybe I'll see you at the hospital sometime."

"Don't!" Lucy lurched toward him, her heels crunching in the glass. "We can just go to my room—"

"Oh, let him go." Jeremy stood in Lucy's path, blocking her way. "You're better off without him. He's only using you for sex anyway. He's *married*."

"I don't think that's any of your business," Lucy said softly. She gazed bleakly over Jeremy's shoulder toward the empty space in the doorway where Pete had just stood. From the front of the house came the click of the entry door closing.

"I don't know why you think you can't do better," Jeremy said, more gently. He smashed another piece of glass underneath the heel of his tennis shoe and ground it into dust.

Claudia was baffled at the strange, antagonistic intimacy that seemed to be playing out between Jeremy and Lucy. When had *this* relationship formed? She was completely lost, a stranger in her own home, a home that had been taken over by this secretive passive-aggressive Peter Pan who called himself her husband and some pathetic, needy girl who was sleeping in Claudia's own bedroom. Suddenly, she couldn't take it anymore.

"*Should* I be jealous?" She found herself blurting out the question Jeremy hadn't answered yet.

Jeremy turned to stare at her, confused. "Of Lucy?"

Claudia angrily pushed the wooden kitchen table, sending it thumping across the linoleum toward Jeremy. "I don't know what the hell is going on here, but I can't deal anymore. I'm done," she said. "I'm sorry, Lucy."

She walked unsteadily out of the room as Lucy began to weep—a frightening, keening sound—and reeled through the living room in the general direction of the front door. She fished her keys out of a silver ornamental bowl that her parents had given them for an anniversary present, intended as a dining room centerpiece but since relegated to holding paper clips and hair elastics and spare keys. Jeremy followed close behind her, suddenly pliant. He watched her as she wrestled with the front door, which had never opened quite right since the day of the earthquake. "Don't *leave*," he said. His voice grew more desperate. "Where are you going?"

Outside, the night was unrelentingly warm, the muggy air offering no relief at all. She stepped through the door and let it fall shut. The last thing she saw through the illuminated crack was Jeremy's face, his eyes wide and wounded. "Nowhere that you can come," she said, to the closed door.

Claudia's didn't really want to be alone. Alone in the car, as it jittered along toward the bottom of the hill, her day kept racing through her head like a bad movie stuck in a perpetual loop: Penelope, blocking her in the closet; the penciled A in her grade book; the guilty expression on her husband's face when Cristina called him *Aoki's Jeremy*, and his distaste as he accused her of being *pretty fucking boring*. Their first real, huge, disastrous fight. She closed her eyes to make it all go away and then opened them again when the car brushed against a hedge. The car made a hideous scraping sound, accusing her of negligent misdirection.

There was nowhere to go. She wished she had a friend in Mount Washington, a safe house where she could go to sleep off the night, but the only people she knew up here were social acquaintances. RC lived across town, in Beachwood Canyon; and she'd be asleep by now, anyway. She could drop in on Esme, who had recently moved into a condo downtown, but she was in New York, doing marketing promotions for an upcoming film about parakeets with superpowers. For the first time, Claudia regretted having chosen to live on a hill, so remote from the rest of the city.

Her shaking hands were making it difficult to drive, so she pulled over to the side of the road, next to a scraggly little public park that had been wedged in the base of a ravine. One lonely streetlight cast a sulfurous glow across a square of cracked concrete. The swing set wobbled back and forth as if occupied by a forlorn ghost child. In the shadows, just beyond the light, lay an abandoned basketball, half deflated. Claudia pulled her cell phone from her pocket and impulsively dialed her mother's phone number.

The phone rang four times. Claudia was about to hang up, having thought better of it, when Ruth picked up the other line.

"Hi, Mom."

"Claudia? Are you OK?" Ruth's voice was phlegmy and sandpapered. She sounded much older than Claudia wanted her to be.

"I'm fine. Did I wake you up?"

"No, I was watching Conan. But honey, why are you calling so late?"

"I just wanted to say hi." She looked out at the barren playground, where the bushes were rattling in a soft wind—the Santa Ana was picking up—and regretted calling. Her mother hadn't been her confidante in years, not since Claudia left Mantanka. It was inevitable. Ruth's world wasn't much greater than the stuffy confines of her own house—where Claudia's semiretired father Barry spent most of his days in a recliner watching the History Channel—and her local Methodist church, where she served as a deacon and all-around do-gooder and, occasionally, the next town over, where she went to deliver noisy plastic toys to her grandchildren. Claudia's parents' home was frozen in time, as if a clock had stopped on some day in the past—roughly June 1986, judging by the fading teal-and-coral color scheme and white wicker furniture—when they had decided youth was officially over and there was no further reason to keep up with changing times. Claudia wasn't sure whether she loved her parents' reliable consistency or feared the terrifying tang of senior stagnation.

In any case, Claudia's life in Los Angeles couldn't be further from her mother's, and their relationship had long ago settled into something affectionate but vaguely distant, as if Claudia were an exotic creature that Ruth couldn't quite believe had sprung from her own loins. At Claudia's wedding, three years earlier, her mother had worn a vaguely perplexed look on her face throughout the entire proceeding, rattled by the cupcakes and the Internet-certified officiant and bridesmaids who were wearing black, of all colors! But that didn't mean she didn't cry, and it didn't mean she didn't love her son-in-law, even if her reasoning stemmed more from the simple fact that Jeremy loved her daughter than any personal connection to him.

"No one calls this late unless something's wrong. Here, let me go in the other room. Your father's dead asleep and I don't want to wake him." In the background the television clicked off and the sheets rustled as her mother climbed out of bed and put on a bathrobe. "OK, tell me what's wrong."

Claudia hesitated for a long time, trying to figure out where to start, and then plunged in anyway. "Do you ever get the feeling," she finally said, "that you've idealized something that never really existed in the first place? That you've been living on the precipice, looking straight ahead at some perfect blue horizon that you'll never arrive at, because instead, right below you is a canyon that you're about to fall into? That the world, as it really is, is a cruel joke and downright abusive?"

"Abusive?" Her mother's voice grew suddenly alert. "Is Jeremy abusing you?"

"No!" She sighed. "No, I just mean . . . I think our ambitions have outpaced what is really possible for us, and now Jeremy and I are paying the price."

Her mother went silent. "Oh, honey, I don't know what advice to give you. All I know is good things happen every time an angel smiles, so you just have to be patient and keep smiling at the heavens and eventually they'll smile back."

Her mother must have said this to her at least a hundred times over the last thirty-four years, and Claudia still didn't think it made any sense, nor did she appreciate the suggestion that her fate was in the hands of some smirking cherubim. "I don't think that's going to help much, Mom," she said.

Static blew through the line, an oceanic buzz that made her mother sound like she was speaking from some great depth. "Is this about Jeremy, honey? Are you two having problems?"

Claudia hesitated. "I'm not sure he's cut out for married life, Mom."

"Oh, now *that's* a story I know," her mother said briskly.

"It is?" She couldn't believe she was talking to her mother about this. But her parents had been married for thirty-nine years, and they had always seemed reasonably happy; maybe not passionately in love, but at least cheerfully complacent. Maybe her mother harbored wisdom on these subjects that Claudia had missed by underestimating her.

Perhaps her own life was still closer to Wisconsin than she had been willing to admit.

"Well, did Jeremy do something in particular?"

Claudia tried to figure out how to put her husband's emotional betrayals into words, and failed. "I don't think he likes my new teaching job, for one," she said, lamely.

"But it's got benefits and health insurance!? Why on earth wouldn't he like that?"

"That's not exactly the issue," Claudia said, growing frustrated again. "It's more like—he doesn't like the direction we're headed. With our lives."

Ruth lowered her voice. "Did I ever tell you what your father did not long after we were married? It had been—oh, dear, maybe six years since our wedding? Your sister was four years old and you were a very colicky baby and the state of our house wasn't very *comforting,* I'll tell you that. Your father started coming home late from the store every night, and I was just absolutely convinced that he was having an affair. Remember Squeaky Holbrook from down the street? Her. Lord knows why—she had fat calves and a laugh like a horse, but for some reason I fixated on the fact that I'd found the two of them in the kitchen together at a party once. Anyway, I went into full battle mode. I decided to ship you and your sister off to my parents for a week, and your father and I went and spent some time in a cabin up on the lake, and there we sat down and made a list of the things we most wanted to do. Together and separately. It was like a second honeymoon, and when we got back home everything was fine again."

"So, wait. *Was* Dad having an affair?"

The note of satisfaction faded from her mother's voice. "Well, I never asked, to be honest. But I think he was just overwhelmed by what it all meant. Marriage and children and taking care of us."

"Oh." Claudia considered this. "So what were the things on your lists?"

Ruth snorted. "I can't remember a one of mine. I think your father maybe wanted to learn how to fly-fish. I believe we did a few of them and then didn't bother with the rest. They didn't matter, really."

Claudia thought this sounded terribly depressing: a list of false promises to each other, never to be redeemed. How was it going to help Claudia and Jeremy to write down on a piece of paper that they wanted to be in a rock band, to direct movies, to backpack across Bhutan, to learn to speak Japanese? Their problem wasn't a lack of articulated desire, it was the inability to fulfill those desires. She understood, in that moment, the futility of ever trying to connect with her mother. She had become unparentable, so completely distant from everything she'd once known that she was now completely on her own. It was silly of her to have imagined that her mother would be able to offer anything but generic platitudes, anyway. How could she? Her mother only knew what Claudia told her, which wasn't much at all. The last vestigial shred of Wisconsin inside her drained away, and she knew she could never go back. But where could she go from here?

The faint wail of a fire engine reverberated down the ravine. The wind was picking up; the swing twisted back and forth in apparent agony. The streetlight flickered in and out, making the park look spectacularly creepy, something from a bad horror movie. Claudia wanted to get off the phone. "You're right," she said. "I guess I just needed to vent. Don't worry."

"Oh, I don't really worry about you that much, honey," her mother said. "You've always been a sensitive girl, too easily wounded, but underneath that you're stubborn as a bulldog. You know how to get something when you really want it. So I know you won't give up anything important without a fight. It's easy to have faith in you."

In the shadows of the park, the deflated ball had begun to roll slowly in the wind, on a wobbly course toward the fence. Claudia let her mother's words—It's easy to have faith in you—sink in. It was the most intimate observation that Ruth had made about Claudia in years, and Claudia grew quiet as she swallowed down a lump that was forming in the back of her throat.

But her mother registered her silence as a hesitation. "Should I be worried about you?" she asked, her voice finally betraying anxiety.

Claudia found her voice again. "Of course not, Mom. Good night," she said, and hung up. She started the car and swung back out into the street, pointing the Jetta back up the hill.

She was going home, of course—there was nowhere else to go. But it wasn't just that: She was incapable of giving up. As her mother observed, it was just her nature. There were things she wanted—and they weren't outrageous things to want—a nice home, a happy marriage, financial stability, the ability to pursue her dreams. A few bad months, one terrible fight, shouldn't mean the end of all that. It shouldn't mean that they suddenly didn't love each other anymore. She would go home and save it all.

Claudia drove slowly back through Mount Washington, passing the darkened homes of her neighbors. She passed a clutch of fading FOR SALE signs and a half-built modern monstrosity whose construction had abruptly halted in mid-September, seemingly doomed to spend the rest of its existence swathed in blue plastic. The neighborhood was changing again, she could feel it, as if a tide had crept up on shore and was now receding again, exposing the dead fish and strangled kelp in its wake.

She thought of her father, probably hiding out in his hardware store just to avoid the screaming kids and demanding wife back at home. Is that what she had become to her own husband, a nag and a bore? Maybe she was being unfair. So what if he couldn't seem to launch a viable career, or let go of his youth, or take their potential foreclosure as seriously as she did? Perhaps she'd unconsciously absorbed her parents' middle-class American values—*husband as provider*—despite everything, and it was *her* job to expunge them, not his to meet them.

By the time she swung her car onto her own rutted cul de sac, she almost felt OK again. It was a silly thing, what had happened—just a painting, a bit of nostalgia, too much stress on both their parts. She'd go home and they'd talk it out. *We'll go to therapy,* she thought. *It can't possibly be as bad as it seemed. We just need to stay the course, communicate better. And maybe once he's happier, he'll be open to selling that painting.* She briefly considered the Lucy issue, and what she might have to say—or, more accurately, get Jeremy to say—to their roommate to keep her from moving out. They couldn't afford to lose the rental income.

She noticed the light first, a red strobe coursing across the horizon, and then the smell of charred wood. A fire engine was parked on their block, with three men in yellow fire jackets winding a hose back into its housing. Water poured down the hill toward her car, a deluge that filled the divots in the asphalt and splashed up against her tires. It wasn't until Claudia was nearly home, and could see Lucy standing helplessly in the street next to Jeremy—balancing the enormous painting upright with his left hand—that she realized that the fire truck was parked in front of her own house.

Jeremy

THERE WERE SEVENTY-EIGHT VARIETIES OF NAILS FOR SALE IN
Home Depot, and Jeremy couldn't fathom the differences between
most of them. He stood there in the carpentry aisle, contemplating the
function of the L-shape flooring nail and the PNI hardened T-nail,
wondering whether he needed $1\frac{3}{8}$-inch nails or $1\frac{1}{4}$-inch nails or
whether he should just buy the 2000-piece PortaNail Complete Nail-
ing Kit and be done with it. The thrum of a forklift reverberated off the
warehouse ceiling, and a red light flashed at the end of the aisle, sum-
moning someone who never seemed to arrive. He hated this place; it
was a reminder of his own inadequacies as a man. Men were supposed
to know how to buy nails, why a wet/dry shop vac was necessary, the
uses of plywood versus pressure-treated lumber. Not Jeremy. Three
years later, he still hadn't opened the forty-eight-bit drill set that his
father-in-law had given him for their first Christmas because, frankly,
the thing terrified him.

He grabbed three boxes of nails at random and turned, nearly collid-
ing into Barry, who had come up silently behind him. His father-in-
law shook his head when he saw what Jeremy held in his hands.

"Those aren't going to do us any good. They're good for stapling
paper together and that's about it." Barry shuffled over to the wall of
nails and selected four different boxes, depositing them in the cart that
sat, laden with lumber and drywall, in the center of the aisle. He
scratched the liver spot that capped the bald crown of his head and then
tugged at the sagging waistband of his pleat-front slacks. "For what

we're doing, we'll also need a nail gun, preferably a Stanley, and some sturdy 3½-inchers. I can't believe you two don't own a nail gun. I could have sworn I gave you one. What have you been using, a regular old double-face?"

It was a pointed question, as far as Jeremy could tell: Jeremy had already given Barry ample evidence that he had no clue as to what was in their toolbox. If the seventy-one-year-old man was trying to show him up, he was succeeding. "I don't know," he said, and smiled to hide his humiliation. "I don't think we've been using anything, actually."

Barry ran his hands authoritatively over a stack of lethal-looking nail guns and chuckled. "You know, when Claudie was four years old she asked me for a hammer for Christmas? She had her very own toolbox, full of little kid-size tools, and she used to play with them just like they were dolls." Jeremy did know this, since Barry liked to repeat this fact rather frequently, as if this one fleeting moment in Claudia's otherwise undistinguished hardware career had bonded father and daughter together permanently. In the three days that Barry and Ruth had been in town, he'd already brought this fact up at least four times. It was quite likely that Barry's memory was starting to go. He was starting to drive Jeremy a little nuts.

But really, Jeremy shouldn't complain, because his in-laws were saving their asses. Barry, who had spent time as a general contractor before opening up two hardware stores in the Mantanka area, was going to do most of the basic repairs on the house—at least, those that didn't require any seriously heavy labor—and it also hadn't gone unnoticed by Jeremy that every time they ran out to buy supplies, Barry and Ruth picked up the bill. For this, Jeremy knew he should be more grateful, especially considering the financial bind that he and Claudia were in now. It was just difficult, he found, to muster the appropriate amount of appreciation for the fact that they were salvaging a house that he secretly wished had burned down entirely.

The smoke hadn't alarmed him at first. If anything, the acrid scent that was drifting into the living room was vaguely comforting; it reminded him of a winter that he and Jillian had spent in Big Sur in an old hunting cabin that was heated only by a stone fireplace. Anyway, he was too agitated to wonder what the smell of smoke might mean. Instead, he sat alone in the living room, drinking abrasive shots of cheap rum out of a coffee mug and ruminating over the frightening expression on Claudia's face as she shut the door on him. He had occasionally wondered if Claudia had a breaking point and somehow taken it for granted that she didn't—had assumed that whatever he did or said, she would always forgive him for it because she was that kind of person: loving to a fault. Apparently he was wrong. *I'm done with you,* her expression had told him, as she left the house. *You are not who I thought you were.* When she shut the door in his face, his self-righteous rage had been subsumed by an alien sort of panic. She was leaving. Was she leaving *him*?

Even though he'd raced out to the front of the house to try to stop her, he had waited a moment too long, and she was already gone. He dialed her cellphone number, but it went straight to voice mail five times. And so he sat there in the living room, drinking leftover rum and getting progressively more drunk. He listened for the sound of Claudia's car turning into the driveway, but the night was silent except for the echo of Lucy's sobs ringing through the heating grates. He had broken something tonight, he realized, and only now that it was sitting in two pieces on the floor before him—a favorite toy, dismembered in a moment of childish petulance—did he realize how much he had loved it in the first place. Why couldn't he just sell the stupid painting, anyway? She was right—it was just a *painting.* He loathed himself for being *that* guy, the bad guy; a better sort of man would have been self-sacrificing and considerate, would put his family and home on a pedestal above everything else. No, this kind of behavior was straight out of his father's handbook: pet lions and three divorces and abandoned children across the world. He wouldn't blame Claudia if she never came home again.

And what if she didn't come home? *He had no one else.* He would be completely alone. He tried to imagine his life without Claudia's comforting, cinnamon-scented presence beside him and saw himself as a boat out in the middle of the sea without an anchor. He finished up the lukewarm dregs of rum from the bottom of the bottle.

It wasn't until Lucy began to shriek in the other room that Jeremy's brain belatedly triggered its alarm. *Something is on fire.* Then: *The house is going to burn down*. That was when something internal took over, some innate chemical impulse that knew exactly what to do in a situation like this, even as his consciousness lagged a few critical steps behind. He was standing, his mind slowly forming the words *fire extinguisher,* but already his feet had moved him toward the kitchen, where the red canister lived among the cleaning products under the sink. Then it was in his hand, covered with a thin layer of grime, banging heavily against his leg as he ran back across the kitchen. A shard of broken glass on the floor pierced his toe and he looked down in surprise, not from pain—that would come later—but at the fact that his left foot was suddenly misbehaving, twisting under him as he raced through the living room and down the hall toward the bedrooms. He turned right and was in Lucy's room, where Lucy stood by the picture window in her silly frilly bathrobe, clutching the white lace comforter from her bed. The curtains were on fire. Orange flames billowed out from the window, and a cloud of charcoal smoke blackened the ceiling, ruining all Jeremy's careful paintwork from years before. The conflagration popped and hissed and spat out sparks as it began its work on the wooden frame of the window. It was curiously beautiful, and Jeremy hesitated before the glory and power of it all.

Lucy swung the comforter at the fire and succeeded only in fanning the flames. Jeremy jolted back to life. "Move!" he screamed at her, and she turned to stare at him, struck mute by the aggression of his command. "Call the fire department!" He stepped in front of her and pulled the pin on the fire extinguisher and released the trigger and just like that—just like something from a movie—a foggy white stream of retardant was spraying across the southern wall of the bedroom. The white clouds mingled with the black smoke and almost blinded him; something like ammonia stung the sensitive flesh of his nostrils. He pointed the extinguisher in the general direction of the wall and shielded his face in the crook of his shoulder, waiting for it to work. *Look at you,* Jeremy's consciousness marveled idly, as he braced himself against the extinguisher's kickback: *Look at you, fighting a fire!* Jeremy felt three steps removed from the scene, as if he were standing back watching a stranger: Who *was* this manly figure with the bleeding foot who was saving this house; saving the life of the hysterical woman beside him; saving the street, the city, the world? *It's you!* he thought, amazed. *You are this man.*

Except that the fire extinguisher was fizzling now, coughing out a few last gusts of chemical powder, but the flames were still growing. The fire had finished consuming the curtains, leaving only blackened webs of fabric behind, and was now eating a hole in the wall, a hole through which Jeremy should be able to see the deck and the view down the canyon, except that the smoke was too thick to see much of anything at all. As he watched, the blaze doubled in size, and climbed north to begin greedily devouring the crown molding. Great bright sheets of flame ascended the wall and then turned left to skim across the ceiling. Jeremy dropped the useless fire extinguisher and let the heat propel him backward, out into the hallway, where a thick layer of smoke had gathered, and farther back across the hall into his own bedroom, where Lucy was clutching the telephone and watching him.

"They're coming," she said, whispering for some unfathomable reason. "The fire department."

"What did you do?" he barked. "What happened?"

"I didn't know! I didn't know they would *burn* like that."

"What would burn?"

"His scrubs."

"You set Pete's scrubs on fire?"

Snot blew from Lucy's nose and lodged on her upper lip. "And some other things of his. I thought if I did it in the trash can. . . ."

Through two doorways he could see the flames advancing across the master bedroom, making their way toward the hallway and the rest of the house. "That was really stupid," he said.

She nodded meekly, and then began to cry. "My things! Can you save my trunk?"

His throat was scorched, his tongue thick and dry; he couldn't summon the saliva to swallow. He was going to lose the whole house, and what would Claudia think of him then? "No," he barked, and then lunged back into the hallway, ducking low to avoid the smoke, this time turning right into the bathroom. There, he closed his watering eyes and blindly felt for the bath towels, dousing them with water from the sink. *(How did he know to do this? Why wasn't he frightened? Who was this fasci-*

nating person who was so calm and efficient in the face of disaster?) He lurched back out and yanked the door to the master bedroom closed, pressing a wet towel against the crack in the door.

"Go outside," he told Lucy, handing her a wet washcloth. She stared at him with moist boiled-egg eyes, clutching her robe around her, then pressed the washcloth against her nose and ran down the hallway. Jeremy followed her.

A thin haze of smoke was collecting near the ceiling of the living and dining rooms. Lucy ran toward the front door and yanked it open. Jeremy watched her flee into the darkness, the marabou feathers that trimmed her robe trailing along behind her like an obedient pet. He didn't follow. He turned in the opposite direction, crossing the living room to the sliding glass doors, and stepped out onto the deck. The clear night air was a balm for his lungs. The black void of the canyon fell away below him. Above, the moon was obscured by a thick cloud cover that reflected the glow of the city lights back down at him. He limped down the deck toward the outer wall of the bedroom, where flames were pouring out through the hole that had burned through the wall. They licked at the outside wall, tasting it and finding it to their liking.

The garden hose was coiled in a pile at the end of the deck, next to the potted tomato plants. Jeremy turned it on full blast, and the hose began to buck and flip, spurting water in every direction. He seized the nozzle and pointed it in the general direction of the house. The jet of water was depressingly anemic compared to the voracious appetite of the fire. Flames were climbing up toward the vulnerable shingles of the roof and out toward the rotting wooden rail of the deck; and so he directed the hose first at one, then the other, and back again, soaking the back of the house with a gentle arcing motion. Water droplets drenched his shirt and cooled his blistered lips and clung to his chin.

Time passed obliquely; he wasn't sure whether he'd been out there for a minute or an hour. He was in a curious meditative state, nearly hypnotized by the motion from the hose. The fire spat at him as it battled to surge forward; he pushed it back with a blast of water. Out here, it was the just the two of them, a battle of wills, and he was determined to win. The world beyond this deck ceased to exist. He forgot that the

fire truck was even coming. He began to feel almost fond of the fire, as
if it were holding up a mirror and showing him something about himself that he'd never imagined before. Even as the flames took hold of
the drenched deck and began crawling toward him, he was strangely
calm, unwilling to flee to the safety of the front yard. His body proceeded mechanically forward, insisting on its moment of victory, while
his thoughts mindlessly trailed behind. *I can still beat this. Claudia will
come home and see that I saved the house and I will be the hero. I will save the
house for her!*

It wasn't until he heard the sirens screaming up the hill that Jeremy
finally broke out of his trance. The fire was dangerously close. He
dropped the garden hose and ran through the sliding glass doors back
into the house. The east end of the house had vanished in smoke, and
he wondered how much was lost. At the front door, he paused: What
else should he save? Looking around the living room, he considered
their possessions: The photos arranged on the wall, the guitars propped
against the couch, the furniture crouching low in the smoky gloom,
Claudia's laptop blinking sleepily on the dining room table. He found
himself standing underneath *Beautiful Boy,* prying it off its hook. He
wobbled under the painting's weight: it would be impossible to carry
anything else. Bracing the canvas against his chest, he awkwardly
steered it out the front door and into the driveway, where the orange
and red lights from the fire truck were illuminating the street like an
apocalyptic disco.

He stood there in the road next to Lucy, with *Beautiful Boy* propped
up beside him, and watched the firemen in their reflective yellow suits
run their flaccid hose in through his front door. Within minutes, water
was pouring down the street in a dirty black stream. Two firemen stood
on the east end of the roof, chopping away the shingles with a hatchet
in order to gain access to the fire below. The sound was like breaking
bones. The fire began to recede, releasing a few last angry clouds of
smoke.

His neighbors had come out to watch the spectacle. Across the street,
Dolores stood in her front yard, wrapping a ratty blue flannel bathrobe
tightly closed around herself even though the night was warm, as if by

doing so she might protect herself against the horrors she was witnessing. They made eye contact; Jeremy managed a weak shrug of acknowledgment, but Dolores's face remained devoid of expression, her mind somewhere else completely. Jeremy took it on himself to fill in the blanks: She was judging him for being so irresponsible as to burn down his house, and for having failed to put out the fire on his own. She didn't know how hard he had tried! *Where was Claudia, anyway?*

It was only now that he was safe from harm that he finally stopped to register what had just happened. His foot throbbed. He coughed dryly, wiping black grit from his face. And then his consciousness arrived back with a rush, throwing him backward with its force as it once again collided with the present moment. What it said to him, with its insidious rationality, with its perpetually self-serving greed, was this: *You could have solved all your problems. You could have just let the damn house burn. How free you could have been!*

According to the fire marshal, Jeremy's quick work with the extinguisher and garden hose had managed to save the house—and, therefore, maybe even the entire hill of tightly packed homes—by confining the worst of the fire to the master bedroom. The kitchen and living room and dining room, at the other end of the house, were relatively unscathed, but the master bedroom was a blackened husk with a gaping hole in the ceiling, and the deck that led off it had been so weakened by the fire that it would need to be rebuilt from scratch; the adjacent guest bedroom and hall and bathroom all had heavy smoke and water damage. Still, Claudia and Jeremy were lucky: The structure remained fundamentally sound, and they could still live in their house by throwing an air mattress down in the living room, even if it was hard to sleep because of the sour, dank smell that pervaded everything.

That was about where their luck ended. The contractor who had come out last Tuesday had offered a staggering estimate of $62,000 for repairs, which at first they thought didn't matter, because they had insurance (not by any foresight on their part; but because it had been required for the mortgage). Except that, as Jeremy discovered on the phone with their insurance agent the next day, their policy came with a $15,000 deductible. *Fifteen thousand dollars*—more than the cost of mixing and mastering an entire album!

Lucy should, of course, be paying the bill; but she'd vanished entirely after the night of the fire, leaving behind her charred belongings, the gluey marshmallows in the fridge, a stack of gossip magazines in the living room. Their furious phone calls had gone unanswered, and the taciturn brother who had arrived to pick up Lucy's floral chaise a few days later had refused to divulge her whereabouts. They could sue her—the lawyer that Claudia had spoken with had said they had a very strong case—but it might take years to recoup their money, and they'd have to cover the cost of repairs in the interim.

The situation was impossible. They had landed back where they'd started in August, only now everything was even more dire. Without the $1,000 rent payment from Lucy there was no way they would make the mortgage payment that was due next week; how many months would the bank give them before it stepped in and foreclosed? In hindsight, the stupidest thing Jeremy had ever done was fight that fire. He was about ready to throw his hands up and tell the bank to just take the fucking albatross of a house already, he was done with it and he'd deal with the consequences. Except that he kept remembering the look on Claudia's face when she finally arrived home that night, a look of confusion that, as he watched, evolved into an expression of personal anguish unlike anything he'd ever seen before. She'd looked from Jeremy to the painting to the smoldering house and back again, and then burst into uncontrollable tears. The sound broke his heart. He gathered Claudia in his arms, torn between relief that she had come home after all and panic that he had just made the biggest mistake of his life. "Don't worry," he reassured her, "it's going to be OK. It's fixable."

And here was Barry to fix it. He and Ruth had arrived in Los Angeles on Thursday, uninvited, two days after Claudia called to tell them about the exorbitant deductible. They settled into a Best Western downtown and arrived on their doorstep every morning at 7 A.M., ready to get to work. "Your pop hasn't forgotten all his old tricks," Barry had said, eyeing the disaster zone with a self-satisfied gleam in his eye, more energized than Jeremy had ever seen him. "Don't forget I'm the one who built that rumpus room in the basement and your mother's garden shed, remember, Claudie?" He could fix up the smoke- and water-damaged guest room and hallway, making the house habitable again, he promised, and probably rebuild the deck too, if Jeremy and Claudia would throw in an elbow. The bigger damage—the obliterated master bedroom, and the gaping black hole in the roof above it—required a professional. But they were making progress, and by mid-week Claudia and Jeremy would probably be able to move their air mattress (the water-logged bed had gone to the dump) into the guest bedroom.

Any time not spent pouring a new foundation for the deck had been spent poring over spreadsheets with Claudia as they tried to figure out where the money for their outrageous mortgage was going to come from now. They'd decided that Jeremy would look for a second job, maybe bartending a few nights a week like he had back in New York when he was still a struggling musician. It seemed he was slipping backward to meet an old half-formed version of himself. This was not the life that Jeremy wanted—there would be, it had gone unsaid, no time for fun at all, and certainly no time for music. It was ridiculous even to consider starting a new band right now. The charred remains of this house was his new jail cell; he was doomed to a life sentence of hard labor in its service. How ironic that he had chosen his own incarceration.

Sometimes he imagined telling Aoki what was happening to his life (*What Would Aoki Think?*) and the look of predictable contempt on her fantasy face made his heart twist. *You could be so much bigger than you are,* she'd told him. So what would she think of him now? It was a relief, he supposed, that he hadn't spoken to her since their coffee. He was tempted to skip her opening this Wednesday entirely, and for a brief moment he'd even considered selling her painting, even though Claudia hadn't said a single word about that. Selling it would rid him of Aoki's voice in his head forever, and dig them out of their financial straits to boot; except that he couldn't quite take that first step toward letting it go. Something inside him was still waiting—maybe until Aoki had finally left town?—to make that last, final break. In the meantime, he gritted his teeth and soldiered on. Yesterday he'd picked up a few job applications at bars downtown, today he would work on repairing that charred deck, and on Thursday, after Aoki's art opening had come and gone, he would try to move on. Become the husband that Claudia wanted him to be.

And so Jeremy pushed the cart through Home Depot, obediently following Barry through FIXTURES and INDOOR PLUMBING. As Barry picked through a box of washers—letting them rain through his fingers—Jeremy stood and watched a young family trudging down the aisle. The parents were just about his age: the father with a Baby Bjorn strapped to his chest, milky spit-up stains on the shoulder of his U2 Popmart Tour T-shirt; the wife makeup-free and dumpy around the hips, furiously chasing a screaming three-year-old down the aisle. The father stopped next to a display of plastic toilet seats, right next to Jeremy.

"Honey," he called. "What's our budget on this?"

"We have forty bucks left," she called, "but don't forget we still need to get the shower curtain." She was trying to tear a plunger from her toddler's insistent grip. The toddler slammed the plunger against the warehouse floor, taking his boundless rage out on the handle. The plunger splintered, and the mother ripped it away, shoving it back onto the shelf.

The man turned to Jeremy with an expression of infinite fatigue. "Hey, dude," he said. "Which brand's supposed to be better, American Standard or Pegasus?"

Jeremy turned to stare at the toilet seat closest to him, imagining the man before him sitting on it, rereading a two-year-old copy of *Popular Mechanics* for the tenth time, lingering over his bowel movements in order to snatch just a few minutes of solitude. It seemed desperately sad. "You're asking the wrong guy." He shook his head, pleased for a moment not to fit here at all. This megastore was a sinkhole for humanity's dreams, replacing lofty ideals and ambitions with soulless mundanity: self-heating toilet seats, faux-wood vinyl siding, and three-quarter-inch plastic piping. *Of course* Jeremy didn't belong at Home Depot; he was an artist! It was a badge of goddamn honor not to know what a PNI-hardened T-nail was! "No, man, I have no clue."

"Whatever, it's all the fucking same." The man grabbed the cheapest one and lugged it back to his wife, as the baby strapped to his chest began to wail.

Jeremy turned and found Barry watching him. "You want a quick lesson about how to seal a pipe joint?" Barry asked.

Jeremy's first instinct was to shake his head—*No, absolutely not*—but something about the hardness of Barry's face stopped him, as if Barry had realized Jeremy was headed astray and was determined to herd him back into his proper position in the pack. "Sure," Jeremy said, weakening.

Barry smiled, revealing square white teeth that Jeremy suspected were dentures. "It's something you really should know about. You'll never have a leak again, I promise you."

"Why don't you show me when we get home," Jeremy said, trying to sound cheerful rather than doomed, trying to sound like a man in charge of his own destiny. "We have everything we need now?"

"Yessirreebob," Barry replied, and let Jeremy push the heavy cart down the carpentry aisle toward the front of the warehouse. There, Jeremy would pay for the supplies with his father-in-law's money before heading back home to Claudia and Ruth for an afternoon of mixing concrete and sanding plaster. He walked as slowly as he could.

Jeremy found Ruth and Claudia in the guest bedroom: Ruth scrubbing soot from the walls with a toxic-smelling cleaning product, Claudia attempting to dry an area rug with a hair dryer. His mother-in-law wore a rubber apron over a pink-collared sweatshirt that was fronted with an appliqué of three frolicking kittens. (She'd worn this sweatshirt nearly every day since their arrival; sometimes, when Jeremy closed his eyes at night, he imagined those three kittens clawing his eyes out.) Gray hair bristled about her head in tight curls. Under the blast of the hair dryer Jeremy could hear a light-jazz song playing on the stereo—was that Herb Alpert? Claudia turned and caught the quizzical expression on Jeremy's face. *Mom,* she mouthed, rolling her eyes. Then: *Save me.*

Ruth wiped her yellow rubber gloves on the front of her apron and shook her head. "I just don't understand how you two could have spent so much on this house," she shouted, over the hair dryer. "It's less than half the size of ours, and ours cost a tenth of yours."

"Well, it's not worth what we paid for it now," Jeremy said. "Maybe we should just move into my convertible. It's probably more valuable."

Neither woman laughed at his joke. Claudia snapped the hair dryer off. "Can you both stop it with the doom and gloom?" she complained. "We're going to repair it. And I'm sure the market will bounce back eventually. Los Angeles is a desirable city and always will be."

"So is Mantanka, if you ask me," Ruth said, directing her words to the blackened patch of wall two feet above the floor.

"A house is a long-term investment, anyway," Claudia continued, ignoring her mother. She walloped the rug with her left hand, sending black dust flying. "It's a *home,* right? Maybe we'll stay here for the rest of our lives, and then it won't matter what happens to the real estate market."

The rest of our lives. It sounded like an ungodly long time to Jeremy. A cellphone rang out in the kitchen and Claudia rose from her seat on the floor, jogging out of the room to retrieve it. From across the house, Jeremy could hear the lilt of her voice, vowels slightly exaggerated, making it clear that she was talking to someone who needed to be impressed. Probably an insurance adjuster.

The rest of our lives. Everything that Claudia said this week seemed to have some coded message that Jeremy couldn't quite decipher. It hadn't started out like this. Their first few days after the fire had ushered in a new, unexpected intimacy: Jeremy and Claudia had clung to each other on the air mattress like disaster survivors, comforted by the presence of each other's bodies. She was so solid, so material, so familiar next to him; nothing else seemed quite as real. They'd had quick, desperate sex on the living room couch and the kitchen table, heightened by the smell of catastrophe around them.

But with the arrival of his in-laws and the dawning reality of their situation, the freeze had crept back into their marriage, as if Ruth and Barry were a magnifying lens that amplified all of Claudia and Jeremy's problems. One of these days, they really should talk about their fight, which still hung in the air in the house, along with the lingering smell of smoke, but Jeremy was happy to avoid it for as long as he could. He was afraid of what might come out of his mouth if he wasn't careful, what he might see if he opened his eyes and gave it all a good hard look.

Late one night, as he lay on the deflating air mattress, he'd had the terrifying thought that maybe love wasn't what he'd once thought it was. You're supposed to love the person you're with just because of who they are, but how are you to know who someone really is when they've still got fifty or sixty years ahead of them? Maybe, when you're young, you love people as much for their potential as for who they are *right now*. And if that's the case, what happens to love when time passes and that potential starts to shrivel and fade? Does love die with it? He was afraid to talk about these things with Claudia, afraid that what he might end up telling her was that he wasn't sure how he felt about anything anymore.

With Claudia in the kitchen and Barry out in the back of the house, Jeremy was left alone with Ruth, a scenario he generally tried to avoid. The passing years had made it clear that the only thing the two of them had in common was a shared affection for Claudia. Conversations between them tended to be as stilted as those between strangers, revolving around generically safe subjects, or else uncomfortably pointed, as if Ruth were using him as a proxy to get a message across to her daughter. Judging by the tight lines that were forming around Ruth's mouth, she was about to attempt the latter.

"It's important to really get this room clean, if it's going to be the kids' room someday," Ruth said. She didn't look at him as she bent to attack a blackened patch near the window. "Kids are much more vulnerable to toxins in the air."

Jeremy could hear Barry downstairs, using the new nail gun ($89.99, on Barry's Visa) to assemble the deck. He wondered if he could excuse himself, claiming that Barry needed his assistance. At least Barry liked to work in comfortable silence, marred only by the occasional satisfied grunt of completion. "I was thinking of turning this room into a video arcade, actually," he told Ruth. "Or maybe an indoor bowling alley."

Ruth stood upright to assess him, her gloved hand pressed into her hip in order to balance herself. "You know, women have a much harder time getting pregnant after they turn thirty-five."

Jeremy took a step backward, toward the door, thinking of the harried family in Home Depot. *The rest of our lives.* "Is that right?"

"I sent Claudia a study about it last summer," Ruth said. "She keeps saying that you're waiting for your careers to stabilize, but I think there's never a bad time to have a baby. Especially now that she's got a real job with health benefits."

Jeremy remembered the study. It had arrived in a manila envelope, along with a collection of other magazine clippings that Ruth considered must-reads: a how-to guide for winterizing your garden, a coupon for $10 off hypoallergenic pillows at Target, an article about an e-mail scam, and six months' worth of marriage announcements from the *Mantanka Bugle,* none of which featured people that Claudia recognized. It was sweet, really, the way that Ruth tried to connect with Claudia, even if her aim was generally a little off. That fertility study, though, might have been a direct hit.

New research has provided the most precise insight yet into when biological clocks start ticking loudly—and it's sooner than once thought. A woman of 27 is already in decline; by age 35, women's fertility levels have plunged nearly by half.

Claudia had examined the article with a pained expression and made a lame joke about her mother wanting her barefoot and pregnant, but she hadn't thrown the study away. Jeremy knew, because he found it in the top drawer of her desk a few weeks later, buried under a box of red pencils and a booklet of obsolete thirty-five-cent stamps. He took the liberty of throwing the clipping away, since Claudia hadn't. It didn't seem healthy to keep it.

Footsteps echoed down the hall and Claudia appeared in the bedroom, much to Jeremy's relief. "That was Samuel Evanovich," she announced. She clutched Jeremy's arm with a slightly sooty hand. Her eyes focused on some point just beyond his shoulder, as if she'd been knocked in the head and was having a hard time focusing. "He wants to meet with me."

Her fingers were leaving black marks on his bare skin. The news seemed unreal, a pronouncement sent from a different dimension altogether; for a moment, he had to remind himself who Samuel Evanovich was.

"That's fantastic," he said, registering her feverish energy. Claudia was flushed, her hand hot on his arm.

"What if he wants to produce my script? It could totally make my career. This could be it, Jeremy. He's a legend. God, if he offers me a good enough deal maybe I could even quit teaching. You wouldn't need to get that bartending job!"

Jeremy patted her hand, curiously hesitant. He wondered, almost from a distance, if it was worth it to get his hopes up again. "What did he say, specifically? Did he say he liked your script?"

She frowned. "Well, *he* didn't say anything, exactly. It was his assistant who called, to arrange a meeting."

"He couldn't have called you himself?" Ruth said, from across the room.

"That's just the way it works in Hollywood, Mom," Claudia said.

Ruth sniffed. "I don't think it's acceptable anywhere."

"Well it's still a really positive sign," Jeremy offered. But he couldn't make himself believe it. Instead, he was skeptical to the point of anger. Wasn't Claudia the one who kept saying that the time for fantasies was long gone? Evanovich hadn't even called her himself; as far as they knew, he might just want to talk about his daughter's grades. Jeremy wondered where his pragmatic wife—the one who wanted him to give up playing music, the one who wanted him to focus on *reality*—had suddenly disappeared to. When had he become the realist in their relationship? She was making a meal out of one pathetic, desiccated scrap: It was just a phone call, some random guy who maybe read her script. She was still a long way away from a studio deal, let alone a massive director's salary that could support them both. *Reality* meant the mortgage that was due next week, and the fifteen grand they needed to repair the house, and the lawsuit against their former tenant. *Reality* meant that fantasies like Claudia's increasingly seemed reserved for indisputable geniuses with charmed lives; people like—for example—Aoki. He reached for the faith he'd always had in Claudia and realized that, for the first time in almost four years, it had vanished. It was a horrid, unwelcome feeling, and he masked it by grabbing Claudia's waist and squeezing tightly.

"So when are you meeting him?" he asked.

"Wednesday, in the evening." Claudia moved Jeremy toward the door, at some remove from her mother. Her voice dropped. "At a restaurant in Beverly Hills."

"I certainly hope he's paying for your meal!" Ruth called.

"*Yes,* Mother."

"Dinner—that's a good sign," he said begrudgingly.

"I'll have to prepare a pitch," Claudia continued, still holding his arm in a vise grip. "I wonder whether he wants to fund the movie himself, through his production company, or whether he plans to go get studio funding? I mean, ideally it would be at least a ten-million-dollar project. . . . I was thinking Penelope Cruz for the sister role, but she's probably going to be expensive, especially if she gets an Oscar nomination this year—"

But Jeremy's attention had already wandered off, toward Aoki. "So, I guess this means you won't be going to Aoki's opening?" Jeremy interrupted. "That's Wednesday night too." It was the first time he'd spoken Aoki's name out loud since the fight, and he waited for Claudia's face to cloud over.

But Claudia seemed too giddy to care. "Oh," she said. "Well, this is more important, obviously."

"Of course. I'll just go by myself," Jeremy said, as a wave of unexpected relief washed over him. Only now could he admit to himself how little he had wanted to take Claudia along. He suspected that nothing good would come from them all being in the same room together; although he wasn't quite sure who, exactly, it was he didn't trust. But was it more dangerous to take Claudia with him, so that her presence would keep him from doing anything regrettable with Aoki (and why did he suddenly think that he might do something regrettable?), or to leave her behind, to save her from Aoki's potential cattiness and the unflattering spotlight of inevitable comparison? "It'll probably be boring anyway."

His response was a touch too quick. Claudia looked at him hard, then shrugged. "Maybe I can drop by for a few minutes before my meeting. The opening is at six-thirty, right? Dinner isn't until seven-thirty."

"Best of both worlds," he offered, not believing this at all.

"Exactly," she said, and smiled, triumphant.

"Who's Aoki?" Ruth called.

"No one," they replied, simultaneously.

They dressed in the living room, in front of a blackened mirror that they'd salvaged from the closet of the guest bedroom. Their clothes still smelled, almost imperceptibly, of charcoal, even after being dry-cleaned. Jeremy had decided three days earlier what he would wear—dark jeans, white button-down, gray sweater under a black jacket with shoulder epaulets; standard male uniform, innocuous enough—and was ready to go in five minutes. It took Claudia nearly an hour to attire herself.

Jeremy sat in an armchair and paged through a water-damaged Richard Price novel he had been reading for six months, absorbing nothing. Human detritus drifted in piles across the living room floor, each precarious island (clothes, books, shoes, linens) representing a group of possessions that had been salvaged from the other end of the house and sorted and stored here, in Jeremy and Claudia's temporary living quarters. In his peripheral vision Jeremy could see Claudia trying on first a silk dress and then a long velvet skirt; a green dress with glittery appliqués at the neck which was far too dressy, and then a pair of jeans with a floral blouse. Everything was slightly wrinkled. She wore a lacy black bra she usually saved for romantic nights out, one that Jeremy hadn't seen in many months.

She caught him watching her in the mirror. "I have to find an outfit that'll work for both an art opening and a business meeting," she apologized, through the filter of the darkened mirror, but Jeremy suspected that wasn't really what concerned her. She was dressing for Aoki, for some illusory vision of her that Claudia had been carrying in her head for the last four years. Jeremy wondered what Claudia's Aoki looked like, whether she was as intimidating and imposing as the real one.

Ruth and Barry were back at their motel room downtown, in all likelihood watching *Animal Planet* from the comfort of their twin beds. Jeremy suspected they were glad to have a night off from hard labor, but the house was dangerously silent without them. Somewhere, deep inside the bowels of the cottage, something was leaking, a maddeningly slow drip. Barry hadn't been able to find the source, even after ripping open the wall in the bathroom and peering down into the guts of the plumbing. "Maybe the house is still draining," he'd said. Jeremy thought it sounded as if the house were crying.

Claudia tried on a snug black dress that Jeremy hadn't seen her wear before. "That's nice," he said, eager to go. "Wear that."

Claudia examined herself critically. "It's too tight," she said. She yanked the dress over her head and flung it on the floor. "Oh, screw this," she muttered. She dug through another pile of clothes and pulled out a knit wrap top and a plain denim skirt, one he'd seen her wear a hundred times. She zipped it and turned to him, pointing her index fingers down at the skirt for his approval. He gave her the thumbs-up, eager to get on the road.

"We're going to be late," he pointed out.

"Aoki can wait," Claudia said to the mirror. But she sat down on the couch across from him and wedged on a pair of heels, apparently finished. Standing, she wobbled slightly, her lips set in a grim line of determination.

"OK," she said. "Let's do this."

In the driveway, their sooty cars sat side by side, streaked with calcified ash and dried morning dew. The days were growing short—daylight savings time would end that weekend—and overhead the sky was momentarily the color of a crossing guard's uniform, a lurid sentinel orange. Jeremy unlocked his car door and then paused as he realized that Claudia was staring across the street.

"Mary?" Claudia asked. It was neither a shout nor a statement, more of a whimper of surprise.

In the road stood a short teenage girl, her hair plaited in two prim braids and an oversized Mickey Mouse T-shirt hanging over her jeans. The girl—Mary?—had just exited the driver's seat of a blue Honda Civic with a sticker that said JESUS ES EL REY on the battered bumper. The girl looked at Claudia, and Claudia looked at her; there was a clear minute when both seemed to be wishing that the other person would disappear, before Mary unleashed a bright gap-toothed smile.

"Hi, Mrs. Munger," she called.

Claudia turned to Jeremy and muttered under her breath. "It's my student. The one who writes those over-the-top essays. This is just creepy. Is she *stalking* me?" Then she turned back to Mary and waved.

Mary walked closer. "Is this your house?" She looked at the house, with the building supplies piled up in the driveway; and then at Jeremy; and then back at Claudia. "Is this your husband?"

Claudia hesitated, visibly flustered by the girl's presence, so Jeremy took it upon himself to make the introduction. "Yes, I'm the husband," he said. "I'm Jeremy."

"Nice to meet you, Mr. Munger," Mary offered.

"What are you doing here, Mary?" Claudia asked, her voice pitching two levels too high.

Mary hesitated in the middle of the road. The horn of the Honda Civic sounded twice, causing all three of them to jump. They turned to stare at the car. In the passenger seat, Jeremy could make out the recognizable bulk of Dolores, staring at them through the windshield. The horn honked again, and Mary backed away.

"My grandma," she said. "She lives over there. I gave her a ride to the doctor. She has lupus."

"Oh." The expression on Claudia's face morphed into one of confused relief as Mary turned away from them and jogged to the Civic's passenger-side door. Jeremy watched as the girl reached in and used both hands to heave her grandmother up from the seat. She nearly buckled under the old woman's weight, enveloped in an acre of floral housedress as she propped Dolores upright into a standing position. The old woman trained her rheumy eyes on Jeremy and Claudia and then turned away, pretending she hadn't seen them. Jeremy thought, for just a moment, that the old lady looked embarrassed.

"Abuelita," Mary said, using the amplified speech that young people

reserve exclusively for speaking to the elderly. "Abuelita, this is my
teacher, Mrs. Munger." But the old lady was shuffling toward her own
front stoop, moving surprisingly quickly considering her infirmities.
Mary followed, lowering her voice. *"Señora Munger es mi maestra. Maestra de cine."*

Dolores lifted a hand in a reluctant acknowledgment without bothering to turn all the way around. It was still the most friendly gesture,
Jeremy thought, that he'd ever received from her. Mary put her hand
out to take her grandmother's elbow, and the old woman leaned into it.
She patted her granddaughter's arm, clutching her tightly, and let Mary
steer her up the path. Beside the sturdy young teenager, Dolores looked
brittle and ancient, as if the elephantine calves holding her upright
might crack and crumble at any moment.

The whole scenario made Jeremy's skin crawl. It was the first time
he'd heard Claudia referred to as *Missus Munger,* and with those two
words she suddenly appeared twenty years older than she was. Even
worse was the fact that this girl—hardly any younger than the girls
who came to see his band!—had called him *Mr. Munger,* a man who by
name alone sounded like he should be mowing the lawn on Saturdays
and buying life insurance policies. So far, he'd been able to regard Claudia's new career as an abstract idea, a vague destination that swallowed
up her time but nothing that tangibly manifested itself in his day-to-
day, but the presence of her student, standing here, brought *Claudia the
Schoolteacher* to life in a way that made him want to run down the hill
as fast as he could.

"We've got to go," Jeremy muttered under his breath to Claudia.
"We're really late."

Claudia tore herself away from the spectacle of the teenager and her
grandmother. She unlocked the door of her Jetta—they were driving
separately tonight—and waved at Mary one last time. "See you tomorrow," she called to Mary. "Don't forget that the David Lynch essay is
due."

Mary nodded. "I already finished it."

"Of course you did." Claudia smiled, a note of indulgence in her
voice, but something about the expression on her face was pinched

shut, as if the existence of the girl was physically painful to her too. But Jeremy didn't have time to wonder about this, as he gunned the engine of the convertible to life, backed out of the driveway, and headed down the hill.

They caravanned in the waning light down the 110 and then across the 10, Jeremy following behind Claudia as her car grew harder and harder to spot. Traffic was heavy. The highway pulsed, then snagged, then came to a near stop. Three of the radio stations Jeremy tuned to were playing the same song, a pop tune by Beyoncé, or was it Rihanna? He couldn't tell the difference. The drivers in the cars on either side of him were talking on their cellphone headsets, having adamant conversations with some indeterminate point on the horizon, hermetically sealed in their air-conditioned luxury bubbles. Jeremy felt as if he were shrinking in size as the urban sprawl spread out before him; just one more set of braking red lights in a vast, convulsing automaton. Near La Cienega, they crept by the wreckage of a horrific car accident, crumpled steel and glass spattered across the road, two tow trucks waiting to hoist the twisted remains to their flatbeds. Someone, somewhere, was probably dead.

He wondered what would happen when he arrived at the opening. Would Aoki be waiting for him at the door, anxious to make a scene or to confront Claudia? Would he be some sort of demi-celebrity, still her most famous subject? Maybe her old New York art friends would be there, a crowd he'd mostly forgotten but still sometimes missed in the abstract. They were probably doing the same things they had five years before—getting falling-down drunk at art openings and then finishing the night at cheap Russian diners, hosting dinner parties that ended as all-night cocaine binges at converted warehouses in Williamsburg, having ugly affairs with each other's significant others. Her friends were rowdy and irresponsible and always in the process of *creating*. Once, he'd fit right into this scene; maybe it wasn't unrealistic to imagine that some things hadn't changed. But it was hard to imagine explaining the mundane, earthly details of his current life to those nomadic butterflies.

He wanted desperately for something thrilling to happen tonight; he wanted, equally, for nothing interesting to happen at all, so he could just move on.

At the gallery, he hesitated only briefly before valeting the car, and then felt guilty when he spied Claudia in her high heels, moving painfully down the street from a parking spot two blocks away. He waited for her on the sidewalk in front of the gallery. It was an enormous white concrete box, sandwiched on either side by luxury boutiques, with a wall of glass windows giving way to the scene inside. Aoki's name hung just inside the entrance in eight-foot-high red plastic letters—just the one word, AOKI, as if her last name had been subsumed entirely by the power of the first. He was perspiring heavily, even thought it wasn't at all hot outside, and he worried that he might appear shiny or even start to smell.

Claudia arrived at his side, reached out for his arm. "That accident," she said, with a shiver.

"I know," he said, moving her toward the gallery door, his pulse beginning to race.

"I'll only be able to stay fifteen minutes, now," she said. Her face was pale and anxious.

"I'm sure that'll be plenty of time," he said, not knowing what he meant. *Time for what?*

The gallery was packed wall-to-wall, the noise level incredibly high, thanks to atrocious acoustics. Waiters passed trays of smoked salmon canapés and champagne in glass flutes. He saw a famous actress and a Grammy-winning musician, and a smattering of artist types with neon-bright clothes and curious hair; but mostly the crowd was middle-aged and wearing conservative attire. Donna Karan and Emporio Armani. Striped ties and linen pants. An elderly lady in an argyle sweater who could have been his grandmother; women in Eileen Fisher dresses that draped over their yoga-mommy bodies. Curators and collectors, he supposed: The only people who could afford Aoki's work anymore. He was strangely disappointed.

Jeremy looked around the room and didn't see Aoki, though he guessed that she was somewhere in the far corner, where the flow of gawkers thickened into a dense clot. He took a glass of champagne and melted into the crowd, drifting aimlessly toward the gallery walls. The show was vast, a mix of old and new pieces. Claudia's elbow jabbed him in the soft spot below his rib cage. "That's you, isn't it?" she asked, pointing to the far wall. It was. Three different times, although Claudia was probably referring specifically to the painting of his profile in orange, rendered from a strange high angle as he looked warily at some point in the distance. There was also a salmon-pink painting of his hand, thickened with calluses from his guitar, and another of his torso, limply splayed across a filthy bed. *Their* bed. He remembered it clearly; the paint-smeared sheets that smelled of unwashed hair, the mattress sitting starkly on the floor of the walk-up, the stains on the ancient ticking. Each painting landed with a visceral jolt, a reminder of a time before, and by the time he'd located them all he was short of breath, as if he'd been shocked back from near death by a defibrillator. Breathing heavily, he pointed each one out to Claudia. He could feel her tensing beside him, registering the blatant sensuality in the images. As he stood there and stared at himself replicated across the wall, he felt as if he were onstage again, the whole world waiting for him to start performing.

"Claudia? Jeremy?" They turned together, too eagerly, but it was only Cristina, weaving through the crowd toward them. She wore a long knit dress that looked purposely homespun and showed off her growing baby bump, with her hair swept behind her in a curling bun. Her cheeks were bright pink with excitement. She arrived before them and gripped them each in turn, hugging them close as if they were already old friends instead of new acquaintances.

"Have you seen the show yet? It's transcendent," Cristina said. "There are three of yours, Jeremy; did you see them?"

"We did. They're very"—Claudia searched for a word—"vibrant. Obviously. They don't look much like Jeremy. Though I'm not much of an art critic, honestly."

Cristina smiled. "I'm sure that's not true."

Cristina's presence seemed to diffuse some anxiety inside Claudia, and she laughed. "Oh, it definitely is. I'd rather not expose my ignorance, if that's OK? I don't want them to kick me out."

"That wouldn't happen," said Cristina. "Art should be democratic. No one person's interpretation is more valid than another's, if you take the universalist approach. Eye of the beholder, la la la." She stepped aside, to let an elderly bearded man who smelled strongly of pot squeeze past.

The clot in the corner had moved down the room, toward the front of the gallery. Jeremy craned his head to see if he could spot Aoki, but she was still engulfed by the crowd, just a flash of shiny black hair hinting at her position. He was crazy to have thought it was possible to have some kind meaningful interaction in this place; he'd be lucky if he even managed to squeeze in the briefest of greetings. He realized he was standing very straight, trying to increase his own profile with an inch or two of height. Would anyone here recognize him from the paintings? He glanced around and realized he might as well be invisible for all the attention being paid him. A young starlet type in a leopard-print dress pushed by, knocking him aside with her elbow.

Embarrassment crept in. Who was he, really? Just a guy in some pictures. He was an outsider here; it was idiotic ever to have imagined anything different. The Jeremy he'd become didn't belong here at all; he understood. Once Claudia left for her meeting and he was on his own, he would probably end up standing lamely in a corner by himself or following Cristina around the room, waiting pathetically for a moment when he could break in and say hello to Aoki. Maybe he would just leave with Claudia. It might even be a relief—honestly, he didn't need any more confusing distractions in his life.

"Is Daniel here?" he asked Cristina.

Cristina shook her head. "I'm here with my boss."

He turned to Claudia. "What time do you have to leave?"

She checked her watch for the third time, visibly twitchy. "Now-ish. Are you going to introduce me to Aoki?"

If they left now, he could avoid that encounter entirely, he realized. They would escape completely unscathed. "If we can find her. I don't even know where she is. Too popular for us, I guess."

"Well, I guess this was a waste of time?" Claudia didn't look like she thought this had been a waste of time; she looked happy, as if the last quarter hour had proved something important to her. Jeremy could guess what it was: that Aoki was no threat to Claudia after all. That here, in Aoki's world, Jeremy was now just as much of a stranger as she herself was. "Are you going to leave too?"

"You can't go yet." Jeremy felt a hand on his arm, freezing cold even through his shirt. The expression on Claudia's face had changed, from relief to cordial wariness. The flush on Cristina's face increased in intensity, to a giddy violet. He looked down to his left and there was Aoki, wedged in just beside him. Her high-pitched voice broke through the din, almost childlike with disappointment. "You just got here," Aoki complained, "and already you want to ditch me?"

She wore a loose white shift that shimmered silver when she moved, tall mirrored gladiator sandals that snaked up her calves, and almost no makeup at all except for a slash of red lipstick. Her hair was twisted into two thick braided buns, which braced her head like apostrophe marks, signing *Here is Aoki!* She looked like a creature you might find dancing in the woods in the moonlight, barefoot. Next to Aoki, all three of them—Claudia, Cristina, and Jeremy too—appeared enormous and ungainly, humans who had stumbled into a fairy's nest.

"Oh, I don't have to leave yet," Jeremy found himself saying. "Just Claudia. She has a meeting to get to." Claudia glanced sharply at him, and he realized that he hadn't introduced her yet.

Before he could, Aoki reached across to grasp Claudia's hand, pulling her in. Claudia tipped over uncomfortably, a strange smile on her face. "So you must be Claudia, then?" Aoki asked.

"And you're Aoki," Claudia said as she pumped Aoki's hand nervously up and down like an overeager discount rug salesman. "Thank you so much for inviting me."

Aoki smiled and released Claudia's hand. "Of course! I was desperate to meet the *mysterious* Claudia. I wish I knew more about you. Jeremy is so reticent sometimes, isn't he?"

You didn't want to hear about her, Jeremy thought to himself. And: *Reticent?*

Claudia blinked. "Oh, I'm not so very mysterious," she said. "It's just that Jeremy likes keeping secrets. Sometimes it takes a crowbar to get information out of him."

"Oh, I remember that well," said Aoki, and rolled her eyes, and then the women both laughed, a touch too loudly.

"How long are you in town for?" Claudia asked.

"I take the red-eye out Friday night, headed back to Europe for a while," Aoki said. "Frankly, it couldn't be soon enough. I loathe Los Angeles."

Jeremy absorbed this with a dismay that startled him; but Claudia was looking looser and more relaxed by the minute. "I used to hate it too, when I first got here," she said chummily. "I know a lot of New Yorkers can't stand the concrete sprawl. But it grows on you after a while. It's a really complex city, so many layers, if you give it a chance."

"It's the cars that get me," Aoki continued, half-ignoring Claudia's explanation. "People here seem to live their entire lives in these rolling leather-lined coffins."

Jeremy was beginning to feel left out. He should have been relieved—the fireworks he'd feared weren't materializing at all; it was all just a cordial meeting between two women who happened to have a person in common—but instead he found himself resenting the fact that he'd been somehow rendered invisible by this conversation. It was as if he weren't standing there at all. Had he *wanted* to be fought over?

"By the way, this is our friend Cristina," he interrupted.

"Such a huge fan." Cristina grabbed Aoki's hand with both of hers and flapped it up and down. "I work at the Modern, here. We have a few pieces of yours in the collection?"

"Yes, a very pleasant little museum." Aoki extricated her fingers from Cristina's grasp.

"I'd love to talk with you sometime about your work, maybe do an interview with you for our patron newsletter?"

"I'm afraid I'm allergic to interviews. I break out in hideous rashes. Doctor forbade them entirely." Aoki turned back to Jeremy, tuning out Cristina. "Come with me. I want to introduce you to a friend of mine, Pierre Powers."

Cristina persisted. "The fashion designer? He's here?"

"He was a huge fan of This Invisible Spot; he's told me many times," Aoki continued, ignoring Cristina's outburst. "He's here and wants to talk to you."

Jeremy battled the murk that had settled in around his brain, making everything Aoki said seem confusing and dangerous. Claudia asked the question that he couldn't quite seem to form. "He wants to talk to Jeremy about what?" she asked.

Aoki swung to look patiently at Claudia. "Working together, of course."

Jeremy found his voice, finally. "He wants me to design T-shirts for him?"

Aoki laughed. "God, no. Music. It's all about cross-platform artistic collaborations these days. I'm painting a line of bags for him. Anyway, he has money and he knows people and he just loves you."

"Really?" His voice was uncharacteristically high; he was giddy. He turned to look at the back of the room, wondering if he would recognize Pierre Powers if he saw him. He knew the name, of course, but had no idea what he looked like in person. His expectations for the rest of the evening took an unexpected, lurching turn, headed toward a much more interesting destination.

Aoki's face was growing pinched with impatience. She took a step away from their cluster. "Just come with me. All the fun people are in the back, in the VIP room. We're going to have dinner after this is over and we want you to join. You don't mind if I steal him, do you, Claudia? You're leaving anyway, yes?"

Claudia's face flickered unhappily. She looked from Jeremy to Aoki and then back to Jeremy again, visibly torn. "It's fine," she said, finally. "I'll see you at home, honey." She leaned over and kissed Jeremy on the mouth, a damply possessive kiss. Jeremy could feel Aoki's cool eyes on them, assessing, patient. He realized he was reddening.

"Don't ground him if he gets home late," Aoki said, her voice as dry as a chilled gin martini. She put a hand on his side and began gently to press him away from the other women.

Claudia's face seemed to freeze, with her smile half-collapsed into a distorted grimace. "Nice to meet you, Aoki," she said, and there was a brief moment while Jeremy waited for her to shake Aoki's hand again, or even attempt an air kiss, but Claudia just stood there, immobile. "Congratulations on a really terrific retrospective," she finished, flatly.

"Oh, this?" Aoki glanced at the walls, gripping Jeremy's waist harder. He felt helpless in her grasp, as if he'd voluntarily relinquished the right to his own will. "Yes, sometimes the oldest things are the best of all."

Claudia

SAMUEL EVANOVICH TUCKED A NAPKIN INTO THE TOP OF HIS shirt, where it protruded straight out from his bulk like a plastic baby's bib. On the plate before him was half a cow, sitting in a pool of its own bloody juices. He smeared butter over the grill marks and then stabbed the flesh with a knife, sawing off a sizable hunk. He chewed it three times, swallowed, and grunted with satisfaction, washing the whole thing down with a slug of watery scotch. Claudia had heard about Samuel Evanovich's legendary appetite, but seeing it in action was something else completely, like watching a private performance by an accomplished maestro. She couldn't decide if she was fascinated or repulsed.

The restaurant was Italian, a wood-paneled den with red leather booths lit from above by yellow glass shades. Waiters in tuxedos hovered just on the periphery, proffering sweaty martini shakers and enormous pepper grinders as if they were holy relics. The clientele was graying, stout, self-satisfied, predominantly male. It looked like someone's approximation of an Old Hollywood hangout. Maybe it *was* an Old Hollywood hangout. Claudia wondered whether it was a sign of her status as an outsider that she'd never heard of it before.

She picked up her fork to prod at her own entrée, pumpkin ravioli with black truffle. It was the sort of decadent treat she would never have chosen if she was picking up the bill herself, but after watching Samuel Evanovich's gastronomical feats she found she didn't have much of an appetite. Instead, she pushed the ravioli around her plate, acutely conscious of the leaden silence at the table. Already they'd spent half an hour on small talk—the discovery of mutual film industry acquaintances (Samuel had once hired RC for a script rewrite), a discussion of the merits of the current Oscar contenders, and a long soliloquy from Samuel recalling a six-month sojourn in Cambodia, shooting a motorcycle movie back in 1978—before running out of comfortable conversation. The only subject they hadn't yet touched was the only one she truly cared about. Was he waiting for dessert to mention her screenplay? Was he waiting for her to bring it up? What was the proper protocol in this scenario?

Samuel Evanovich sopped up a puddle of congealing *jus* with a golf ball of baked potato and then sighed, as if the effort of dining was almost to much to take. "It's like this," he began. "Your script is a smart piece of writing, but it's absolutely unmakable. It's not going to play in France or Germany, so you can forget foreign financing. Your leads are teenagers, so there goes your shot at getting a bankable name. And the love interest goes off to Iraq in the end? Investors are going to run screaming. Three years ago, I might have been able to scrape up ten or twenty million, but dark little dramas like this are going the way of the dodo bird."

"I don't need ten or twenty million. I'm sure I could make it for five," she offered. "Maybe even less, if I had to."

Samuel grunted and rummaged around in the bread basket, coming up empty-handed. A trail of sesame seeds led across the tablecloth from the basket to his plate, a clue to the fate of the missing loaf. He sat back in his seat and rubbed at the place where his cardigan strained across his paunch, and then took a long swallow from his scotch and soda. "Even six months ago, I would have said let's take this around to the indie divisions, see if we can pitch a development deal," he continued. "But honestly, I know what they're going to say already, and I don't want to waste my time."

"I could revise it," she offered, growing frantic. "I'll make any changes you think I should to make it more commercial."

Evanovich shook his hand. "Pointless. It is what it is."

Claudia took a sip of wine, trying to blink back the unprofessional tears that sprang to her eyes. Stupidly, she had not prepared herself for this outcome; had naïvely assumed that their dinner could only have a positive result because why else would he want to meet? She should have known better; she *did* know better, and yet she had somehow let herself get swept away by the old, alluring dream. Now she wished Samuel had waited until dessert to deliver the bad news, because she wasn't sure she could sit here for another half hour and make polite small talk without breaking down entirely.

Samuel continued on, explaining the current state of the film industry—*DVD market in collapse, half the indie financiers closing their doors*—as if Claudia was a naïf who'd just arrived on a plane from Poughkeepsie, but Claudia wasn't paying attention anymore. Instead, she let her thoughts drift naturally back to the anxiety she had been suppressing since she walked in the door of the restaurant. *Aoki.* For the hundredth time, she regretted having left Jeremy behind at the art gallery. She blinked, and the momentary image that danced on the back of her eyelids was of *that woman,* steering her husband away. Her intestines twisted sourly, insisting that she had made a terrible mistake.

For the first fourteen minutes at the gallery, she'd been able to convince herself that all her fears about Aoki had been misplaced. Despite the portraits of him on the wall, the flesh-and-blood Jeremy looked awkward and incongruous at Aoki's opening. He didn't know a soul there, despite her fears that he might somehow find himself surrounded by long-lost friends, and he held himself stiffly, acutely self-conscious. Aoki hadn't been waiting to pounce on him; in fact, she hadn't come to find them at all, and Claudia was able to convince herself that this was because Jeremy wasn't very high on Aoki's priority list after all. Her jealousy suddenly seemed unmerited—it was, she decided, simply the exaggerated insecurity of a woman who, all her life, had feared that she didn't measure up. Just because Aoki was famous and wealthy—just because that one valuable painting held some special resonance for Jeremy—didn't mean he was going to run off with his emotionally unbalanced ex-girlfriend.

Coming here was the right thing to do, she had thought to herself. *He's letting go of something, accepting the fact that the past is gone forever. There's nothing exciting for him here at all. We'll finally be able to move on. Maybe he'll even sell the painting.*

Even when Aoki did finally present herself, Claudia didn't panic. Certainly the woman was stunning, if you went for that whole petite Asian thing, but her appearance was so contrived, her airs so self-consciously dramatic, that it seemed difficult to take her seriously. The Jeremy Claudia knew always gravitated to laid-back types, people who didn't press him too hard or demand too much of him; Aoki, on the other hand, was clearly a lot of work. With just a few words, Claudia could see why that entire relationship had imploded so violently; it was impossible to imagine them ever being compatible in the first place. And so Claudia had let her guard down, had let herself believe that, if anything, Aoki was someone with whom *she* now shared more in common than Jeremy did. Weren't they the only two women in the room—in the world, really—who had spent years of their lives trying to understand his maddening ways? It was a relief to hear that Jeremy had been just as—what was the word Aoki used? *Reticent*—with Aoki as he sometimes was with her. *It's not just me,* she thought to herself, happily.

It wasn't until the end of their conversation that the warning bell began to clang. It was Aoki's hand. Aoki had placed her palm low on Jeremy's waist as if she had every right to put it there, touched him with the possession of a girlfriend or wife. Women simply did not touch their estranged ex-boyfriends' bodies that way. Claudia's breath had stopped in her throat. And then, with Aoki's blithe dismissal of her—"don't ground him if he gets home late"—she recognized a new dynamic that Aoki had somehow forged, with Aoki as exciting lover and Claudia as nagging (*pretty fucking boring*) mom. Before she could figure out how to respond, Aoki simply steered Jeremy away, and he passively *let her do it.*

That was when she knew: Aoki wanted Jeremy back.

She stood there, for a beat too long, watching Jeremy disappear into the throng at the rear of the gallery. When she looked back, Cristina was staring at her. "Well," Cristina said, clearly wounded, "Aoki lives up to her reputation."

"She's a pathological narcissist," Claudia replied, but the insult was a weak rally against a formidable opponent. Even then, she knew she should have chased them down, forgone her meeting, glued herself to Jeremy's side for the rest of the night. *He is vulnerable right now, and that woman is not to be trusted,* she thought. But no. She'd stupidly put her career first and fled here, to this stuffy restaurant, trying to convince herself that Jeremy loved her and would never betray her. On the car ride here, she realized for the first time how pitiable positive thinking really was: an avenue of last resort, a candy-coated mirage for powerless people who had no other options at their disposal. Who had no other way to prevent a husband from cheating.

She'd done that, for *this:* Evanovich's blithe dismissal of her work. She should have known better. She considered flagging down the waiter and asking for the bill, fleeing back to the gallery before it was too late, but she couldn't quite bring herself to be so rude, despite the emotional injury Evanovich had just inflicted. What had this whole charade been about? *At least he liked the script,* she consoled herself. *At least he validated the fact that I have some talent, even if it is a completely wasted talent.* She took a sip of Pellegrino to moisten the dry paste that glued her tongue to the roof of her mouth, and realized that Samuel Evanovich was awaiting her response.

"Well, I appreciate your honesty," she said stiffly, aware that she didn't sound appreciative at all.

"Oh, don't get all touchy artist on me, kiddo," Samuel said. She wondered when she'd been demoted from *Mizz Munger* to *kiddo.* "Shelve the script for a while, and we'll try again in a few years. The industry always goes in cycles. Just think of what we got stuck with in the 1980s. *Captain EO. Howard the* fucking *Duck.*"

We. She revived at his unexpected use of the pronoun. "So what do you suggest I do, then?" she said, deciding to take a chance. What did she have left to lose? "Because honestly, I'm stumped. My film career has stalled completely."

"You know how many working feature directors there are in the United States, ones who actually make a good living doing it?" Samuel said. "My guess, less than two hundred. You have a better shot at getting hit by lightning. It's not a profession for sensitive types. You sure you really want this? What's wrong with the teaching thing?"

"It's not what I want to do."

"Ah, that old story. Let me tell you something: No one gets to do what they really want to do all the time. That's just a pretty fairy tale.

Real life is just a never-ending string of compromises that you make in order to survive."

Claudia picked up her fork and prodded at an oily pillow of ravioli, sending orange squash squirting across her plate, and then pushed it away. The rich, loamy scent repulsed her.

"Not good?" he asked, pointing at her pasta with his fork.

"Not hungry," she replied.

Samuel began to guffaw, a rolling, churning sound that reverberated across the restaurant, ending only when Samuel choked on his own laughter. "Ah, women," he gasped. "Four wives and not a one who didn't worry about her weight."

"I'm not on a diet," she said, growing indignant. "Can we get back to the subject of my career?"

Samuel stabbed at his eyes with the bottom of his napkin, drying invisible tears. "Of course, of course. I apologize. Let's keep this professional, no?" He placed two meaty fists on the table, framing his plate, and leaned in. "Soderbergh."

"Soderbergh?"

"He's got a handle on his career. A smart kid, wife's a real looker, even if some of his films are self-indulgent snores. Anyway, this is the way it works. You make a movie with big mainstream appeal so you can bank a reputation with the studios as someone whose name means box office. *Then* cash that in to make your quirky indie drama. You alternate, like Soderbergh. One for them, one for you. See?"

This wasn't particularly useful advice, she thought. "You make it sound so easy—just make a movie with commercial appeal, like he does? But that's precisely the problem. I'm *not* Soderbergh. I'm ready and willing to make a big mainstream movie but no one will give me that chance in the first place. It's a Catch-Twenty-two."

"Yes, I understand." Samuel sat back in his seat with a frown. "But let me tell you. I wanted to meet with you because I have a project I think you might be right for, a project that calls for a female director. It's not as serious as what you have here, of course, not as edgy, but I think you'll find the themes are universal. The screenplay's got a lot of promise, and you could do a rewrite if you have ideas. I've got it set up at Spyglass; it's a go film, and they're planning on plugging it into their summer lineup. They want it to be a vehicle for Jennifer what'sherface. Looking at a twenty million budget, in all likelihood." He quaffed the last of his scotch while simultaneously gesturing for another one with his index finger.

Lightness, like a soap bubble, rose up in her chest. Working together! It wasn't what she'd expected—it wouldn't exactly be *her* movie—but it certainly wasn't anything to sniff at. *A go film!* "What's it about?" she asked, not bothering to mask the eagerness in her voice.

Samuel shook his head, dislodging bread crumbs from his beard. "I don't pitch. Look, you read it; you tell me what you think. We'll work it from there."

He rummaged around in a battered leather satchel on the banquette next to him and withdrew a script, sliding it across the table. Claudia read the title page upside down: QUINTESSENCE. A felicitous name. She smiled, drawing it toward her. "I'll get back to you in the next day or two," she said.

"I need an answer early next week," he said. "Preproduction is scheduled for late November. We had a director signed on already but she got herself knocked up and had to drop out."

She looked down, a new lump lodging in her throat. "Why me?" she blurted out, before she could think better of it.

Samuel sat back in his seat and flung an arm across the back of the banquette. "You're a talented kid." He shrugged. "I liked that film of yours. What was it called? Funny. Showed promise. Not a lot of women directors out there. And honestly, new talent is a hell of a lot cheaper on the bottom line."

This time the infantilization didn't even bother her. "Thank you," she offered, sincerely. "I really appreciate your enthusiasm."

She smiled helplessly around the room, wanting to share her joy; she found herself directing her grin at the eager waiter who was pushing a dessert cart in their direction. Gelatin confections jiggled on their plates as the cart made its bumpy way across the ancient carpet. The waiter whisked a chocolate pudding under her nose, tempting her—"*Budino cioccolato,* madam, *con panna*"—as Claudia thought, *Everything will still all be all right after all. We're going to make it. I'm going to make another movie. I'll get home tonight, and Jeremy will already be there. We'll celebrate together.*

Samuel grunted. "My daughter," he said.

"Your daughter?" She startled, realizing that she'd forgotten about Penelope entirely.

"She says she's getting an A in your class. Is this true?"

She hesitated. "Yes," she finally said, wondering what Penelope had told him. What part was the bogus grade playing in all this? It didn't matter now, she supposed. The A had clearly done whatever good it could do; she could assuage her guilty conscience that she had made the right decision after all. Perhaps someday the three of them would even be able to laugh about the whole episode together. For now she could put it out of her mind, forget it ever happened.

"Good." Samuel pulled the napkin from the neckline of his shirt and dropped it on the table, waving for the bill. He patted Claudia's hand on the script, absently. "I'm glad it's all working out."

EXT. CONSTRUCTION SITE: DAY

A high-rise construction site in downtown San Francisco.

BETH

walks briskly down a plywood walkway in heels and skirt, a baby strapped to her front and back, pushing a triple stroller with three more, all wearing little hard hats.

A group of male WORKERS walk with her, led by the contractor, GUY (pronounced "ghee").

BETH

points to sections of the half-built lobby as Beth's ASSISTANT strides next to her, writing down her every word.

                              BETH
              This is unacceptable. You're going to
              have to rip out this wall and redo it.

> GUY
>
> But we're already over budget—

> BETH
>
> But it's not right!

The baby on her back starts to cry. She stops abruptly, making a loud shushing sound, jiggling up and down. The men wait, exasperated. The baby calms.

> BETH
>
> White noise. Simulates the womb.

Then the other four start to cry.

> GUY
>
> You know, it might be better if you left them at home next time—?

> BETH
>
> You sound like my ex-husband.
> Anyway—I had to let another nanny go.

> GUY
>
> Now? We got the city inspector in two days!

> BETH
>
> Well, when your babies aren't receiving the care they deserve, you act quickly.
> (sighs)
> It's impossible to find anyone you can trust more than yourself.

She notices the men staring at her silently.

BETH

What?

Guy points to her chest: It's wet.

WORKER
What, one of 'em piss himself?

Guffaws in the group. BETH slips her hand inside her blouse, checking her breasts. The men like this.

BETH

Shit, I'm leaking.
(to group)
That wall better be history or you're
fired.

She rushes off with the babies. GUY watches her go.

WORKER
(coughs under breath) Bitch.

INT. OFFICE ROOM: CONTINUOUS

BETH

drags the stroller into an unfinished office space, juggling her five crying kids. She sits down on a stack of plywood, undoing her nursing bra.

She attaches a baby to one breast, works open the other side, and latches on another one. The other three start crying.

BETH
What do you want, I've only got two!

She juggles babies, her breasts hanging in full view, when she hears a catcall. She looks up.

The ceiling is incomplete. Above her, sitting on a girder, are a dozen construction workers, applauding.

                        CONSTRUCTION WORKER
                    Brings back mammaries of my youth.

The group cracks up. Another worker holds up an Oreo he's eating with his lunch.

                        CONSTRUCTION WORKER #2
                    Hey sugar tits, how 'bout some milk
                    with these cookies?

BETH

sits, smoldering, as the cacophony of her babies competes with the men's laughter.

By the time she finished reading the script, it was eleven-thirty and there was still no sign of Jeremy. She lay back on their makeshift bed and stared up at the ceiling, thinking. Back in its old position on the living room wall, *Beautiful Boy* leered down at her; she rolled on her side so she wasn't looking at it, and the plastic air mattress squeaked under her weight. The living room furniture cast menacing shadows in the glancing light from the lamp in the corner. Her footprints were visible in the dust that had settled on the hardwood floors. She imagined herself floating on an inflatable island, surrounded by sharks, buoyed by air that was slowly leaking out beneath her. Jeremy should have been home by now, even if he had gone to dinner with Aoki afterward. It didn't bode well.

She flipped back to the first page of the script and began—reluctantly—to read it again. The elation she'd felt in the restaurant resolved itself into a tight knot of heartburn the further she read. Surely this was some kind of joke. Surely Samuel Evanovich, of all people, didn't think that a script with *universal themes* and a *lot of promise* would feature eleven boob jokes? *Quintessence* was a 102-page high-concept chick flick about a divorced career mom who hires a male nanny to take care of her quintuplets. It was assembled out of every Hollywood cliché ever conceived, every wooden piece of dialogue and forced plot contrivance, every toothachingly sweet "meet cute" and banal character stereotype. The male lead lived on a sailboat and rescued stray puppies; the female was a controlling architect who needed to learn how to relax. Claudia counted four gags involving women's underwear. There was a makeover montage and a drunken sing-along to a classic seventies song. The movie ended with a chase scene, the woman rowing after the love-interest nanny as he sails away, eventually repudiating her high-powered job to spend more time with her improbably adorable kids.

Skimming the pages for a second time, Claudia could see the glimmer of promise that had once lived at the center of this script—a sly inversion of gender roles, an examination of the meaning of parenting and domesticity in the twentieth century. What remained was probably just a remnant left over from the first draft of the script, before subsequent layers of development executives and producers and hundred-thousand-dollar-a-week script doctors took their stab at making the story more "audience-friendly," the leads more "relatable." Claudia looked at the title page again. There were four credited screenwriters, nine drafts dating back three years.

Was it still salvageable? With a new ending, and a dialogue polish, maybe it could be decent, if not great. Maybe Evanovich was hiring her specifically *to* salvage it; *You can do a rewrite if you have ideas,* he'd said. And yet—was it possible that he himself had played a role in the neutering of this script? Maybe he didn't even *realize* it was bad; maybe he was deadly serious about his belief in the project after all. Because, to be honest—and as the clock ticked toward midnight, she acknowledged this for the first time—hadn't Claudia kindly been overlooking the fact that he hadn't produced a truly great movie in over a decade?

Maybe he'd once been the undisputed King of Quality Cinema, back in the seventies, but his more recent filmography also included best-forgotten titles like *Crazy Girls* and *Crazy Girls 2, Sherrie and Mary Go Shopping,* and *The Defeater.* She saw him, suddenly, as a has-been cling-ing to the victories of his youth, regaling her with outdated wisdom in order to prove his continuing relevance. Aligning herself with him would get her nowhere.

And I gave Penelope that A for this, she thought. Then*: Maybe this is what you deserve for doing that.*

Nonetheless, it was a directing job. And a high-profile lucrative one at that. She didn't have any other options. What was worse, directing a sub-par movie or resigning herself to teaching for the rest of her life? There were plenty of terrible movies made by great directors, she re-minded herself, many of which were commercially successful. Un-doubtedly the best business decision she could make right now was to direct a big marketable movie with a well-known producer. *One for them, one for you,* she thought. *Maybe ten for them.*

The clock clicked past midnight. Where was Jeremy? She imagined the things he might be doing (with Aoki?) that very minute: sitting in a trendy bar with an exclusive guest list, getting drunk with Pierre Powers; having an intimate heart-to-heart reminiscence about the old days at some all-night diner; even (she let this vision flash quickly be-fore she banished it from her mind) having mind-blowing sex in Aoki's suite in some hip design hotel in Beverly Hills. And yet. Jeremy had never cheated on a girlfriend in his life, he'd once told her; he didn't have it in himself to hurt someone that way. Why would he start now? (*Because you're not Aoki,* she answered her own question.) She flipped off the light and lay there in the dark, thinking. The night was silent—no helicopters, for once; no cars or alarms or police sirens—except for the wind that swept the fronds of their ancient palm tree across the roof, gently brushing back and forth across the charred shingles. Deep in the house, something was dripping, and she noticed a creaking sound from underneath the floorboards. The basic repairs on the house were almost finished—her parents were leaving in four days—yet something deep in the bones of their home felt permanently altered, ir-reparable.

The wind picked up outside, sending a loose palm frond clattering down to the almost-finished deck, where it rested for a minute, before dropping farther, into the shadowy depths of the canyon below. She picked up her cellphone and typed out a message to RC: *Career advice required. Can I come over tomorrow eve and pick your brain?* She sent it off into the night, rolled over, and closed her eyes.

By the time headlights splashed across the living room, signaling Jeremy's arrival back home, Claudia had fallen asleep.

When her alarm went off at five-thirty, Jeremy was unconscious beside her on the air mattress, snoring and reeking of alcohol. She lay there for a while in the dark, watching him sleep, wishing she could read his mind, dreading what she might learn if she did. Eventually she rose and clattered around the house, brewing coffee, dressing for work, flipping through the paper. Jeremy rolled over on his back and flung an arm across his eyes to block out the light spilling in from the kitchen.

"Uggggh," he muttered. "Can you keep it down?"

She stood in the doorway, watching him from a safe distance. "So was it fun? You got home awfully late." Her words emerged stiff as planks.

"It was OK," he muttered. The arm across his face made it impossible to decipher his expression. "I drank too much."

"Obviously."

"I had to take a taxi," he continued. His breath was ragged and labored. "It was expensive. I'm really sorry."

He moved his arm to squint at her with bleary red-rimmed eyes. The anguish in his face was clear even from across the room; Claudia softened, weak in the face of his misery. "God, Jeremy," she began, and then stopped, knowing that whatever discussion needed to happen, it couldn't happen now, when she was already running late.

"Really, I feel bad." It sounded almost like a plea.

"It's fine," she said. "We may not have to worry about money for much longer." She stood there, waiting for him to wonder what she meant by this; to link her words to the previous night's meeting with Samuel Evanovich.

Jeremy pulled his arm back over his face. "Right," he mumbled. He lay on the mattress, as still as a stone. It seemed vitally important that he remember to ask her about Samuel on his own, but as she waited it grew clear that he'd fallen back asleep. She gathered her belongings and made for the front door. Just as she was about to shut it behind her, she stopped, hearing Jeremy's muffled voice drifting across the house.

He remembered, she thought. "What?" she called.

His words were muted, filtered through the skin of his forearm. "I love you," he said, to the crook of his elbow.

RC's house was an argument against the existence of gravity, a can-tilevered modernist cube that seemed to float on the edge of a ridge overlooking Beachwood Canyon. The architect had avoided right an-gles entirely, designing the building as an interlocking puzzle of obtuse slopes and unexpected turns and circular steel staircases that seemed to hover without any support at all. The walls facing the view were floor-to-ceiling glass, which opened up so that the home's inhabitants could live among the clouds (on hot days, the smog layer). Floors were poured concrete, polished until they reflected the sky. The swimming pool on the terrace melted into the horizon, vanishing against the Pacific in the distance.

It was a home that would have belonged on the cover of *Architectural Digest,* were it not for the chaos that reigned inside. The living room was a makeshift garage used primarily for the storage of skateboards and bicycles; smears in hues of grass, mud, Sharpie, and ketchup marred the slipcovers on the couches; a ring of smudgy fingerprints, waist high, encircled the glass façade. Tumbleweeds of canine hairs, shed from the twins' beloved chow-collie mutt, drifted along the concrete floors whenever a draft blew through. Ten-year-old boys had wrested control of this house, and RC and her husband had long ago given in to that inevitability. "We'll get it back someday," RC had told Claudia. "For now, it's a fight we'll never win, so I might as well embrace the chaos."

Claudia settled into a Corbusier lounger that was losing its stuffing—Claudia couldn't quite tell whether the chew marks at the seam were human or canine—while RC fixed her a lemonade. She wondered how much RC paid on her mortgage every month and was depressed to realize that it probably wasn't much more than her own, since RC had purchased this house long before the real estate boom began. Back when a million-dollar house was actually a *million-dollar house*.

"*Mom!* I need you to sign a permission slip. *Mom?*" One of the twins—Lucas or Otis, Claudia could never tell them apart—drifted into the living room, sucking on a grape popsicle. He was closely followed by the dog, his focus trained on the ground by the boy's feet. The boy's knees were capped with raw scabs; his short brown hair was mashed flat from where he'd been wearing a baseball cap. While Claudia watched, a purple iceberg sheaved off the popsicle stick and landed on the floor; the dog swiftly lapped it up. (*And that is why RC doesn't bother with rugs,* Claudia thought.)

RC appeared in the doorway, holding Claudia's lemonade. "What for?" She passed the glass to Claudia and glanced at the crumpled paper in Lucas/Otis's hand.

"Field trip?" the twin offered hopefully. "Just sign it."

RC pulled the paper from his hand, examining it. "You want to go bungee jumping? When hell freezes over, darling beastie." She tucked the paper in the pocket of her cargo pants.

The twin scowled. "Justin's parents are letting him do it."

RC kissed the boy on his rumpled head. "A valiant effort, Otis. Next time, try your father. He's a bigger sucker than I am."

"I'm a sucker?" Jason stood in the doorway, holding a can of charcoal lighter. He was bearded and tan from his travels, with ethnic cotton pants rolled up to his knees to reveal hairy calves and bare feet. "Thanks, honey. You're supposed to be helping me convey manliness, not emasculating me in front of the kids, remember?"

"What's emasculate?" Otis asked. The popsicle in his right hand sagged, and the dog dutifully lifted a tongue to finish the melting remains.

"It means your mother wears the pants in this family. Which shouldn't come as a surprise to anyone, considering her sartorial

choices. Hi, Claudia," Jason said. "I'm grilling steaks. Will you be staying for dinner?"

"Not tonight, but thanks," Claudia said.

RC sat down across from Claudia, pushing aside a PlayStation con-
sole to make space for her legs on the couch. "I'm declaring the living
room a no-tread zone for the next half hour, OK? Claudia and I need
some alone time, so go create your vortex of destruction somewhere
else for a while." The twin conceded and ran from the room, the dog at
his heels. Jason disappeared in the direction of the garden.

"Can I borrow your life for a while?" Claudia asked. "You make it
look easy."

RC laughed. "Look at my house. I live in a war zone. My children
are conniving heathens. I sleep three hours a night. Nothing is ever
easy."

"I hope at least it gets easier." Claudia knew she sounded bitter.

"Don't kid yourself." RC rolled a basketball underneath her bare
foot, her brow crinkling as she registered Claudia's mood. "It's all about
coming up with your own coping mechanisms. So what's the crisis?"

"I was offered a job," Claudia said. "A directing job, on a go movie."

"And this is a crisis?"

"It's not a good script."

"Oh." RC leaned forward, bracing her hands on her knees. "What's
the project?"

"*Quintessence,*" Claudia said. "Samuel Evanovich is producing. Know
it?"

RC winced. "It's been bouncing around the studios for years. In fact,
I was asked to do a rewrite on it ages ago. Couldn't do it because I was
busy with pilot season. But I see your dilemma."

Down the hall, the dog barked and the boys shrieked with pleasure.
Claudia felt strangely safe here, cradled inside the familial chaos. "So
should I take the job?"

RC kicked the basketball away and it rolled across the room, bouncing against the far wall. "Tell me why you wouldn't want to do it," RC
said.

"Credibility," Claudia began slowly. "Pride. The desire to make
something great instead of something subpar."

"Vanity." RC nodded. "Idealism. Which is a good-enough argument, considering the soullessness of the industry we work in. OK, now tell me why you *would* take the job."

"Money, obviously," Claudia said. "Keeping my career alive, no matter the cost. Because I have no other options." She hesitated, then bit back the last and perhaps most compelling reason, the one that had taken root in her mind that morning and grown ever since: *Aoki.* In a world full of Aokis, a mundane schoolteacher couldn't compete. It was just a matter of time before Jeremy drifted off, caught in a more alluring wake. But *Quintessence* would keep Claudia in the game. No woman would dare steer her husband away from her if she were a wealthy, successful director. And if freedom from financial obligation was what Jeremy was longing for—and it certainly seemed like this was the case—she could buy it for him: With her salary, she could support him, let him quit his day job, help him go back to making music full time. It would bring an end to *pretty fucking boring,* once and for all.

RC was watching her, waiting. "And?"

"And that's it."

RC tipped her head back and stared at the ceiling, transfixed by a faded blotch that appeared to be dried orange juice. "Don't take the job. It's not going to be a good movie."

Something heavy crashed at the other end of the house; followed by a suspicious silence and then a keening wail, which RC ignored. Claudia fell back in the leather lounger, realizing that this was not the answer she'd wanted to hear. "But maybe I could elevate the material. Rewrite the script. Hire great actors and an amazing DP. Put my own spin on it."

"It's possible," RC said. "But I have to say, I've been paid to polish up bad scripts a hundred times and never truly succeeded."

Claudia considered this. "And if I don't succeed. Would it really be so horrible to work on a bad movie?"

RC picked up the PlayStation joystick and used the hem of her T-shirt to wipe a sticky smear off it. "Well. *I've* worked on plenty of awful projects over the years."

"Yes! And you've survived," Claudia pointed out. "In fact, your career is in great shape. You use a Golden Globe as a toilet paper holder!"

"But I'm fine, morally speaking, with lowering my standards every once in a while, and I'm not sure you are. And directing is different from screenwriting—as director you'll end up taking full responsibility if the film bombs. It could kill your career." RC dropped the joystick and leaned forward, her T-shirt falling around her narrow frame. "You're still so young, Claudia. Do what you love while you still can, before you have to take kids and aging parents and all that into consideration. Do what will make you happy."

"Right. Just do what will *make me happy.*" She tried to imagine what this might be. *Happy* had once seemed like a baseline emotion from which all other states deviated; but right now she couldn't even remember what *happy* felt like.

Jason marched back through the living room, this time with a plate of meat in his hand. "I think the boys are trying to murder each other," he said. He tipped the platter to show the steaks to Claudia. "Grass-fed beef. These cows lived a finer life than any of us have. You sure I can't tempt you?"

A cloud of barbecue smoke drifted in from the garden. The familiar smell of carbon landed with a visceral twist, and Claudia was momentarily unable to breathe—*something is burning!*—until she reminded herself that her own house wasn't on fire anymore. Looking at Jason, Claudia thought of Jeremy and wondered if he was also cooking her dinner right now. She realized that, for the first time in nearly four years, she didn't trust that he would be there when she got home.

"No, I have to get going." She pushed herself upright, removing a few strands of dog hair from her skirt. "Thanks for the advice, RC."

RC stood. "I don't think I was very helpful."

"Of course you were." Claudia lied, now aware that she'd made her decision long before she ever arrived at RC's home. She thought of Evanovich's words: *Real life is just a never-ending string of compromises that you make in order to survive.*

Her compromise would be her career ideals in exchange for her marriage. Honestly, wasn't she halfway down this path already anyway? She just needed to take the final step.

She barely waited until RC's front door was shut behind her before pulling her cellphone out of her purse. There in the driveway, her hands still shaky with charcoal-fueled anxiety, she typed out an e-mail.

Samuel—Read the script: great possibilities. I'm in. I'll call your office tomorrow to get the ball rolling on the legal work. Thanks—Claudia.

Jeremy

SLEEP ELUDED HIM, DESPITE A HALF AN AMBIEN AND A PAIR OF earplugs, despite the black sock he had draped over his eyes to block out the sun that streamed through the sliding glass door, despite his complete and utter exhaustion. Claudia had departed for work hours before, her parents had been dispatched for the day with a phone call to their hotel, and the faint noontime bell had come and gone. He was really pushing it with Edgar, bailing on work yet again, and there was also the troubling fact that his car was sitting with a valet in Beverly Hills. But still Jeremy lay motionless on the air mattress, the afternoon passing as he parsed through the events of the evening before.

He tried to understand where everything had begun to unravel, but most of the night remained a blur. Perhaps that could be blamed on the two glasses of champagne he drank at Aoki's opening; and then the bottles of expensive burgundy that he shared at dinner with her friends, at a French restaurant whose name he could not recall; and the multiple martinis that he polished off in the lobby of the Château Marmont, where Aoki and her entourage were staying. Or perhaps it was because of the adrenaline that raced through his veins all night, an obliterating high that had nothing to do with alcohol at all. Maybe it was the relentless stimulus of new people and places and sounds and ideas that left him so addled.

Or maybe it was all inevitable in the first place, and there was nothing to be faulted at all. It was just the way things had to be.

Regardless, he couldn't pick out a coherent narrative from the previous night, nor could he really remember any prolonged conversations or a clear sequence of events. What was left in his head, as he lay there on the air mattress, was a fuzzy recollection of prolonged pleasure.

But a few specific moments did keep returning to haunt him:

1. Aoki, steering Jeremy toward her friends at the back of the gallery and talking about Cristina. "God, that museum woman was awful. Remember what I was saying about sycophants? That's what I meant. There's nothing interesting about being drooled over." She says nothing at all about Claudia.

2. Pierre Powers falling to one knee in mock adulation, pressing Jeremy's hand to his forehead. Murmuring "a rock God" in accented English, as the rest of the people standing around them titter: a small man with a Dalí-esque pencil mustache and exaggerated biceps, wearing something resembling a pirate costume, with a ruffled white woman's blouse over tight black leggings. "I design my last collection to the sound of your music. I listen to it so many times I wear a hole in the—what do you call it?"—turning to a woman standing next to him and conferring with her in French—"lamination. I did not realize that was even possible!" His breath smelling like milk and cloves. "Aoki says you want to make a new album, yes? I would like very much to be a patron, like Medici. I have too much money. I will help you." Beside him, Aoki smiling, victorious.

3. The back of Aoki's town car, drinking more champagne en route to the restaurant. A strange new view of Los Angeles, from deep leathery bucket seats. A famous actress on one side, Aoki on the other; the flash and snap of a camera shutter as a photographer from *Vanity Fair* takes photos from the front seat. A slice of the southern sky through the tinted windows, neon reflections on the top of buildings, the night illuminated by a full moon. Everything so bright he can't see any stars at all.

4. Dinner. Eating snails drowned in butter and parsley. Speaking about Japan with the fashion editor on his right, photography with the

artist across from him, and the history of R&B music with Pierre. At one point realizing that he has unconsciously slung his arm around the back of Aoki's seat and left it there. Eating a dessert Aoki chooses, something lemony and sour. No one talking about the collapsing economy, or their day jobs or mortgages; money being a perpetual assumption they all seem to share.

5. Sitting in an armchair in the lobby of the Château, Aoki perched in his lap because the hotel has run out of seats. She weighs almost nothing. A new group of people around him, whose names he can't remember, whose conversations he can't hear over the music anyway.

   Aoki's breath on his cheek. Aoki's hand on his thigh, almost painful; his jeans far too tight. They are making a spectacle of themselves, but no one seems to notice. Aoki whispering in his ear: "Come to Paris with me."

6. Kissing Aoki in the women's bathroom, pressing her violently against a white-tiled wall. The sound of water running in the sink, a low-tempo throb from the lobby DJ vibrating the stall where they hide. Stooping to meet her upturned face, his back almost bent in two; her leg flung around his waist so he can touch the bare skin of her inner thigh. Everything so agonizingly familiar: how cool her lips and sharp her tongue, the strange way they always fit together despite their different sizes. Realizing that nothing again will ever be the same.

He cried as he kissed her.

Waking up on that air mattress next to Claudia, knowing what he knew and she didn't, was a special sort of torture. For the first time since August, he was thankful for Claudia's job and the merciful reprieve that her early departure for work gave him. And she was going to be late coming home, too—she'd e-mailed him that she was dropping by RC's house after school—which gave him enough time to banish both the remorse and the exhilaration and settle himself into a Zen sort of state where each moment existed in a vacuum, divorced from the past and the future. Enough time to gather up his remaining fortitude and generate the best distraction that he could: cooking dinner for Claudia. (A distraction for himself? Or her? Perhaps both, he decided.)

He rose around four. Showered and dressed. Drank two cups of coffee, then a beer to calm his nerves. Foraged in the fridge and cobbled together a gourmet feast, a greatest-hits collection composed of Claudia's favorites: salmon in shallot-mustard sauce, roasted butternut squash soup, grilled asparagus with lemon aoli. He put a Flaming Lips CD in the stereo and then tuned it out completely as he cooked. The onion browned in the bottom of the soup pot; the food processor emulsified the eggs into a thick cream as he slowly added in a cup of olive oil; the roasting squash sizzled in the oven. He almost felt OK. And then he didn't feel OK at all.

Come to Paris with me.

He looked in the freezer again, discovered a bag of frozen blackberries, threw together a berry crumble. He set the table for two, but not with the good china; opened a bottle of wine, but not the Pinot Blanc that they'd bought in Santa Barbara and were saving for a special occasion. He didn't it want it to be obvious that something had shifted.

He drank another beer and stirred his soup with a broken wooden spoon. By the time Claudia's keys rattled in the lock, he'd finally taken the edge off his agitation and settled into a mild buzz, so that when she appeared in the kitchen he was able to look at her straight on and offer what felt like a sixty-three percent genuine grin.

"Hi," he said. "How was your day?"

He wasn't sure what he was expecting, but it certainly wasn't the exultant smile that Claudia offered him in return. She was wearing her usual conservative teacher outfit—knee-length skirt, average heels, cardigan sweater over a blouse—but she looked different than she had when she left that morning. More pulled together, maybe, even a half inch taller. Her face was flushed; her eyes, usually a dark hazel, were a vivid green. She was radiant, as if she'd just claimed some victory; or maybe just had a roll in the sack. A vague stir of hopeful desire passed across him.

She stood there in the kitchen doorway, silhouetted by the lights of the dining room, holding her book bag in one hand and her purse in the other. "We can stop worrying," she announced. "About *everything*. I got a directing job. I'm going to make another movie."

The meeting with Evanovich—he'd forgotten all about it. *Evanovich is going to make her movie after all?* For a moment, he thought she was lying; that she had somehow sussed out his misbehavior of the previous evening and had come up with this deception to disarm him. And then he hated himself for doubting her. *Of course Evanovich wants to make her film!* All the old familiar faith in his wife flooded back, and he was almost dizzy with love and pride and shame. For just an instant, it seemed possible that the last twenty-four hours could be entirely erased; that the last three months could be rewound like a faulty film spool, and they might find themselves back in early July, with possibility still spread out before them, the two of them poised to take on the world.

He stepped forward, wooden spoon still in his hand, ready to gather Claudia in a celebratory embrace, ready to disavow Aoki once and for all. "The human trafficking script? He's going to make it!"

Claudia hesitated. "Not exactly," she said. "No."

Butternut-squash puree was dripping off the spoon and onto the floor. He cupped his hand underneath it and turned back to the stove. "What is it, then, a different film?" he said, not quite understanding.

She dropped her purse and book bag on the kitchen table and smiled again. "It's a comedy, called *Quintessence*. It's a go film, and he needed a director."

The garlic for the sauce was burning; he scraped at the sauté pan with the dirty soupspoon, trying to salvage the least charred bits. Something about Claudia's reaction felt suspect, slightly forced. "What's it about?"

Claudia rummaged in her book bag and pulled out a script in a pristine red cover. She tossed it on the table. "Kind of a . . . high-concept romance," she said, staring down at it. "It needs a little work, but it's got a lot of promise. With a strong actress, I could really say something about gender roles in the modern age. It could be my . . . my *Working Girl*."

Jeremy put down the spoon and picked up the script. "That's so great," he said. "It's unbelievable."

She kissed him on the cheek and walked to the sink to wash her hands. "I know! Preproduction starts in a few weeks, so I'll be quitting Ennis Gates soon. And once the checks start rolling in you'll be able to quit your job too. That's what you want, right?" She turned to smile at him.

"Unbelievable," he repeated. It *was* unbelievable; something about the whole scenario didn't quite feel real to him, but maybe that was just because of his blurry mental state. He opened the script and flipped through it, half expecting the pages to be blank. "So I guess you didn't have to worry about Penelope's midterm report card after all. Or did her dad not receive it yet?"

"Oh," Claudia said, her voice growing fainter. "No, they went out a few weeks ago."

"So he doesn't blame you for the fact that she's flunking your class?" Jeremy glanced down at the script and read the last page.

BETH

rows frantically, the five babies in their life vests cooing with excitement as seawater splashes their faces. She docks alongside the sailboat just as MARK comes aboveboard. His dog barks frantically at them.

MARK
What are you doing here?

BETH
Before you sail away. . . . I just needed to
say—you were right.
(off MARK's *skepticism*)
I see now that my priorities were all

wrong. Why do I need big dreams about
changing the world when my family is
already this big? So I'm giving up my
architecture practice to stay at home
with my kids. That's enough for me. I
was thinking I'd open a day-care center
in the house.
(beat)
But I could really use some help from a
professional. Will you give me a second
chance?

MARK

looks out at the Golden Gate Bridge, then flings an anchor over-
board. He leaps over to her rowboat.

                    MARK
        Beth, you know I'll always be your
        Manny.

He holds her in one arm, hugs a child with the other. MARK
and BETH kiss as we pull back to see the sun setting over the
San Francisco skyline.

THE END

That was enough. Jeremy dropped the script quickly, as if the exe-
crable dialogue might infect him, just in time to see Claudia's face turn
a curious shade of violet.

"Right. No. Yeah. Circumstances changed," she mumbled. "So what's
for dinner?"

Lying did not come naturally to Claudia. She leaned down and took
off her shoes, unwilling to meet Jeremy's eyes. He closed the script and
stared at her, understanding that something critical was going unsaid.
"Wait. You *didn't* flunk her?"

"It doesn't matter now." Claudia wandered over to the stove, her back to him. "I smell fish?"

"Did you . . . ?" He didn't finish his sentence, already understanding how the whole scenario had played itself out. The good grade, a bribe to the father; the script, his wife's reward. She'd sold out—for *this* piece of crap? He couldn't fathom why.

He looked up at Claudia, who had turned to measure his reaction. She leaned back against the stove and twisted her engagement ring back and forth, as if it trying to loosen it on her finger. Or maybe testing to make sure it still fit. *She's doing this for me.* He suddenly understood. *Somehow, this is intended for me.* He wanted to throw up, finally feeling his hangover kick in for the first time that day.

"Yeah, salmon," he said, instead.

"Yum," Claudia peered in the oven. "Oh, the kind I like, with the mustard sauce?"

Jeremy looked down at the table, set for a romantic dinner for two people he didn't know anymore. Who was he kidding? Even without the special wine and good china, it was all so obvious; if Claudia hadn't been so distracted by her news, she'd have known instantly what had happened the night before. All that was missing was candles and a big rose bouquet with a card that read: *I betrayed you. Don't be mad, OK?* He wished he'd stayed in bed instead of cooking up this charade; he wished he could just go back to bed now and sleep the rest of his life away.

Come to Paris with me.

He could hear that annoying dripping again, under the floorboards, and Claudia's careful breathing as she stared, for far too long, into the oven. His soup had come to a high boil, burping orange droplets of squash goo all over the stovetop.

He walked over and turned the burner off. "Yes," he said. "I made it for you."

Claudia

"HELLO, STRANGER!"

Claudia paused, coffee in hand, as Brenda lurched down the length of the teacher's lounge to catch up with her. Brenda's hemp tote had swollen over the course of the semester, spilling over into new bags, so that now three amorphous lumps hung from her shoulders, each more distended than the last. Their combined weight forced Brenda to walk with the shuffling gait of a prisoner in full-body chains. Claudia checked her watch impatiently—she had only half an hour before her senior seminar began.

Brenda arrived by Claudia's side, groaning, and dropped her bags on the floor. "I swear the parents should be paying for my chiropractic bills," she muttered. She peered into the pastry box that sat on the counter next to the coffee machine and selected a cranberry muffin, taking a bite. "Ew. Vegan. Must have come from the Hoyts." She glared at the offending lump in her hand and then held the remains out to Claudia. "Want the rest? I'm not going to waste my calories."

"I'm not hungry." Claudia squirted a packet of creamer into her coffee and stirred it. She glanced over to the tables, where Jim Phillips (Gym) was mixing protein powder into a thermos of nonfat milk while flipping through a *Runner's World,* and quiet Hannah Baumberg (Classic Literature) sat underlining passages in *Jude the Obscure.* Evelyn Johnson (Political Systems) lay back on a couch with a student essay tented over her face, her orthopedic shoes dangling over the arm of the couch as her feet flexed back and forth.

"I swear you're the only new teacher to lose weight during her first semester here." Brenda took another bite of the muffin, made a face, and kept chewing. "You're looking skinny."

"Let me guess." Evelyn lifted the term paper from her face and peered over the back of the couch at them. "The brats have given you an ulcer. My first year here I spent a fortune on Xanax. Would pop two with breakfast every morning, another two for lunch."

Claudia's coffee tasted like wet ash. She steeled herself and drank it anyway, desperately in need of the extra caffeine jolt. "It's not that. I needed to drop a few pounds anyway." Brenda raised a questioning eyebrow. "Really, I'm fine," Claudia reiterated, although she didn't particularly feel fine today. This *should* have been her day of triumph—the beginning of a promising new chapter in her life, and the end of her brief tenure at Ennis Gates—but she'd been in a foul mood since she woke up that morning. Maybe it had something to do with dinner with Jeremy the night before, which seemed intended as some sort of mutual reconciliation and yet had been dominated by a freighted silence, as if the number of subjects they were afraid to discuss now officially outweighed the safe ones. They'd gulped down Jeremy's salmon in less than ten minutes, and, rather than talking about the events of the previous twenty-four hours, they rehashed a debate about replacing the damaged bathroom linoleum with subway tile. Finally, they gave up any pretense of romance and ate dessert in front of the television set. Jeremy passed out on the couch by nine, and Claudia let him stay there, while she moved to the air mattress to sleep alone.

She didn't ask what had happened with Aoki; she didn't want to know. *He's here, isn't he?* she'd told herself. *That's what's important. We'll figure out the rest with time.* Or so she tried to convince herself as she lay sleepless on the mattress, in the same room as her husband and yet a world apart.

Brenda had opened the fridge and was peering in. "I also saw a fruit salad in here somewhere, if you're doing the dieting thing, although I really don't think you need to be," she offered.

"That fruit is mine," called Jim Phillips from across the room. He lifted a finger and waggled it in reproach. "And I would appreciate it if you'd stop eating my lunches, Brenda. I'm on a special diet for my ultra-marathon."

Claudia began to edge her way toward the door. "Sorry." Brenda rolled her eyes at Claudia, following her toward the exit. "Anyway, I wanted to confab with you before the school board meeting this week. I think the teachers need to present a united front against this new fascistic code of conduct the administration wants to implement. I'm sorry, but this is supposed to be a *liberal* arts school, don't you agree?"

Claudia glanced at the clock on the wall again. The minutes were disappearing fast; she wanted to check her e-mail before class began to see if Samuel Evanovich had responded. *Codes of conduct*—thank God she'd never have to worry about the administrative arcana of high school teaching again, or about kissing the asses of her kid's meddlesome parents. She almost felt sorry for Brenda and the rest of the teachers, trapped in a world where these banal worries were paramount. "I'd love to talk but I've got to get to class," she said. "Maybe later?"

But Brenda was looking through the swinging glass doors that led out to the quad. "Speak of the devil," she muttered. Claudia followed her gaze down the purple hallway to where Nancy Friar, the principal, was marching straight toward them. She wore a cerise pantsuit and a determined expression. Nancy saw that she'd been spotted and raised a hand in greeting.

"That's my cue," Brenda said. She melted away toward the other side of the lounge and began fiddling with the mail in her cubbyhole, leaving Claudia alone in the entry as Nancy pushed through the swinging doors.

"Just the person I was looking for!" Nancy chirped, as she approached Claudia. "Can I steal you for a moment?"

"I have to prep for my senior seminar," Claudia objected. Nancy was the last person she wanted to talk to right now. She hadn't yet decided how to break the news to her friend's mother that she was going to be quitting before the semester was over. She imagined that it wouldn't go over well.

"Don't worry," Nancy said. "This will only take a few minutes."

Nancy drew her away from the door and into the corner of the lounge farthest from the other teachers. Impatient, Claudia wondered what Nancy could possibly want; it was the first time the head of school had ever bothered to seek her out. *Could she already have heard about* Quintessence *from Samuel Evanovich?* she wondered.

"I want to start by asking if you've been having problems with Penelope Evanovich," Nancy began.

It took a minute for Claudia to realize what Nancy was talking about, and when she did, it felt as if a giant hand had just smacked her in the chest, sending her body backward and leaving her breath behind. "Nothing that comes to mind," Claudia answered, wondering what Nancy knew. Had Penelope gone to talk to her about the illicit A? But why on earth would she do that? "Why? What did you hear?"

Nancy glanced over her shoulder at the other teachers and then dropped her voice. "OK, I'll level with you. Penelope has been bragging to other students that she doesn't have to do any of the work for your class because she has some sort of *special* arrangement with you. Do you know what that's about?"

Claudia's body, from temple to toe, felt as if it had been strung together with taut rubber bands. She struggled to find the appropriate response, aware that each passing moment of hesitation would simply cement her guilt. She glanced around the room, where the other four teachers were doing a bad job of concealing the fact that they were listening in. Brenda lurked by the fridge, slowly stirring her tea; Jim was fiddling with the drawstring waistband of his sweatpants, tucking his shirt in and then untucking it again; Hannah had stopped turning pages in her novel; Evelyn was holding the term paper over her face again, but her hands quivered with the effort to keep it there.

"I have no idea what that's about," Claudia finally said. "Have you asked Penelope what she meant?"

"I wanted to address it with you, first," Nancy said. She fussed with the drape of the cherry-print silk scarf around her neck. "I'm sure it's all a false alarm—this kind of thing happens more often that you'd think."

"Teenagers aren't exactly known for being forthright, are they," Claudia said, and offered her employer a commiserating shrug. Nancy didn't know anything specific, she tried to reassure herself; it was all just secondhand rumors. And in a she-said she-said situation, wouldn't the teacher always win by default?

"They certainly aren't," Nancy agreed. "But we'll need to investigate further, just in case parents get wind of it and kick up a fuss. You know how they are. Anyway, I hope you won't be offended, but may I look at your records?"

Claudia swiftly calculated the possible outcomes of this. If they discovered that she had been blackmailed into doctoring Penelope's grade, she would lose her job—which wasn't the end of the world, of course, since she was quitting to direct *Quintessence* anyway. Except that Penelope would undoubtedly be punished by Nancy—perhaps even expelled—and for that Claudia would surely incur the wrath of Samuel Evanovich and lose the movie. No movie, no job: Penelope's big mouth was about to cost her her entire future. What on earth had possessed her to brag?

She glanced around the room. No one was bothering to hide their curiosity now. Jim Phillips was doing some runner's stretches in the middle of the room, staring blatantly; Brenda was standing with her hands on her hips, as if ready to barge in on the discussion; Evelyn had let the term paper fall to her chest as she watched. Even Hannah Baumberg had finally looked up from *Jude the Obscure,* marking her place with one finger.

"You know," Claudia bluffed, "if you wait here, I could go grab a few of Penelope's old assignments for you. Right now. Just to show you that she's been doing the assigned work."

Nancy smiled. "That would really clear things up."

"I'll be right back," Claudia said, already moving toward the door.

"I'll wait here," Nancy said. Over Nancy's shoulder, the rest of the teachers settled in to their seats, planning to wait for the finale of this show. She wondered whether they were on her side in this dispute and realized that, by keeping to herself this semester—and considering this job just a setback en route to loftier goals—she had pretty much guaranteed that they weren't.

Claudia turned and fled.

Out in the quad, the marine layer overhead was growing dark, signaling the arrival of the first fall storm. A few students meandered across the campus, toting skateboards and iPhones. "Heya, Munger!" called one, a sophomore from her Film Noir course. Claudia jogged across a small patch of grass toward her classroom, passing underneath a polished steel sculpture that distorted her silhouette against the flat sky.

The keys slipped in her fumbling hands, requiring three tries before the door finally opened. Inside, she flipped on the lights and headed for the utility closet. There, Claudia took a deep breath, and another, trying to calm herself. The air was hot and staticky. She tore into her bag, shuffling through a batch of essay assignments, until she found what she was looking for: the most recent offering from Mary Hernandez. "Post-Structuralist Elements in David Lynch's *Blue Velvet*" was a twelve-page tome that name-checked Foucault, Wittgenstein, and Benjamin, followed by three pages of footnotes. Emblazoned on the last page, in teacherly red ink, was an A+. She tore off the cover page and hid it in her drawer.

Digging further, she located Penelope's submission: "*Blue Velvet* by David Lynch," an unfinished three-page essay with no thesis to speak of. Quickly, before good sense overcame her, Claudia gently removed the cover page and stapled it to the front of Mary's essay. Voilà! If you examined the new essay closely, you might notice that the two paper stocks didn't quite match, and that the cover page was typed with a slightly different font, but was Nancy really going to study the essay that closely? Claudia rifled through her drawers, looking for more evidence to doctor. There: her own answer sheets for the last three multiple-choice pop quizzes. She penciled Penelope's name on each one, and then graded each with a red-ink A. It would have to be sufficient.

She gathered her papers and raced back to the lounge. Students were arriving quickly now, gathered in clusters by their lockers, sending last-minute texts to friends who were standing just a few feet away from them. Two girls in regulation blue blazers were huddled in a corner by the entrance to the teacher's lounge, twirling their hair around their fingers as they stared at a boy Claudia didn't know, who was carrying an enormous plaster bust of his own torso, probably the latest assignment from Sculpture and Life Drawing. The hallways smelled like pepperoni pizza, wafting out from the cafeteria's ovens.

Back in the teacher's lounge no one had moved, the four teachers apparently far more riveted by the spectacle unfolding before them than by any urgency to get to their classrooms on time. Only Nancy had switched her position, from the corner of the lounge to a sentinel position by the window, where she could oversee the migrations of the kids outside. She made notations in a notebook, perhaps tracking wardrobe infractions that would later need to be addressed.

Claudia handed the stack of forged assignments to Nancy just as the first bell rang. "This is all I could find in my files," she apologized.

Nancy examined the papers. Outside, the thundering of a thousand pairs of tennis shoes pounded through the corridors. Students shrieked and shouted in the courtyard, oblivious to anything but the melodramatic minutiae of their small sheltered lives. It was almost too much for Claudia to bear.

Nancy glanced briefly at the cover of Mary Hernandez's essay and then turned the page, scanning the text. "They're quoting Foucault now? Good grief. I didn't study him until grad school. I just can't keep up with these kids anymore."

"They're very bright." Claudia held her breath as the principal riffled quickly through the rest of the papers. Nancy gave a brief glance at each quiz and then handed the stack of papers back with a smile. And it was done.

"Well, that's a relief. I'm glad to see it was all just a misunderstanding. I swear, this group of seniors is so gossipy, I don't know where they get it from. Their parents, I imagine."

Jim Phillips let out a small wheeze, perhaps of disappointment, and picked up his gym bag. Hannah Baumberg was already halfway out the door, followed in quick succession by Evelyn Johnson. Only Brenda remained, lingering near the coffeepot.

"I'm happy I could clear it up," Claudia said faintly, rolling the offending papers into a tube before Nancy could examine them further.

"So am I." Nancy reached out to grasp Claudia's hand. Her palm was warm and well-moisturized, just like Esme's. "You know, it's been great having you as part of the team, and the kids certainly seem energized by your courses. We're really glad you're here."

"It's been a pleasure," Claudia heard herself saying, and then Nancy was gone. Through the window, she could see the principal crossing the quad through a crowd of students, a veteran salmon battling against the prevailing current.

I won, Claudia thought, as relief turned her bones to gelatin. *I won.* She backed up from the window, blindly bumping into a sofa. She grabbed the armrest to stabilize herself.

"I just want you to know that I have your back," she heard Brenda saying in her ear.

Claudia turned to face Brenda, who stood just behind her, bags in hand. "Excuse me?"

Brenda stepped in closer, dropping her voice to a near-whisper even though the lounge was completely empty now. "I had the Evanovich girl for Modern Thinkers last year, and she was a nightmare. Contradicted me constantly, always in pursuit of some private agenda, a lazy little girl with a chip on her shoulder looking for the easy way out. I'm not sure what she's got against you, but I count myself lucky that she never decided to go after me."

"Thanks," Claudia said. She realized she was tearing up in appreciation of Brenda's support. *I don't deserve this,* she thought. "But I think everything's OK now."

Brenda shook her head and hoisted the bags back onto her sloping shoulders. She pushed her cat's-eye glasses back up the bridge of her nose with a free forefinger. "I hope for your sake that it is," she said.

Claudia returned to her classroom just as the final bell rang, settling into her usual position behind the podium onstage. It was still difficult to breathe. The kids entering the room impressed Claudia as no more than a colorful, noisy smudge. Only one person in the entire room was distinct: Penelope. The girl scuttled into the classroom last, chewing on a jawbreaker that stained her lips blue. Claudia watched her select a seat in the far corner of the classroom, at safe remove from—who, her peers? Her teacher? She pulled out a pen and began to doodle unconcernedly on her notebook, seemingly unaware of the crisis she had nearly ignited.

Rain pattered against the windowpanes; the storm had arrived. The students had hauled their jackets and umbrellas out from hibernation, and a path of damp footprints led from the door down the aisle, vanishing just before the stage. Claudia gathered homework assignments with shaking hands, as her stomach began to sour with guilt. *You only did what you had to do to survive,* she reminded herself. *There was no other option, barring total disaster. It was the only way to save* Quintessence. *To save your entire way of life.*

She queued up the DVD of Robert Altman's *The Player,* part of a weeklong lesson plan about the portrayal of Hollywood in the movies. The male half of the class busied themselves watching the girl's gym class suffer through a game of basketball on the soggy courts just outside the window. In the back of the classroom, Jordan Bigglesby and Lisa Yang texted furiously on their portable devices. Claudia couldn't be bothered to stop them.

"Let's start by discussing what the title of this movie means," she addressed the class. She was met by a profound silence. Rain battered the campus, amplified by acres of polished concrete. "Did no one care for this film?"

Theodore Kaplan flung a hand over his head, tearing his gaze away from the wet T-shirts of the girls outside. "I liked it," he said.

"What did you like about it?"

Theodore's mouth twitched with concentration. "Um. I thought the Tim Robbins character was pretty bad-ass. Killing a guy and then sleeping with his girlfriend."

From the side of the classroom, Penelope snickered audibly. "*Bad-ass, dude,*" she muttered, and then rolled her eyes so far into the back of her head that Claudia momentarily hoped they might get stuck there, forever blinding the supercilious brat. Theodore turned to stare at Penelope, furious. Next to him, Eric Doterman wadded up a ball of paper that Claudia was fairly certain would be aimed at Penelope's head the next time Claudia turned her back. She twisted deliberately away, letting him do it.

"So you admired the murderer," Claudia repeated. "Did anyone else feel the same?"

Mary Hernandez, a row over, shook her head. "I thought it was a fairly hypocritical movie," she said, lisping slightly.

"Hypocritical how?"

"Well, he's making fun of cinematic tropes, like sex scenes and happy endings and a three-act structure, but then he gives the movie a sex scene and a happy ending anyway. So it's as if he's pandering to the lowest common denominator but also complaining about it at the same time. He's having his cake and eating it too, so to speak." She grabbed a rope of black hair and pulled it over her shoulder.

"A good observation, but maybe that was his point," Claudia responded, finding it difficult to meet Mary Hernandez's eyes. She thought of the effort that the girl put into her work, week after week—God knows when Mary slept, between slinging chicken buckets at Chicken Kitchen and the hours she apparently spent perusing French philosophy books for fun—and felt sick that she had credited Mary's work to her most problematic student. The girl spent her free time driving her sick grandmother to the doctor, for chrissakes; and Claudia's first callous response when she ran into Mary outside her house had been to suspect her of *stalking* her? *Maybe Mary does try too hard,* she thought, *but that doesn't mean I'm not a terrible teacher and an even worse human being.* She pivoted and walked across the stage. "Let me ask another question. What do you think Altman is trying to say about the film industry in this movie?" She waited. On the edge of the room, Penelope cackled—maybe the paper ball had hit its mark?—but even she had nothing to offer for once.

"No one? OK. This is a movie about the moral bankruptcy of the film industry. Altman used it as a way to vent about his own demoralizing experiences in the studio system. It's no coincidence that the screenwriter gets murdered, and the producer is the one who kills him; this is a symbolic expression of the death of creativity in Hollywood at the hands of executive power."

Again, silence. Claudia looked out at the room and saw a sea of faces staring at her with confusion. Or was that silent accusation that she saw? Because who was she to lecture about the moral bankruptcy of the film industry, when she'd just sold out her star student (a scholarship student, at that!) in order to secure a job directing the biggest piece of trash she'd read in years? She gazed around the room and finally landed back at Penelope, who now had her back turned to the front of the room. She was holding up a piece of paper for Theodore and Eric's benefit, some sort of sign with words written on it in capital letters.

"Penelope?" Penelope turned, startled, and dropped the paper. "Would you care to share your sign with me?"

Penelope fiddled with her pencil, examining her handiwork under a curtain of sticky bangs that she stroked, absently, with her free hand. She was wearing a studded, spray-painted leather jacket that looked like it belonged in the bargain bin of a gutter punk supply store; it was definitely not regulation uniform, and the fact that she could get away with wearing this was yet another sign of the Evanoviches' exalted position within Ennis Gates. It was utterly unfair.

"No," Penelope said. "Not really."

A palpable current of shock washed across the classroom: a fellow student so openly defying the teacher? Claudia felt her face growing pink. Months of hot fury at the girl bubbled on the surface, dangerously ready to erupt. *Control yourself,* she thought. *The last thing you need is a confrontation.*

"Fine," she said, slowly. "Then why don't you just tell me whether you agree with my assessment of Altman's film?"

Penelope slouched back in her chair and stared at Claudia. "I don't know. I wasn't listening."

"Clearly," Claudia said, through her clenched teeth. She knew she should just move on to the next student—she had already prevailed today, hadn't she? Penelope wasn't a threat any longer, she could just ignore her for these last remaining days at Ennis Gates and everything would be fine—but she couldn't make herself do it. Something had cracked open inside her, and rage was leaking out. The sarcasm fell off her tongue before she could shut her mouth to stop it. "In that case, why don't you pull from your *vast* experiences in the film industry and simply tell me how talent is treated in Hollywood."

"I have no idea," said Penelope. "Do you? Honestly?" She giggled and looked around the room, an invitation for the rest of the class to join her. A nervous titter started at one side of the room and passed across it, finally undoing in five seconds what Claudia had spent all semester trying to build. Her class disliked her, after all, and it didn't respect her, either.

Worst of all: The students were *right*.

She stared at Penelope and thought of the deplorable *Quintessence*.

What was she thinking? There was no way she could put her name on *Quintessence* and feel proud of herself. If that trite piece of shit was what would get her on the inside track in Hollywood, then she wanted nothing to do with Hollywood. There were better ways to win back her lost career, better ways to distract Jeremy from the glittery toy that was Aoki. She'd gone into film because of her love for a well-told story; because she wanted to make audiences feel something authentic and original, not to be a disposable hack for hire, generating garbage for America's cultural trash heap. It was better to be broke and anonymous than to be wealthy and famous for making dreck. RC was right—she didn't have the stomach for this. She would rather give up entirely.

She tried to remember the person she'd been, the idealist just out of film school who carried a notebook jammed with script ideas; the woman who patched together *Spare Parts* with tenacity and duct tape; the "gimlet-eyed auteur" who went an entire week without sleep in order to capture just the *right* moment when the winter light would convey the pensive air her movie required. Who had she become? Why was she letting herself be tortured at the hands of the Evanovich family for the sake of a miserable chick flick? Father and daughter were tearing away her last vestiges of self-worth. But she didn't have to let them do it anymore.

"What Altman is saying," she said, very slowly, "is that to be an insider in Hollywood—a player, so to speak—you have to sacrifice your principles."

"Yeah," announced Penelope, meaningfully. "Assuming you have principles in the first place."

Claudia was at Penelope's seat in three strides.

She hadn't intended to tell Penelope to go fuck herself; the words just slipped out of her mouth, a good three seconds before her brain was conscious that this was even what she was thinking. For two electrifying seconds after she tenderly muttered the words into Penelope's ear—"Go fuck yourself, kiddo"—teacher and student were both frozen in time, with Claudia's breath stirring a few fugitive tendrils of curly hair, the flush of mortified blood rising up from Penelope's neck just inches away from Claudia's face. The girl smelled of expensive scent, a sickly lavender that burned Claudia's nose, and her skin was caked with a sallow concealer that failed to conceal a fresh speckling of pimples. In those two seconds before time caught up with her, Claudia was touched by her student's surprising, ineffectual little vanities: Her fury abruptly vanished, and instead her heart swelled with painful empathy. She almost reached out and stroked Penelope's cheek: She wasn't the enemy after all, just a pathetic little girl who was buckling under pressure put on her by her parents; a girl who hadn't had enough love, who wasn't as smart as she was supposed to be, and who erected a confrontational façade in order to conceal the pain of rejection by her peers. It wasn't too late for them to understand each other.

And then Penelope jerked her face away, breaking the electric moment, and Claudia's awareness finally caught up with her. She straightened up in horror, noting now the sound of Mary Hernandez gnawing wetly on her pencil, the rubber squeak of the basketball game thumping across the courts, Jordan Bigglesby tapping away at her BlackBerry—all the familiar little noises that had been the soundtrack to her life here for the last few months. The whole class was staring: She could feel it, even though she purposely looked out the window and up toward the rain-spattered sky. They had all heard.

She knew she was fucked even before Penelope twisted her face up and around to meet Claudia's and hissed, "You're so screwed."

Claudia stood upright and turned back toward the front of the classroom. "See if I give a damn," she said.

Driving home, she felt free for the first time in months. It was all incredibly clear. She should have listened to Jeremy back in August. They would sell the house, even if they had to take a loss on it. Hand it over to the bank. Whatever had to be done to get rid of it. She would tell Jeremy to quit that job at BeTee, and instead they would head off to Barcelona, just as he had suggested all those months ago. They'd get jobs as bartenders, or waiters, or au pairs, and write screenplays and make music on the cheap; maybe they'd apply for art grants or find European financial backers who were more open-minded than their American counterparts. So what if they were on the downhill slide toward forty, the time in their life when they should be popping out babies and installing central air-conditioning and contributing to IRAs? That could wait another five years. Ten, even. They might be broke, starting at zero again, but they would at least be doing what they loved. At least they would be able to say they were sticking with their principles. At least they would be *together.*

Thinking of how close they had come to disaster, she almost wept with happiness. The wipers squeaked against the glass of the windshield; water dripped through the faulty seal of the moon roof. The brake lights of the cars in front of her reflected red in the oily pools on the road. She passed through sodden West Hollywood and Miracle Mile and Koreatown, Silver Lake and Glassell Park, heading east and homeward.

No one was home when she arrived back at the bungalow. Someone—her father, probably—had draped blue plastic over the back of the house, in order to prevent the rain from coming in. *Went to Home Depot for more tarps* read a note on the fridge, written in her mother's neat cursive. Wound up with excitement, Claudia drifted through the empty house, examining it with fresh eyes: the patches in the plaster from the earthquake, the water damage on the walls, the smoke stains that were still visible despite her mother's best efforts. It had been a great house once, but now it was a wreck, just four meaningless walls full of charred memories. She would be glad to see it go. She thought of calling up her parents and telling them to go back to Wisconsin today, to stop trying to save her house for her. They certainly wouldn't approve of the step she was about to take and she didn't want to face their approbation. It was better if they just left her alone with Jeremy.

When she returned to the living room, she stopped. The air mattress still lay on the floor, blankets in disarray on the couch from where Jeremy had slept the night before, and the furniture was exactly where it was supposed to be, but something felt wrong. She looked out the sliding glass door, to where soaked bougainvillea leaves were plastered on the new planking of the deck, and farther, to the darkening hills across the canyon, but couldn't quite place where this feeling had come from.

She turned slowly in a circle, examining the room more closely. All at once, she was terribly frightened.

The painting was gone.

Jeremy

THE PLANE LURCHED SLIGHTLY AS IT PULLED BACK FROM THE
Jetway, and then the dark form of LAX began to glide slowly away. It
was drizzling, and the orange hazard lights of the airplane, reflecting off
the pools of rain on the runway, looked like watery beacons illuminating the way out. Jeremy could see nothing beyond the airport, just a
veil of mist, shrouding the rest of Los Angeles in an inky fog. It was almost as if the city no longer existed, as if he were being propelled forward from a vast nothing into some kind of wonderful dream.

Jeremy sat back in his seat, put his feet up on the footrest, and lifted
his champagne flute.

Jeremy had never been the kind of person who longed for a life in
the first-class section. Instead, he'd marched gamely through the aisle of
the airplane toward the economy seats in the back, feeling like a man
of the people. The big leather seats up front were for those overstuffed
titans of industry in their wool worsted business suits, reading the *Wall
Street Journal* and washing down their complimentary cocktail with a
Maalox chaser. He couldn't see how anyone thought that a miniature
bottle of scotch, a foot or two of extra legroom, and *Toy Story 2* on demand could possibly be worth the extra thousand bucks you'd drop on
the ticket. Not when the same money could pay for a new Ricken-
backer, or a month of his band's studio rental, or three hundred
bean-and-cheese burritos. Jeremy didn't mind it in the back, with its
more egalitarian outlook on humanity; he belonged in the portion of

the plane where the reasonable people—the people with the right priorities—sat.

Or maybe this is just how he'd *wanted* to imagine himself. Maybe his whole image of himself as a complacently impoverished artist, a populist and proud of it, was just a form of self-justification, a way of deflecting any shame over being thirty-four years old and still making less than your average new college graduate. Because now that he was here—nestled in the cushiony leather seats of first class, sipping on a little flute of pretty good champagne, with his feet swaddled in a pair of cozy complimentary slippers—any argument in favor of sitting back in cattle class seemed ridiculous. He'd misjudged, radically, how wonderful first class (or, rather, *L'Espace Première*) really was. Up here the food actually smelled edible. The foie gras and lobster entrée were designed (according to the menu he'd been given) by a famous French chef whose Michelin three-star restaurant had a two-year waiting list. There were 112 channels of entertainment available on his own personal monitor. To be watched using his seat's Bose noise-reduction headsets ($400 a pair—he'd priced them out once before settling for a cheaper brand). He had to fully extend his arm in order to get his hand anywhere remotely near his seatmate, and when he wanted to nap the stewardess would turn his fully reclining seat into a real bed with a feather duvet. *Of course I wanted all this,* he thought. *I just didn't admit it to myself.*

"Meester Munger," a voice cooed in his ear, and he looked up, smiling involuntarily. A soignée blond flight attendant (did they keep the prettiest ones up front, too?) was leaning over him, offering a tray of Grand Marnier truffles. Her neckline was just low enough to reveal a crack of freckled décolletage, artfully framed by a silk scarf printed with the airline logo. She smelled faintly of jasmine perfume; her lashes, perilously close to his face, were heavily laden with black mascara. "Would you like to schedule a massage with our in-flight masseuse?" she murmured in accented English.

"Why, yes," he said, knocking back the last of the champagne and proffering the empty glass for a refill. "Yes, I would."

The runway was backed up due to the storm. The airplane idled in an endless queue of jumbo jets, the entire world apparently trying to flee Los Angeles at once. Jeremy didn't care. He was already tipsy. He killed the time with a selection of complimentary magazines, blowing through a *Business Week* (irrelevant) and a *Time* (depressing), before settling for the escapism of an Angelina Jolie action film.

Cold fingers knotted themselves in his and he looked to his right, where Aoki was peeking around the curved edge of the pod wall that separated their cubbies. She was wrapped in gray cashmere, a soft fuzzy thing that encased her from chin to toe in a luxury cocoon. A biography of Max Ernst sat in her lap; the text was German and Jeremy wondered how she could possibly understand it since she didn't speak a word. Her face was scrubbed clean, pale and glowing like the moon. Looking at her, he had another one of those electric surges, and he wondered if he could just blame everything that was happening on some kind of irrefutable chemistry that had rendered him otherwise impotent.

She squeezed his fingers. "I know of this great little studio in the fourteenth arrondissement where you could set up a practice space. It used to belong to a Russian sculptor but he committed suicide over the summer, and now it's just sitting there empty."

"That's awful," he said.

Aoki let go of his hand. She flipped a page of her book and examined a surrealist print of an eagle hungrily eyeing a baby lizard. "He was a mediocre artist and unfortunately, by the time he figured that out, he'd wasted most of his life at it. My sympathy is limited."

"Remind me never to commit suicide. I wouldn't want to read the epitaph you'd write for me."

Aoki laughed. "See, that's why I love you. I know you would never commit suicide."

The use of that word—*love*—was startling; though shouldn't he have expected it? Wasn't that why he was here? Coming from her mouth it sounded like a rusty engine, revving to life for the first time in years. Jeremy smiled, skipping lightly across its presence. "You never know. I might surprise you."

"Don't try, please. Oh, look, Pierre is so shameless; he's hitting on the man sitting next to him even though it's perfectly obvious that the guy is straight. He's wearing Brooks Brothers, for God's sake." She pointed to a seat two rows up, where Pierre—today wearing some sort of haut sailor suit—was carrying on an earnest conversation in French with a man Jeremy's age. "This is going to be great for you, you know. He's just filthy rich and loves to spend money on people he admires. It's like he collects *people* as his hobby. He funded my last art installation, and all he asked in return was that I invite him to hang out with my friends once in a while." She laughed. "Just don't let him tell you that you have to suck his dick."

"Excuse me?" Jeremy was jerked momentarily out of the pleasant fizz of anticipation.

"I'm kidding," she said. "Sort of. Anyway, he knows you belong to me so he'll keep his hands off."

"Oh, I belong to you, do I?"

"You always have," she said, then vanished into her cubicle as the plane finally began to accelerate up the runway. The raindrops on the windows slid sideways as the plane picked up speed and then lifted off the ground. Jeremy let the force of the ascent drive him backward into his seat, happily relinquishing himself to the momentum.

He'd had to rent a truck to get the painting to the gallery. The fact that it wouldn't fit in his convertible was only half the problem, considering that the car was still (presumably) parked with the valet from the other night, anyway. Instead, he summoned a taxi for a ride to the Ryder Rent-a-Truck downtown and then drove the truck back to the house, where he carefully wrapped the painting in a batik quilt that had once belonged to his mother. He wedged the package in the truck bed between stacks of bubble-wrap boulders and then drove this precious cargo across town, arriving at the back entrance to the gallery ten minutes before his appointment with Louisa Poppinopolis.

Only when Louisa Poppinopolis herself came out into the alley, with an expression of mild surprise on her face, did Jeremy realize he'd wasted his entire morning (not to mention the $79 rental fee). The gallerist—a compact older woman with white-streaked Susan Sontag hair—approached the driver's side window, one hand planted on her cardigan-wrapped waist, the other holding an umbrella aloft. "I thought you were bringing slides," she said, "not the whole damn painting."

"I thought you would want to see it in person," he said.

"Slides would have suffered. Anyway, next time you decide to transport irreplaceable art across Los Angeles, keep in mind that we *do* have our own truck. Specially designed to move large canvases. We would have picked the painting up, or even come to visit in person, if we'd realized you planned to bring it here shoved in the back of a rental."

"It wasn't a big deal," he said.

"Let's just hope it survived the trip unscathed."

A swarm of gallery staff had gathered at the back of the truck, waiting for its contents to be revealed. Jeremy rolled up the door and then stood in the rain, his jeans growing soaked from the knee down, as they extricated the batik-swaddled painting from the back of the truck and carried it into the building. Louisa herded them along, waving her umbrella and barking orders, an officious sheepdog.

Louisa was right, of course. Even Jeremy knew the proper way to do this was to shop the painting around—have slides made, set up meetings with the major auction houses, organize home visits so that gallerists and collectors could make appraisals, and then take the highest bid. But he didn't have time for any of that. Once he'd made his decision, at a groggy four o'clock in the morning, he wanted to get it all out of the way as quickly as possible before he changed his mind or otherwise came to his senses.

Sell it, the voice had said. He'd thrashed about on the couch, worried that his spasms would wake Claudia, who slept on the air mattress below him. *Sell it. It's the only way.* And as aware as he was that this was the kind of decision that required the clear light of day and a well-considered pro–con list, he was determined to stick to that middle-of-the-night impulse. *Sell it:* The most cogent thought he'd had in months.

So here he was, still giddy with insomniac certainty, still intoxicated by the madness of his decision, sipping chai from a porcelain cup with a handle shaped like a human femur while staring at his painting. Louisa and three of her minions—earnest-looking young women with severe hair and minimal makeup—stood silently beside him, as politely distant as strangers at a museum. Propped against the vast white expanse of Louisa Poppinopolis's gallery wall, *Beautiful Boy* looked diminished, just a little square of cheap paint in a dusty frame, and he wondered whether Cristina's estimate of the painting's value had been vastly overstated.

"Normally we wouldn't do something like this, but when you said you were *that* Jeremy . . ." Louisa began. She stopped abruptly and took four steps back from the painting, tilting her head slightly to the left as if righting Jeremy's twisted torso in her mind. The art minions, each cradling her own teacup, stepped backward with her, staying respectfully out of Louisa's field of vision. Louisa straightened and walked briskly toward the canvas. She pulled bifocals out of the pocket of her cardigan and pushed them up her nose as she peered at its texture; she put her hand up and let it hover there, an inch above the surface, tracing the path of Aoki's paintbrush with her palm. Then she stepped away from the painting and reached out to take Jeremy's hand, shaking it as if congratulating him on the birth of a son. "Well done," she said, smiling for the first time. "It's an astonishing painting, really. Better than the Jeremy Series pieces we currently have up in the show, quite possibly the best of the whole series. I'm surprised Aoki didn't clue us in to the existence of this one. We would have loved to borrow it for the retrospective, if nothing else."

"Aoki and I were out of touch until this month."

"So last night was a reunion? A shame. Had we known we could have used you as a talking point for the event: *Aoki and Jeremy reunited.* It would have caused quite a stir. We could have pitched a feature to *ArtForum.*"

He could envision this feature; a whole photo spread of the two of them, sitting in her studio covered with paint, tangled in sheets in her hotel room, all very Nan Goldin. . . . A visceral memory—*Aoki's cool, smooth thigh under his palm*—flash-flooded his mind, momentarily drowning out any other thought, and he flushed, as if riding a fever. A silent minion appeared at Jeremy's side, refilling his mug with tea. He glanced impatiently at his watch, wanting to get this transaction over quickly so he could just move on to the next step.

"So, how much do you think you could give me for it?"

Louisa removed the bifocals and tucked them back in her pocket. "Normally we'd do something like this on a consignment basis," she said.

He did not have that kind of time. He did not have any time at all. "I'm hoping to make a cash deal."

Louisa turned to stare at the painting again. "It's too bad. Six months ago I could have asked seven figures for this, but with the art market the way it is now, the best I'll be able to do for you is low-to-mid six."

He drained the second cup of tea, surprisingly calm in the face of such unreal figures. He was fairly sure he was being low-balled. According to Aoki, Louisa had sold out the entire show at the opening party; the gallery couldn't keep up with the demand. "Can you be more precise?"

The minions disappeared quietly into the depths of the gallery, leaving him and Louisa alone to talk business. Louisa walked around the back of a tall white counter toward her desk. Jeremy followed and sat down in a molded plywood chair across from her. From here, he could see into the main room of the gallery, pristinely restored from the party Wednesday night. In the stark light of day, without the distracting crowds, Aoki's paintings looked even more monumental. *I have the upper hand,* he realized. *The painting is a museum piece.*

Louisa flipped through papers on her desk, and then typed something into her laptop, frowning at the result. "More tea?" she asked.

"No, thank you."

She punched some numbers into a calculator with the tip of a pen and nodded. "OK. I can offer you three-eighty."

The only time that Jeremy had come up against a similar figure in his life was when he'd taken out a mortgage three years before; but this was *cash money,* not an illusory figure that passed from bank to bank. Something fluttered disturbingly in his chest, like the first tremor of an incipient heart attack. "You can do better," he said.

Louisa raised her eyebrows. "Can I? That's news to me."

Jeremy took a deep breath and plunged forward, resisting every impulse to just give in without a fight. *It's the least you can do for Claudia,* he reminded himself. "You have paintings on the wall in the other room that you're selling for far more than this. And you said yourself, this is better than anything else in your show. It will complete the retrospective. And I know you have collectors crawling all over your gallery right now, dying for an Aoki original; you'll sell it in a hot minute."

Louisa smiled. A web of tight wrinkles crept out across her face, less mirthful than annoyed. "Tell me what you were hoping for," she said.

The edge of the Danish modern chair sliced into his vertebrae, and he shifted back and forth in his seat, wondering whether the uncomfortable chair was a negotiating tactic on Louisa's part. His clothes were still damp from the rain, his jeans had pasted themselves to his shins, and his feet, encased in soggy sneakers, were freezing. "Six," he said. "Six hundred thousand."

Louisa laughed. "You're insane. The gallery needs to make a profit too."

"Six," he repeated, more firmly this time.

Louisa was silent for a long time. She leaned forward, waggling the pen between her fingers. "I can do five-seventy-five, and that's it."

Jeremy smiled. "Could you wire it directly into my bank account?"

"It's a deal." She offered her hand across the desk. He grasped it, feeling Louisa's papery skin in his own firm grip. "I'll have one of my assistants draw up the paperwork right away."

Jeremy stood up, still amazed by himself. He turned to look at *Beautiful Boy* leaning against the wall, no longer his, and waited to tear up, to feel some kind of grand remorse; but for the first time in five years it held no allure for him at all. It was just a painting. Instead, he felt freed, as if the painting had somehow hypnotized him, held him in thrall for the better part of his adult life, and he had only now managed to break its spell.

"One more thing." He turned back to Louisa. "Do you think one of your assistants could return the rental truck for me?"

For Jeremy's thirty-second birthday, two years before, his bandmates had taken him skydiving. It was one of those perfect mornings—the van drive out to Palm Springs, beers before noon, vistas across the sun-bleached San Jacinto Mountains—but when it came time to actually jump, he froze completely. He stood motionless in the open doorway of the rattling airplane, staring down at the desert plains from 14,000 feet in the air. Behind him, the instructor was awaiting his cue, and his friends were screaming into the wind—"Jump!" "Do it, you pussy!"— but all Jeremy could focus on was the patchwork of dirt and sand below and his own brains splattered across them like a Jackson Pollock paint- ing. And then, finally, he felt Daniel's hand on his shoulder, heard his voice tearing across his ear—"You don't have to do it if you don't want to, Jeremy, we won't be upset"—and he closed his eyes and signaled and then somersaulted sideways out of the plane toward certain doom.

Except, of course, that he didn't die. He opened his eyes to see the ground racing up to meet him and at first it felt as if his body had sep- arated entirely from his soul, a sensation of unadulterated terror but also of complete release: He had relinquished himself to gravity and there was nothing left to be done but accept his fate. And then the parachute exploded out of the pack and jerked him upright, transforming his vi- olent descent into an idyllic drift; everything suddenly reconnected and was clear, as if the meaning of the word *life* really made sense for the first time. He laughed hysterically the rest of the way down, thrilled to be alive and to be safe, and it didn't even bother him when he landed with his knee in a cactus that required a trip to the emergency room to remove the spines.

This felt like that: a sweet, free, pure sensation of complete release. He'd sold *Beautiful Boy,* jumped from that plane, and now everything was going to be OK. Having unburdened himself of the painting, it would be easy to relieve himself of everything else. He was doing something radical, dangerous, intoxicating, possibly lethal—and he mostly felt elated. As he raced home in his convertible, belatedly re- trieved from the gallery valet, the rain thundered across the retractable canvas roof, drowning out the radio. The city flew past as a smear of car dealerships and corporate high-rises and condominiums with views of the freeway, as he crossed town twenty miles over the speed limit.

The part that Jeremy had not thought through, however (if he could be said to have really thought through anything at all) was how he would tell Claudia. Nor, for that matter, had he decided *what* he would tell her. The optimist in him—that portion of him that felt like it was floating six inches off the ground—thought she might empathize. Sure, things had been magical there, for a while—they had been really lucky to have the time they'd had—but even Claudia had to know that things weren't great these days; she clearly wasn't any happier than he was. He couldn't live here anymore, trapped with a woman who could so easily sell out her principles, when there was a whole free world out there just waiting for him to explore. And clearly Claudia couldn't live with his choices either. They were incompatible. It just hadn't worked out, and that was that.

Maybe Claudia would even be *appreciative*—especially with the money he was about to give her. He would be saving her from having to direct that awful script—assuming she even understood that it was awful. So really, he was setting them *both* free.

He kept one eye on the dashboard clock, thinking that maybe if he made it home before Claudia returned from work, he could just leave her a letter explaining the situation. Expressing himself articulately had never been his strong suit, not without the protective insulation of a microphone and a stage and a set of composed lyrics; it would be easier to be concise and definitive if he didn't have to look Claudia in the face and see, reflected back at him, everything that he didn't have in him to actually say.

He swung up the hill toward the house at two, a good two hours before Claudia usually made it home from work: Plenty of time to pack and scribble a note. He was roughly composing the letter in his mind— *Claudia, I'm going away for a while. You're amazing and I don't want you to think that I don't love you, but I think we have different priorities these days*— when he swung into the driveway and realized, too late, that a car was already parked there: Claudia's Jetta, glistening in the rain. He glanced at the dashboard clock again, wondering whether his eyes had played a cruel trick on him, but no, it was only two.

And it wasn't until he had already turned off the ignition and was sitting there immobile in the front seat of his car, trying to suppress a full-tilt panic attack, that he had an even more horrifying realization: The rental car belonging to Ruth and Barry was parked just across the street.

"Shit," he said, to no one in particular.

It was still possible to turn the car around, reverse his journey back down the hill, and pretend he had never been there, but the only person he would be kidding was himself. The occupants of the house would have seen his car pull in; even if they hadn't, they would have at least *heard* it. Thus far, he had managed to convince himself that he wasn't doing anything problematic but was merely taking the appropriate path toward securing his own future. But fleeing from his in-laws? That was irrefutably spineless.

The rain had turned to hail. It pinged off the hood of his car, knocked insistently against the windshield, slashed at his tires. Jeremy took a long, rattling breath and got out. He splashed his way toward the front door with his hands in front of his face, fending off the pellets of ice, and let himself in his house for the last time.

Claudia sat on the couch in the living room, staring at the spot on the wall where *Beautiful Boy* had recently hung. Jeremy stopped a careful ten feet away, watching her consider the void. Hail fell off his clothes onto the hardwood floor and melted there, in tiny puddles. He could hear the sound of a power drill in the other room, grinding away at drywall; the low murmur of Ruth and Barry, benignly arguing about something inconsequential. The house was overheated, and the sliding glass doors to the deck had clouded with condensation.

Claudia refused to look at him. Somehow that didn't make this any easier, after all.

"You're leaving," she said. It wasn't a question. It should have been a relief that she already knew, but instead those two words felt like cactus needles penetrating his skin, and he remembered suddenly how painful that trip to the emergency room had actually been.

"Yes," he said. It was harder to maintain his equilibrium than he'd anticipated.

She kept gazing at the ominous square on the wall where the paint hadn't yet faded. "Did you fuck her?"

"No," he said, relieved that this was technically true.

"But you're leaving me for her."

"No!" he said. Again, *technically* true, and certainly less cruel than admitting the alternative. Anyway, he wasn't leaving specifically for Aoki; he was leaving for a new and improved life, one that just happened to include her. "I mean, she's going to be where I'm going, but I'm not going *for* her."

Claudia finally turned to meet his gaze. There was something new, something *hard* in her face that stopped Jeremy cold. Her eyes were raw and feline, drowning in an angry expanse of hot skin. He took an unbalanced step backward. The drill in the other room whined on and off, on and off. Hail clattered against the windows, threatening to break through. "Cut the bullshit," she said. "You owe me more than that."

He looked at her, trying to figure a way out of this that wouldn't involve her hating him for the rest of his life. "I just need some time off. The last few months have been. . . . Look, you're incredible, and I don't want you to think. . . ." He kept getting tangled in his own words and finally just gave up. *You're leaving. It doesn't matter what she thinks of you,* he realized. He was tired of worrying about how people perceived him.

"Look," he said, more firmly. "For too long I've been living my life for everyone else around me. Now I've got to go live it for myself for a while."

"Oh, please," she said. "Living your life for everyone else around you? You made all your own choices. You're delusional."

He flinched. "This will be better for both of us. But I'm sorry if that hurts you. "

"I'm sure you're sorry," Claudia said. "But that doesn't make it any less of a horrible juvenile cliché."

"I'm a bad guy," he admitted, and it felt good to finally settle into this fact, almost like he'd been given a hall pass.

"You're not a bad guy. More like . . . a coward. You just gave up when it turned out everything wasn't as easy as you wanted it to be."

"If that's what you need to think, go ahead," he said, feeling magnanimous. *Almost done,* he thought. *Just pack and go.*

She didn't seem to appreciate this. Instead, she picked up a couch cushion and hugged it to her chest. "So are you going to tell me where the painting went?"

The power drill ground to a halt in the other room. In its absence, the house was watchfully quiet; even the hail had subsided into a hush, as if listening in on their conversation. Jeremy lowered his voice so that Ruth and Barry wouldn't hear. "I sold it."

Claudia began to laugh, a low-keening cackle. "Of course you did. You don't need it now that you have the real thing." She palpated the pillow under her palms, manhandling an invisible cat. "Financing your fancy new life with Aoki? You'll be living high on the hog, now."

"No! It's for you." he said, hoping this news might somehow steer the conversation in a more promising direction. "I sold it so you could pay off the house. You'll be free and clear. No more financial worries. You can do whatever you want."

Claudia flung the cushion at the empty space on the wall. It hit the plaster and thumped to the floor ineffectually. Jeremy stepped back, surprised. "You've got to be fucking kidding me," she said.

He found himself offended by her lack of gratitude. "Isn't that what you said you wanted?"

Claudia shook her head. "God, you're stupid."

He thought about defending himself, but objectively he knew this was his moment to accept blame. He was abandoning his wife. And yet he didn't feel nearly as guilty as he knew he should. He wished he could split himself in two, be both Jeremys at once and somehow satisfy everyone. "I won't be gone forever," he said, keeping his voice low.

"Right." Claudia shrugged. "Do what you think you have to do. But you're going to regret it."

Jeremy couldn't think of anything else to say. He looked at his clothes lying in heaps across the living room floor and thought that he should start to pack, but found that his feet were rooted fixedly in place. Steam rose off his T-shirt as it dried. A thick burr scraped at the back of Jeremy's throat; he couldn't clear it no matter how many times he swallowed. Unexpectedly, he felt like crying; as if she were the one who was leaving him, instead of the other way around. "Don't be like this, Claude."

She flapped a hand at him, waving him away. "Why don't you just go, Jeremy. Please?"

"Go where?" Ruth stood in the doorway, her hair white with plaster dust. The three kittens tumbled on her sweatshirt, giddily oblivious. "Where are you going, Jeremy?"

Jeremy looked away, out the sliding glass door, hoping that someone else might answer this question so he wouldn't have to. Condensation dripped down the inside of the glass. He watched a drop gather, swell, and dart erratically down toward the casement, leaving a clear snail trail in its wake. Another one gathered in its place. No one said anything for him.

"Nowhere special," he said, finally.

"Oh." Ruth ran her fingers through her hair, sending a shower of dust dandruff over the frolicking kittens. "Well, do you want some microwave popcorn then? Your father and I were feelish snackish."

"He's running off with another woman, Mother," Claudia said. "He doesn't want any popcorn."

"That's not funny, sweetie." Smiling starchily, Ruth turned to scrutinize Jeremy, and then Claudia, and then Jeremy again, her face collapsing further with each swivel. "Oh. Oh, dear."

And then Barry was in the room too, still holding the power drill. "I think we need to pick up a new power pack if anyone wants to make another run to Home Depot with me," Barry began, and then stopped, as it dawned on him that something was amiss. "What's going on in here?" he demanded.

Six eyes fixed on Jeremy, waiting for him to begin his performance. He realized that he was standing on stage; the smallest yet most important stage of all. For the first time in his life, this was not a pleasant feeling. "I'm sorry," he said. "I think I'm just going to go now."

He backed blindly toward the front door, abandoning his clothes, his guitars, his books and papers, his wife—the assorted accumulations of thirty-four years of personal history. It didn't seem necessary to pack anymore; Jeremy felt like he'd already immolated everything of importance, anyway. He realized he was tiptoeing, as if by being very very quiet he might somehow avert further damage.

"I don't understand," Ruth was saying, as Jeremy wrestled the door open and escaped back out into the rain. "He's not really *leaving* leaving, is he?"

And Jeremy hesitated, just a fraction of a second, to hear Claudia's answer before he closed the door behind him. "It doesn't matter, Mom," she said. "He was never really here in the first place."

Driving off, he realized he was shaking, and for a moment he thought it was fear until he realized that it was actually his body uncoiling, finally relaxing in relief. The carnage was in his rearview mirror now, and as he made his way down the hill he decided only to look forward, toward the road ahead. He'd survived the worst possible things in life— death of a mother, demise of a marriage—and everything else from here on would be easy.

And indeed, the rest of it *had* come easily: just one phone call to Edgar to quit his job at BeTee; another three to coordinate the purchase of a first-class plane ticket to Paris (paid for with Pierre's black AmEx); a quick trip to his father's apartment to stash his car until an undetermined date ("Took my advice after all, eh?" Max had laughed. "Good for you. Just stay away from Norway. That country is bad news"). As he was leaving his father's home, he experienced an unfamiliar sensation in his sternum, like the flutter of a moth's wings, and for a moment he wondered whether he was about to throw up, until he realized that what he was experiencing was the weightlessness of being completely unfettered by obligations, by possessions, by expectations. *I'm free,* he told himself. Light seemed to crack through the cloud cover, illuminating the sky above him, settling in around his chest. *I can do anything I want.*

His cellphone rang as he was hailing a taxi.

"You could have got Louisa up to six hundred," Aoki said. "You caved too soon."

"Or maybe you're not worth as much as you think you are."

Aoki laughed. "You know I think I'm priceless," she said. "Are you coming over now? I ran into that actor again, in the lobby, and he wanted to grab a drink with us before the town car comes to take us to the airport."

"I need to stop at the drugstore and buy a toothbrush first," he said. "It looks like I'm going to be traveling light."

He waited for her to ask about Claudia, but she didn't. *What didn't involve her didn't really happen at all, as far as Aoki is concerned,* he realized. This didn't bother him; in fact, it was a relief not to not have to think about what he'd just done. It certainly made it easier to forget; like he'd been granted a mercy lobotomy. *So simple just to slip into something new,* he thought; *the kind of pleasure that comes from putting on a brand-new shirt and realizing that it fits you perfectly.*

"They sell toothbrushes in France, you know," Aoki scoffed, as if it were ridiculous that he would even consider dental hygiene at this moment. She was right, of course. He didn't have to think about those kinds of things anymore, nothing mundane or ordinary. She continued: "Except there they don't call it a toothbrush; they call it a *brosse à dents.*"

She purred the term as if it were a form of sexual foreplay. "Say that again," he commanded.

"Brosse à dents," she murmured. "Now, hurry up."

"I'm almost there," he said.

When he woke up the airplane was dark, the cabin illuminated softly by reading lights. The hour was indeterminate—it could have been midnight or five in the morning, as far as Jeremy could tell. They were flying through a thunderstorm, the plane bouncing as it passed over choppy air. Throughout the rest of the cabin the passengers lay inert in their sleeping pods, wrapped in blankets, blinded by silk sleep masks, knocked out by sleeping pills. Jeremy's television flickered with the credits of the movie that he'd been watching when he fell asleep. The flight attendants were nowhere in sight: The only person who was awake was Brooks Brothers, two rows up, working over Excel spreadsheets with a glass of wine by his hand.

Jeremy fumbled to remove the Bose headphones. White noise filled the cabin—the high-pitched whine of the engines, the hissing air vents, the chattering cutlery in the galley. And there was one more, unexpected, sound: the unmistakable contralto hiccup of a sobbing woman. A very familiar hiccup.

Jeremy sat up. He leaned across his seat and peered over the edge of the wall that separated him from Aoki. She lay motionless on her side, facing away from him, clearly asleep. Except that she wasn't. As he watched, her back shuddered with a suppressed convulsion.

"Are you OK?" he whispered. The plane jerked sideways as the turbulence grew worse. Jeremy braced himself against the seat back before him.

Aoki froze. "I'm fine," she said, in a voice muffled by blankets.

"You're not fine," he said. "What is it?"

The engines droned as the plane began to ascend, working to rise above the storm. Throughout the cabin, the passengers were grumbling awake, jarred by one inconvenience that not even a $10,000 plane fare could circumvent. "If you don't know already, I'm not going to tell you," Aoki whispered. She rolled over to look at him, revealing a puffy, tearstained face—not at all beautiful, not like this—and then turned away again. She yanked the blankets tightly around her and pulled a sleep mask down over her eyes. Jeremy reached out to touch her back, tying his brain in knots as he tried to figure out what he should already know.

And then, slowly, he withdrew his hand.

Above his head, the seat-belt sign was illuminated. A woman back in cattle class shrieked as the plane suddenly plummeted, then righted itself. The soothing voice of a flight attendant came over the loudspeakers as the plane jolted up and down, right and left, buffeted by unpredictable currents. "Ladies and gentlemen, we are experiencing some light turbulence," she said. "Please make sure your seatbelt is fastened. There is no cause for alarm."

But the hair on Jeremy's arms was already standing on end, stirred to life by an old, long-forgotten dread.

Claudia

Day One

Jeremy has only been gone twenty-two hours, according to the clock on the living room wall, but for Claudia time is just an abstract concept, the clock a torture device marking off interminable minutes of hollow pain that promise to stretch indefinitely into the future. It feels like she will be in this room forever, looking out the window at the rain while her parents fuss and flutter around her. It feels like time has gotten itself stuck, and she is doomed to live in some horrible limbo for the rest of her life.

She waits for the tears to come, longs for the terrible catharsis of a meltdown, but what she feels instead is even worse: a crawling numbness, as if all her nerves have been frozen, and she realizes she has been anticipating this departure for some time; it's not a surprise at all. In some ways, she's been expecting Jeremy to leave her since the moment they first met. She thinks—and has always thought—that this is what she deserves.

Instead of hating Jeremy, the person she hates most is herself.

She recalls the Emily Dickinson poem about death—*After great pain, a formal feeling comes*—and even though the comparison may be overwrought (Jeremy is not dead, just gone of his own volition), she understands what the poet meant. *The feet, mechanical, go round . . . a wooden way.* This is how it feels, as she moves from couch to kitchen to bathroom to bedroom, and finally back to the couch, where she flips on the

TV and watches something without absorbing it at all. Her heart is an empty cage where a living creature once resided, that now holds nothing meaningful at all.

"Pancakes," Barry announces, coming in from the kitchen. "I'm making you pancakes."

"You don't need to, Dad," Claudia says. "I don't even think we have flour."

"You need to eat something," Ruth chides. "You're going to make yourself sick this way. It's flu season." Ruth stands at the dining room table, sorting Claudia's underwear into piles: She has done the laundry, without asking. Claudia wants to demand that she stop folding Jeremy's T-shirts into neat rectangles—her mother's Mantankan-born housewifely efficiency is not going to make Jeremy come back (*that* least of all; *that* being half of Claudia's problem in the first place), and even if he did come back, he certainly wouldn't notice the effort Ruth has put into ironing his clothes.

But she refuses to say this, because at this moment Ruth and Barry seem terrified of saying Jeremy's name. It's as if the mention of his existence might break something apart, tip them all down into an abyss. Instead, they tiptoe around Claudia, while she retreats behind her fortification of stony resignation. Her parents have already mopped her floors and washed her dishes and cooked her dinner while she watched TV, surfed the Web, took a sleeping pill and a twelve-hour nap. She senses that she has accidentally landed back in some sort of extended adolescence, once again a ward in her parents' care. This is a special kind of hell reserved for those who have failed at life.

"I'm not hungry," she snaps at her mother, which just makes everything worse, because now she even sounds like a peevish teenager.

Ruth turns to look at her, an expression of infinite forebearance. She walks over and sits down next to Claudia, extends her hand as if she were going to grip Claudia's fingers, and then drops her palm to the couch. "It's OK to go ahead and cry, honey," she says, in a soft voice. "I know it hurts."

And her words *almost* work—they almost jolt Claudia from her stupor. But she recovers herself quickly, biting the inside of her cheek. She realizes that even if she wants to cry, she *can't*—because she won't be able to stop, and right now it is critical to show her parents that their concern for her well-being is unnecessary. Hysteria will just prove to them that she is incapable of taking care of herself, and then they will stay here forever.

Barry appears in the kitchen doorway. "There *is* flour. But no syrup. I'll go to the store. Do you want blueberries too?"

"Blueberries! Doesn't that sound good?" Ruth looks at Claudia expectantly. "Blueberry pancakes were always your favorite."

Claudia shrugs, too tired to fight them. "Sure, Dad. If it will make you happy."

Barry smiles, pleased to have a purpose. Ruth waits for him to leave the room again and then leans in and clutches Claudia's hand. "You know," she says. "I know that we're supposed to fly home tomorrow, but we could change our flights, if you want."

Claudia stands up, disentangling herself. "I really appreciate what you're trying to do for me," she says. "But you have your own lives to get back to. I'll be fine, Mom."

Once she's uttered these words, she wishes she could take them back; she wishes they *would* stay here forever, cosseting her with their undemanding devotion, saving her from being alone. But it's too late.

Day Two

She comes home from the airport to find a message on her voice mail. "Hi, Claudia," it says. "This is Nancy Friar. I've spoken to Samuel Evanovich and am troubled by some inappropriate behavior he told me about. I think it's best if you don't come in to school tomorrow. Or for the rest of the week. Not until the board meets to discuss the situation. I'm very sorry about this. I'm sure that Penelope has been a rather *trying* student, but we do have certain codes of conduct that we really need our teachers to abide—"

Claudia presses DELETE, cutting Nancy's voice off.

There has been no contact from Samuel Evanovich about the status of *Quintessence*, which isn't surprising in the least. Claudia knows better than to e-mail him herself. She has been dumped twice in one week: Hollywood, her other longtime lover, has also fled to more alluring pastures. She is not sure where she went wrong, what another person in her situation might have done. Probably her failure was due to some innate character flaw, one that followed her all the way from Wisconsin and was inescapable despite her best efforts. (*The same flaw that caused Jeremy to leave,* she thinks.) Probably she was doomed from the start. She was never going to make it in an industry so fixated on *hot* and *cool,* no matter how hard she tried, not when she so clearly lacked either.

"You can always move back home," her mother said at the airport, gripping Claudia tightly, just before she and Barry boarded the plane. What had, in the moment, sounded like a last act of desperation now seems—as she stands alone in her half-repaired house—like a possible path of least resistance. *Maybe I belong in Mantanka after all,* she tells herself. *Maybe I should have gotten on that plane with them.*

Day Four

She has finally summoned the courage to look at her bank balance on-line: *five hundred seventy-five thousand dollars.* This is what Jeremy has left behind, his parting bribe. She sits at her laptop with a bottle of gin at her elbow, and counts the zeroes three times, sure that the alcohol is deceiving her, but no—it is over half a million dollars, all hers. No strings attached, until you consider the fact that the money is intended as a substitute for spousal love.

And that, for some reason, is what triggers the great deluge. She finds that she is crying at last. Crying so hard she thinks her tears might fry the circuit board on her laptop. Heaving, painful, blubbery sobs. If her life were a movie, she would instruct the actress playing Claudia to tone the hysteria down a little bit, maybe lose some of the snot and drool and effluvia. She would call her own performance overwrought. Even Dolores, across the street, can probably hear her. But she can't seem to stop herself: everything that has been bottled up over the last few days has finally erupted.

He's gone, she thinks, and it feels like the first time she has really understood this. *And I don't think he's ever coming back. My entire life has vanished, just like that.*

The tears aren't cathartic in the least.

Day Eight

Today, she is trying to decide what to do with the ring.

Claudia never expected Jeremy to give her an engagement ring. She certainly didn't expect the princess-cut diamond solitaire that he picked out at a downtown jewelers. The stone is a tiny half-carat speck that is dwarfed by its platinum pronged setting, and the delicate narrow band rattles against Claudia's knobby knuckle. When Jeremy presented the ring to her, a week after their spontaneous engagement, she at first suggested that he return it. It seemed a waste of money, this fussy, traditional memento that suited neither Claudia's hand nor Jeremy's budget. Looking at the ring wedged in its velvet coffin, Claudia had experienced an unexpected wave of disappointment—in the ring, whose exceedingly modest size would be a permanent advertisement for their penurious state; in herself, for noting this and for still being so shallow and old-fashioned as to lust secretly for a wastefully frivolous two-carat token; and in her new fiancé, for trying to read her mind and failing.

Over time, she came to love it *because* of its modesty; came to see all the emotion and sacrifice and intention on Jeremy's part that it did represent. Or so she thought. Because now, when she looks down at it on her finger, what she sees is *Claude the Clod,* the type of girl who *did* want a traditional diamond ring. The type of girl who Jeremy had maybe once thought he wanted to be with but clearly changed his mind about.

Aoki would never lust after a diamond engagement ring, she thinks. *And Jeremy would never think to buy her one. She probably doesn't even want to get married.*

If only she had insisted that he return it to the jeweler where he bought it. If only they had done something reckless and silly instead—like getting matching tattoos or buying novelty rings in plastic eggs from a supermarket vending machine or just spending the money on a trip to India. Maybe he would still be here now.

It is an idiotic, reductive thought, but one she can't quite banish from her mind.

The ring is suddenly a symbol of everything that was wrong with their marriage, right from the start. Wearing it is unbearably painful.

Should she take it off? Jeremy said he was coming back. Maybe he will; maybe he *is* just "taking a break," a period with a finite end. And yet— the irreducible fact is that he has gone off with another woman. It feels farcical to still be wearing it, this carbonized promise of eternal faithfulness.

She removes it from her finger and tucks it away in a drawer.

An hour later, she retrieves it from the drawer and puts it on again.

Day Thirteen

Her house is knee-deep in plastic and drop cloths. The contractor has moved in with his cavalry of plumbers and carpenters and electricians and roofers and painters, so that the only part of her home that is not currently a construction zone is the kitchen. She has handed over fifteen thousand dollars to cover her insurance deductible, the first check to be written on her new bank account. Her contractor, a diminuitive Salvadoran man named Santos, has sketched out plans not just to repair the essential fire damage but also to remodel the bathrooms, install new floors and windows, add French doors in the master bedroom and living room, and paint the whole house for good measure. He will also undo the mistakes that Barry has made, which apparently are numerous.

Hiring the contractor is step one in Claudia's End the Pity Party Plan, but that's where the plan ends. There is no step two yet. Logically, what she should do next is figure out what to do with the rest of the *Beautiful Boy* money that sits in her bank account, torturing her. But what does one do with half a million dollars? Her first impulse is to give all the money to charity, as some sort of self-punishing, to-hell-with-it gesture, but that seems impetuous and unwise. Then she thinks she'll just pay the mortgage off in its near-entirety, as Jeremy instructed her—but that would be giving him the upper hand. *Screw him,* she thinks, growing angry. *Who is he to tell me what to do with my life?*

Instead of feeling hollow and frozen, she finally melts into a simmering fury.

Giving in to an impetuous impulse, she flees the chaos of her occupied home and goes on a spending spree. She starts at Bloomingdale's and buys herself new clothes for the first time in nearly a year, squandering $2,000 on a leather trench coat that she will never wear. She books a day at a Beverly Hills spa, has her back massaged with hot stones and her face steamed with eucalyptus and her feet entombed in paraffin, and then finishes it out with a $400 cut-and-color from Jennifer Aniston's hairdresser. She has a leisurely lunch at an obscenely trendy restaurant, ordering $40 lobster salad because it's the most expensive thing on the menu, even though she doesn't particularly like shellfish. Every time she slaps down her bank card, she experiences a sort of fury-fueled high, as if each dollar wasted is a fuck-you gesture to the man who has just tried to bribe her not to hate him. As if Aoki herself were paying Claudia's bills. It almost obliterates the pain.

By the end of the day, she looks better than she has in years, which is supposed to be its own form of revenge, if you go by the lessons taught by chick flicks and bad paperback romance novels. Not surprisingly, though, she doesn't actually *feel* better. Lying on the massage table having her scalp rubbed, or sitting in the salon chair drinking organic mint tea, or ringing the dressing room bell to have a different size dress brought to her, she feels instead as if she has become a stranger to herself. She is escaping Claudia and trying on a completely new identity: a self-indulgent person living a life of pampered indolence, someone who cares nothing about the world around her and what it might think of her.

She decides she doesn't like this person very much, either.

Day Eighteen

It's nearly midnight and she has just bought herself a plane ticket to Paris, leaving the following morning. She is drunk, blunted by a $119 bottle of Pinot Blanc that she and Jeremy bought during an anniversary trip to the wine country of Santa Barbara, a bottle they'd been saving for a special occasion. In her inebriation, she has had the following epiphany: *Jeremy wants you to try to get him back, even if he doesn't know it yet. It is exactly the kind of impulsive, extravagant gesture that he won't expect from you, and that's exactly why you should do it.*

She opens another bottle and reserves a car service pickup for 10 A.M. *I will fly to France and retrieve him from Aoki!* she thinks, wobbling as she stands up from the computer. She trips over a pile of tile that the contractor has left in the middle of her living room and lands on her knee. It's bleeding but it doesn't hurt at all—she is strong, invincible! *I will show up in Paris and he will realize what a horrible mistake he made!*

A third bottle, and she passes out on the couch.

Day Nineteen

Someone is pressing the doorbell, over and over again. Claudia wakes up on the couch, fuzz-tongued and lead-headed, and for a moment she can't imagine who could possibly be at the door. And then she hears the idling town car out front.

She thinks she's going to die, right here, in this construction zone of a living room, with plastic sheeting over the windows and the smell of roofing tar making her stomach churn unhappily. What was she thinking? Jeremy is gone of his own free will; he has left her for someone else he loves *more than her.* Buying a plane ticket to France will change none of these intrinsic facts.

The phone starts to ring, and the car service dispatcher leaves a peeved message on her answering machine. The chauffeur bangs on the door one last time before finally departing. She hears his town car rolling slowly down the hill, bumping over the potholes. Only then does she rise from the couch, take two aspirin, and go back to sleep.

And that is where she will stay for the next few weeks: deep in a fugue state, motionless and depleted. To rise from a prone position is unthinkable; to wash and dry her new haircut, impossible; to move Jeremy's belongings from their resting place on the floor of the closet, absurd. So how could she possibly even consider what to do with the rest of her life?

Day Twenty-three

A sign has appeared on Dolores's front door; a binder-paper-sized official notice affixed there with a strip of blue painter's tape. It's been flapping there, yellowing, for nearly a week. From her vantage point in the living room window, using a pair of binoculars, Claudia can make out the largest type: NOTICE OF INTENT TO FORECLOSE, it reads. Has Dolores even seen it? From what Claudia has seen (and she's been sitting here, doing not much of anything, all week), Dolores hasn't exited her house since the notice was posted there, nor have any visitors—not Mary, not Luz—come by to take it down. In this, she feels a strange kinship with her neighbor, both of them cloistered in their own homes, growing increasingly out of touch with the world outside their front doors.

Claudia hasn't changed clothes since Thursday. When she wants to eat, she orders pizza. Mostly, she sleeps and stares out the window into the street.

Thanksgiving is just days away. Despite the apparent acceptance of her heartfelt apology to Esme about the whole Ennis Gates fiasco, an invitation to Thanksgiving dinner has yet to be issued; but there's always RC, who is hosting a catered meal for thirty at her house. Claudia's mother has informed her that it's "unhealthy" to be by herself on the holiday, but Claudia can't bear the thought of being with anyone, either. She can just see those limpid, sympathetic smiles, highlighting the fact that someone is notably not in the room this year.

The wildfires have returned, just twenty-five miles away this time, and today the stinging winds are blowing across the canyon, whipping the chaparral into a chattering frenzy and spackling the top of Claudia's car with pallid ash. *That's someone's home,* she thinks, as she watches the particles rain down on the road, *reduced to a dirty smear on the top of my hood.* The sunlight is thick and golden and magical through the smoke, beautiful with terrible destruction.

On television, the local newscasters report winds of eighty-two miles an hour in Sylmar. Claudia watches videos of the fire being propelled along by this invisible force, devouring entire neighborhoods in a matter of minutes. It makes her weep inconsolably.

By the end of the day, the notice of intent has blown away.

Day Thirty-nine

There is a new sign in front of Dolores's house. This one appears on a frigid Sunday in December, a signpost plopped into the parched earth like just another pinwheel. MOTIVATED SELLER, it says. OPEN HOUSE TODAY! MAKE YOUR BEST OFFER. The listing belongs to RE/MAX, the fourth one on this street alone. The sign is faded and coated with a thin layer of grime; it sags as if overcome by exhaustion, having put in too much time this winter already.

Claudia watches from her living room window as the real estate agent—a middle-aged blond woman in a purple suit with green lizard-print pumps—parks her car in the driveway at promptly one o'clock. She heaves a second OPEN HOUSE signboard out of the trunk of her Honda CR-V and props it open on the curb. She ties three helium balloons to the mailbox. Then she lets herself into Dolores's house and closes the door behind her.

Claudia sits in the window watching the house across the street, idly waiting for the first buyers to arrive. Around two-fifteen, Dale—the violinist from up the street—drives by in his dented Volvo, but no other cars appear on the hill. By three o'clock, it is growing clear that no one is coming.

She isn't sure if it is pity for the real estate agent, curiosity about Dolores's fate, or the realization that her legs are falling asleep from being stationary for so long that finally propels her to tie on her tennis shoes and put a jacket on over her wrinkled T. By three-fifteen she is standing on the doorstep of the beige stucco cottage. The sign out front is, of course, an invitation: *Come right on in! Make yourself at home! This house could be yours!* But old habits die hard; it just seems rude to barge in on her neighbor's home without knocking. Finally Claudia hedges her bets by rapping with her knuckle twice before opening the door and letting herself in.

At first she thinks the door is stuck; it won't quite open all the way. Claudia peers around the entrance, quickly realizing that the problem isn't the door itself, but a pile of indeterminate *stuff*—FedEx boxes, Spanish-language newspapers, dusty baby clothes—that is lodged behind it. The door leads into a short hallway, and Claudia's first impression is of a bat-infested cave, shadowy and musty and claustrophobic. As her eyes adjust, she begins to understand why. The hallway is lined on both sides, from floor to ceiling, with mountains of yet more *stuff*. Mexican dolls in ceremonial garb, staring out from plastic boxes. Religious cartoon pamphlets. Used manila envelopes, addressed to Dolores and Mario Hernandez, dating back thirty years. Men's underwear folded in piles. Unpopped bubble wrap. Years of the *Mount Washington Monthly*—the same free newspaper that Claudia often moves to Dolores's front doorstep—still tied in blue rubber bands. Stuffed animals missing critical limbs, spilling cotton entrails across the mostly obscured carpet. The precarious edifices wobble as Claudia squeezes past, drawn toward a faint light at the end of the hallway.

She peers into the first doorway—a kid's bedroom, though the twin beds, stacked four feet high with detritus, have clearly not been used in years—and then turns to see the real estate agent rushing down the hallway toward her with a hand extended. In the other hand, she clutches a cellphone.

"Marcie Carson," she says breathlessly. "Nice to meet you."

"Claudia." She accepts the real estate agent's dry palm, squeezing it encouragingly. When she takes her hand away, there is a business card nestled there: MARCIE CARSON, YOUR REAL ESTATE PROFESSIONAL FOR TWO DECADES!

"So," the real estate agent begins. She gestures vaguely at the mess surrounding them. "As you can see, this is a house that requires a little bit of. . . . imagination. But I guarantee you that once you remove the previous owner's belongings you'll see that the house is structurally quite sound. It's not a issue of *maintenance* so much as housekeeping."

"I understand completely," Claudia says.

"Can you tell me what you're looking for?"

This is the moment to tell the real estate agent that she isn't looking for a house at all, but why ruin Marcie's day? "Oh, you know," she says. "Someplace that speaks to me."

Marcie ushers her into the living room, judging by the plastic-covered velour sofa, which cowers beneath a mountain of storage boxes. The room reeks of stale smoke, ineffectually masked by lemon air freshener. "Well, this neighborhood is exceptional," Marcie says. "Very up-and-coming. Lots of young professionals like yourself. And this house is an absolute bargain. Worth well over four but we're listing it for three-seventy-five. You know, the owner's been here for thirty-two years and never remodeled, so the home still has all its original period details. That's very rare these days."

A mound of junk by the window has collapsed, and the ensuing landslide of expired coupon books and Christmas tree ornaments and dog-eared board games clears a space through which Claudia can see across to her own house. It is strange to look at it from this perspective, as if she were a stranger observing someone else's life. From inside this dingy lair, her newly remodeled home—the fire-retardant synthetic shingles as yet unfaded, the gray-and-red paint job still fresh from the work that the contractor finished just two days before—looks like a bright beacon of logic and order. How long would it take for her own house to fall into similar disrepair? How many months of failing to throw away the supermarket circulars or take out the garbage? At what point on this road she is already on will she officially become a house-bound hermit too?

Your life could get so much worse, it dawns on her. *You could be Dolores.*

"What happened?" she asks, fingering the business card.

Marcie lowers her voice. "It's a foreclosure," she says.

"Was it the lupus?" Claudia asks.

Marcie looks confused. "I'm just representing the bank," she says. "I didn't even know she had lupus. But sure. I see that all the time these days. These older single women with no real income and depleted savings, they were told they could basically get free money out of their house. They have medical problems, so they take out a second mortgage or a home equity line and use the money to pay their bills. And then it's gone and the payments balloon and they can't afford to stay."

"That's horrible."

The phone in Marcie's hand begins to vibrate. Marcie glances at it, growing distressed. "Well, it's certainly leaving an opportunity for the right person."

"Where will she go?"

"I have no idea," Marcie says. "I'm sorry, but I have to take this call. Why don't you look around for a bit and I'll be right back?" She flips open her phone and rushes out of the living room, talking in a hushed voice.

Claudia follows her out to the hall. She wants to leave, but Marcie is in conference by the front door, preventing a stealthy escape. Instead, Claudia turns right, delving deeper into the house. There isn't much room to maneuver, but there isn't much to see anyway: The house, only slightly smaller than Claudia's, has been reduced to a postage stamp by the presence of so much detritus. In the three years that they've been neighbors, Claudia has never once imagined what Dolores's home might look like inside; even if she had, she would never have envisioned *this*. Claudia can't help but push on farther, mordantly curious to see how bad things could possibly get.

There are photographs on the wall in the hallway. The biggest is a framed black-and-white photo of a grandly mustachioed Mexican man: her husband? Claudia wonders. Portraits of assorted babies taken over the last few decades, one of them undoubtedly Luz. A framed watercolor of Jesus. And a seventh-grade school photo of a gap-toothed girl with twin black ponytails, her starched white shirt and stiff back slightly too formal for a class portrait, as if she has far grander ambitions than surviving junior high: Mary Hernandez.

Looking at the picture, Claudia recalls the college recommendation she never wrote—it's far too late now—and hates herself even more. Only now that she has lost her Ennis Gates job does she see how woefully she squandered that opportunity. Teaching could have been a great career. It might even have brought her fulfillment, if she had let it. Instead, Mary, too, is probably better off without her.

She squeezes into the kitchen, which bears a marked resemblance to her own—the same avocado-colored linoleum, the same vintage stove, the same wooden cabinets splintering at the corners—except for its dismal state of repair. Dusty flats of canned frijoles sit in the corner. Crayon children's drawings are stuck to the fridge with yellowing tape. The sink drips yellow water from a water-stained faucet. The light in the room is dim; when Claudia looks up, she realizes that this is because the overhead fixture is filled with a layer of dead bugs.

From the back door, Claudia gazes out into the garden. A path lined with colored glass bottle bottoms leads up the hill, vanishing into a tangle of dust-strangled ivy and thorny succulents and overgrown thistle. Buried deep within the ivy is a prefab children's play set, spotted with rust. Claudia steps out the back door, drawn toward the one patch of sunshine.

When she looks to the left, she stops. In that little beacon of sun, Dolores has staked her final claim—a folding lounge chair missing two plastic slats, a withered pot of petunias, an overflowing ashtray. She sits there now, clad in a floral housecoat, fanning herself with a PennySaver and smoking a foul-smelling cigarette. Both activities come to an abrupt halt when she sees Claudia standing in her backyard.

"You," she says.

"Me," Claudia agrees.

The cigarette resumes its trajectory toward Dolores's mouth. The ash collapses under its own weight en route, landing in her formidable cleavage. Claudia imagines Dolores sitting here by herself every day, a lonely old woman with nothing to keep her company but some dusty piles of junk, the skunks skittering about under the house, and the occasional obligatory visit from her children and grandchildren. The sadness of this small empty life makes Claudia want to weep.

"I'm sorry," she says. "I was just leaving."

But Dolores is heaving in the chair. Her bosom bounces from her failed attempt to lift her mass upright. She gives up and settles back, looking up at Claudia. "You buy my house?" She jabs the cigarette for emphasis.

"I already have a house," Claudia says.

"This house ees good house," Dolores continues, her sandpapered voice rasping. "I leeve here *thirty-two* years. Three kids."

She bares her teeth at Claudia, revealing nicotine-stained teeth. It is the first time that Claudia has ever seen her smile, and it seems to hurt her; the muscles of her upper lip tremble with the effort of lifting her mouth into an upward curve. It appears that she is trying not to cry.

"I don't want two houses," Claudia says, once again feeling like she is supposed to apologize. She sees what she must look like to the old woman: the vulture from across the street, swooping in to pick over her ailing carcass. Does Dolores mistakenly think she is rich, Claudia wonders? Is that why she has always hated them? *But you* are *rich,* she realizes suddenly. *You have over half a million in the bank. And you were still rich, comparatively speaking, even when you didn't.*

"There you are!" The real estate agent bursts out the back door, still wielding the cell phone. She grips Claudia's jacket, tugging her gently back toward the door. "I see you've met Mrs. Hernandez. Don't worry, she knows she has to vacate before the property goes into escrow."

Dolores takes another drag of her cigarette. Her face collapses, her bushy gray brows beetling toward her nose, the corners of her mouth curling toward her chin. She looks up the hill, as if absorbed by something in the ivy, determined to ignore the interlopers in her garden. Claudia lets Marcie Carson steer her back to the dark interior of the house, leaving the old lady alone in the garden.

Once inside, Claudia makes a beeline for the front door. The hand falls from her elbow as the dismayed real estate agent watches her flee. "You have my number!" Marcie calls after her. "Think about it. The bank is very motivated to move this house. We're willing to be flexible on price."

Claudia turns to wave goodbye without breaking her stride, careening sideways as she dodges piles of junk. Her hip knocks into one of the teetering pillars, sending its contents sliding to the floor. Claudia stares down at Dolores's belongings as Marcie crouches besides her, struggling to upright a stack of tattered *People en Espanol* magazines dating back to 1998. A cardboard box full of curling family photographs cascades across the hallway floor, and Claudia bends to pick one up.

It's a faded snapshot of Dolores and the mustachioed man with three teenage children, standing in front of this house in the 1980s. Dolores is almost unrecognizable: a trim woman in a plaid dress, her long hair woven up in braids, radiantly smiling as her husband tucks his arm around her waist. The house behind her is painted yellow—the same paint job that will eventually fade into its current colorless beige—and the first of the garden gnomes is already positioned amid the begonias in the front yard. One of the teenage girls (possibly Luz, though it's hard to tell) holds a pinwheel, caught in the act of blowing into it to make it spin. The family looks happy, confident in the permanence of their surroundings, secure in their belief that their future will be like this one perfect frozen moment.

What happened to that family? Claudia wonders. What other seemingly flawless moments happened here, in this decaying house? She looks at the squalor surrounding her, and suddenly understands that this isn't *junk* after all. To Dolores, these odds and ends are memories she is unwilling to separate from, no matter how seemingly inconsequential. She is preserving the comfort of continuity.

Claudia swallows hard and stuffs the photo back in the box before hurrying back home.

Day Forty-five

"Weren't we supposed to be living in paradise? What happened to our weather?" Esme shivers and pulls her cardigan around her shoulders, moving closer to the heat lamp that is irradiating them with propane. The twinkling fairy lights, strung in the overhead olive trees, shiver as arctic fog blasts across the patio. Despite the chilly December evening, the outdoor tables surrounding Esme and Claudia are all packed with bar patrons, everyone pointedly ignoring the fact that LA's celebrated balmy winters have apparently migrated south with the birds this year.

"It's the middle of winter, Esme." It is so cold the ice in Claudia's gin and tonic isn't melting. The marine layer overhead traps the light from the city, illuminating the patio with a ghostly luminescence. It is only six o'clock but it feels like midnight.

"Technically, winter doesn't start for one week. Anyway, we're not *supposed* to have winter in Los Angeles."

"We could always go inside," Claudia observes.

"That's not the point," Esme says. "The point is that we moved here so we wouldn't have to make that choice."

"You didn't move here," Claudia points out. "You were born here."

"Maybe we should go on a trip together," Esme says. "Someplace warm and beachy and restorative. Tulum? Hawaii? Interested?"

Claudia shrugs and fishes an ice cube out of her glass, wishing she had stayed home. But Esme has been pestering her about a "girls' night" for weeks, and Claudia has run out of excuses. A "girls' night," as far as Claudia can tell, mostly involves Claudia listening to Esme's upbeat chatter—anecdotes about her job, the men she is dating, the condo she is decorating, lightweight subjects that seem expressly designed to take Claudia's mind off her seeping melancholy. Or perhaps her friend's just dancing around the awkward fact that Claudia managed to completely sabotage the opportunity that Esme's mother gave her? Regardless, while Claudia appreciates the intention behind this gathering, she would have preferred to be at home, watching reality show reruns on standard cable (movies are just too painful these days) or staring blankly out through her newly installed double-paned windows into the depths of the canyon. And yet she knows it is time to start facing the world again; it's been six weeks since Jeremy's departure, and it's occurred to her (in the abstract, but still) that she can't stay in her house forever.

She feels like an amputee learning how to walk again.

Esme's babble grows more frantic by the minute, as if she were a depth finder charting the fathomless bottoms of Claudia's depression. Esme's face flickers with concern as it registers Claudia's misery, her friend's forehead corkscrewing tightly as she musters up a new round of false cheer. It's clear that whatever anger Esme might still feel about the Ennis Gates debacle, it's been trumped by pity. Not that Claudia finds the latter emotion any more bearable.

"So, anyway, I'm thinking mint, for the living room," Esme says, abruptly returning to a previous conversation. "With coral and ivy as accent colors. I'm basing it on this wallpaper that I found on sale at a design store on Beverly. A kind of fern pattern. The big conundrum is, Do I go for a kind of contemporary beach-house feel? Or try for more of a Miami deco aesthetic? What do you think?"

"I don't know," Claudia said. The ice cube melts painfully on her tongue. "Neither sounds particularly natural for a fourteenth-floor condo in downtown LA, if you ask me."

"You think it's stupid for me to be worrying about this kind of stuff." Esme deflates. "It *is* stupid of me to be worrying about this. I'm sorry. I'll shut up."

"It's not you. It's me. I'm bad company tonight." Now she feels even worse—her friend is at least *trying* to be cheerful.

But Esme already looks equally morose. "I used to read fashion magazines and spend my weekends buying shoes. Now I obsess over design blogs and furniture reproductions on eBay and eco-friendly rugs," she says. "I guess by your midthirties you've realized the limitations of your own body. The new frontier to decorate is the home. Not that it's any less shallow."

Claudia nods, wishing she could muster the same enthusiasm for her own newly redone home. The two women sit in silence, examining the other customers of the bar. A few feet away, a group of men their age are staring at them. The men splay out at their table, leaning back in their chairs, legs positioned open in greater-than wedges that sign directly to their crotches. Cocktail waitresses weave between the tables, pints of beer slopping pools of froth across their trays. This bar is usually empty until the dinner hour; Claudia wonders if business is up because people are unemployed and have nothing better to do than get drunk before dark, or because Happy Hour beer is five dollars cheaper.

Esme shivers and peels the label off her beer bottle. "So," she says, her words measured and cautious. "Have you heard from Jeremy at all?"

"No." Claudia isn't at all sure that this is an improvement on the previous conversation. "I'm not sure I really want to talk about him."

"You need to talk about him with *someone*," Esme says. She picks at the sticky label residue with a ragged fingernail. "You'd tell me if you were getting divorced, right?"

It's the first time Claudia has heard this word spoken out loud, let alone let herself think it, and the harsh resonance of its syllables jolt her alert. *Divorce.* It sounds like something that happens to people much older than they are. Only now, hearing that word coming from her friend's mouth, does Claudia realize that she's never really felt *married* in that way she'd always assumed one did. That if certain benchmarks are the classic markers of middle-class adulthood—marriage, kids, mortgage, all maintained by a financially stable career—she came close but ultimately fell too far from the mark to really feel like a grown-up.

But *divorce?* It just seems like she's moving farther and farther away from life's golden ring. She is on the verge of having to start at the beginning again, on all fronts of her life, at an age when her own parents were celebrating their twelfth anniversary, with two kids in school and the jobs they'd have for the rest of their lives. For a moment, she wishes she'd never known that a life outside of Mantanka was even possible: She could have stayed, married an accountant, become a stay-at-home mom, and lived in a modest, affordable tract home near her parents. Everything would have been so much easier if she'd never known about the other sort of happiness available to her. Then she would never have had to lose it.

"I haven't even heard from him," she tells Esme. "I don't know what's going on. With anything, honestly."

"Oh." Esme considers this. "What about the money? Have you decided what to do with it yet?"

Claudia shrugs. "Maybe I'll give it to charity."

"What charity?"

The wind blows a stack of cocktail napkins off their table, scattering them across the patio. "I'm not sure," she says. "Maybe a breast cancer charity."

Esme watches her. "Why breast cancer?"

For a moment, even Claudia isn't sure why she's said this until she remembers: *Jeremy's mom died of breast cancer.* His grip on her seems inescapable, even from thousands of miles away. This has to stop. "Or maybe I'll just save it and live off it for a few years. Take a sabbatical from life."

Esme stares at her. "So you'd just do . . . nothing?"

"Got a better idea?"

Esme finishes peeling the beer label off and tries, unsuccessfully, to affix it to the paper tablecloth. "Why don't you do something fun to take your mind off everything? Go travel. You never did that after college. Train around Europe. Get stoned on the beach in Thailand. Go on safari."

The very thought of this—of packing a suitcase and getting on a plane, of talking to strangers and scouring travel guides, of taking tours for one and eating dinner at restaurants by herself—exhausts her. "I'm thirty-four, Esme. I'd look ridiculous camping out on the beach in Thailand."

"Book a hotel room, then." Esme flags down the waiter, pointing to their empty drinks. "Maybe you're just not ready yet, but *I* think you should take advantage of the situation you're in. The sooner the better."

"The situation I'm in? You mean, having destroyed two careers and my marriage on the same day?" She glances at Esme. "It's worth repeating, by the way, how sorry I am about that. The whole mess with your mom. I really screwed that one up."

"No need to apologize again. You weren't yourself. I get it." Esme punctuates her words with a stiff shrug, then smiles beneficently. "The point is, you can do anything you want now. You have the financial freedom to try anything that crosses your mind. Right now, that's a pretty rare opportunity."

Her words painfully mirror Jeremy's parting shot: *You can do anything you want.* And they are both right. But Claudia can't think of anything to *want* right now, except for something that is completely intangible and unattainable: What she really wants is to be *wanted.*

She leans forward, bracing her head in her hands, her elbows on her knees. "You know what I think? I think we just know too much now. We all got too much too fast, and then we lost it even faster, and now the only thing that's clear is that we never had any control over anything in the first place. Our generation was supposed to be young and optimistic and full of pioneering ideas about the future, right? Well, life's scraped that right out of me. All I feel these days is jaded." She scratches at her forehead with a fingernail. "The truth is, we're older than we've been willing to accept."

"It kind of sounds like you're looking for an excuse to avoid starting something new," Esme says. "At least you have the *possibility* to figure all this out. I wish I could say the same thing."

"You're doing just fine," Claudia tells Esme. "You're a high-powered marketing executive."

Fresh drinks arrive on the table. Esme drinks half of her beer before she answers. "Honestly? I hate my job. I hawk crappy kids' movies for a living, convincing hard-working, possibly broke Americans to shell out twelve dollars for cynical, brainless, disposable crap that I wouldn't ever watch myself. You know, last spring I was starting to think about quitting to try my hand at writing again? But there's no chance of that now. I haven't been able to save a dime. And I live in an overpriced condo that I bought just two months before the real estate market crashed, in a building that's half-empty because the developers can't sell the rest of the units. So I can't move even if I wanted to. I'm stuck. You, however, are not."

Claudia stares at Esme, noticing for the first time that her friend has gray hair sprouting in her part, a tiny crop of wrinkles nests along her cheekbones, and she looks like she's gained a few pounds in her hips. Is it unhappiness or stress or is it just that Esme is starting to look her age? It seems too soon for them to be already heading toward bodily deterioration. "I'm sorry. You should have said something sooner."

Esme shrugs. "It's all anyone talks about anymore—how screwed they are. I'm tired of all the whinging. I'm lucky to have a job at all."

Claudia thinks about Esme's words. *You could do anything you want.* "So where do you propose I start with reimagining my life?" she asked.

"You need to do something drastic, right? Well, you could start by getting laid. Have cheap, tawdry sex with an attractive stranger. Get your mind off Jeremy." Esme tilts her head in the direction of the men who sit a few feet away. "Him, for example. The guy in the plaid shirt with the beard. He's been staring at you."

"I think he's wearing a wedding ring."

"So are you."

Claudia looks down at her hand. Esme and Claudia stare at the ring together. What is she *doing*? Jeremy is off with Aoki, God-knows-where; he has started an entirely new life with another woman and—judging by his lack of communication—doesn't miss her in the least. And she is sitting here with Esme at the same bar she's been to a hundred times, still wearing Jeremy's ring as if it's a talisman that will magically eradicate the events of the last few months, and spending her days wallowing in apathetic self-indictment.

She finds herself thinking of Dolores, moldering away amid her memories—widowed, probably dying from a painful disease, and helplessly counting down the moments until her home is taken away. *That* is real misery. Who is Claudia to feel sorry for herself?

She finishes her second gin and tonic. Then she tugs at the ring, wedging it over her knuckle and drawing it off her finger. "You're right," she says. "I need to do something drastic." She gazes over at the men. They have registered Claudia and Esme's interest and are now blatantly staring. The bearded man makes eye contact with Claudia and then looks coyly away. Hidden speakers in the bushes crackle as Billie Holiday serenades the customers with heroin-honeyed blues.

"I'll give you five dollars if you go talk to them," Esme whispers. "Ten if you go home with the beard."

"Save your money," Claudia says. "I'll call you soon, OK?" She stands, tucking the ring in the pocket of her jeans. The three men watch Claudia as she picks her way between the chairs, heading directly toward their table. The bearded man smiles at her—the facial hair and plaid shirt combined with Converse high-tops give him the appearance of an urban lumberjack, someone who would be good at fixing broken doors and capturing dangerous spiders. This isn't entirely unattractive. The man leans forward as she approaches, and his two friends sit back respectfully, giving him the floor. He isn't wearing a wedding ring after all.

"Hey, there," he says, as she sidles up beside him, and then the invitation in his face changes to an expression of bewilderment when he realizes that Claudia isn't coming for him after all; she is passing their table entirely. The fairy lights tremble overhead, battered by wind and fog. Waitresses swivel their hips, dancing a dangerous flamenco between the tables, trays lifted aloft for a finishing flourish. The whirring propane heaters hum a sound track for her departure as Claudia makes for the exit.

The Chicken Kitchen where Mary Hernandez works is in outer Silver Lake, across from a trendy café that sells six-dollar cups of coffee. Claudia deposits her Jetta in the restaurant's parking lot. Crime-deterring floodlights wash the concrete patch with sterile white light. In the shadowy recesses near the back of the lot, a dreadlocked homeless man rummages through a Dumpster. He removes an empty gallon jug from the bin and shakes it three times before depositing it gently atop the piles of garbage in his shopping cart.

The evening traffic is picking up, and roving packs of hipsters throng the street, weaving between an art gallery opening, a gourmet wine shop, and a French restaurant on the corner. There is a long line at the café, the yearning for exquisite artisinal caffeine managing to trump the realities of the new economy.

The Chicken Kitchen sits between a Salvation Army thrift store and a gay porn shop. She pushes the entrance to the restaurant open, still unsure what she is doing here. *Maybe I can help Dolores,* she thinks, as she heaves the swinging door open and feels a wall of air-conditioning numb her face. *Maybe Mary doesn't even know what's going on with her grandmother.* Her mind works through a half-baked math formula, in which the rescue of Dolores will somehow equate to her own personal salvation.

You need to do something drastic.

Unlike the artfully lit yuppie palaces across the street, the Chicken Kitchen is illuminated by bare fluorescent tubes, which reflect off orange-painted walls and sanitized white tile. Neon signs advertise a bucket of flame-grilled chicken for $5.99, a sampler of BBQ wings for $2.99, party catering, everything *Fresh! Breezy! Meaty!* Overhead, metallic HAPPY HOLIDAYS streamers spin slowly in the draft from the air-conditioning unit. Young families sit in plastic booths, noshing on unidentifiable chicken parts that have been broken down and remolded into perfect spherical nuggets.

Claudia spots Mary at the end of the counter, manning a register. "Mary!" she calls softly, from her position at the end of the line. Mary turns to locate the voice, her face registering confusion, then pleasure, and then mild concern. She glances quickly behind her, where her manager—a middle-aged Middle Eastern man in tight orange poly-ester slacks—is lurking by the soft drink machine. Claudia waves. Mary smiles and waves back tentatively.

Claudia hesitates, considering the impulse that has driven her here. Surely Luz already knows about Dolores's foreclosure. And how exactly is Claudia planning to offer support? She should have just gone home with the beard, a far more clear-cut response to Esme's challenge. The longer Claudia stands there, the more muddled her intentions become, until finally the line before her has cleared and it is too late to dart back off into the evening.

Claudia steps up to Mary's register. Mary's braid is tucked up into a hair net that she wears underneath an orange Chicken Kitchen baseball cap. She is sweating slightly, under the band of the cap. A painful-looking pimple punctuates the tip of her nose. Mary offers up her di-astemic grin, looking far too young to be working at a fast-food restaurant on a Monday night, and then turns to the boy working next to her.

"This is my film teacher, Mrs. Munger," Mary tells him, in a low voice.

The boy nods, uninterested, and turns back to his customer.

"Not anymore," Claudia corrects Mary.

Mary leans over the register until it presses into the top of her polo shirt. *My name is Maria!* reads her name tag, and Claudia wonders whether the anglicized *Mary* is for the benefit of the girl's Ennis Gates classmates, another sign of her striving, or whether the *Maria* was a mistake on the manager's part. "You know, I thought it was great that you told Penelope to go"—Mary glances behind her at her manager and mouths the words *fuck herself.* "I bet there are a lot of people who wished they'd said it first."

"It still wasn't appropriate," Claudia says, growing uncomfortable. There is no possible way Mary could ever learn about her own small role in the Penelope debacle, she reassures herself. But it is more difficult to look at Mary's guileless face than she'd expected it to be.

"Mr. Wilson is teaching the class now," Mary says. "It's really tedious. He keeps making us watch Spaghetti Westerns. I mean, I appreciate that those films contributed to the revitalization of the genre, but they're so racist."

"The Mexicans are always the bad guys," Claudia agrees, feeling somehow responsible for this affront.

Mary nods. "And they're not even played by real Mexicans."

"You know, I never had a chance to write you that UCLA recommendation," Claudia offers. "I've got more free time now, if you still need it."

Mary gingerly touches the pimple on the end of her nose and then pulls her hand away. "Thanks," she says, "but it's too late. I got someone else to do it." There is no bitterness in this, no accusation, just a statement of fact, but this doesn't make Claudia feel any better.

Norteño Christmas carols blast over the loudspeakers, the *oom-pa* of the accordion forcing cheer into the otherwise mundane proceedings of the chain restaurant. *Oom-pa oom-pa oom-pa!* The racket doesn't make Claudia much want a chicken bucket; she can only imagine how the music would grate after an eight-hour shift. "How are you doing, Mary?" she asks, stalling.

Claudia is holding up the line. The manager wanders close, watching, and Mary lowers her head. "What can I get for you, ma'am?" she says loudly. Claudia looks up at the overhead menu, with its laminated pictures of suspiciously fake-looking chili-cheese fries, oozing shiny Day-Glo goo. "Crispy chicken sandwich," she says.

"Would you like our manager's special with that? Side of mashed potatoes, ninety-nine cents?" Mary's face pinks over with embarrassment. Claudia understands her mortification, understands how separate this flame-grilled world is from Mary's days at Ennis Gates, sees suddenly how hard Mary must work to maintain two simultaneous lives. *This was a bad idea,* she thinks. *Awkward for both of us.*

"You sold me." Claudia smiles broadly to the hovering manager to reassure him that Mary is an exceptional saleswoman. The manager grunts and disappears into the back of the kitchen to scold the sweating teen managing the fryer.

"Sorry," Mary whispers. "He's kind of a fascist."

"Why do you work here?" Claudia asks. "You should be working at a bookstore or a museum, something more intellectually challenging."

Mary laughs, not happily. "Those jobs are all going to grad students these days," she says. "But the pay here is really good, actually, and it's easy work so I can focus more on my studies. Plus I'm writing a script; you know, based on my experiences here." She steps away to collect Claudia's meal and returns with a cardboard box. The sandwich nestled inside it has been sitting under a heat lamp for some time, and the crispy coating has ossified into a dried-out crust. Mary slides it over to her on a tray alongside a tub of glutinous mash. Claudia's stomach turns.

"Can I get you anything else?" Mary asks, eyeing the line. "I'd love to talk, but—" She shrugs apologetically.

Overhead, tinsel Christmas presents twist in the draft. The dinner rush is gathering behind Claudia, impatient for their sixty-nine-cent drumsticks. "What's happening to your grandmother? " Claudia asks quickly.

Mary stares at her, startled. "Mama Dolores? What do you mean?"

Already Claudia regrets having said anything. Under the fluorescent lights of the Chicken Kitchen it seems like a family matter that has nothing to do with her. Besides, Claudia doesn't even *like* Dolores. Still, she perseveres, compelled by some force she doesn't understand. "With her home?"

Behind Claudia, a man in carpenter's overalls is clearing his throat to convey his dissatisfaction. Mary looks flustered. "She's moving in with us," she says. "I'm going to have to share my bedroom with her."

The mental image that this news conjures up—the seventeen-year-old sharing a room with her smoking, wheezing, perpetually sour-faced grandmother—is unbearable. However hard it has already been for Mary, it is about to get a lot harder. "That's awful," she says, without thinking.

"I'll survive." Mary's face tightens with cool determination.

For a brief moment, Claudia loses her breath. Instead of an insecure, hopelessly sincere sycophant, Claudia suddenly sees a focused teenager who plans to force her will on the world, despite the hurdles in her path. *Don't flatter yourself—Mary never really needed you,* she realizes. *Someday, she will probably do all the things you haven't.* The girl who stands before her, unconcernedly hawking chicken drumsticks as a matter of course—even using it as a "teachable moment" for a movie—would not be deterred by the setbacks that Claudia herself has suffered this year. Claudia is reminded of a younger, better version of herself, a Claudia she suddenly misses, a Claudia she only now realizes that she has lost.

"I'm sorry," Claudia says. She isn't sure whether she is apologizing for barging in on Mary's world without an invitation, or for failing to take the time to get to know her, or for the unwritten recommendation, or for any of a number of unintended condescensions and personal failings.

Mary gazes at her with curious, mascara-fringed eyes. The pancake concealer she's used to cover the acne on the end of her nose has caked into flakes of makeup that threaten to peel off. "Why are you sorry? It's not your fault. It's just the way things are." She looks at the line and smiles at the next customer. "It was really nice to see you, Mrs. Munger. Thanks for visiting Chicken Kitchen."

.   .   .

By the time she arrives home, darkness has fallen and the moon is rising over the hill. It stares baldly down at her through the eucalyptus
trees. Claudia stands in her driveway for a long time, looking at the
house across the street. Blue light flickers inside Dolores's living room;
she can almost make out the old woman parked on her couch, in front
of the television set.

Her own house, when she goes inside, is freezing cold. It smells like
fresh paint and lumber, like a place where no one has ever lived at all.
Claudia flips on the new recessed overhead lighting and stands in the
living room for a long time, without taking off her coat. In the kitchen,
the freezer buzzes and rattles as the icemaker spits out fresh cubes.
Claudia looks at the spot on the wall where *Beautiful Boy* once hung;
the square patch of unfaded paint has been completely erased by the
contractor's steady brushwork. Gone, too, are the cracks in the plaster
from last summer's earthquake, and the rough splinters in the floor that
used to snag her tights, and the pervasive dripping sound. The house
that once seemed cozy for two people now feels unbearably large for
one.

For five months she has put so much energy into saving this house;
and now that it is safely hers, she realizes, she no longer wants it.

Somewhere high up in the hills, the coyotes are howling; a dog answers, defending his territory. She wishes she could hear the sounds of
human existence: a party nearby, or a neighbor's music, even the sound
of traffic. But all that has been consumed by the void of the canyon. For
the first time in the three years that she's lived up in Mount Washington, Claudia feels she is on an island far out at sea, cut off from the rest
of civilization. She is truly alone. And she senses that it's time to learn
how to live with that.

You need to do something drastic.

She walks over to the silver catch-all dish on the table by the front
door. She fishes through the junk stored there, pushing aside abandoned pennies and keys that open doors that no longer exist and old
rubber bands before she finally locates Marcie Carson's business card.

It is far too late to call: Marcie's phone goes straight to voice mail.
Claudia leaves a message, her voice echoing across shiny hardwood

floors, newly installed bathroom tile, double-paned windows still covered with manufacturer's stickers.

"Hi Marcie, this is Claudia, from Dolores Hernandez's house yesterday," she says. "Could you call me back as soon as possible, please? I'd
like to put in an offer."

Jeremy

THERE WAS A NAKED WOMAN SLEEPING IN HIS BED. JEREMY STOOD in the hotel suite, the key card in his hand, staring at the Teutonic blonde splayed across the mattress, draped in silk damask linens. A flaxen thatch of pubic hair peeked out from behind the sheet that was wedged between her legs. A green jewel winked from her belly button. One erect nipple pointed jauntily toward the ceiling; the other slid sideways on the woman's chest to stare at Jeremy, alert to his presence in the room.

Even six floors up, he could hear the early afternoon traffic in the streets below, the screams of an ambulance, and the caterwaul of a busker harassing the tourists down on the piazza. The open balcony doors offered a view across the street to a department store housed in a seventeenth-century palazzo, its façade hung with Italian flags. Outside, it was threatening to rain again, but this hotel room was sweltering; moisture gathered in Jeremy's armpits, trapped underneath two layers of fine Italian wool. The table lamp in the corner of the hotel room spotlit an empty jar of Nutella sitting on an abandoned lunch cart, alongside a ravaged basket of pastries, a congealing pitcher of milk, and two espresso cups ringed with violet lip prints. It was his third day in Rome, or maybe his fourth; he couldn't remember anymore.

The woman stirred, opening one eye to assess Jeremy. "Ciao," she said.

Jeremy removed his coat—a Pierre Powers original, still fresh from the designer's showroom, like the rest of his wardrobe—and dropped it on one of the armchairs. He sat down, covertly scrutinizing the shadowy region below the woman's pubic mound. "Where's Aoki?" he asked.

The woman turned on her side, haphazardly tugging the sheet up over her body. It slid right back off, landing in a puddle below her breasts. "Who eez Aoki?" she asked, in an indeterminate accent.

"The Japanese woman," Jeremy said. "The artist."

The woman smiled, revealing crooked milk teeth, and rolled onto her back. "She wanted *fromage*. She went to Roscioli."

A little shock of excitement shot through him—*Aoki is finally back*—as he unwound the scarf from around his neck. He folded the scarf in thirds with fumbling hands. "So, who are you, where are you from?" he asked, in a voice as colloquially neutral as he could muster. "Are you Italian? German?"

"I am Ulla." The woman pulled a feather pillow toward her and hugged it, demurely, to her chest. "You like to take a sleep?"

"No, thank you," Jeremy said, unsure if this was an invitation. He wondered whether Aoki had just seduced this woman, or whether she had invited a stranger to take a nap in their bed for more altruistic reasons. Perhaps Ulla was a prostitute, or a homeless person, or a famous European actress in need of a disco nap. Any of the above was possible with Aoki. That's why life with her was so exciting, wasn't it? It was astonishing how quickly he was adjusting to this, the strangers that drifted in and out of their hotel suites, pieds-à-terre, vacation villas. Two months in Europe, and he felt as if he'd been drunk for a decade—as if existence had become an endless, intoxicating whirlwind that kept him always slightly off balance and perpetually giddy, but without the wicked hangover in the morning.

They'd lasted only twenty-six days in Paris before Aoki packed them up and sent them on a cross-continental scavenger hunt, in pursuit of an elusive art dealer from Cannes they'd never located. Instead, they'd ended up at a black-tie gala at a London museum, where Aoki had been invited as the guest of honor but left early after she slapped Damien Hirst; then Berlin, to iron over some sort of conflict with Aoki's gallerist there; and finally a ski resort in Moldavia for the Christmas holiday, where they connected with an alcoholic journalist from *Vanity Fair* who was writing a profile of Aoki. In order to recover from *that,* Aoki required a recuperative stay at the Positano villa of an Argentinian photographer she'd met the previous summer. It rained, and the two women argued about food and fascism and the meaning of the word *obscene.* They left Positano abruptly and landed here, in Rome, for no good reason whatsoever.

Jeremy hadn't seen Aoki since they checked into the hotel on Tuesday evening. She vanished at the concierge desk, just as a bellboy wearing a little blue fez trundled their luggage away. "I have to meet an old friend for drinks," she said, and stood on tiptoe to kiss Jeremy. "I'll be at this *enoteca* by Piazza Navona if you need me. We can have dinner later—there's a place in the old Jewish ghetto I want to take you, run by this deaf old grandmama who makes the most pornographic fried artichokes." And then she vanished back out into the night, leaving Jeremy standing alone on a flat field of marble in the chilly hotel lobby, where a pianist was mournfully playing a Liszt étude to an elderly couple swaddled in minks.

Aoki never returned. Jeremy went down to the Piazza Navona around midnight that night, thinking she might still be there with her friend, and quickly realized that there were about fifty wine bars in the three-block radius surrounding the square. Aoki was at none of them. When he woke up the next morning to see that her side of the bed was still made with crisp hospital corners, her Vuitton weekend bag still zipped closed, he realized he'd been abandoned. Temporarily? Permanently? Should it matter? It crossed his mind that she could have had a relapse and be passed out in a drug den somewhere, just like the old days. But she'd barely even touched a drink since they'd arrived in France; she instead seemed to be surfing some kind of ecstatic natural high. Really, knowing Aoki, she could be anywhere, doing absolutely anything.

The ensuing adrenaline rush kept him up all night. *You are starting each day as a blank slate,* he thought, not for the first time during this trip; *No two days will ever be the same.* That very unpredictability was why he'd come, wasn't it? To escape the mundanity and tedium of domesticity? Maybe other guys would be upset that their lover had up and vanished with no explanation, leaving them alone in a foreign country, but not Jeremy: He was cut from different cloth.

Not that he was using this sudden independence to do anything particularly notable. Without Aoki as his social planner, Jeremy found himself settling into the role of your standard American tourist. He visited the Roman Forum during a lightning storm, eating a Magnum bar as he huddled underneath two-thousand-year-old colonnades. He took a four-hour tour of the Galleria Borghese, learning more about baroque sculpture than he ever cared to know. He threw all his spare change into the Trevi Fountain, relinquishing five euros to have his picture taken with a guy in a gladiator costume who brandished a plastic sword over his head. He thought about giving the photograph to Aoki as a joke, before deciding that she wouldn't see the humor in it. (*You're enabling the virulent spread of vulgarity,* he could hear her say.) He threw it away instead. To avoid the unbearable desolation of a bottle of Chianti for one, he ate most meals in their hotel room while watching CNN on satellite cable.

Even after three nights without Aoki, he was able to maintain a nonchalant attitude about her absence. He knew she would come back eventually. Besides, wasn't their mutual freedom the whole point of this reunion? He wasn't beholden to her, nor was she to him. It was about *passion,* about *adventure,* about being *young and wild and free.* "A symbiosis of mutualistic reinvention"—that's what Aoki had called it on that night in Moldavia when he got drunk and asked her what she thought was going on between them. He wasn't quite sure what that nonsense really meant, but whatever it was, Aoki seemed to be thriving on it. There had been no crying episodes since the night on the airplane; instead, upon landing at Charles de Gaulle, Aoki had reverted back to her most compelling, animated self. In Paris, they flung themselves into a series of personality-studded cocktail parties, dinners that ended at three in the morning, VIP art openings, all part of a spinning social circle that never seemed to recycle the same people twice. Aoki spoke haphazard French these days, as well as select bits of three or four other languages, and just watching her work a room in her polyglot tongue—her dazzling persona a weapon that dared anyone to misunderstand her—was an aphrodisiac in its own right.

And then there was the *art*. During those few weeks in Paris, Aoki vanished into her studio for days at a time, returning back to her pied-à-terre with paint in her hair and a feral, consumed expression in her eyes. "I'm doing the best work I've ever done, and it's because of you," she told him, when she climbed into bed at four in the morning. "I'm doing a canvas that's twenty feet long. It's an allegory about art as sex and the importance of the masculine gaze. I painted you into it. You're naked and masturbating."

"You probably had to add a whole extra foot of canvas just to fit my penis," he joked, feeling slightly exploited but also wildly titillated, as if he'd once again located his proper place in the world, memorialized in flesh-colored oils.

"Two," she said, reaching for him.

His own artistic endeavors were bubbling along, albeit a bit slower. He'd moved his new recording equipment—paid for with money that Pierre had transferred into Aoki's bank account—into the Russian sculptor's studio, set a stack of empty sheet music by the window with the view down into Montparnasse cemetery, tuned the borrowed Gibson and then sat there, for days on end, mostly noodling on his guitar. He became intimately familiar with the way the light crested the ornamental crosses at twilight; with the pigeons coating the ledge of his window with calcified birdshit; with the raspberry-filled mille-feuilles from the bakery downstairs, which he ate thrice daily. Sometimes, he'd take the pastry into the cemetery and sit among the graves, watching the old ladies sweep leaves off the stones. Watching them, he was overwhelmed by immense but blunted emotion, as if the world had expanded before him and there wasn't enough room in his heart to understand everything he was feeling. He just wished he could translate this into notations on paper. *Give it time,* he'd think, before going to meet Aoki for martinis on the rue Saint-Honoré.

Pierre came to visit him at the studio sometimes, and Jeremy always tried to look busy. He would play music for him, acoustic versions of the songs he had written for Audiophone, to keep the impression of fresh genius alive. Pierre would clasp his hands to his legging-clad thighs and close his eyes and listen as if it were the most blissful sound he'd ever heard. Sometimes he brought friends—models, assistants, other musicians that he knew, some of whom invited Jeremy to jam with them, none of whom produced music that Jeremy particularly liked. The chunk of money Pierre had put at Jeremy's disposal was unfathomably huge: They'd spoken, early on, about Jeremy performing new material at Pierre's fashion show in the spring but that was the extent of their makeshift business agreement. Jeremy wasn't quite sure what the diminutive designer really expected of him. Sometimes he suspected that he was being paid mostly to be a new friend, a novelty for Pierre's cabinet of curiosities. He almost hoped this was it, because he was starting to worry about how he would single-handedly produce an album's worth of original songs by March, especially without a lyricist to write the words.

He just needed to be patient, he reassured himself. He was still adjusting to a distracting new life, coming up with a new sound, trying to understand who Jeremy-the-solo-artist was going to be. Sometimes he felt like a child who had been dropped into an enormous playground and didn't know where to start his playtime. It was almost a relief when he came back to Aoki's apartment one afternoon in early December and found her packing their belongings into suitcases. "We're going to Cannes," she announced, and he shrugged and happily accepted this fate, thrilled by the spontaneity. He would use the trip as a kind of creative palette cleanse; take the opportunity to collect some new musical inspirations. He didn't pack his guitar, assuming that they would be gone only a few days. Maybe that hadn't been such a good idea, because here they were, five weeks later, in Rome, and it was unclear when—or if—they'd ever go back home.

Home. This word was the only hitch in an otherwise dreamlike existence. Every time it popped up in his head—as in *I'm tired of traveling and ready to go home now*—the image that came with it was not Aoki's eclectic Beaux Arts pied-à-terre in Paris, piled high with art books and half-finished canvases and gold-painted scarves and musty-smelling antiques rescued from Les Puces, but the modest little bungalow in Mount Washington with the chipped IKEA coffee table and the old leather couch with a permanent indentation in the cushion from his own ass. He wondered if Claudia's parents were still in LA, helping her finish the repairs on the house; he almost hoped they were, so Claudia wouldn't be alone. The thought of her in their house all by herself—quite possibly unhappy, because of him—made him itch all over. Occasionally, when he was falling asleep, he would hallucinate her into being, standing on the edge of their half-finished deck, teetering on the precipice of the canyon, about to fall in. *You're supposed to be there to catch her*, he would think, right before he fell asleep.

Eventually these images would pass into fogged memory. Or so he hoped. For now, they remained a wound on his conscience, and in quiet moments he couldn't help picking at the scab and making it bleed anew. Sometimes when he rolled over in the middle of the night and woozily pressed himself against the body on the other side of the mattress, he would startle awake. *That's not Claudia!* he'd think, realizing that his body hadn't latched into a soft and yielding wall of flesh but had landed against something hard-edged and sharp-boned and tiny. Resisting the thought, he'd wake Aoki up, and they'd have rough, burning, breathtaking sex that made the memory of Claudia disappear for the rest of the night.

You chose this, he would think. *You wanted this.* And certainly, right now, looking at the naked stranger in his hotel bed, his body stirring as this fact sank in—*there's a naked woman in your bed*—he found it hard to locate the will to complain. What right-thinking man would? There was the distinct possibility of a memorable sexual experience if he just waited this out, waited for Aoki to come back with the cheese, waited for any misgivings about his new life to pass, just as they always did. *This is why you're here,* he reminded himself. *For moments just like this one.*

"I'm going to order some champagne from room service," he told the woman in his bed. "Would you like anything?"

Later, after Aoki returned with two big wedges of aged pecorino and a fresh loaf of *ciabatta* under her arm; and after the three of them—Aoki, Jeremy, and the naked Ulla—ate this modest repast together, as if there were nothing abnormal about a nude Swiss woman eating cheese with two fully dressed adults; and after two bottles of champagne had been demolished, while Aoki and Ulla embarked on a long and rather titillating story about how they'd met the previous evening at an illegal burlesque nightclub; and after the three of them somehow quite naturally ended up in bed together with their clothes off, as if this had all been predestined from the start; and after Jeremy had the appealing mid-coitus epiphany that he was almost exactly reenacting a scene from a porn movie he had once watched in his midtwenties—after all that, when Ulla had finally departed with the second wedge of Pecorino stuffed in her purse, Jeremy turned to Aoki.

"So, are you going to tell me where you've been for the last few days?"

Aoki lay facedown on the bed. She was reading Musil, which struck Jeremy as a strange choice for post-coital reading material. The television hummed in the background as two reporters discussed the bailout of the American auto industry. The bed was full of bread crumbs, which stuck to the drying sweat that pricked Jeremy's back. The unventilated room smelled oceanic and sour.

Aoki tilted her head sideways to look at him. At some point during their bedroom acrobatics with Ulla, her hair had fallen out of its topknot, and long black strands now stuck to her eyelashes. She swiped them off her face with the back of her hand. "Nowhere particularly interesting," she said. She leaned over and kissed the bare flesh of his shoulder as consolation.

"I'm not supposed to ask," he said.

"No, you aren't." Aoki turned a page in her book, pretending absorption in German modernist literature. "It's better for both of us that way. Besides, you could do the same thing if you wanted to."

"I know," he said. "Maybe I will." *I should,* he thought, and tried to conjure up his own equivalent adventure—hunt down Ulla and take her off for a weekend sex romp in Lausanne? Embark on a three-day drunk in Amsterdam's red-light district? This struck him as being unlikely, unsanitary, unfathomable.

Aoki shrugged. "Anyway, you know the important thing."

"The important thing?"

"I'm always going to come back. So why worry?"

Jeremy nodded, conscious that it was to his benefit to find this explanation not only acceptable but perfectly reasonable. Would it help him to know that she had disappeared into someone else's bed, had a drug relapse, checked herself into an insane asylum? This was what had driven him mad before: the gaping voids in her life into which he could not enter, in which he had no place at all. This time around, he needed to be a more sanguine person, more comfortable with letting the unknown variables remain unknown, relinquishing logic and order in exchange for other, more unpredictable rewards.

Except that he wasn't.

Petulance gripped him. It struck him that the variables in this new equation were lopsided and balanced entirely in Aoki's favor. While he was roaming around Rome by himself, bored—let's face it—this woman who was supposed to be his partner of some sort was having wild adventures she wouldn't even tell him about. Maybe she'd come back pregnant or with some kind of disease. Where was the excitement in that? Instead, he felt unclean, as if he needed to take a shower as quickly as possible.

He picked the remote up and clicked the television set off. Without the illuminated cube on the wall, the room descended into rainy evening gloom.

"Why am I here?" he asked the ceiling.

Aoki closed her book, marking her place with one forefinger, and rolled over onto her back. "One of my major collectors is in from Milan and wants to have dinner. I could use the sale, so I really need to stick around and make nice, play the part of Aoki, so he can go home believing he's received his obligatory chunk of my flesh. Except that I've had to postpone three times. Anyway I think we'll be able to leave by Monday. I *do* need to get back; I've got to finish two more paintings before the end of the month or Berlin is going to have my head on a platter. And Pierre's probably having a conniption that you've been gone so long."

"That's not what I meant," Jeremy said.

Aoki frowned. "Don't tell me you're not having fun."

A worm of bankrupt pleasure crawled up his spine as he recalled the afternoon's exploits. "It's definitely been fun," he agreed. "But I still don't know why you came to LA to get me in the first place."

She reached up and gripped the loose hair that fell across her cheek, twisting it up into a knot that she anchored with the free hotel pen from the bedside table. Her mascara was smeared above and below her lids, so that she resembled a badly used Kewpie doll. "Because I love you," she said. She reached across the bed and put a hand on his thigh, pinning him in place. His leg broke out in goose bumps as five chilled fingers pressed into his flesh. He didn't understand how she could be so cold in a room that felt to him like an overripe terrarium.

He pushed himself upright, propping himself against a pile of unpleasantly damp pillows. "I'm fairly certain that's not the only reason," he said, understanding for the first time that this was true. "It took you four years to have this epiphany. So why now?"

"I don't know why you're doing this," Aoki said.

"I'm not doing anything," he said. "I only want to understand what's going on here."

Aoki reached over the edge of the bed and retrieved an undershirt, a ribbed boy's tank top. She pulled it over her head, letting it fall loosely over her narrow chest, and then flipped her book open again. "I was stuck," she said. "I hadn't painted a new canvas in six months."

Jeremy climbed out of bed and walked to the window. The streetlights below were coming on; they glimmered diffusely under a layer of fresh rain. The Italian flags on the department store across the street flapped in slow motion, dripping water from laden folds. "And you thought I would somehow remedy that?"

Aoki ran her palm across the open page of her book and began to speak to it, as if she were addressing Musil rather than Jeremy. "You know, when I first started painting I did it because I felt *compelled* to," she said. "I absolutely had to convey these enormous emotions that were tucked inside me. But after you left me, after my career really exploded, art became about something more than just exposing my heart on canvas. I became a kind of factory, manufacturing valuable widgets ruled by strict mathematical equations. Size of canvas plus medium used plus time spent painting minus forty-percent gallery commission equaled value of artwork. See? I had become a *commodity*. And pretty soon the very smell of my oils made me gag. And then there was rehab, and all that *talking* I was supposed to do. . . . By last spring, I couldn't even remember who I'd ever been in the first place. Something finally just emptied inside me: I was completely drained, as though someone had pulled my plug in the night. I couldn't think of a thing to paint; nothing that felt like authentic *Aoki*."

"I'm still not understanding how this relates to me," he said stubbornly.

"I came to get you because the last period in my life where I felt truly *inspired* was when I was with you. It was like—you were the only person who knew who I was *before,* and who didn't put any demands on me or try to shape me into something I wasn't. And I thought if I could just see myself through your eyes again, maybe it would all come back to me. That feeling of emotional inspiration." She smiled, triumphant. "And see? It did."

With the balcony doors closed against the rain, the street noise six floors below was entirely absorbed by the hotel's thick Persian carpeting and damask drapery. "So you saw me as a value-add business proposition. A small financial outlay for a big back-end return." He knew he sounded bitter. "How much am I worth to you, a million? Two? Ten?"

"That's a cynical way to look at it," she said. "I came because you were my *muse.* And frankly, because I was yours too. You needed me; I *knew* that. You hadn't exactly been thriving since I last saw you."

Coming from her mouth, the indictment of his previous life in LA felt unfair; he had to resist the urge to defend himself and the life he'd had there with Claudia. Those four years weren't a total waste. In fact, from the vantage point of this stuffy hotel room, they were suffused with the bucolic haze of selective memory: Cocktails on the deck on Sunday afternoons and jamming with his friends in the studio in the Valley and cooking goat-cheese omelets for Claudia and painting the bedrooms cerulean blue. Having sex in the kitchen, amid broken glass, while the house shivered around them. As for inspiration—well, he'd written more music in the last few months in Los Angeles than he had since he'd arrived in France. Julian Bragg had called his work with Audiophone *brilliant*—he might even have worked with him, had he stayed in Los Angeles—and Aoki could make no claim on that.

"I freed you," Aoki continued, without waiting for him to respond. "This is what a liberated relationship is like, Jeremy. It's about doing what you want, when you want to do it, being able to fulfill all your dreams and urges without worrying about anyone else's demands. And knowing that love is something completely separate from that—love is just an *emotion,* it shouldn't be a *trap.* You know, acting in your own self-interest isn't the horrible thing that our world makes it out to be; it's actually the best way to become an individual. To avoid a life of averages and conformity. That's what you wanted, isn't it?"

It was, he thought, and then corrected himself—*It is.* But for some reason he didn't want to gratify Aoki with this answer. "So what if I'd needed you while you were off living your liberated life for the last few days?" he asked, instead.

Aoki groaned loudly. "Are you having a little-boy tantrum like you did last time around? Because I thought you were grown up enough to handle this now."

He turned from the window and walked slowly back to the bed. He stared down at Aoki, a tiny little lump in the vast overupholstered bed, and found he didn't have the energy to pursue this argument to its end point. He was afraid to know what the end point even was. "Forget I said anything," he said. He climbed under the covers and rolled on his side so he was facing the wall.

"Fine," Aoki said. She snapped the bedside lamp off, plunging them into darkness.

He woke to a dark room and an empty bed. For a moment, as he fumbled for the light switch, he thought Aoki had vanished again. But he could see, once the lamp was on, that her clothes were still in a heap by the side of the bed, her suitcase was open in the corner, and her purse sat on an armchair.

On the far side of the suite, a bright bar of light under the bathroom door offered a clue to Aoki's whereabouts. Jeremy climbed out of bed and crossed to the door. He knocked softly. "You in there?" he asked.

There was no response. Jeremy recalled, as he stood there, the evening five years earlier when he'd come home to their New York walk-up and found Aoki naked in the bathtub, bleeding profusely from her wrists. He couldn't recall exactly why she tried to commit suicide—something to do with his spending the previous evening talking to a female drummer he'd met at a gig—but he did remember the heart-stopping sight of the nail file in her hands, sawing away at her artery. He understood, now, the artifice in the entire setup: how Aoki must have chosen to remove her clothes before climbing in the tub, anticipating the aesthetic jolt provided by her pale naked body and scarlet blood against the stark white porcelain. She must have known, too, that a nail file was a weak weapon of choice, and that if she *really* wanted to die she would be cutting down the vein instead of crossways. She probably even timed it so that the deepest, most dangerous gashes happened as his key rattled in the door, giving him plenty of time to call an ambulance. It was all so obviously a cry for attention. But that hadn't occurred to him then. He'd seen her death wish as an indictment of his own behavior: He was accountable to her and had somehow failed her. So even though he had already been starting to wonder whether their relationship was a healthy one, he'd stayed with her for nearly a year after the suicide attempt before he finally made his break.

Could their fight tonight have tipped her over that edge again? This time, would it be for real? He knocked again, louder. "Aoki? You OK?"

"It's not locked," Aoki called, her voice echoing across bathroom tile.

He pushed the door open, ready to leap for the tub or the telephone, whichever seemed more urgent. But the bathtub was empty. Instead, his gaze went straight to the floor of the bathroom, where black webs of human hair lay scattered across peach-colored tile. The trail of hair started near the bathroom door and ended by the sink, where Aoki stood in her underwear, her bare feet buried in shiny black cuttings, nail scissors in her fist.

She'd chopped her hair off, trimmed it all the way to the scalp. And the bizarre thing was that even nearly bald, even with the remaining tufts jutting out at strange angles from the spots she'd missed, Aoki was breathtakingly beautiful. Perhaps even more so: Her features looked huge against her exposed skull, dewy and precious as a fawn's, and her eyes burned hot and a little insane with excitement.

"I got tired of it getting in my eyes," she said, in a faraway voice. "What do you think?"

"You look great," he said, honestly.

"I've always wanted to do it." She blew out her lips like a horse to unglue the strands that were stuck to her face. They tumbled to the floor, joining the rest. He noticed that her bare scalp was bleeding in the back, dribbling down the vulnerable base of her skull toward her neck. "I'm thinking I'll save the hair and use it for a sculptural piece. I've already got a name: *Artifice.* Or maybe *Abandonment.*"

Jeremy sat on the edge of the claw-foot tub, watching Aoki as she smoothed her hand across the back of her head, feeling for uneven sections. Her fingers forged across the blood trail and then left smudgy red fingerprints across her denuded nape. She pulled her hand away and stared at it, slightly baffled, before sticking a gory forefinger in her mouth and licking it clean. She winked at Jeremy as she did it.

This self-abuse was intended as a message for him, he knew it; he just couldn't figure out what the message was. And suddenly he didn't care enough to *want* to figure it out.

He knew, as he watched her, that this would never end; that as long as he was with her, he'd be anticipating the moments when she disappeared, or started crying for no discernable reason, or slit her wrists in the bathtub, or took up drugs again, and this unpredictable life no longer struck him as thrilling but as tedious. His job here was to pick up after her, to always be waiting when she returned; and he didn't really want to do it after all. Maybe Aoki had liberated herself from a life of responsibility, but rather than releasing Jeremy from *his* fetters, Aoki was actually saddling him with a whole new set of even more constricting ones.

"I'm going to order room service for dinner," Aoki offered, as she snipped an errant strand near her earlobe. "Caviar and French toast?"

"Get whatever you want." Jeremy stood and walked out the door of the bathroom. He headed to the armchair where he'd deposited his jeans during their earlier sexual escapades, and began to tug them over his shins. Aoki followed him out of the bathroom, still clutching the nail scissors.

"Where are you going?" she asked.

"For a walk," he said. He tied on his shoes and grabbed his coat.

"Oh, for God's sake. Are you still upset about what we were discussing earlier? It's really not a big deal." Aoki's face was shut tight, shrouded in the shadows cast by the light of the lamp.

Maybe it *wasn't* a big deal. Maybe he'd known all this the night that he decided to kiss Aoki at the Château Marmont or the evening he'd boarded Air France with her. Maybe this was the calculation *he'd* done, believing that the sum would end up net positive. Maybe he would leave and return, the way he always had in the past. All he knew was that right now, he couldn't stand to be closed in this room with Aoki's logic planted there between them. "I just need some fresh air," he said. "I'll be back in a few."

"You're the one who wanted to talk about our relationship," she said. She was looking over his shoulder to a gilt-edged decorative mirror on the wall, turning her face to the left and the right so she could examine her own profile. "Don't ask for honesty if you can't cope with it."

"Don't tell me what I can cope with," he said, and left.

Outside, the rain had stopped and the clouds were clearing, and all of Rome was taking advantage of the reprieve to do their evening perambulations. In his Pierre Powers wardrobe, Jeremy looked exactly like everyone else here—no American brand names, no baseball cap or skate shoes to give him away—but as he wandered aimlessly through the stone streets, he felt both invisible and out of place: an imposter in innocuous wrappings, a pretender who hadn't mastered any Italian beyond *buon giorno* and *per favore*. He didn't even have his passport on him. He could die out here, in some kind of freak accident involving a Fiat or a bucket of tortelli or a collapsing Renaissance cornice, and he would be unidentifiable. Could Aoki be trusted to come looking for him eventually? He didn't count on it.

He walked by the Pantheon, where the tourists were drinking watered-down cocktails in the shadow of the ancient dome, and then headed west. He ended up at the foot of the monument to King Victor Emmanuel, a gaudily illuminated fin-de-siècle confection plopped down in the middle of a busy intersection. He sat there on the steps, blinking against the glare of the spotlights and watching matchbox-sized cars weave frenzied patterns in the street below. After a while, he wandered back up the Corso. It was past eight, and the shops were closing, grates falling shut all around him. He knew exactly where he was and yet couldn't help feeling completely lost.

He ended up at a café in a pedestrian zone near the Navona, ordering a glass of wine he couldn't pronounce from a waitress who looked like a young Anjelica Huston. The restaurant was packed and hot so he took his wineglass out to a streetside table, wiping the water from a chair with a damp paper napkin. Across the street was a bookstore; next to that, a delicatessen with hairy boar legs hanging from hooks and packages of pasta tied with raffia in the windows. As he watched, a young family trundled out of the delicatessen. The mother pushed an empty stroller, whose seat was occupied by a long salami and a string bag full of vegetables. The rightful tenant of the stroller stumbled alongside: a toddler in a puffy pink snowsuit, walking thanks to the assistance of her father, a leather-clad young man who was behind her holding her arms aloft. The little girl bumped across the earth, her unsure feet touching the ground only temporarily before her father lifted her up again. The family paused as they hit the chilly night air. The father bent to zip up the pink jumpsuit while the mother chattered in rapid Italian. And then they both laughed as the little girl threw her arms up toward the sky, begging to be borne aloft and rescued from the burden of gravity. The father lifted the toddler up again, this time raising her all the way to his shoulders, where he deposited her. She gripped his hair and howled with terrified pleasure as he locked her legs into place across his chest. In this fashion, the threesome wandered off down the street, toward home and dinner.

Jeremy watched them go. *That's what love is,* he thought, *knowing implicitly that it's your job to lift up your kid, and never caring that it's a job in the first place.* He tried to recall a time when his parents had carried him like that, and although he could conjure up a clear memory of Jillian dragging him by his hand as they hurried to catch a train somewhere in Southeast Asia, he couldn't remember being raised high like that;

certainly not by his father. Maybe he would have been too young to remember.

For a fleeting, aching instant, he wanted desperately to be responsible for someone else; to sacrifice himself entirely to someone else's
needs. It wasn't Aoki that he thought of. Instead, a clear thought crossed
his mind: *I'm going to carry my kid around on my shoulders, whether he knows*
to ask for it or not. And he had a sharp visual of it too—of the laughing,
adoring toddler on his shoulders and the amusement of the mother beside him, and he realized, as he conjured up this image, that the face of
the woman he'd envisioned beside him was Claudia.

"Another glass?" The waitress stood in front of him, speaking in
nearly perfect English. "We have snacks inside, if you like. It's warmer
there." She cocked a hip toward him as she emptied his ashtray, sliding
in an empty one in its place, and then smiled flirtatiously. The implicit
promise of a three-day jaunt to Neverland, no strings attached, crossed
his mind. He could do it, if he wanted; he could do anything he
dreamed of right now.

"No, thank you," he said. "I think I'm done."

He thought of Aoki, back in his hotel room, examining her bleeding
profile in the mirror. He stood, pushing a ten-euro note under the ashtray. And then he crossed the street, drawn to the lights of the bookstore and the handwritten paper sign in the window that announced,
modestly, INTERNET POINT. It was nearly closing time, and he was the
only customer in the shop. A few young clerks wandered the floor,
straightening stacks of paperbacks and chatting in Italian as they cashed
out the register. One of them accepted a coin from Jeremy and directed
him toward a computer terminal against the back wall.

The computer keyboard was in Italian, and a PC to boot, so it took
Jeremy a few minutes to figure out how to load the Internet browser
and type a URL without making any grievous errors. When he finally
logged in to his e-mail account, it was bloated with several weeks'
worth of messages. There was one from Edgar, telling him that BeTee
had been acquired by a Japanese men's clothing company and was ex-
panding. A note from Julian Bragg, checking on Audiophone's
progress. And there was a longer e-mail from Daniel, in response to Jer-

emy's previous apology for having missed his December wedding to Cristina. They'd found out that the baby was going to be a girl, Daniel wrote; they were naming her Allegra, they'd bought a house in Eagle Rock, they were planning to have the baby at home. He missed playing music, but not as much as he'd thought he would; he hoped Jeremy was making a go of it, for both of them. The last two lines of the message felt like an addendum, a momentary ray of skepticism breaking through a message otherwise dictated by good intentions: *I hope you know what you're doing, Jeremy,* Daniel wrote, *because from here it looks like you're acting like a crazy man.*

There were a few invitations to Los Angeles New Year's parties that he'd missed, and a smattering of Facebook invitations, and one petition forwarded by his father demanding the legalization of medical marijuana, but there was nothing from Claudia. *There was no reason to expect anything,* he thought. Still, Jeremy clicked through to the end of his mailbox, through two months' worth of archived e-mail, just to make sure. And then he sat there, overwhelmed with disappointment.

The overhead lights began to click off, one by one, until the only light left in the store was coming from the front window displays. The last clerk stood directly behind Jeremy and read over his shoulder, not bothering to mask his impatience.

Ignoring him, Jeremy opened a new window. He typed Claudia's e-mail address and then paused, unsure of himself. The clerk cleared his throat and said something incomprehensible, and before Jeremy could think better of it, he wrote three words, hit SEND, and stood up.

I miss you.

I love you.

I am sorry.

I was wrong.

As he exited the bookstore, he couldn't recall which three words he had written, but all of them felt true.

Claudia

CLAUDIA MOVED INTO HER NEW APARTMENT ON ONE OF THOSE sunny, crystalline winter days, a day that had been plucked out of bucolic May and planted serendipitously at the end of January. It hadn't rained since December and, in the papers and on TV, meteorologists were offering ominous predictions of an impending drought, but up here, within the double-paned central-air-conditioned safety of her sixteenth-floor loft in downtown Los Angeles, Claudia felt she could ride out the weather.

Her new home was one of fifty-three units in The Luxist, an Art Deco bank building that had spent time as a Mexican movie palace after World War II, a flophouse during the decline of the 1970s, and then abandoned entirely, before it was finally reincarnated as a luxury condo conversion during the recent real estate boom. The building was in a state of permanent near-completion, construction having halted when funds ran out the previous fall. That unintentionally left Claudia's one-bedroom loft with exposed heating ducts overhead, flaking plaster friezes above the windows, and a sink in the open-plan kitchen that didn't actually run hot water. Upstairs was a rooftop swimming pool, surrounded by an empty framework of cabanas that had yet to be built; in the basement was a gym, where CNBC played on television sets over a row of Stair Masters and nonfunctional treadmills. And yet there was free building-wide Wi-Fi, a doorman in the lobby, and sustainable bamboo flooring in the hallways. Besides Claudia, and Esme in her condo two floors below, only eighteen other units in the building were occupied. Claudia had rented hers for a bargain, since the building's developers were on the verge of bankruptcy and desperate to milk every dollar from their prerecession folly that they could.

Moving here had been Esme's idea. When Claudia put her house on the market in December, Esme had begged her to move into her building. "I could use the company," Esme said, "and frankly, so could you." She wasn't wrong. After two months of staring nightly into a dark canyon, wearing her solitude like a second skin, Claudia was looking forward to life in an urban center, to peering out at orderly grids of yellow squares glowing in the buildings around her, each cube filled with the promise of humanity. She was ready not to be isolated anymore.

She hadn't quite expected everything to move so quickly, though. Her house in Mount Washington had sold almost instantly, thanks to the aggressive pricing and savvy marketing of Marcie Carson. The fire turned out to be an asset in the end; all that brand-new construction brought up the value of the house, and she'd ended up listing it for only $36,000 less than they'd bought it for in the first place—a minor miracle, considering the state of the real estate market. She was in escrow with an environmental scientist and his pregnant wife before the bank had even accepted Claudia's final offer on Dolores's house across the street.

As for Dolores's house, Claudia had bought *that* outright, using the money from the *Beautiful Boy* account, knowing she'd never be approved for another mortgage. Buying Dolores's home for her may have been a stupid move, financially speaking, but it wasn't going to be a completely losing proposition. The monthly rent that Dolores would be paying her should cover nearly half of Claudia's rent for this condo. Someday, far down the line, if and when the market ever bounced back, she might even be able to fix the house up and sell it at a profit.

Not that this was the goal, it never had been. Nor had it she bought the house as a bid for ego-affirming gratitude; she knew better than to expect Dolores to be appreciative. Rather, Dolores had reacted to Claudia's proposal—that Claudia buy Dolores's home out of foreclosure and let Dolores rent it back from her—with her usual display of curmudgeonly skepticism. "Better to own," she grumbled. "Not paying deposit, OK?" She then proceeded to bargain Claudia down on the rent, from $700 a month to $650.

And it wasn't a form of revenge, either—though Claudia had imagined how horrified Jeremy would be to know that Aoki's museum-quality masterpiece had gone to pay for a house for Dolores, of all people. *Take that, Aoki,* she found herself thinking, as she signed the final documentation at the escrow agents' office. *Your precious painting paid for an aesthetic travesty.* And yes, maybe that *did* feel good, but it certainly wasn't what had driven her to call Marcie Carson in the first place.

No, the only way she could explain her actions was that they were a form of secret penance only she would ever understand. Karmic compensation, as it were, for her own contributions to the world gone awry, for betrayed principles and blind self-interest. Up here on the sixteenth floor, she could think of Dolores rotting contentedly away among her dusty memories, of Mary writing college admission essays in her quiet bedroom, and feel that she'd restored some sort of order to an increasingly unpredictable world. Even if her own life still teetered on the fine edge of a precipice, she was preserving balance where it was needed even more.

If Mary knew about the exact details of her grandmother's new living situation, Claudia hadn't heard about it. Maybe it wouldn't make a bit of difference in her life, in the end, but that didn't seem to matter either. Claudia suspected that she would never hear from or see Mary again, unless it was to read about her former student's achievements in the paper some year in the future. That felt like enough.

Frequently, these days, she thought of a term that the commentators on TV kept using: *moral hazard.* Even though Claudia wasn't quite clear what this meant in pure economic terms (something about the reckless behavior of banks that insulate themselves from risk), the phrase felt apt and true to her own situation. *Everyone pretends that their lives exist in a vacuum,* she thought, *but the truth is that our individual lives exist in an intimate relationship to the rest of the world. Our actions have consequences in places we are too willfully blind to imagine.* Everyone was interconnected after all, and only now was the world waking up to that fact and realizing that this collectively self-centered state of perpetual adolescence—the gimme gimme era—might actually be ethically flawed. *No one realizes the moral hazards of their ambitions,* she thought. *Not even me.*

The movers had left her belongings in one massive heap in the middle of the floor, ignoring the labels that Claudia had marked on the top and bottom of each box. Claudia found one marked GLASSWARE and unpacked a solitary tumbler. She filled it with warm soda and went to gaze out the floor-to-ceiling windows at her new view. A few blocks to the east of The Luxist was a homeless encampment the size of the town she'd grown up in, and a few blocks west was a brand-new gourmet food store paved in marble and brass that blithely sold fifty-dollar lemon tarts and baseball-sized orbs of *burrata* mozzarella as if the economy had never crashed. In between were blocks of crumbling Art Deco buildings that had been converted into Spanish-language theaters and iron-grated toy stores selling counterfeit SpongeBob SquarePants dolls; and splashy glass-clad bank buildings with OFFICE SPACE AVAILABLE NOW! banners flying across their fronts. Gazing directly to the south, she could see the blinding electronic billboards that fronted the new entertainment complex and convention center. In forty-foot-high LED lights, the billboards pleaded with her to drink Coke Zero, to attend a Lakers game, to visit the cineplex, to spend money she no longer had. She found it comforting to stand here, looking out at the epicenter of Los Angeles's demise, rebirth, and demise again. These stately old buildings had survived booms and busts for a hundred years or more and were still standing, confident that they would be reinvented in perpetuity, always accommodating the world's changing whims.

Sixteen stories below, Claudia could see office workers scurrying along to their lunch meetings, jackets flung over their shoulders, and a fruit cart vendor selling coconut and mango chunks to women in seasonally ambitious sundresses. Claudia finished her soda and turned away from the window. She stepped over a stack of bubble-wrapped appliances and walked to the kitchen table. There, underneath a pile of hanging bags, was her laptop case. She turned on the computer and loaded up her Screenwriter program, quickly finding the place where she'd stopped writing the day before.

Four weeks in, and she was already a third of the way through a first draft; at this rate, she'd be done with the screenplay by late spring. She still wasn't sure exactly what the ending was going to be, but she knew it would be an intimate movie, something that could be inexpensively shot on a hand-held camera with only three characters and a few locations. It would be a relationship story but not a love story; a chronicle of modern life, and probably the most personal thing she'd ever written. She might even be able to finance the production herself, with the last dregs of the *Beautiful Boy* money, if she put herself on a tight budget and tracked every penny she spent.

Sometimes she felt like she was winding the clock back a decade, returning to a simpler ideal from a long-forgotten time. It was odd—she was renting instead of owning, she was writing a tiny indie movie instead of parading across a studio lot, descending the Hollywood ladder rather than climbing it, living on a burrito budget with no sign of financial relief in the future. And yet, instead of feeling like a failure, she mostly felt liberated to reimagine her existence, to do something she cared deeply about. She felt more like *Claudia* than she had in a long time.

It was possible that she was finally starting to be OK again.

Afternoon had crossed over into dusk by the time she finally disengaged from her computer screen. She loaded up her e-mail program and sent the day's pages to RC.

Thirty pages down, seventy or so to go. Do you think this scene is too expositional? Willing to trade free babysitting for your expertise, as long as you'll provide full body armor and all-you-can-eat Valium.

She hit SEND, hesitated, and then clicked CHECK NEW MAIL. Her e-mail program churned away, retrieving her correspondence. She could feel her heartbeat picking up momentum, from steady kick-drum to high-hat cymbal, as the messages began to roll in.

There it was. Another e-mail from Jeremy. The third this week, the ninth since his initial contact two weeks before. She hadn't answered any of them, not trusting herself, and yet they still poured in, each one longer and more confessional than the next. It was as if she were being courted by a stranger, someone who little resembled the husband who had walked out the door into the rain three months ago. At first she had been upset, and then angry—she'd deleted e-mails four and five without reading them at all—and then simply confused. But by this one, the ninth, she was mostly just curious to see what he had to say next.

> *I'm in London now. Still alone, in case you're wondering. And I know you'll probably never forgive me—and if you don't, I deserve it—but I hope that you will. I could write a ten-page e-mail here trying to explain why I did the stupid things I did—I'm guessing a therapist would charge me thousands of dollars to tell me it had something to do with abandonment issues, or fear of commitment, or the rootlessness and impossible expectations that Jillian and Max instilled in me—but what's really important is that I now know how deluded I was. And I've finally figured out what I want: a real family, for the first time in my life. With you and me at the center.*
>
> *Claude—the rules that circumscribed our world seem obsolete now. And where before I thought it was impossible to live up to rules at all so why bother trying, now I realize we should be making up our own as we go along. Define our own principles, ones that can coexist with what the world demands of us. Just—I want to make them together, with you. And I'm ready to compromise if that's what it takes.*
>
> *I'm booked on a flight back to Los Angeles, arriving in town tomorrow afternoon. I could probably stay with Max, but I'd rather stay with you, if you'll have me. I can sleep on the couch, or in the guest bedroom if it's been fixed up by now?*
>
> *I love you. I hope you know that.*
>
> *Do you still love me?*
>
> *Jeremy*

Claudia spun in her chair and surveyed the loft. She hadn't located any of her lamps yet, so the room was illuminated only by the refracted lights of the city. The piles of boxes loomed in the eerie glow, the contents of her entire life encased in packing tape and old newspaper. She knew she should get a move on and unpack, but something held her back. It just seemed like such a monumental job, one that she couldn't possibly imagine tackling on her own quite yet.

And wasn't it Jeremy's fault that she was having to unpack at all? He didn't even know where she was living. How unfair of him to expect to show up and be let in the front door. There was no room for him here; there was barely enough room for herself.

She turned back to the computer and typed quickly, letting the anger write for her.

Hi—
I sold our house, so don't show up on the front doorstep and expect to find me there. You'll just annoy the new owners.
Claudia

She clicked SEND and stood up. Took three steps toward the kitchen before spinning around and moving toward the loft stairs, and then stopped again, having already lost track of what she planned to do.

She'd always thought that there would be some clarity at this point in her life, something concrete she could point to that might explain where she had been and was going, but all she could see from here was a tangle of infinite complexity and complications, a snarl of abandoned dreams and naïve ideals and lingering hopes inextricably woven with flinty reality. She held this knot in her hand, realizing for the first time that she might never be able to realign it into a logical, linear rope.

Did she still love Jeremy? Of course she did. That wasn't something that could just be shut off like a broken water main or a bloody nose. Did she still need him? That didn't seem to be the right question either. Anyway, for the first time in more than four years, she felt like maybe she didn't. At least, not for the reasons she used to.

No, the relevant question was whether she still wanted him.

She sat back down at her computer and typed quickly, before she could think better of it.

Hi again—

If you need a place to sleep for a night—ONE NIGHT—you will find me in The Luxist, downtown. Apartment 1621. This is not an invitation to move back in, but you do own half the couch so I guess you have the right to sleep there if you need to.

She paused, then added a few last lines.

I appreciate what you've said. Don't think it has gone unheard. But I reserve the right to see if anything has really changed. Frankly, you have to give me a good reason to trust you again.

The e-mail sent, she stood in the middle of the darkening room, surveying the task before her. She located a desk lamp hidden behind the couch, but none of the wall outlets seemed to be hooked up to the electrical grid. As she was on her hands and knees, crawling around the baseboards in search of a working plug, her phone rang. She let the caller leave a message on her answering machine.

Thees is Dolores Hernandez and I need you to fix toilet, OK? Also, ees not good smell in sink. There was no please or thank you, just a fumbling click and a long buzz of telephone static.

Despite this, despite everything, Claudia found herself smiling.

The light from the curtainless windows woke her up at dawn, a golden sunrise reflecting off the mirrored façade of the office building across the street. She spent the morning frantically unpacking. In the light of day, it seemed critically important that Jeremy not arrive to see her world in disarray, but to present a unified front of one. *I'm doing just fine without you,* the loft needed to say.

It took longer than she thought to put everything away, considering the diminuitive size of the space and the diminished state of her post-fire belongings. Sixteen floors below, the city came to life, the police sweeps moving the stray homeless back toward the invisible confines of skid row, the buses groaning through with morning commuters, the echo of horns ricocheting off walls of sixty-story-high skyscrapers. The sun passed over from the east side of the street toward the west and was creeping its way into her loft by the time she finally hung the last picture on the wall.

The doorman buzzed up to let her know she had a visitor just as she was breaking down the remaining cardboard boxes. She splashed cold water on her face—there was no time to change—and then sat waiting on the couch for her husband to arrive.

She counted to eleven before the doorbell rang, and then added another five just to keep him waiting, and still had to remind herself to walk toward the door in a measured manner. She knew Jeremy would be able to hear her footsteps from the hallway and would use them to try to read into her state of mind, and as yet she wanted to give him nothing. She felt as if she were about to open a door to a blind date. Even as she opened the door she half expected not to recognize the person who stood behind it.

"Hi," Jeremy said.

He wore well-tailored clothes that looked like they belonged to someone else—someone more put together and self-assured than the Jeremy she remembered. His hair was shorter too; the long curls that used to fall across his eyes had been trimmed away to expose pale temples and vulnerable pink earlobes. He looked like a prom date who had dressed up to impress someone's parents; all he lacked was an orchid corsage in a clear plastic box. And yet beneath this new formality he was still, somehow, the old Jeremy, with his wry half-smile and hesitant slump to the left.

"Hi," she said, and stepped a few feet back, giving him room to enter. She could see him measuring the distance she had put between them, trying to discern whether she was going to allow him to touch her and deciding not to gamble on it. He walked politely through the space she left and entered the loft.

He walked toward the living space and stood there, still holding his bag. He looked down at their old leather couch and chipped coffee table, and then up at the air ducts overhead, as if trying to make sense of these half-familiar surroundings. It felt, to Claudia, like a leaded weight had landed on the room and was pushing down on them both from above, the pressure making it difficult to feel anything clearly.

Jeremy cleared his throat, as if about to deliver a prepared speech. "I just want to start by saying—" he began.

Claudia realized that she wasn't ready to hear what he had to say. "I only have a few minutes—" she interrupted.

He frowned and tried again. "I've really missed you—"

"—I have to go fix a toilet at Dolores's house," she finished.

Jeremy set his bag on the floor. "Why are you fixing Dolores's toilet?"

"It's a long story," she said curtly.

She knew she was being cruel, and she waited for him to grow indignant. But he mostly looked baffled, and a little bit wounded. *Maybe he* has *changed,* she suddenly thought.

"Anyway—"

Claudia picked up her keys and her laptop bag, anxious to escape the tension in the room. "I should go. Dolores is waiting." This *did* feel like a blind date, the bad kind, a strained encounter between two strangers who could find no way to intersect with each other. "I'll be gone for the rest of the day, but feel free to stay here without me. Or go out if you need to. I'll leave a key with the doorman."

"Wait." Jeremy sat down on the couch. "Can we try this again? I didn't want it to be like this."

"What did you *expect* it to be like?" Her words were a thinly veiled threat, and she watched him slump under the accusation in them. She stood there, daring him to respond, but she wasn't enjoying her moment of victory at all. Instead, she fixated on a new expression of weariness that hung from the tender thin skin below his eyes. He looked older, as if he'd lost his joy, and—without thinking—she felt the urge to hug him tight, like a child, just to make him laugh again. She resisted the impulse.

"I don't know. Not this awful," he said. "*Everything* can't be dead, can it?"

"It might just be too late for us, Jeremy," she said.

"I know. But aren't you willing to at least try?"

It wasn't until his face changed—lightening with a faint ray of hope—that she realized she'd put down her keys and her laptop. She moved to the sink to pour herself a glass of water and then stood in the dark recesses of the kitchen, looking at Jeremy silhouetted against the windows. "Are you thirsty?" she asked, instead of answering his question. "I have beer and soda."

"Water's fine," he said.

She handed him a glass of tap water and they both drank in silence. Jeremy politely cupped the underside of the glass in his palm to catch any drips of condensation. He was trying too hard; it made Claudia uncomfortable. The sun poured through the wall of windows, casting parallelograms of light across the bamboo flooring, and the air-conditioning clicked on as the loft began to warm up.

"You look great," Jeremy said softly. "It's good to see you."

She looked down at her sweats and dirty T-shirt, her skin covered with dust from the move. "Thanks," she said. Now that she wasn't escaping out the door, she wasn't sure what to say. "Anyway. What are your plans? Do you have any?"

"I'm not sure. There was this guy, Julian, before I left. He does music licensing, and he wanted to work with me. I thought I'd give him a call, see if he could give me an entry-level job. There's good money in it."

"But you're still planning to play music?"

Jeremy shrugged. "I don't know. Maybe it's time to give up on that."

"Don't," she said, surprised by the softness of her own voice. "That would be a terrible waste."

Jeremy nodded absently, absorbing this, and then stood to wander restlessly around the loft. He let his hand trace along the surface of the chairs, the couch, the table, as if he were testing whether or not they were really there.

"So. You sold the house," he said.

"Yes."

He was quiet for a minute. "I don't understand," he burst out. "I thought you loved our house. I thought the whole point of . . . everything that happened . . . was about trying not to lose it."

"There's a difference between losing your house involuntarily and choosing to leave it," she said.

"No, no. Of course. I see." The expression on his face suggested that he didn't, but was trying his hardest. He gazed around him, looking at the photos of Claudia's family that hung on the wall. Unease filled his face as he realized that the documentation of their life together—the wedding photos, his portrait of Jillian—had been amputated from this new home. Claudia wondered whether he had expected her to bring his belongings along with her to display, like artifacts in a museum.

"Your things are boxed up and stored downstairs, in the garage," she explained. "I didn't throw anything away." She hesitated, recalling several trash bags' worth of odds and ends that had ended up on the curb. "Well, maybe a few things. I got a little worked up one afternoon, and . . . felt the need to pare back. You know."

"*Pare back*. Uh-huh." Jeremy raised a skeptical eyebrow, and against her better judgment she found herself smiling. He smiled back, finally relaxing into a person she recognized. "I guess this place—it's kind of small, isn't it?"

"It's plenty big for one person," she said.

"Right." He moved to the bottom of the stairs and gazed up at the sleeping loft. Then he turned around and walked over to the windows to take in the view. "But it could probably fit two, if you wanted it to?" he asked, looking out over downtown.

She heard a strange hiccup in his voice and realized he was on the verge of tears.

"*Don't.*" It came out as a sort of wail. "I don't think I can take it if you start crying now. I've already cried too much, Jeremy."

He pushed a thumb into the corner of his eye, pressing his tear duct closed. "I'm sorry, Claude," he said. "I'm so sorry—"

"I know," she said. "But I'm just not ready to talk about everything yet. I don't know when I will be. If I ever will be."

But she came and stood beside him at the window, and together they looked out at the city set before them. This far inland, you couldn't see the blue expanse of sea, but if you squinted hard at a slice of horizon wedged between two skyscrapers, you could almost make out the coastline in the distance. Claudia let herself adjust to Jeremy's presence again, surprised at how he could feel both familiar and new at the same time. The plate glass fogged from their combined breath, and then cleared again, bringing the view in and out of focus.

"So," he began, turning to her. "So this is where we live."

Acknowledgments

I am indebted to those who helped me get to the finish line a second time.

Once again, I couldn't have done this without the Hive: Darcy Cosper, Colette Sandstedt, Benj Hewitt, and Greg Harrison, plus the much missed Carina Chocano. Dawn MacKeen was the best writing partner a woman could ask for, and kept me honest on those days when I just didn't feel like showing up.

Dan Crane and Brian Cleary shed light on the life of an indie rock musician in Los Angeles; Ted Walch and Brian Wogensen offered their insights into teaching at private schools; and Crystal Heatherly and Mike and Kristina Hart shared their inside knowledge of Mount Washington life and real estate.

As always, I received invaluable instruction and encouragement from the divine Susan Golomb and the brilliant Julie Grau. I am fortunate to be in your hands. Much gratitude to the whole support team at Spiegel & Grau, including Maria Braeckel, Laura Van der Veer, and Sally Marvin.

And finally, to my daughter, Auden, who allowed me no wiggle room on deadlines; and to my husband, Greg, again, because I can never thank him enough.

ABOUT THE AUTHOR

JANELLE BROWN is the author of *All We Ever Wanted Was Everything*, a novel. A journalist who has written for *The New York Times*, *Vogue*, *Wired*, and Salon, she lives in Los Angeles.

ABOUT THE TYPE

This book was set in Bembo, a typeface based on an old-style Roman face that was used for Cardinal Bembo's tract *De Aetna* in 1495. Bembo was cut by Francisco Griffo in the early sixteenth century. The Lanston Monotype Machine Company of Philadelphia brought the well-proportioned letter forms of Bembo to the United States in the 1930s.